PRAISE FOR THE NOVELS OF

EMILIE RICHARDS

"Well-written, intricately plotted novel...."
—*Library Journal* on *Whiskey Island*

"A multifaceted charmer...Richards's characters evince
impressive depth...."
—*Publishers Weekly* on *Whiskey Island*

"Richards's characterization and plotting are all on target."
—*Publishers Weekly* on *Beautiful Lies*

Beautiful Lies is "a romance in the best sense, appealing
to the reader's craving for exotic landscapes, treacherous
villains and family secrets...."
—*The Cleveland Plain Dealer*

"A multi-layered plot, vivid descriptions and a
keen sense of place and time."
—*Library Journal* on *Rising Tides*

"...intricate, seductive and a darned good read."
—*Publishers Weekly* on *Iron Lace*

"A fascinating tale of the tangled race relations and
complex history of Louisiana...this is a page-turner."
—*New Orleans Times-Picayune* on *Iron Lace*

"Emilie Richards makes a tale of class, culture and color
come alive with her emphasis on the flavorful sights,
sounds and languages of New Orleans."
—*Tallahassee Democrat* on *Iron Lace*

EMILIE RICHARDS

FOX RIVER

MIRA

ISBN 1-55166-806-8

FOX RIVER

Copyright © 2001 by Emilie Richards McGee.

All rights reserved. Except for use in any review, the reproduction or utilization of this work in whole or in part in any form by any electronic, mechanical or other means, now known or hereafter invented, including xerography, photocopying and recording, or in any information storage or retrieval system, is forbidden without the written permission of the publisher, MIRA Books, 225 Duncan Mill Road, Don Mills, Ontario, Canada M3B 3K9.

All characters in this book have no existence outside the imagination of the author and have no relation whatsoever to anyone bearing the same name or names. They are not even distantly inspired by any individual known or unknown to the author, and all incidents are pure invention.

MIRA and the Star Colophon are trademarks used under license and registered in Australia, New Zealand, Philippines, United States Patent and Trademark Office and in other countries.

Visit us at www.mirabooks.com

Printed in U.S.A.

Dear Reader,

I've been fortunate to live in wonderful places I can share in my novels. I started my writing career in New Orleans, the setting for *Iron Lace* and *Rising Tides*. I made two extended trips to Australia, the setting for *Beautiful Lies*, and I spent many years in bustling Cleveland, the home of *Whiskey Island*.

When it came time to move again, I was as interested in a unique and colorful setting for my next novel as I was in school systems and health care facilities. When northern Virginia appeared on my family's horizon, I knew I'd found another home rich in history, culture and natural beauty.

From my front door I can easily drive to mountains and beaches. Or I can take a shorter drive to some of the most beautiful rural scenery imaginable: Virginia horse country, where farms and million-dollar estates rise from rolling hills, and Thoroughbreds graze inside miles of winding stone fences.

It only took one visit to Loudoun County to know I'd found the setting for my next book.

So this time come with me to the world of foxhunting and steeplechasing, and a society that values the way a man sits a horse as much as it values his family name. I hope you'll find it as fascinating as I have.

I always enjoy hearing from my readers. Please write me at P.O. Box 7052, Arlington, Virginia 22207.

Emilie Richards

From the unpublished novel *Fox River*, by Maisy Fletcher

Today, when I think of Fox River and all that happened here so many years ago, I am unwillingly wrapped in shades of green. The fresh, sweet green of pasture deepening toward the horizon, the evergreen of forest shading inevitably to the blue-green of Virginia hills until, at last, mountains merge with a misty sky.

It is the same sky, more or less, that others see. The sky that stretches over California and China and the farthest regions of Antarctica. It is the sky under which I was born, under which I lived the events told in this story. The same sky that sends sun and rain to make the grassy hills of Fox River as verdant, as lush, as any in the world.

But I, Louisa Sebastian, am the only person who sees the proud man silhouetted against this Fox River sky, the man erect on a stallion that no one else will mount, a man so wedded to the horse beneath him that I am reminded of the mythical centaur, and my breath, despite everything I know of him, catches in my chest.

Today, when I am forced to think of the events that happened at Fox River, I am swallowed by shades of green and by the blood that so long ago stained blades of grass a bright and terrible red. In the many years since, the grass has grown and the rain has washed away visible traces of blood, but I know the earth beneath has yet to recover, that if I were to dig in that very place, the dirt beneath my fingernails would be rusty and tainted still.

Had I only known what awaited me as I rode to Fox River that first afternoon, I would have galloped back to my cousin's estate to seclude myself. I would have pleaded illness or injury and asked that my trunks be packed immediately for my return to New York.

But, of course, the future is never ours to know. Only the past is ours to contemplate and mourn forever.

1

The citizens of Ridge's Race, Virginia, claimed that Maisy Fletcher lived her life like a pack of foxhounds torn between two lines of scent. She had worn many disguises in her fifty years, each of them clearly revealing the flighty, distractible woman beneath. Jake Fletcher, her husband for twenty years, disagreed. Jake claimed that his wife had no trouble making up her mind.

Over and over and over again.

Today, those who knew Maisy would have been shocked to see the purpose in her stride and the lack of attention she paid to everything and everyone that stood between her and the front door of the Gandy Willson Clinic, just outside historic Leesburg. She ignored the horsehead mounting posts flanking the herringbone brick sidewalk, the magnolias flanking the portico. She paid little attention to the young couple sitting stiffly on a green bench under the magnolia to her left. More tellingly, she brushed right past the young security guard who asked for her identification.

"Ma'am, you can't go in there without my seeing some ID," the young man said, following close at her heels.

Maisy paused just long enough to survey him. He looked like an escapee from the Virginia Military Institute, hair shaved nearly to the scalp, acne scars still faintly visible. He had the same hostile stare she associated with new cadets, a product of exhaustion and harassment.

Normally she might have winked or stopped to question him about his upbringing, his opinion of the Washington Redskins' chances this season, his take on the presidential election. Today she turned her back. "Don't try to stop me, son. I'm as harmless as a butterfly in a hailstorm. Just go on about your business."

"Ma'am, I have to—"

"My daughter's a patient here."

"I'm going to have to call—"

She reached for the door handle and let herself in.

She had never been inside the Gandy Willson Clinic. Through the years, acquaintances had disappeared into its confines for periods of "rest." Some of them boasted of time spent here, adding "G.W.S." after their names like an academic achievement. "G.W.S." or Gandy Willson Survivor, was a local code, meaning "Don't offer me a drink," or "Give me the strongest drink in the house," depending on the length of time out of treatment.

Maisy wasn't surprised by what she saw. Gandy Willson catered to the wealthy elite. The chandelier gracing a cathedral ceiling was glittering crystal, the carpet stretching before her had probably robbed a dozen third world children of a normal adolescence.

The security guard hadn't followed her inside, but another, older, man strode from his office to head her off as she stepped farther into the reception area. He was in his sixties, at least, bespectacled, perfectly tailored and attempting, without success, to smile like somebody's grandfather.

"I don't believe we've met." He extended his hand. "I'm Harmon Jeffers, director of Gandy Willson."

She debated taking it, but gave in when she saw the hand wavering with age. She grasped it to steady him. "I'm Maisy Fletcher, and my daughter Julia Warwick is a patient here."

"Julia's mother. Of course." His unconvincing smile was firmly in place.

There was no "of course" about it. Maisy and Julia were as different from one another as a rose and a hibiscus. For all practical purposes they were members of the same general family, but the resemblance ended there. This month Maisy's hair was red and sadly overpermed. Julia's was always sleek and black. Maisy had gained two unwanted pounds for every year she'd lived. Julia survived on air. Maisy was average height. Petite Julia barely topped her shoulder.

And those were the ways in which they were most alike.

Maisy drew herself up to her full five foot four, as the small of her back creaked in protest. "I'm here to see my daughter."

"Shall we go into my office? I'll have tea sent, and we can chat."

"That's very old Virginia of you, Dr. Jeffers, but I don't think I have the time. I'd appreciate your help finding Julia's room. I hate barging in on strangers."

"We can't let you do that."

"Good. Then you'll tell me where she is?"

"Mrs. Fletcher, it's imperative we talk. Your daughter's recovery depends on it."

Maisy lifted the first of several chins. The others followed sluggishly. "My daughter shouldn't be here."

"You disagree that your daughter needs treatment?"

"My daughter should be at home with the people who love her."

The young couple who'd been sitting on the bench entered and shuffled lethargically across the carpet. He put his hand on Maisy's shoulder to steer her away from the door. "Mrs. Warwick's husband feels differently. He feels she needs to be here, where she can rest and receive therapy every day."

Maisy cut straight to the point, as unusual for her as the anger simmering inside her. "Just exactly how many cases of hysterical blindness have you treated?"

"This is a psychiatric clinic. We—"

"Mostly treat substance abusers," she finished for him. "Drug addicts. Alcoholics. My daughter is neither. But she might be by the time she gets out of here. You'll drive her crazy."

"There are people who will say your daughter is already well on her way." He lifted a bushy white brow in punctuation. "There is *nothing* wrong with her eyes, yet she doesn't see. For all practical purposes she's totally blind. Surely you're not trying to tell me this is a normal event?"

She drew a deep breath and spaced her words carefully, as much for order as for emphasis. "My son-in-law brought her here directly from the hospital because he didn't want Julia to embarrass him. She *came* because he threatened her. She's not here because she believes you can help her.''

''She's not receiving phone calls just yet. How do you know this?''

''Because I know my daughter.''

''Do you, Mrs. Fletcher?''

That stopped her, as he probably knew it would. She supposed that with all the good doctor's training, finding an Achilles' heel was as elementary as prescribing the trendiest psychotropic drug.

She took a moment to regroup, to focus her considerable energy on what she had to do. ''I will see my daughter.'' She surprised herself and said it without blinking, without breaking eye contact. ''Either you can help me, or you can help me make a scene.''

''We'll sit and talk a few minutes. If you're still inclined to see her, I'll send a message. But if she doesn't want you here, you'll have to leave.''

She threw up her ring-cluttered hands.

He led her down the hallway to the door he'd come through. His office was much as she'd expected. Leather furniture, dark paneled walls covered with multiple framed diplomas, a desk as massive as a psychiatrist's ego. She always wondered if professional men measured the size of their desks the way adolescent boys measured their penises.

''Make yourself comfortable.''

She had two choices—to perch on the couch's edge like a child in the principal's office or settle back and appear completely defenseless. She was sure the stage had been set that way. She settled.

Dr. Jeffers sat forward, cupping his hands over his blotter, and nodded sagely. ''So you don't believe this is the right place for Mrs. Warwick?''

Maisy glanced at her watch. It was an insubstantial rhinestone-and-pearl encrusted bauble, and she wore it with everything. Now she wished the hands would move faster.

''This is my daughter we're talking about. No one knows her better than I do, which is not the same as saying I know everything about her. But I do understand this. She's a private person. Her strength comes from within. She will not want to share those strengths or any weaknesses with a stranger. You are a stranger.''

''And she'll want to share them with you?''

''I do wish you'd stop putting words in my mouth.''

''Correct me, then, but I'm under the impression you think you can help her and I can't.''

''Being with people who love her will help her. I know she's desperate to see Callie—''

''You can't possibly know these things, Mrs. Fletcher. Perhaps you're projecting? Your daughter's spoken to no one except her husband since she arrived.''

''I know she's desperate to see Callie,'' Maisy repeated a bit louder. ''Are you listening or aren't you? She'll be frantic to see her little girl. If you think a frantic woman is a good candidate for therapy, then you need to go back to medical school.''

''There is only one frantic woman in this clinic, and she's sitting across from me,'' he said with his pseudograndfatherly smile.

With some difficulty Maisy hoisted herself to her feet, but before she could say anything the telephone on his desk rang. As he picked up the receiver, he held up a hand to stop her from leaving. When he'd finished, he glanced up and shrugged.

''It seems you're not the only frantic woman in this clinic, after all. Your daughter knows you're here.''

Maisy waited.

He rose. ''She's demanding to see you. Her room is upstairs. Follow the corridor to the end, turn left, and you'll see the staircase. At the top, make your first left, then a right. Her room is at the end of the hall. But just so you know, it's my responsibility to notify Mr. Warwick that you've visited Mrs. Warwick against medical advice.''

''Dr. Jeffers, are you a psychiatrist or a spy?''

''Dear lady, you have some mental health issues you need work on yourself.''

It was a testament to her mental health that she left without responding.

* * *

Julia knew her mother had come. Maisy and Jake's pickup had a bone-jarring rattle as audibly distinct as the belching of its exhaust system. For years Bard had tried to convince Jake to buy a new truck, but Julia's stepfather always refused. He was a man who would do without comfort rather than spend money foolishly, not a stingy man, simply one who believed in taking care of what he owned.

At the sound of the truck in the parking lot, Julia had found her way to the window to confirm her suspicion. She wasn't sure what she expected, a sudden lifting of darkness, a sneak peek at a world she hadn't seen in weeks. She felt the cool glass under her fingertips, traced the smooth-textured sill, the decorative grids. But she wasn't allowed even the pleasure of an afternoon breeze. The window was locked tight.

She had realized then that she had to ask for help. Practical help, not the kind she had supposedly checked herself in to receive. After the first day she had realized that the Gandy Willson Clinic was the wrong place for her and that her sessions with Dr. Jeffers would be nothing more than a battle of wits. She would hide her feelings, and he would subtly berate her for her lack of cooperation.

Luckily there was at least one staff member who seemed genuinely interested in her. Karen, the nurse on duty, agreed to call Dr. Jeffers and relay Julia's demand. If Maisy Fletcher had come to see her daughter, he was not to send her away. If he did, Julia would be the next to leave.

When Maisy turned into the hallway, Julia knew her mother was coming by the bustling of her footsteps. Maisy was always in a hurry, as if she had somewhere important to go, although, in truth, destination was never a priority.

"Julia?"

"In here, Maisy."

The door swung open, a welcome whoosh of fresh air followed by a gentle bang.

"Sweetheart."

Julia heard and smelled her mother's approach, and in a moment felt Maisy's soft hands against her cheeks. Then she was wrapped in the overpowering fragrance of violets and the soft give of her mother's arms around her.

Julia slipped her arms around her mother's waist as Maisy joined her on the bed.

"How did you know I was here?" Maisy said.

"I heard the pickup. I guess it's a good thing Jake hasn't gotten a new one."

"That's not what I was thinking on the way over. I almost left it by the side of the road. Darn thing has never liked me."

"That's because you push it too hard." It was the story of Maisy's life.

"How are you?"

Julia straightened and folded her hands in her lap. For once Maisy seemed to take the hint and moved away a little to give her daughter breathing room. "No better, no worse," Julia said.

"Dr. Jeffers is an officious little bastard who probably couldn't cure a hangnail."

"Don't be so easy on him."

Usually at this point Julia would have gotten up to roam the room. Only now, that particular escape was fraught with danger. She had carefully memorized the layout, but she wasn't sure she could navigate it with her mother watching. For a moment her heart beat faster and her breath seemed to come in short gasps. The world was a black hole sucking at her, threatening to pull her into its void forever.

"What are you doing here, sweetheart?" Maisy asked.

Julia willed herself to be calm. "One place is exactly like another when you can't see."

"That simply isn't true. You need to be with people who love you, in a place you know well. Not with strangers."

"Look around. It's almost like home. I have my own fireplace, a room full of antiques—so I'm told. The view is undoubtedly priceless."

"The only priceless thing in this room is my daughter, and she doesn't belong here."

Julia's sightless eyes filled with tears. She rose. It was safer to risk butting up against the furniture than her mother's love. "Bard thought it would be best for everyone."

"And you agree?"

"He doesn't always get his way, Maisy. I just thought that this time, he might be right."

"Why is that?"

"He's afraid for Callie." Julia stretched a hand in front of her and was disconcerted to discover that she wasn't as close to the wall as she'd expected. She inched forward until she could touch it before she spoke again.

"He says my...condition is confusing and upsetting her, that she feels somehow to blame—"

"Ridiculous."

Julia faced her, or thought she probably did. "How would you know?"

"Because I'm her grandmother. I've called her every day since the accident, and we went out for ice cream after school yesterday. Callie knows it isn't her fault that Duster balked at the jump and you took it headfirst without him. Those are the chances anybody takes when she's training a new horse."

"Right after the fall Callie told me she was sure Duster balked because she'd startled him with her pony."

"But didn't you explain that Duster had balked half a dozen times in the past and would again? That's what she told me. I don't think she feels guilty anymore, she just feels lonely and afraid you aren't coming back."

Julia swallowed tears. "Did you tell her I'm coming back as soon as I'm well?"

"She's eight. At that age a grandmother's word isn't quite as good as a mother's."

"The fall had nothing to do with this...this condition. Did you tell her that, too?"

"I did, but that's harder for her to understand."

"How can she? I don't understand it myself. One minute I can see, the next I can't. Only there's nothing wrong with my eyes. There's nothing wrong with any part of me except my mind."

Maisy was silent, waiting, Julia supposed, for her to bring herself back under control. One thing mother and daughter did have in common was a mutual distaste for emotional fireworks. Julia began to prowl the room, hands extended. She found a desk chair and held on to it. "I'm not crazy," she said at last.

"Are you afraid I think so?"

"Bard says it's all about mind over matter. He wants me to be a big girl, square my shoulders and go about my business. If I put my mind to it and work hard while I'm here, I'll see again." She thought she managed a wry smile. "That's what he would do, of course."

"He might be surprised. There are some things in life that even Lombard Warwick has no say in."

"I close my eyes, and every single time I open them again, I expect to see, but I can't. I've fallen off horses plenty of times, but this was different. When I flew headfirst over that jump, I remember thinking about Christopher Reeve. His horse balked, and now he's confined to a wheelchair for the rest of his life. When I hit the ground I was afraid to move, afraid I might not be able to sit up or walk again. I must have blacked out. When I woke up..."

She felt her way around the desk, then over to the window. She faced her mother again. "When I woke up I didn't open my eyes. I raised a leg, then an arm. I was so relieved. I can't tell you how relieved I was. I hadn't even broken anything. Then I opened my eyes."

"And you couldn't see."

Julia had told her mother all this in the hospital where she'd been taken after the accident, but she continued, needing, for some reason, to repeat it. "I thought, how strange. I must have been here for hours. Callie must have ridden back to get help and they can't find me. I thought it was night, but such a black, black night. As it turns out I was unconscious for less than a minute."

"Does it help to go over this again and again?"

"Nothing helps. The fog doesn't lift. It doesn't even waver. And you know what the worst moment was? Worse than waking up blind? When they told me there was nothing wrong with my eyesight. Conversion hysteria. I'm a hysteric."

"You're a wonderful, sensitive, intelligent woman. You're not a psychiatric label."

"I'm in a psychiatric clinic! Maybe it has fireplaces and antiques, but it's still a clinic for the mentally ill."

"You shouldn't be here."

Julia realized she had to tell Maisy the rest of it. "There are things you don't know."

"Well, you're not the first to say so."

Julia tried to smile but couldn't. "Before this, before I even saddled Duster that day, things hadn't...hadn't been going well."

Maisy was silent. Julia knew that if she could see her mother, Maisy would be twisting her hands in her lap. The hands would be covered with rings. Maisy loved anything that sparkled. She loved bright colors, odd textures, loose flowing clothing that made Julia think of harems or Polynesian luaus. She was a focal point in any crowd, the mother Julia's childhood schoolmates had most often singled out for ridicule, a bright, exotic flame in a community of old tweeds and perfectly faded denim.

"You don't want to hear this, do you?" Julia asked.

"Julia, I'm sitting here waiting."

"You never want to know when things aren't going well, Maisy. If you wore glasses, they'd be rose-colored."

"No doubt," Maisy agreed. "Cats'-eye glasses with rhinestone frames, and you would hate them. But trying to keep a positive attitude isn't the same as refusing to see there's another side of life."

Julia felt ashamed. She loved her mother, but there was a gulf between them as wide as Julia's twenty-nine years. She had never quite understood it and doubted that Maisy did, either. How two women could love each other and still be so different, so far apart in every way, was a mystery.

"I'm sorry. I didn't mean to criticize." Julia started back toward the bed, or thought she did. "It's just that I don't want to make this worse for you...."

"Let's make it better for *you,* instead. Tell me what's been happening. And move a little to your left," Maisy directed her.

Julia adjusted; her shin contacted the bed frame. "I'm going to need a white cane." The last word caught.

Maisy took her hand and helped her sit. "Has Dr. Jeffers given you a prognosis?"

"No. He rarely speaks during our sessions, and when he does, he just asks questions. Why didn't I seek help when the problems started? Why do I think I'm being so defensive? Why don't I want my husband involved in my treatment?"

"Would Bard like to be involved?"

"I doubt it, but I'm sure he's never told the doctor outright."

"Tell me about the problems you mentioned before."

"I was having blinding headaches." She smiled grimly. "Pardon the pun."

"The doctors know this?"

"Yes. They've scanned every inch of my brain, done every test a neurologist can dream up, called in every specialist. They can't find anything physical."

"What else?"

"I..." Julia tried to decide how to phrase the next part. "My work was suffering."

"Your painting?"

Julia nodded. "I had a commission for a family portrait of the Trents. You remember them? They have that pretty little farm down toward Middleburg, just past the Gradys' place? Two very blond children who show their ponies with Callie? A boy and a girl?"

"I think so."

"We had three sittings. I never got things right."

She wasn't sure how to explain the next part. She'd had no success with Bard or Dr. Jeffers. Bard told her she was simply overwrought and making her problems worse. Dr. Jeffers scribbled notes, and the scratching of his pen had nearly driven her crazy.

She tried again. "It was worse than that, actually. I did preliminary sketches. The Trents wanted something informal, something with their horses and pets out in the countryside. The sketches were fine. I had some good ideas of what I wanted to do. But when I tried to paint..."

"Go on."

"I couldn't paint what I saw. I would begin to work, and the painting seemed to progress without me. Mr. Trent is a stiff, formal man who's strict with the children. That's all I was able to capture on canvas. He looked like a storm trooper after I'd roughed him out. At one point I even found myself painting a swastika on his sleeve.''

''Maybe you weren't painting what you saw but what you felt. Isn't that part of being an artist?''

''But I had no control over it.'' Julia heard her voice rising and took a moment to breathe. ''And it was true of everything I painted in the month before the accident. I would try hunting scenes, and they weren't lovely autumn days among good friends anymore. We chase foxes for the fun of it, not to destroy them. But every painting I attempted seemed to center on the hounds tearing a fox to bits. They were…disturbing, and when I was finished with a session, I'd feel so shaken I was afraid to start another.''

''Maybe it was simply fatigue. Maybe you needed a break.''

''Well, I got one, didn't I?''

Maisy was silent, and Julia didn't blame her. What could she say? If Julia's sight was not restored, she would never paint again.

''When you were a little girl,'' Maisy said at last, ''and something bothered you, you would go to your room and draw. It was the way you expressed yourself.''

''It still is. But what am I expressing? Or what *was* I? Because I won't be able to do it again unless something changes radically.''

''Come home with me, Julia. If Bard doesn't want you at Millcreek, come back to Ashbourne. You know there's room for you and Callie. We can find a therapist you trust. Jake wants you to stay with us, too. You know he does.''

Julia loved her stepfather, who had brought balance to Maisy's life and gentle affection to her own. He was a kind, quiet man who never ceased to marvel at his wife's eccentricities, and Julia knew he would welcome her with open arms.

For a moment she was tempted to say yes, to return to her childhood home and bring her daughter to live there, too. Until her sight was restored or she'd learned to live with her impairment. Then reality got in the way.

She shook her head decisively. ''I can't do that. My God, Bard would be furious. He had to pull strings to get me admitted here. He's convinced I need to be away from everything and everyone before I'll get better.''

"And what do *you* think?"

"I hope he's right. Because I don't think I can stand being here very long. I feel like I'm in prison. I know how Christian—" She stopped, appalled at what she'd nearly said.

"You know how Christian feels," Maisy finished for her. "It's been a long time since I've heard you speak his name."

Julia stiffened. "I haven't been thinking about Christian. I don't know where that came from."

"You've lost your sight, he lost his freedom. Both of you are living in places you didn't choose. The connection is there."

"I don't want to talk about Christian."

"You never have."

There was a rustling noise at the doorway. With something close to gratitude, Julia turned her head in that direction.

"A nurse is here," Maisy said.

"Mrs. Warwick?" Karen, the nurse who had made the telephone call for Julia, entered the room, making enough noise as she did to help Julia know where she was. "Dr. Jeffers thinks you need to rest now."

For once Julia had to agree with her psychiatrist. She was suddenly weary to the bone. She felt the mattress lift as Maisy stood.

"You do look tired. I'll be back tomorrow," Maisy said. "Is there anything you'd like me to tell Callie?"

"Tell her I love her and I'll be home soon. Tell her I can see her in my dreams."

"You'll think about what I said?"

Julia nodded, then realized her mother might not be looking at her. It was just another of those small things the sighted took for granted.

"I'll think about it." Her throat was clogged with words she hadn't said. A part of her wanted to beg Maisy to take her home to Ashbourne, to the quaint stone cottage where she had lived until her marriage. Another part insisted that she stay and suffer here at Gandy Willson, that if she suffered hard enough, she might find a cure.

Karen spoke. She had a soft, husky voice and warm hands. Odd observations, but the only ones Julia was equipped to make. "I guess you know Mrs. Warwick isn't supposed to have any visitors except her husband, but unfortunately, Dr. Jeffers has a meeting tomorrow afternoon at three, so he'll be away and unable to monitor things closely. Anyone could slip right in."

"I see," Maisy said.

"Thank you." Julia understood what Karen was trying to do.

"Goodbye, sweetheart." Julia felt her mother's hand on her shoulder, then Maisy's lips against her cheek. When Karen and Maisy were gone, the room was as empty as Julia's heart.

2

Like their counterparts in Great Britain, the great farms and estates of Virginia were often given names. Ashbourne was one such, a large, distinctive house and three hundred acres made up of serpentine hills and rock-strewn creeks. The Blue Ridge Mountains were more than shadows touching the land; they were a presence that anchored it and coaxed the hills into craggier peaks and wider hollows. Maisy never ceased to be amazed at Ashbourne's natural beauty or the twist of fate that had brought her here as the young bride of Harry Ashbourne, master of the Mosby Hunt.

Harry was gone now, dead for nearly twenty-five years. Ashbourne lived on, holding its breath, she thought, for Harry's daughter Julia to reclaim it and restore it to its former glory.

The main house at Ashbourne was a gracefully wrought Greek Revival dwelling of antique cherry-colored brick and Doric columns. Symmetrical wings—two-story where the main house was three—gently embraced the wide rear veranda and flagstone terrace. In Harry's day the gardens of hollies and mountain laurels, Persian lilacs and wisteria, had been perfectly manicured, never elaborate, but as classic and tasteful as the house itself.

Over the years the gardens had weathered. Ancient maples, mimosas and hickories had fallen to lightning or drought; the boxwood maze that Harry had planted during Maisy's pregnancy had grown into an impenetrable hedge obstructing movement and sight until a landscaper had removed it. Over the years the meticulous borders of bulbs and perennials had naturalized into a raucous meadow that ate away at grass and shrubs, spreading farther out of bounds each season.

Maisy preferred the garden that way. The house was empty now, and the black-eyed Susans, corn poppies and spikes of chicory and Virginia bluebells warmed and softened its aging exterior. Neither the house nor the gardens had fallen to rack and ruin. She made certain all the necessary maintenance was done. Jake did much of it, a man as handy as he was good-natured. But the property was simply biding its time until Harry's daughter decided what should be done about it.

Maisy and Jake lived in the caretaker's cottage, a blue stone fairy-tale dwelling that was the oldest building on the property. The cottage perched on the edge of deep woods where foxes and groundhogs snuggled into comfortable dens and owls kept vigil on the loneliest nights.

The cottage was two-story, with a wide center hallway and cozy rooms that huddled without rhyme or reason, one on top of the other. The furnace and the plumbing groaned and clattered, and the wind whistled through cracks between window frames and ledges. Maisy and Jake were in agreement that the house's idiosyncrasies were as much a part of its charm as its slate roof or multitude of fireplaces.

The sky was already growing dark by the time Maisy returned from her visit to the Gandy Willson Clinic. Inky cloud layers lapped one over the other, shutting out what sunset there might have been and boding poorly for a starry night. She often darted outside two or three times each evening to glimpse the heavenly show. She made excuses, of course, although Jake was certainly on to her. She fed the barn cats, three aging tortoiseshells named Winken, Blinken and Nod. Sometimes she claimed to check gates for the farmer who rented Ashbourne's prime pasture land to graze long-horned, shaggy Highland cattle. No excuse was too flimsy if it kept her on the run.

She traversed the wide driveway and pulled the pickup into its space beside the barn, taking a moment to stretch once she was on the ground. Every muscle was kinked, both from sitting still and the lack of functioning shock absorbers. She vowed, as she did every time she drove Jake's truck, that she would have it hauled away the very next time he turned his back. She had her eye on a lipstick-red Ford Ranger sitting in a lot in Leesburg, and in her imagination, it beeped a siren song every time she passed.

As she'd expected, she found Jake in the barn. There were several on the property. The one that Harry had used to stable his world-renowned hunters was at the other side of the estate, empty of horses now and filled with artists and craftsmen to whom Maisy rented the space as a working gallery.

This barn was the original, smaller, built from hand-hewn chestnut logs and good honest sweat. Jake used it as his repair shop. There was nothing Jake couldn't take apart and put back together so that it ran the way it was intended. People from all over Loudoun and Fauquier counties brought him toasters and lawnmowers, motor scooters and attic fans. Mostly they were people like Jake himself, who believed that everything deserved a shot at a miracle cure, people who were wealthy enough to buy new goods but maintained a love affair with the past.

When she arrived, Jake was bent over his workbench. Winken crouched at the end, lazily swatting Jake's elbow every time it swung into range. The three felines were right at home in the barn. Like so much that Jake repaired here, they had been somebody else's idea of trash. Maisy had found them one winter morning as they tried to claw their way out of a paper bag in the Middleburg Safeway parking lot, tiny mewling fluffballs that she'd fed religiously every two hours with a doll's bottle, despite a serious allergy to cat dander and a craving for an uninterrupted night of sleep. Now, years later, they kept the barn free of mice and Jake company. Cats, she'd discovered, were serious advocates of quid pro quo.

"I'm back."

Jake turned to greet her. When he was absorbed in his work he forgot his surroundings. He had the power of concentration she lacked, so much that she often teased that a burglar could steal everything in the barn, including the cobwebs, while he was working on a project.

He wiped his hands on a rag before he came over to kiss her cheek. "Did you see her?"

"Yes, I did. But not without a fight." She knew he wouldn't ask what she'd learned. He would wait for whatever information she wanted to reveal. She glanced over his shoulder. Blinken had joined her sister, and the two were investigating Jake's latest project. "Work going well?"

"Liz Schaeffer brought me a mantel clock that's been in her family for three generations. Ticking fifty beats to the minute."

"Can you fix it?"

"I'll have to see if I can find a new part, but most likely." He swallowed her in his arms, as if he knew she needed his warmth. "I made chili for dinner. And corn bread's ready to go in the oven."

"You're too good to me." She relaxed against him, looking up at a face that was growing increasingly lined with age. Jake had never been a handsome man, but he had always been distinguished, well before the age the adjective usually applied. His hair was snow-white, but still as thick and curly as it had been the first time she saw him—and still, as then, a little too long. His eyes were the brown of chinquapins, eyes that promised patience but of late showed a certain fatigue, as well. Sometimes she was afraid that he was simply and finally growing tired of her.

"Let me put things away and I'll be in to finish the meal."

She moved away in a flurry of guilt. "Don't be silly. I'll put the corn bread in the oven and make a salad." She paused. "Do we have lettuce?"

He smiled a little. "Uh-huh. I shopped yesterday."

"Where was I?"

"Holed up in your study."

"Oh..."

"I like to shop, Maisy. I always see somebody I know. I do more business between the carrots and eggplant than I do on the telephone. Go make a salad."

She made it to the doorway before she turned. "Would you mind if Julia and Callie came to live with us?"

He looked up from his workbench. "Was that Julia's idea?"

"I made the offer." She paused. "I pushed a little."

"Like a steamroller on autopilot."

"She shouldn't be there, Jake. You know that place. She's miserable."

"You know Julia and Callie are welcome here."

"Was I wrong to push?"

"You're a good mother. You always do what you think is best."

She knew the dangers of acting on instinct, yet she was pleased at his support. "I'm going back tomorrow."

"Bard won't be happy if you interfere."

She stepped outside and peered up at the sky, now a seamless stretch of polished pewter. The temperature was dropping, and she shivered. Autumn was exercising its muscle. Maisy decided that after dinner she would ask Jake to make a small fire in the living room, then she would tell him in detail everything that Julia had said.

She wondered, as she did too often now, if he would find the recounting of her day too tedious to warrant his full attention.

Julia knew Bard would visit after dinner, not because his schedule was predictable but because he needed to see for himself that everything at the clinic was under control. In the early days of their marriage, that quality had reassured her. She was married to a man who had answers for everything, and for a while, at least, she had been glad to let him have answers for her.

She felt a vague twinge of guilt, as she always did when she had disloyal thoughts about Bard, the man who had stood beside her at the worst moment of her life. Bard could be overbearing, but he could also be strong and reassuring.

In some ways Bard was the product of another era. He was older than she, almost twelve years older, but it was more outlook than age that separated them. Bard would have felt at home in King Arthur's court, a knight happiest slaying dragons. But Bard would never be a Lancelot. He wasn't motivated by religious fervor and rarely by romance. Dragons would fall simply because they stood in his path.

At seven o'clock Julia found her way to the dresser where her comb and brush were kept. Her black hair was shoulder-length and straight, easy enough to manage, even when she couldn't see it. She brushed it now, smoothing it straight back from the widow's peak that made it difficult to part.

She didn't bother with cosmetics, afraid that lipstick poorly applied was worse than none at all. Earlier she had changed into wool slacks and a twin set because her room was cooler than she liked. Maisy always insisted she'd feel warmer if she gained weight, but Julia doubted she was destined to add pounds at this particular juncture of her life. The clinic food was exactly what she'd expected, low-fat and bland—garnishes of portobello mushrooms and arugula notwithstanding.

She was just buttoning her sweater when a gentle rap on the door was followed by Karen's voice. "It's chilly in here. Would you like a fire tonight? Dr. Jeffers has given permission."

She supposed permission was necessary. After any time at Gandy Willson, even a patient in her right mind would want to throw herself into the flames.

"You're smiling," Karen said.

She realized it was true. "It's the thought of a fire," she lied. "What a nice idea."

She fumbled her way across the room and sat on a chair by the bed, listening as Karen brought in logs. The sounds were all familiar, as was the burst of sulphur when the match was lit.

"Just a tiny one," Karen said. "Nothing more than kindling. But it will warm you. We're having trouble with the heat in this wing."

Julia thanked her, then sat listening as the wood began to crackle.

In the hospital, immediately after the accident, she had found it impossible to measure time. Without visual clues, one moment still seemed much like the next. The sun or the moon could be sending rays through her window and she wouldn't know. The overhead lights could be on or off, the news on her neighbor's television set could be either the morning or evening edition.

Little by little she'd learned new cues to guide her. The buzzing of the fluorescent lamp in the corner when light was needed in the evening, or the scent of disinfectant when the hallway was mopped each morning. The cues were different here, but just as predictable.

She had also learned that time passed more slowly than she realized. Without the constant distractions of a normal life, each second seemed to merge in slow motion with the next. She had never understood Einstein's theories of time and space, but she thought, perhaps, she was beginning to.

After she was sure she'd been sitting for at least a day, she heard Bard's perfunctory knock. He always rapped twice, with jackhammer precision. Then he threw open the door and strode purposefully across the floor to kiss her cheek.

Tonight was no different. He was at her side before she could even tell him to come in. She smelled the Calvin Klein aftershave she had helped Callie pick out last Christmas, felt the rasp of his cheek against hers.

"You look tired." He had already straightened and moved away. She could tell by his voice.

"Sitting still all day will do that to you," she said.

"You need the rest. That's why you're here."

She was here to keep from embarrassing him. She suspected that not one of their mutual friends knew exactly what had happened to her, and she wondered what story he was telling. "I would get more rest at home. I could find my way around. Get a little exercise. I'd feel more like sleeping."

"We've been over and over this, Julia."

The forced patience in his voice annoyed her. "*You've* been over and over this, Bard. I've had very little to say about it."

"I understand your sessions with Dr. Jeffers aren't going well."

"If you mean that I haven't miraculously regained my eyesight, then yes. They haven't gone well."

"I didn't mean that."

She could feel her frustration growing. "Bard, stop talking to me like I'm Callie's age, please. I'm blind, not eight. Exactly what did you mean?"

"Dr. Jeffers says you're not cooperating. That you're resistant to treatment."

"I am resistant to spilling my guts so he'll have something to write on his notepad."

"How do you know he writes anything?"

"I can hear the scratching of his pen. I have four senses left."

"Why are you resisting his help?"

"He isn't offering help. He's a Peeping Tom in disguise. He wants to see into every corner of my life, and I don't see any reason to let him."

"You'd prefer a guide dog?"

She clamped her lips shut. As he barreled through his days, Bard had developed a theory that life was an endless set of simple decisions, for or against. Accordingly, he had boiled down Julia's recovery. Either she let Dr. Jeffers cure her or she remained blind. He didn't have the inclination to consider the matter further.

"I guess that means no." He sounded farther away, as if he'd taken up her favorite spot at the window.

"What do you see?" she asked. "I'd like to know what's out there, so I can imagine it when I'm standing there."

For the first time he sounded annoyed. "That sounds like you're making plans to live with this."

"It's a simple, nonthreatening question."

"I see exactly what you'd expect. Trees, flower beds, lawn. A slice of the parking lot. Hills in the distance."

"Thanks."

"I hear Maisy came to visit today. Against orders."

His voice was louder, so she imagined he was facing her now. She pictured him leaning against the windowsill, long legs crossed at the ankles, elbows resting comfortably, long fingers laced as he waited for her answer. She remembered the first time she had really noticed Lombard Warwick.

She had known Bard forever. The town of Ridge's Race—nothing much more than a gas station, post office and scenic white frame grocery store—was named for an annual point-to-point race that extended between two soaring ridges on either side of town. It was also the address of dozens of million-dollar farms and estates, including Ashbourne and Millcreek Farm, which was Bard's family home. Ridge's Race had a mayor and town council, churches along three of the four roads that intersected at the western edge of town, and a community as tightly knit as a New England fishing village.

Because of the difference in their ages, she and Bard had never attended school together. Even if they'd been born in the same year, their educational paths wouldn't have crossed. Bard was destined for the same residential military school his father had attended. Julia, the product of an egalitarian mother who believed class segregation was nearly as harmful as racial segregation, was destined for the local public schools.

They hadn't attended church together, either. There was a plaque listing generations of Warwicks on the wall at St. Albans, the Episcopal church where the most powerful people in Ridge's Race convened on Sunday morning. There were Ashbournes on the plaque, as well, and Julia had been christened there, a squalling infant held firmly in the strong arms of the father who had died when she was only four. But for as long as Julia could remember, on the rare occasions when Maisy took her to church, Maisy drove into Leesburg or Fairfax and chose congregations and religions at random.

Even without common churches or schools, Bard had been a presence in Julia's life. Millcreek Farm was just down the road. As a little girl she had seen him pass by on sleek Thoroughbreds or in one of a series of expensive sports cars. She had seen him in town, discussed weather and local politics while waiting in line at the post office, watched him shop for bourbon and bridles in Middleburg. Until she was twenty he had been a local fixture, like miles of four-rail fencing and Sundowner horse trailers.

Then one day, when her whole world lay in pieces at her feet, she had finally taken a good look at Lombard Warwick, sought-after bachelor, son of Brady Warwick and Grace Lombard, heir to Millcreek Farm, graduate of Yale law school, owner of champion hunters in a region filled with exquisite Thoroughbreds.

She thought now that Bard had been at his peak that year. He'd been thirty-one and appallingly handsome. His dark hair hadn't yet been touched by gray; his green eyes had been clear and untroubled. He had a long, elegant jaw shadowed by a jet-black beard, and hatchet-sharp cheekbones that defined a face as confident as it was aristocratic. He had a way of looking at a female that had taught more women about their sexuality than Mama's muddled lectures or high school health class.

She hadn't fallen in love with him, but she had been drawn to his strength and self-assurance, something nearly as powerful that had, in the end, changed her life.

Today Bard had much of the same physical appeal. He was heavier, following in the footsteps of his father, who had seriously taxed the county's sturdiest quarter horses. So far the extra pounds merely made Bard more a man to be reckoned with. He was tall and big-boned, and he carried himself with military bearing. He was rarely challenged and even more rarely beaten in any endeavor.

The other changes were subtler. The eyes were still untroubled, but troubling. The silver at his temples was attractive, but misleading. Age hadn't brought with it serenity. He was intelligent, but not necessarily insightful, able to bide his time but never, never patient.

Now was no exception. "Julia, I'm waiting to hear why Maisy was here. This new push to go home...that wouldn't happen to have come from her, would it?"

"Is it suddenly necessary to report all conversations with my mother?"

"I don't want her upsetting you."

His voice had risen a tone. She could visualize him tugging at an earlobe, the one visible vice he allowed himself when he was angry.

"Bard, *you're* upsetting me."

"Why?"

"Because you're trying to run my life."

"Dr. Jeffers thinks she'll set back your recovery. This is Maisy we're talking about. I'm surprised she was able to find her way here, that she didn't end up on some side road sorting autumn leaves by size and color."

She was torn between outrage and a vision of Maisy doing exactly that. "She loves me. And she's worried."

His voice softened. "We're all worried, sugar. And that's why I want you well as soon as possible."

"I don't want to stay here. I can see a therapist privately. We can hire someone to help me. It would be enormously less expensive than keeping me here.''

"But not as beneficial.''

She knew it was time to remove the kid gloves. She straightened a little, carefully turning her head until she was certain she was looking at him. "You don't want me at home because you're embarrassed. You don't want anyone to know that a wife of yours has gone off the deep end and manufactured her own personal handicap.''

"You're completely forgetting about Callie. Do you think it's good for her to see her mother like this? She's upset enough as it is. She doesn't need a daily dose of you walking into walls and tripping over doorways.''

Her frustration blazed into full-blown anger. "What's the sudden concern for Callie, Bard? Most of the time you don't think twice about her.''

"I'll assume that's coming directly from your mother, too.''

"It's coming directly from *me*.''

"I don't fawn over Callie. That certainly doesn't mean I don't care about her.''

"I said you don't think twice about her. Callie is my job. I make the decisions. I give the attention.''

"And because it's been your job, Callie expects you to be well and able to take care of her.''

"She needs me with her, whether I can see or not. Children imagine the worst if the grown-ups in their lives aren't honest.''

"I've reassured her.''

"Are you spending time with her? Have you taken her out to eat? Taken her to a movie? Helped with her homework?''

"I have a job. I'm doing what I can.''

Bard's job had never been a source of tension before, because Julia had always been home to fill in the gaps. He was a real estate attorney for Virginia Vistas, one of the area's largest development firms. When he wasn't closing and negotiating deals, he worked with the developers both as an attorney and a private investor. He had a gift for knowing when to buy and sell God's green earth that made the substantial holdings he'd inherited from his wealthy parents a mere line or two in his financial portfolio.

"Are you spending any time with her?" she asked. "She loves to ride with you. Have you taken her riding?"

"The last time she rode with one of her parents wasn't exactly a roaring success."

"More reason. She needs to see that my accident was a fluke."

"I'm doing what I can."

"She needs more."

"Then you'll need to get better quickly, won't you? Callie's welfare should be an incentive."

"You can be a bastard, can't you?"

He was silent. Without visual cues, she could only imagine the expression on his face. But the possible range wasn't pretty.

"I'll take her riding this weekend," he said at last.

It was a concession, but not much of one, since today was only Monday. "Bard, nothing that's happened to me is under my conscious control. And it may not go away quickly. If it doesn't, I have no intention of staying at Gandy Willson just because you want me out of sight."

"I'd like you to stop saying that. You need to stay here to get well."

"You can catch Callie before she goes to bed. Please go home and read her a story for me."

He was silent a moment. "All right. But I'll let her read to me. She needs practice."

It was an old argument. Callie had a form of dyslexia that made reading a struggle. Bard believed if the little girl just read out loud enough, her disabilities would disappear. No matter how much she hated it or how much it upset her.

"Will you read to her instead, please?" Julia asked. "She can practice reading when everything else is back to normal."

"You want me to spend time with her, but you want to tell me exactly how to spend it."

"If you spent more time with her, I wouldn't have to tell you."

When he spoke, he was standing directly in front of her. She hadn't even heard him move. "If it will make you feel better, *I'll* read to *her*. But will you stop fighting everything and everyone and concentrate on seeing again?"

She didn't repeat that all the concentration in the world wasn't going to bring back her eyesight. She recognized a compromise when she heard one. "I'll do whatever it takes," she promised.

"That's my girl." He bent and kissed her, not on the cheek but full on the lips.

"I'll see you tomorrow?"

"That would be wonderful." His voice was husky. "I hope you *will* see me tomorrow."

"Me, too."

"I'm flying down to Richmond early in the morning, and I won't be by until after dinner. Sleep well."

That was a promise she couldn't make. "You, too."

He closed the door gently enough, but moments later it still resounded. She was left with an assortment of feelings.

She had never dealt well with her own emotions. Only rarely had she understood what fed the creative well inside her or sealed it completely. She had found it best not to tamper. Painting or drawing, even sculpting—something she'd only done infrequently—had become her outlet. Perhaps she didn't understand anything better when she'd finished, but she felt better. And that was good enough.

Now a desire to sketch seized her with a force that almost took away her breath. She got to her feet and felt her way around the room until she came to the desk. She slid her fingers underneath, feeling for a drawer. She was rewarded with what felt like a wooden knob, and when she grasped it, she felt the drawer sliding toward her. When it was open, she poked her fingers inside and felt for paper or a pen, but the only thing residing there was what felt like a slender telephone book, despite the fact that her room had no telephone.

To prevent theft, Bard had taken her purse. At the time she hadn't thought that he was also taking pens and memo pad, her only means of drawing. Why would she have? How odd to think that a blind woman would want to draw something she couldn't see.

Yet she did. With such an intensity, such a hunger, that she felt, for a moment, that she might starve if she couldn't.

Before she could think what to do, Karen knocked and entered.

"I saw your husband leave. Will you need help getting ready for bed, Mrs. Warwick?"

She wanted to weep with relief. "Karen, this probably sounds ridiculous. But I'm an artist, and even though I can't see, I need to draw. I don't need anything fancy. Just a notepad, if you have one. A pencil or two, even a pen. Would that be too much trouble?"

Karen didn't answer for a moment, just long enough to let Julia know she wasn't thinking about where she might find supplies.

"Mrs. Warwick, the thing is, Dr. Jeffers has forbidden it. He ordered the nursing staff not to provide you with art supplies."

Julia still didn't understand. "What possible reason could he have for that? Is he afraid I'll slit my throat with a pencil?"

"I think...I think he believes it's an escape from reality. That he wants you to face your problems directly."

Julia drew a startled breath.

Karen hurried on. "Do you want me to call him at home? I could tell him what you've asked and see if I can get permission. He might want to come and talk to you about it himself."

Julia slashed her hand through the air to cut her off. She knew what Dr. Jeffers would say. He was locked firmly in the psychiatric past, when psychoanalysis was the only therapy worth mentioning.

"I'm so sorry," Karen said. "I don't agree with him. But if I helped you..."

"I'll get myself ready for bed."

"I really am sorry."

Julia didn't trust herself to answer.

"I'll just scatter the wood. The fire's almost out anyway."

Julia stood stiffly and waited until Karen closed the door. Anger was now a boiling cauldron inside her. Rarely had she felt so unfairly treated. At this, the most frightening moment of her life, she was locked away among strangers she couldn't see, the prisoner of outdated therapies and psychiatric whims.

She had never been a rebel. In all areas of her life, her choices were usually fueled by concern for others. Even as an artist, she had never rocked the boat. She painted traditional portraits and landscapes. At William and Mary she had been the despair of art professors who had praised her talent and urged her to break free of convention.

She wanted to break free now. She had followed all the rules, and look what had happened to her. Her own body had betrayed her.

She took a deep breath to calm herself, but it was like a gust of wind fueling glowing embers. From the other side of the room she heard a faint pop from the fireplace. She wondered what was left of the fire Karen had made. The nurse had scattered the logs. Nothing more than kindling, she'd called them. There might not be anything now except coals.

Or there might be a stick or two, partially burned and black as charcoal. She abandoned the idea immediately, but it formed again, a foolish, dangerous rebellion that could burn down the clinic. At the very least she would never have another fire in her room, no matter how cold the weather.

She made her way to the fireplace and placed her palms against the opening. It was glass, as she'd expected from the noises Karen had made opening and closing it. She found the handles to pull it apart and was rewarded with a screech as the panels parted. She knelt on the hearth and held her palms against the opening. The heat was minimal. The fire must have been small, just as Karen had said.

She knew she might get singed, but she didn't care. She lowered her hands and felt along the seam between the tile hearth and brick lining. At first she was unsuccessful, but as she inched forward, she felt a piece of wood that was cool to the touch. She investigated it carefully with her fingertips. It seemed to be about two inches in diameter, more kindling than log. She gripped it in her right hand and inched her left along its length. It grew hotter as she progressed, until she drew scorched fingertips back in alarm.

She guessed that the tip was still glowing. She lifted the stick higher and gently ground the tip against the floor of the fireplace for a moment. Then she inched her hand along its length again. She repeated the ritual several times until she was finally satisfied. She lifted it higher and waved it in front of her face. The kindling was barely smoking now, not actively alight, and most likely well on its way to becoming ash.

What did it matter if she was imagining what this makeshift charcoal pencil could do? She couldn't see the result. It was the motion that mattered, the translation of the visions in her mind.

She stood and realized she was trembling with excitement. How much of it was the thrill of the mutineer and how much the thrill of the artist? She didn't know or care. She was about to transform an unthinkable situation.

She chose the widest stretch of wall, one without pictures or shelves to block her movements. She stood an arm's length away and wondered what color the wall was painted. She wished that she had asked Karen or Bard. She imagined it as white and realized it didn't matter, since she would never see what she was about to draw, except in her own mind.

And she doubted that Dr. Jeffers would hold showings.

She spoke out loud. "I'm just glad it's not wallpaper."

She took another deep breath, and the glowing embers of her imagination burst into flame.

3

On the morning after her visit to Julia, Maisy was awakened by pounding on her front door. She was at her most energetic and creative late at night. Unless she was forced to, she rarely rose before ten. The bedside clock said seven.

She rolled over and felt for Jake's warm body, but the other side of the bed was empty. For a moment she thought she might ignore the summons, then it sounded again, louder and more insistent.

She sat up and tried to remember what day it was. When that proved an impossible task she swung her legs over the bedside and felt for her slippers. She grabbed a royal-purple satin bathrobe on her way out the door and fluffed her perm with stiff fingertips as she navigated the stairs. When she peered out the stairwell window and saw who was standing at the front door, she sighed. But it was nine years too late to crawl back under the covers.

The door wasn't locked. She swung it open and peered at her son-in-law through heavy-lidded eyes. Bard Warwick was convinced that if Maisy simply adjusted her time clock, the rest of her life would fall into place.

"Has something happened to Julia or Callie?" she asked.

"You tell me."

She stepped back and he entered. He was dressed for business in a dark suit and patterned tie topped with a navy London Fog.

She noticed for the first time that it was drizzling and his dark hair was beaded with moisture.

In Maisy's mind Bard was the best and worst Virginia had to offer. He was athletic and intelligent, self-disciplined and stuffed with both Southern manners and charm. What he wasn't was particularly straightforward or altruistic.

Bard's view of himself was like a humorous tourist map. The city in question was the center of the universe, towering above other inconsequential dots like Los Angeles, Hong Kong or London. From birth he had been given everything a boy could ask for, and while those advantages might humble another man, to Bard they were simply tools that had been provided for his convenience.

She was afraid Julia was yet another blessing placed in his path. A man to whom everything came too easily was often a man without a frame of reference.

"Since I'm up now, we might as well have coffee." She trudged toward the kitchen, aware that her son-in-law had already judged her early-morning attire and found it wanting.

"I don't want coffee. I'm on my way to the airport. I just want a quick chat, Maisy."

"I can't talk without coffee in my hand. Not before noon."

She supposed he was following her as she wound her way through a hallway cluttered with odds and ends she'd picked up along life's amazing journey. She turned right and heard him behind her. In the kitchen she gestured toward a seat at the table, then opened the freezer to remove the coffee.

"To what do I owe the pleasure of your visit?"

He sat gingerly, as if he wasn't sure what he would find if he swung his legs under the table. The house was never dirty, but the hallway wasn't the only part that was cluttered. Maisy was a collector. Not a pack rat with bundles of newspapers or old cardboard boxes, but a collector of ceramic figurines, scraps of lace, buttons, gloves and quilt squares, lithographs and discarded books. She saw stories in everything, felt vibrations of lives lived and emotions experienced when she held someone's beloved treasure in her hands. Bard saw it as one step from mania.

"I'm told you visited Julia yesterday."

She carried the coffee can to the pot and fished in the drawer below it for a filter. She scooped away birthday candles, coasters, balls of string and pizza coupons before she realized she was looking in the wrong drawer. "I did. You've filed her away like yesterday's mail, Bard."

"That's a colorful way to put it, but not one bit true. She needs help, and I don't know what else to do."

For a moment she was taken aback. He sounded genuinely overwhelmed, something she hadn't expected. "She needs to be with people who love her, not with strangers."

"Maisy, in the years I've known you, you've been a musician, a Mary Kay spokeswoman, a publicist for some Eastern guru with bad breath and dirty feet, a vegetarian and a holy roller. When were you ever a psychologist?"

"It doesn't take a psychologist, Bard. It takes good common sense."

To his credit he did not point out that no one thought common sense was Maisy's strong suit. "Do you know what your daughter did last night?"

"I feel sure you're about to tell me."

"She scratched pictures on her wall. She took a piece of firewood out of the fireplace—the God damned fireplace I'm paying a fortune for her to enjoy—and she scratched pictures. Like some sort of cavewoman."

This was so unlike Julia that Maisy had to rearrange everything she knew about her daughter to fit it in.

He gave a short, humorless laugh. "Well, I guess I took you by surprise."

"Why didn't she just ask for paper and pencils?"

"Hostility? Do you think?"

She had to admit it sounded like the act of a pissed-off woman. "Did she have access to art supplies? If she'd asked for them?"

"Dr. Jeffers feels she needs rest and quiet."

She was beginning to understand. "And not art supplies."

"Julia doesn't need to draw. She needs to talk. Besides, damn it, she can't see! She's blind, or at least pretending to be!"

She was stunned. "You don't believe her? You think she's making this up? My daughter isn't perfect, but she doesn't lie."

"No? There are a few things in her past she sure doesn't bandy about."

"Bard, Julia can't see. If you think she can—"

"I know she *thinks* she can't. I believe her. But there's nothing wrong with her eyes! Nothing!"

"Except that she can't see through them."

He pounded his fist on the table, another highly uncharacteristic show of emotion. "You wouldn't know it after the way she acted last night, would you?"

"This is just another example of why she shouldn't be there."

"Enough." Bard rested his head in his hands. "I don't want you to see her again while she's in the clinic, Maisy. Dr. Jeffers thinks you brought this on, and so do I. He called me about an hour ago, and he was very upset." He lifted his head. "I want you to understand, this isn't personal. I just can't have you interfering with her treatment. She's my wife."

"She's my daughter."

He pushed back his chair and rose from the table. "You need to listen to me. Closely. Most of the time you're harmless, but not in this instance. I don't want you near her until her sight's been restored. Julia has a lot of thinking to do, and you're going to get in the way." His voice dropped. "I won't have it."

A man spoke from the doorway. "What won't you have?"

Maisy turned and saw a bareheaded Jake dressed in a canvas raincoat. No matter the weather, Jake started each day with a long walk. She supposed after living with her all these years it was a way of pumping some predictability into his life.

"I want Maisy to stay away from Julia." Bard started toward Jake. "Will you make her listen to reason?"

Jake didn't smile. "Maisy doesn't take orders well. It's one of her finer qualities. If she needs to see her daughter, she will."

Bard's face was a mixture of emotions. Maisy was too fascinated to be angry he was trying to rally her husband against her. She made another plea. "Look, I offered to have her come here if you don't want her at Millcreek. I'm home all day. I can help her get her bearings—"

"She doesn't need to get her bearings! For God's sake, Maisy, she needs to see again! And with you fawning all over her and waiting on her hand and foot, why should she?''

Jake stepped forward to meet him. ''You think your wife lost her eyesight because she wants to be taken care of?''

When Bard answered at last, his face was expressionless. ''You have ties to her. I understand that, but right now, I'm in charge of her recovery. Stay away from her. Please. Until she's ready to come home. Then we can talk about what's best for her.''

''Julia is in charge of her own recovery,'' Maisy said, spacing the words carefully.

Bard shook his head. ''If you won't agree, I'm going to have to make my feelings clear to Dr. Jeffers.''

''I suspect you've already done that,'' Jake said. ''Is there anything else you need this morning?'' He stepped aside to make his point.

Bard started past him. ''I'll talk to you later.''

Maisy didn't respond, and Jake didn't speak again until their front door closed. ''Are you all right?''

''I'm trying to remind myself that for the sake of my daughter and granddaughter I have to be nice to Lombard Warwick, even when he's in a suit.''

''This has been hard on him, Maisy. He's trying to cope as best he can.''

''By giving orders and making decisions.''

''He's not so bad. He thinks he has Julia's best interests in mind.''

Maisy filled the pot with fresh water before she flipped on the coffeemaker. ''Well, he *did* say that usually I'm harmless.''

Jake chuckled. ''He doesn't know you as well as he thinks.''

She smiled, but it died quickly. She told Jake what Bard had said about Julia sketching on the wall. ''I'm going to see her again today.''

''Do you want me to come along?''

Maisy considered before she shook her head. ''No. One of us needs to stay in Bard's good graces. If you don't come, we can preserve the illusion that you don't completely agree with me.''

''And that's an illusion?''

"Do you agree?"

He came over and took cups out of the cupboard, setting them on the counter in front of her. Then he went to the refrigerator for the cream. "If you're going because you want to be sure she has choices, you have my full support."

"I just want the best for Julia."

He set the cream in front of her. "You sound remarkably like Bard."

The warm glow of Julia's rebellion only lasted until the early hours of the next morning. She awoke when the morning nurse came in to check on her. She heard the woman's soft gasp and hasty exit.

The jig was up.

By the time she had showered and finished breakfast, she knew she was overdue for a visit from her psychiatrist. She had to commend his self-control.

When Dr. Jeffers finally arrived, she was sitting by the window, listening to the rain falling on a wet landscape. She could picture the autumn leaves, heavy-laden and resistant. But they couldn't resist for long.

"So, Julia, we have here a little protest."

She had been contrite until she heard Jeffers' tone. Had he not sounded as if he were talking to someone with the IQ of an earthworm, she might have apologized.

Now she was angry again. "I will not be kept from doing the things I need to in order to get better."

"And you think defacing our walls will make you better?"

She was teaching herself not to play his game. "When I checked myself in, I expected rules. This particular whim of yours was simply cruel. You're unhappy with my so-called lack of cooperation, so you're taking away the things that mean the most to me."

"You sound suspicious of my motives."

She considered that. "You may well think you're doing this for my benefit, but the result is the same."

"And the result would be?"

"Let's stop dancing around. I'm not going to improve if I

spend my whole time butting heads with you. I'm willing to stay, but I want to be able to have visitors and art supplies."

"Supplies you can't see."

"I see pictures in my head as clearly as I ever did."

"Tell me about them."

She considered that, too. "Not until I can trust you to hold up your end of the bargain."

He gave a dry laugh. "Oh, so it's a bargain, is it? Is that how your life works, Julia? You withhold favors until you get what you want?"

"A healthy person doesn't give too much without the confidence she'll get something in return. I'm asking for simple things anyone else would take for granted."

"It's difficult to tell exactly what you had in mind when you were drawing. I'm sure it would be clearer if you could see, or if you'd had better tools. But I think I'm looking at a landscape of some sort. Hills? Perhaps a stream?"

"I don't think we've reached a decision."

She thought he sighed. "I'll have to give this some thought."

She heard the scrape of a chair, as if he was standing up. She ventured one parting shot. "Dr. Jeffers, let's face the fact that this might not be the best place for me. If we can't come to an understanding, then I'll check myself out. No hard feelings."

"I'm not sure I can let you do that."

She was taken aback. "I admitted myself voluntarily. You'd have trouble painting a blind woman as a threat to anyone."

"You might well be dangerous to yourself, as that stunt last night proved. I'm surprised you didn't burn down my clinic."

A touch of panic gripped her, an old friend by now. "The fire was out and I was careful."

"But what comes next? I think you're seriously depressed and capable of acting out. A bad combination."

Oddly, instead of anger she experienced a surge of relief, which pruned the panic at its roots. Now she knew what she had to do. "I think we're done here."

He was silent, and she wished she could see his expression. When he did speak, he was farther away, at the door, she guessed. "You have an appointment this morning with our internist."

"I had a physical at the hospital."

"Will you argue about this, too? We like to be thorough. Then you and I have an appointment at four-thirty. I'll see you, then."

She wouldn't see *him*. She would be gone by then. Any ambivalence she'd had about leaving had disappeared in the wake of his threats.

At three o'clock Julia heard Jake's pickup. By three-fifteen she knew Maisy had run into trouble, because she still hadn't arrived at Julia's door. Julia rang for Karen and waited impatiently until the young nurse came to her room.

"Karen, my mother's here again to visit. Would you find out what's keeping her?"

Karen sounded unhappy. "They aren't going to let her up here to see you, Mrs. Warwick. Dr. Jeffers says it runs counter to your treatment plan. Security has orders. I'm sorry."

"Is she still here?"

Karen hesitated, then she lowered her voice. "I'll find out. Do you want me to give her a message?"

"Yes, tell her to wait for me."

"Wait?"

Julia was on her feet. "I'm coming down. I'm going home. This is outrageous."

"But you can't do that. You signed yourself in."

"I'll sign myself out. And I'm going to do it right this minute, so don't ask me to wait."

"Dr. Jeffers isn't here to—"

"Good."

"But we can't take you down there. We have orders—"

"Damn it, I'll find my own way, then. And if I break my neck while I'm at it, my mother can sue Gandy Willson." Julia started toward the door. She felt her way past the desk and dresser before she bumped into Karen.

Now Karen was pleading. "You're going to get us in real trouble."

Julia hesitated a moment; then she shook her head. "I'm sorry. Just tell Jeffers the truth. You tried to reason with me. I refused to listen. I *am* refusing, that's no lie."

"Let me call him."

"Do whatever you want. But he can't get back before I leave."

"Let me talk to your husband."

"Good luck. He doesn't listen very well."

Karen's voice caught. "Please, don't do this. Wait until—"

Julia was a small woman, but she drew herself up to her full height. "Please get out of my way."

"But you're going to get hurt," Karen wailed.

"I hope you've moved." Julia started forward, feeling for the doorway. She brushed Karen as she wiggled through.

In the hallway now, she realized how disoriented she was. There was an elevator by the nurses' station, but she remembered being told that operation depended on a key. Dr. Jeffers had apologized for not having any vacant rooms on the first floor, which were state-of-the-art and handicapped accessible. He had promised her the first one that became available. At the time it hadn't mattered. Now she realized how convenient this was for him. She was a prisoner of her own sightlessness. She was going to have to navigate the stairs alone.

"I don't suppose you'll tell me which way to go?"

"I can't," Karen said clearly. In a much lower voice she said, "Are you absolutely determined?"

"I'm leaving."

She lowered her voice still more. "Go right. At the end, go left. The stairs are on your right, at the very end of that corridor. I'll meet you there."

Julia understood. No one would fault Karen for giving in at that point and helping her patient to the first floor. She would be negligent to do anything else. But first Julia had to make it to the stairs alone.

Julia took a deep breath, buoyed by the knowledge that at the very least she wasn't going to tumble headfirst down a full flight of steps. She turned and took a step, then another. The hall was eerily silent. She wondered where the other patients were. Making pot holders or brownies in occupational therapy? She'd met no one since she arrived. No one had attempted to make her socialize. As she adjusted, Dr. Jeffers had wanted her to be alone with her thoughts.

She slid her hand along the wall beside her, taking another shuffling step. Each time she put her foot down, she expected anything but solid floor. She was falling into darkest space, disoriented and more frightened with each step. But the alternative frightened her more. If she was forced to stay, the depression Dr. Jeffers had cited would grow to be as real as the blindness that held her in its sway.

The wall dropped away, and startled, she jerked her hand back. Her feet were still planted firmly. She stood still for a moment, trying to picture her predicament. She realized that she must have encountered an open doorway, that there would probably be more than one on the hall. She lifted her left foot and replanted it in front of the right, feeling first with her toe to be certain the floor hadn't suddenly dropped away, as well. Satisfied she kept moving. After what seemed like several yards she felt the wall again, but closer than it had been, as if she'd veered off course.

She straightened and continued on. She had no idea how far she would have to travel. The hall could be a few more yards or many. She had driven by the clinic a thousand times, and now she tried to picture the building. Were the wings long? They were additions to an antebellum mansion, which was now the central reception area, but the additions were old, as well.

She didn't know how long she took to find her way to the end. She counted six doorways before she sensed something in front of her. She was sweating, even though the hallway was chilly. She was also trembling, afraid that each step would pitch her into space. Too well she remembered the terror of flying through the air, the sudden vision of total paralysis, the knowledge that she was about to hit the ground.

The realization that she could no longer see.

She stretched out her hands, but she touched nothing. She inched forward, arms extended, until her palms contacted glass. She was at the end of the hall, at a window, she guessed, and now it was time to turn left.

She turned, right hand still touching the window to help orient her. Relief was seeping through the fear. She was going to make this terrible journey in time to reach her mother. Maisy wouldn't leave without a drawn-out fight. But she had to hurry.

Julia took a step, then quickly, another. Her toe caught on something just in front of her, and before she could steady herself, she pitched forward to her knees.

Her cheek rested against the branches of a tree. She stifled a cry, then felt for her bearings. She had stumbled over a plant of some sort, a small tree in a pot. An interior decorator's vision.

She didn't linger. She used the pot to steady herself and got to her feet. She had fallen and lived through it. She had gotten back up. She was moving. She might trip again. She would keep moving.

Nearly at the end of the second hallway, she heard a warning just before she stumbled over what felt like the edge of a carpet and sprawled chest down on the floor. This time it took her a moment to catch her breath. Pain shot through her right knee, but before she could find her way to her feet, she felt strong arms helping her up.

"Damn it!" Karen sounded as if she wanted to weep. "I don't care if I lose my job. There have to be better places to work. If your mother's gone, I'll drive you home myself. I have a little boy at home. I just didn't want—"

Julia felt for Karen's hands. "I'm going to need help. Come with me. At least until you can find a job you like better."

"I'd like flipping hamburgers better than this."

"Let's go find my mother."

"Can you make the stairs?"

Julia managed a smile. "I'll do anything to get out of here."

"Don't forget I'll have my arm around you. Just put one foot in front of the other."

Julia found that was a lot easier with Karen walking beside her.

4

The inmates at Ludwell State Prison left Christian Carver alone. That hadn't always been true. When he had arrived as a frightened twenty-three-year-old, he had snagged more than his share of attention. Athletic and strong, he was also lean-hipped and slim. And at twenty-three Christian hadn't yet learned the importance of feeling nothing, so that he truly had nothing to hide.

In a matter of months he had learned—the hard way—everything he needed to survive a life sentence. Who to befriend and who not to let out of his sight. How to tolerate the noise and the smell. How to find some common denominator with men who had broken into houses or set them ablaze, maniacs who had murdered old women and raped small children. The right balance between anger and hate, so that he could endure but not be consumed by the fire within him.

He had made a peace of sorts with his life. One of the guards had taken an interest in young Christian's welfare and moved him into a cell with an old man convicted of murdering his wife. Alf Johnson had smothered his beloved Doris at her own request when the cancer eating away her lungs made every breath a torment. In the pre-Kevorkian days of Alf's trial, Doris's death had simply been premeditated murder.

Alf had used his years in prison to pursue the education his life on the outside had never allowed, and he had taken the young man under his wing. Before his death a year later, he'd taught

Christian how to have a life behind bars, as well as one important motto to live by.

Only one man can imprison your spirit.

Now, as always, Christian was employing everything he'd learned.

"I don't give advice." Christian examined the golden retriever puppy at his feet. Seesaw had a coat as shiny as polished nuggets and liquid brown eyes that noticed absolutely everything. "Seesaw, sit."

The dog sat obediently, her plump puppy body wiggling with pent-up energy. But Seesaw stayed where she was, despite instincts that told her otherwise.

Christian reached down to pet and praise her.

The man beside him spoke. "I don't need advice, man. I just need to know how to get Tyrell off my back."

"Same thing." Christian snapped the leash on Seesaw's collar. "Heel, Seesaw."

"Hey, you been here a long time—"

Christian straightened. "And I'm going to be here a lot longer. So I know better than to say anything that might get me in trouble."

"How'd telling me what to do get you in trouble?" The young man walked beside Christian as he and Seesaw slowly paced the indoor track that the prison dog trainers used for walking their canine charges. Timbo Baines was new to Ludwell, young, black and terrified. He had chosen Christian as his mentor, a job Christian didn't want but wasn't quite embittered enough to refuse.

"Look, Timbo. Tyrell has friends here. Friends talk to friends. You'll talk to some of them. You'll mention me."

"So what if I just stay out of his way?"

"Make it a priority." Christian stopped to gently scold the puppy, who was beginning to strain at the leash. "He has a short attention span."

"He? I thought Seesaw was a girl."

"Not Seesaw. Tyrell."

"Yeah? Oh, yeah. I get it. Okay."

"Think you can take over? Don't raise your voice. Praise her if she does what you want her to. Don't jerk on the leash."

"Don't know how I got stuck training dogs."

"Guess you were just lucky." As well as convicted for selling cocaine to middle-class teenagers who'd been sight-seeing in Richmond's inner city.

Christian started back toward the kennel.

"Christian?"

He hadn't noticed the Reverend Bertha Petersen at the end of the first run. An overweight woman in her fifties, she wore jeans and a sweatshirt with a bandanna covering her closely cropped salt-and-pepper hair. A barrel-chested guard stood stiffly nearby, watching every move Christian made.

Christian approached her, stopping several yards away so as not to worry him. "Hello, Pastor. We weren't expecting you."

"It's good to see you. How are the new puppies?"

"It's too early to tell. But no real problems so far. The Lab's a little excitable. She may calm down, but we'll watch her."

Bertha Petersen was the director of Pets and Prisoners Together and an ordained minister in a small fundamentalist sect with a long name. While many of her cohorts were busily converting the heathen, Bertha had turned her own considerable energy to good works.

The purpose of Pets and Prisoners was to raise and train helping dogs for the physically or mentally challenged. Ludwell was the first prison in the program to train dogs for the blind, turning over two dozen a year to organizations that did the final portion of the training and placed them. Christian had been in charge of the Ludwell program for two years.

"So, did you just drop by to check on us?"

"I like to keep up with everybody if I can." Bertha's gaze traveled to the guard, then back to Christian. "Why don't you show me the dogs in training? How many do you have right now?"

Ludwell had two separate programs in progress. A new program, of which Seesaw was a part, evaluated puppies who had been bred to become guide dogs. The second and more established, brought in young dogs who had already been socialized by a host family and trained in good manners and family routine.

They received intensive training from the prison staff for three months before they were passed on to one of several programs.

Christian would have liked to finish the training of each animal, but the final month involved working with the dog's new master, often on city streets. And no one felt safe sending the blind to a prison or prisoners to the blind.

But what did that matter compared to everything else the men were denied?

"We have four dogs left," Christian told the pastor. "We started this session with ten."

She turned to the guard. "Officer, we're going over to the other kennel. Will that be all right?"

He didn't answer directly. Instead he picked up his two-way radio and spoke into it, then he gave a brief nod.

The second kennel was on the other side of solid steel doors. Christian and Bertha waited as the doors opened, then closed behind them. They walked down a short corridor flanked by video cameras. The second kennel looked much like the first, but the track was considerably larger, and a yard fenced in mesh and topped with razor wire was visible through a window.

The guard on duty here was used to Christian and hardly gave him a glance. He was busy watching one of the other inmates walk blindfolded through an obstacle course. A chocolate Lab wearing a leather harness led him through the maze. Javier Garcia, a huge man in blue jeans, walked confidently behind him.

Christian and Bertha strolled over to the guardrail overlooking the course and watched.

Christian explained what they were viewing. "That's Cocoa. She's had a little trouble with overhead obstacles." The dogs had to be trained not to lead their new masters into low-hanging obstacles like tree branches and awnings, even if their masters urged them forward. Guide dogs were trained to practice "intelligent disobedience." Their own good instincts had to supplant their blind master's commands.

"She's catching on?"

"Cocoa's a winner. Very bright. She'll make it. But we had one of her litter mates who flunked out the first week. He jumped at loud noises. Very distractible for a Lab. Hopefully by checking out the puppies earlier, we'll avoid these problems.''

The pastor was silent for a moment as she watched Javier and Cocoa move flawlessly along the track. Then she turned so she could see Christian's face. "Christian, I've been considering this conversation carefully.''

He waited stoically, another survival skill he'd learned.

"I've heard something.''

He supposed Bertha heard lots of gossip as she moved from prison to prison. Ludwell wasn't the only penal institution that trained helping dogs.

She continued. "I suspect I could be accused of interfering with proper procedure for telling you this. Certainly for jumping the gun.''

"I'm listening.''

"Have you heard of a man named Karl Zandoff?''

Christian devoured the newspaper whenever he could. Anyone who could read had heard of Karl Zandoff. He gave a short nod. "He's on death row in Florida. His appeals are almost up.''

"His execution date's been set for December.''

"Yeah, and it looks like a date he'll be keeping.''

"He's been talking to the authorities.''

"So?''

"Apparently he's confessed to another murder, one they didn't suspect him of.''

"Nothing like a rendezvous with Old Sparky to get the juices flowing.''

"I'm told he might confess to more before this is over.''

Despite himself, Christian was growing curious. "Maybe confession's good for the soul. You'd believe that, wouldn't you?''

"How about you?''

"I haven't seen much God in here, Pastor. If we were ever on speaking terms, we haven't been for a long time. If I had anything to confess myself, I'd do it to my lawyer.''

She didn't miss a beat. "Zandoff told them where to look for the body, and they found it. A case solved. The girl's parents can finally put her to rest.''

"Girl?''

"A college student in Tennessee. She disappeared ten years ago."

"I thought all his crimes had been committed in Florida."

"Now they're looking at other unsolved murders in the South. Turns out he drifted for a while. Worked construction, followed the jobs. Then he settled in with a wife and couple of kids in the Sunshine State. But he didn't stop preying on young women."

Christian knew Zandoff had been caught with a young woman's monogrammed barrette and a brand-new shovel covered with Tallahassee's sandy clay loam. That was the crime he'd been arrested for. And when the body was finally located, the two in shallow graves beside it had earned him the death penalty.

Christian searched the pastor's face impassively. On the track beyond them he could hear Javier praising Cocoa for a job well-done. They only had another minute at most to finish the conversation before Javier joined them.

"I'm unclear as to why you're telling me this. I'm not Karl Zandoff. I didn't kill one woman, much less an interstate sorority. If you think his example is going to stir my conscience, forget it."

"Christian." She shook her head, as if she really was disappointed in him. "I know you as well as anybody does. You didn't kill Fidelity Sutherland."

He studied her. "There were people who knew me as well as they knew themselves, and they questioned it." One woman in particular, whose face he still hadn't been able to erase from his memory.

She glanced at the track. "I'm telling you because there's a rumor Zandoff spent time in northern Virginia between nine and ten years ago. He's hinting that he murdered a woman here, as well."

For a moment Christian didn't make the connection. Then he shrugged. "Lots of people disappear or die mysteriously every year."

"He worked construction. They're looking at records."

"How do you know all this?"

"Somebody working the case told me. I want to call your attorney. Your interests should be represented."

Javier reached the railing with Cocoa in tow. He had black hair that fell straight to his shoulders and an incongruously narrow face that didn't fit his broad body. "Did you see that? She's catching on, and she goes with a real light touch. She'll be perfect for a woman."

"Hello, Javier." Bertha greeted him warmly. "I spoke to your wife last week."

The big man beamed. "She doing okay, Pastor?"

"She says you have a good chance with the parole board. Should I start scouting out a job for you?"

"You'd do that?"

"I sure would."

There wasn't much Bertha Petersen wouldn't do for her inmates. She believed in every one of them, despite all evidence to the contrary. She was as comfortable with murderers as she was with Bible-thumping evangelists. She wasn't foolish, she simply believed that God held her life in his hands.

"About that phone call?" She turned to Christian.

He shrugged. He was dismayed to find that for a moment he had almost been suckered by hope. But unlike the good pastor, he had no illusions that God cared one way or the other what happened to Christian Carver. The prison walls were too thick for lightning to strike here.

"I'll take it that's a yes," she said with a smile. "I'll leave you gentlemen to your work."

"She don't know what bad asses we really are, does she?" Javier said, once the minister was out of earshot.

"Oh, she knows. She just doesn't care." Christian grimaced. "God doesn't deserve a woman like that one."

"Hey, man, you could go to hell for saying that."

"Been there, doing that." Christian walked away.

5

Julia longed to pace, but that was a recipe for disaster. She'd been raised in this house, but nothing had ever stayed the same. As a child she might return home from school to find that Maisy had rearranged bedrooms or turned the dining room into an exercise studio. Furniture mysteriously traveled from room to room, and carpets soared to new locations like props from the Arabian Nights.

With her eyesight intact, the changes had been mere annoyances. Now they were lethal. She didn't know where to step or sit. Even with Karen's help, she hadn't yet mastered the small first-floor bedroom where Jake had made her welcome.

"I'm facing the window that looks over the front driveway." Julia lifted her arm cautiously, but if she was indeed facing the window, it was still more than a length away.

"Good." Karen's voice sounded calmer than it had since their escape from the clinic.

Julia felt sympathy for the nurse, but right now she was too worried about Callie to offer much support. Maisy had gone to Millcreek to fetch her, and Julia was afraid there might be trouble. "I've got it right?"

"You're right on target. We'll get this room memorized, then I'll talk to your parents about setting up the rest of the house so you can move around easily." Karen paused. "This really isn't my area of expertise, Mrs. Warwick. You'd do better to hire someone who has experience with the blind."

"Call me Julia. And you have a job with me as long as you want one."

"Your eyesight could return tomorrow. I hope it does."

"Me, too. And if it does, then you automatically become my personal assistant. And don't think I don't need one. I've been threatening to hire somebody, and now I have."

"Just remember I warned you."

"Didn't you tell me you have a son at home? Do you need to get back to him?"

"Brandon. My mother takes care of him."

"Why don't you go ahead and leave for the day? You've done more than enough. But we'll see—" She stopped and wondered how long she'd continue to use that expression. "We can expect you in the morning?"

"Eight? Nine?"

"Nine will be terrific." Julia managed a smile. "I'm turning now and facing the bed." She started forward, stopping after several steps. She put out her hands but didn't touch anything. Karen wisely kept silent.

She took two more steps before feeling for the bed again. This time she felt the spread under her fingertips. "I can make myself comfortable. Go on, now."

"Nine, then. I'll come right after I get Brandon off to school. Sleep well."

"Better than I have in weeks."

"If you have trouble, try herbal tea or warm milk."

Julia liked that prescription better than the ones the doctor had issued. "A shot of whiskey in the milk might work wonders."

Karen squeezed her shoulder. In a moment Julia heard the door close behind her.

She was home. But not in the upstairs room where she had danced to Depeche Mode and Michael Jackson's "Thriller," where she had sketched a thousand portraits of her schoolmates and landscapes of her beloved hills, suffered over trigonometry defeats, talked on the telephone for hours to Fidelity...and Christian.

Her hands rested in her lap, but she felt them ball into fists. She hadn't slept under this roof since her marriage. Even though she'd only been twenty when she married Bard, she had packed away her childhood and stored it in the attic of her unconscious.

She remembered it, of course. If she had the need she could pull pieces of it from mental suitcases and trunks. When Callie asked, Julia told stories of growing up at Ashbourne, of the winter when she'd had the chicken pox and to cheer her Maisy had dressed up like Santa Claus to deliver Valentine candy nestled in a lavender-and-yellow Easter basket.

She thought now that she had been a pensive child in a happy home. A quiet child in a home where nothing ever went unsaid. A secretive child in a home with no mysteries. No one here had belittled her or tried to change her. She had been accepted and loved, and though at times she had yearned for the more traditional households and parents of her friends, she had also realized just how lucky she was.

Until the day her world turned upside down.

Her reverie was broken by a knock at her door. "Come in," she called too loudly, grateful to be interrupted.

"I brought you some tea. I remember the way you liked it as a little girl."

She smiled in the direction of Jake's voice. "You're too good to me." She heard his footsteps.

"No one could ever be too good to you, Julia." He set something, probably her cup, on the table beside her bed. "It's our largest mug, about half full. I baked cookies last weekend, and there are two on the saucer beside it. Shall I put the mug in your hand?"

"Please." She extended her hand and closed it around warm pottery, probably one of Maisy's projects. Maisy had gone through an unfortunate ceramics era, and the cupboards were still filled with lopsided mugs and plates that couldn't survive the microwave.

Jake waited until she was secure before he released it. "Two lumps of sugar and plenty of milk."

"I haven't had it that way in years. What a treat."

The bed sagged. She could tell he was sitting at the foot now. "You've had quite a day."

She hadn't thought of it for years, but now she remembered

the many times Jake had come to her room as a teenager, making himself available if she wanted to talk, departing without comment if she didn't. He never probed, never criticized. Jake had always simply been there. No real father could have been kinder.

"Dr. Jeffers was threatening to have me committed if I didn't agree to stay there on my own."

"Could he do that?"

"I don't know the law, something I'm sure he was counting on. I guess he thought that was his ace in the hole."

"Well, about now he's playing fifty-two pickup, isn't he?"

"I couldn't get better there. But maybe I won't get better here, either."

"What would be the worst thing that could happen?"

"I might never see again."

"Highly unlikely, but let's say it's possible. Then what?"

"I learn to live with being blind."

"Could you?"

"Would I have a choice?"

"Only a very extreme one."

She realized he was talking about suicide. "This is terrible. Unthinkable. But I still have my life, my family. I'm not going to do anything foolish." Tears filled her eyes. "Jake, what is Callie going to think of me?"

He was quiet a moment. "I believe we're about to find out."

She heard the pickup, too. "I don't want her to see me crying."

"Drink some tea and wipe your eyes."

The tea tasted like childhood, like rainy afternoons and Black Stallion novels and the wind whistling through evergreen hedges. She had regained her composure, at least outwardly, by the time she heard the old heart of pine floors creaking with excitement.

Then her door burst open. She felt Jake remove the cup from her hands, and she opened her arms wide just in time to catch her daughter's soft body in a fierce bear hug. She pictured her as she held her.

Callie Warwick had pigtails the color of butterscotch and brown eyes rimmed with thick black lashes. Like her mother she was small-boned and petite. Unlike Julia, she was spontaneous, open and unafraid to show her feelings.

"Mommy!"

Julia wondered if she would ever see her daughter's sweet face again. "I'm so glad you're here!"

"Maisy came and got me. And she got Feather Foot, too. I mean she told Ramon to get her and bring her here so I can ride at Ashbourne. Isn't that neat?"

Feather Foot was Callie's pony. At eight, like most local children, Callie was an accomplished rider. "Maisy is the world's best grandma," Julia said.

Callie giggled. "We played hide-and-seek with Mrs. Taylor."

Julia imagined it was more like hide, then hide some more. She was sure that once Callie's suitcases were packed, Maisy hadn't wanted to run into Millcreek's housekeeper.

"Everything go okay, Maisy?" Julia lifted her face from Callie's hair. She knew her mother was standing there by the scent of violets.

"No problems at all. And we stopped by the stables to make arrangements to have Feather Foot loaded and delivered within the hour."

"Are we really going to stay here, Mommy?"

Julia brushed Callie's bangs back from her forehead. "Yes, we are. Maisy and Jake say they want to take care of us until my eyesight returns, but I think they just want more time with you."

"Is that true?" Callie said.

"Your mommy's too smart for words," Maisy said. "She always was. I could tell you stories."

"And will if there's even one moment of silence to give you a foothold," Jake said.

"Maisy said I can pick out any room I want upstairs. Do you want to help?" Callie was silent as Julia tried to think how to gently remind her that picking things out right now was a difficult task. "Oh, you can't," Callie said matter-of-factly. "I forgot."

Julia felt a weight lifting from her shoulders. She had nearly bought Bard's warnings that her blindness would be an insurmountable hurdle for Callie.

She hugged Callie again, then released her. "I could go along anyway and tell you what I remember. Like the time I hid under the bed in the room beside the bathroom because I didn't want to go to school.''

"You did?''

"Uh-huh. And Maisy pretended nothing was wrong all day. Nobody even looked for me.''

"Is that true?'' Callie asked.

Maisy answered. "Absolutely. I figured if she needed a day under the bed, I'd let her have one.''

"Is the bed still there?''

"Don't get any ideas,'' Julia said. "You'll be going to school every day. Besides, it was dusty and boring.''

"I'm going to see if it's still dusty.'' The clatter of feet disappearing down the hall announced her departure.

"Well,'' Maisy said, "piece of cake.''

"She didn't find it odd that you were practically kidnapping her?'' Julia said.

"Not at all. She did wonder what Bard would say. Then she said maybe he wouldn't notice.''

"He'll notice,'' Julia said. "The telephone will be ringing shortly.''

"How would you like us to handle it?''

"There's a phone on my table, right?''

"I moved the cordless in here. It will be easier for you to use,'' Jake said.

"Then I can handle Bard.''

"He's always welcome here, Julia.'' Maisy's tone sounded sincere enough.

"When Bard is under stress the worst parts of him come to the surface. He gets more rigid and more assertive. But he'll come around once he sees I mean business.''

"Will you go home, then?''

She was home. As strange as it felt, it also felt right. She wondered what that said about her. She was a grown woman with a husband and child of her own, but she needed the parents she had left behind. She had crawled back into the womb.

"Let her take it one step at a time,'' Jake said, when Julia didn't answer.

"Maisy, will you help Callie get settled upstairs?" Julia said.

"With pleasure. If she wants your old room?"

"It's a room, not a shrine."

"Maisy!" Callie's voice drifted down the stairwell.

"Would you like your tea again?" Jake said.

Julia wanted her life again. She did not want to be a tormented, hysterical, sightless woman who was forced to depend on her stepfather to put a mug of tea in her hand.

She shook her head. "No, I'm going to find it on my own, thanks."

She waited for someone to argue. No one did.

"We'll leave you to it, then," Jake said. "And just so you know, if you happen to knock that particular mug to the floor, that would be fine with me."

"Not one of my better efforts," Maisy agreed.

"Definitely not."

Julia could picture Jake, his arm slung over Maisy's shoulder, leading his wife from the room. Tears filled her eyes again.

She took a moment to mourn all she had lost. Then she swallowed her tears and began her search.

6

Fidelity Sutherland, her long blond hair woven in a flawless French braid, came to Christian that night. Her smile was as sassy as ever, her throat a gaping caricature, a hideously grinning half-moon that spouted a river of blood down the front of a tailored white shirt.

He awoke without a sound and sat up quickly, but Fidelity would not be purged. In death, as in life, she was tenacious. As a young woman she had found ways to have everything she wanted. Dead almost ten years, she hadn't lost her touch.

By the faint lightening of the sky Christian saw that dawn was perched on the horizon. There was a small barred window in his cell, too high for any purpose other than to let in slivers of light. He'd often wondered why windows had been included in the prison's design. To remind the refuse of society that the sun rose and set without them?

Christian pillowed his head on his arms and stared up at the window. One year a red-winged blackbird had taken a liking to the narrow ledge and landed there intermittently all summer, vo-calizing his own version of "nevermore," which had seemed all too appropriate to Christian. He'd found himself looking for the blackbird whenever he was in his cell, but the moment Christian had begun to count on finding it there, the bird disappeared.

Blackbirds had darkened the skies at Claymore Park. Christian had grown up with them. Telephone lines crowded with glisten-ing feathered bodies like endless ropes of Tahitian pearls. Once he had told Julia Ashbourne that her hair reminded him of a blackbird's wing.

Once he had been a foolishly romantic young man with no idea of how quickly everything in his life could change.

"You awake?"

Christian didn't take his eyes from the window. His cell mate, a man named Landis, always woke early. Landis, not yet twenty-one, was getting a head start on a lifetime of mornings like this one. Like Christian, his chances of encountering dawn any place else were almost nonexistent.

"Go back to sleep," Christian said. "You have time."

"Shit, I don't sleep. You don't know what can happen to you when you're sleeping."

"Nothing's going to happen in here. You're not my type."

"You got a type?"

Christian's type had been female and deceptively fragile, black-haired, blue-eyed and much too serious. In the company of the more flamboyant Fidelity Sutherland she had been easy for some people to overlook. He hadn't been one of them.

He thought the sky was growing lighter quickly, which was too bad. "My type is female. Which means you're safe."

"Shit, most people got that idea when they come in here. But look what goes on."

"Don't look. You'll be better off."

"How you get to be so bored with all this? You don't care about bein' here?"

"What good would it do to care?"

"I never met nobody as alone as you." Landis continued, buoyed by Christian's silence. "You got no family?"

"All gone."

"No woman waiting?"

"That would be a long wait, wouldn't it?"

"You get mail, but you don't even read it."

Christian shifted, easing the pressure on his forearms. "You're paying attention to things that aren't your business, Landis."

Landis bristled. "So? You gonna make something out of it?"

"I don't give a rat's ass what you notice, but other people might."

"So?"

"I've seen men stabbed for less."

"I just said you don't read your mail. That's all I said. How come you don't?"

"No reason to."

"It makes you homesick, don't it? Mine makes me homesick."

On a night when he'd been high on drugs and sure he was invincible, the young veteran of the streets of Southeast D.C. had killed a cop in a car chase, just within the Virginia border. Unfortunately he was also the proud owner of a rap sheet as long as the list of foster homes he'd paraded through from the time he was three. This wasn't Landis's first time in jail, but it would almost certainly be his last.

"I got me a girl back home," Landis said. "I'm gonna get out of here someday. She'll be waiting."

Christian was silent.

"Your mail from a woman?"

Maisy Fletcher was certainly that. A warm earth mother who had taken Christian under her wing the first time she laid eyes on him. Now, all these years later, she hadn't given up on him, even though her daughter had tossed him away like so much spoiled paté.

Maisy wrote Christian faithfully, averaging a letter a month. The letters appeared as regularly as beans and corn bread on Wednesday nights. There was nothing else Maisy could do for him.

He had gotten one yesterday, hence Landis's question. He never read the letters anymore. In the first years of his sentence, he had read them all until he realized that the letters were like acid burning holes through his thickening defenses. She talked about people he'd grown up with, talked *around* Julia's marriage to Lombard Warwick, told funny stories about life in Ridge's Race. As a letter writer Maisy, who in everyday life was often inarticulate and unfocused, came into her own. She captured the life he'd left behind too perfectly.

"Chris, you awake?"

"What chance do I have to sleep with you talking?"

"I'll stop reading letters, too, won't I? One day, I'll stop reading them. Just like you."

Christian closed his eyes.

"Heel, Seesaw." Seesaw obediently took up her place beside Christian and started down the track.

She was a particularly pretty puppy, clever and bursting with energy. But Christian knew better than to get attached to any of the dogs who came through the Pets and Prisoners program. He had grown up with dogs and horses. He'd seen both at their best and worst, trained them, nursed them, even put them down when required.

He kept his distance here. The dogs he trained went on to new masters. He knew from reports how well they were cared for and how invaluable they were. Sometimes he found himself wishing he could watch a puppy like Seesaw grow up, but he knew how lucky he was to have this chance to work with her at all. Training guide dogs was as close to his past as he was liable to come.

Timbo signaled from the side of the track, and Christian stopped and turned. Seesaw waited beside him as he unsnapped her leash. Timbo called her name, and she trotted toward him. Christian followed.

"Okay, Timbo. If you had to rate her chances of getting through the advanced training, what would you say?"

Timbo studied the puppy as he petted her. "Good. No, better than good. I'd say nine out of ten." He looked up. "What do you say?"

"Eight out of ten. She's a party girl. We may have some trouble teaching her to ignore other dogs. But it's a small problem at this point, and I expect it will go away as she matures. I'll mention it to her new family."

"They're taking her tomorrow?"

"In the morning. We'll get another batch of puppies next week. I'll finish the paperwork tonight."

"She'll have a good home?"

Christian raised a brow. For a man who couldn't imagine how he'd been assigned to train dogs, Timbo was evolving fast. "All the homes are good. Most have children and other pets to play with. She'll be fine. And we'll see her back here in a year.''

''Just wondering.''

''You've done your job with her.''

''Never had me no dog. But I fed some, you know? Dogs in the neighborhood nobody took care of. Used to buy sacks of dog food and leave 'em in the alley at night.''

''You're all heart, Timbo.''

Timbo grinned. ''That's me.''

''Do a good job here, and when you get out Bertha will help find you a job on the outside.''

''What, shoveling dog shit at some kennel?''

''You might aim a little higher than that.''

''I got big plans.''

Christian squatted beside the little retriever, scratching behind her ears. ''A man's plans have a way of changing.''

''Yeah? Looks like yours are about to.''

Christian glanced up and saw the guard on duty motioning for him. He stood. ''Take her back to the kennel, would you? Then go on over and help Javier. I'll see what he wants.''

''What he wants is to make you feel like you nuthin'.''

Silently Christian handed Timbo Seesaw's leash.

Mel Powers was a skinny man who perspired like a heavy one. He wore an extravagant hairpiece, expensive suits that always looked cheap and gold-rimmed glasses with lenses that were as thick as his New Jersey accent. The effect was more ambulance chaser than high-powered attorney, but Mel Powers was the revered Great White of shark-infested waters. Mel, considered the best criminal attorney in Virginia, had been hired by Peter Claymore to represent Christian. He still took Christian's conviction as a personal affront.

Peter Claymore, of Claymore Park, was a study in contrasts. At sixty, he was twenty years older than Mel, and if he sweated at all, it was only after hours of riding to hounds. His silver hair was thick and his eyesight so perfect he could detect movement in the forest when everyone else believed a fox had gone to ground. When he wore a suit, it was tailored to highlight the breadth of his shoulders and the good taste of his ancestors. Claymore Park, the largest and most successful horse property in Ridge's Race, had been home to Claymores long before the War of Northern Aggression.

Christian hadn't expected to find either man waiting for him in the tiny visitors' room. Neither the guard who had summoned him to the warden's office nor the warden who had brought him here had given him any indication. After shaking hands, he seated himself on the other side of the small rectangular table and waited for them to speak.

"You're looking well, Christian." Peter sat with one arm on the table, the other thrown over the back of his chair. He looked at home in this unlikely place, but in all the years Christian had known him, Peter had never seemed ill at ease.

"I'm doing as well as you could expect, sir." Christian's gaze flicked to Mel, who was patting his forehead with a folded handkerchief.

"I get the heebie-jeebies every time I come." Mel wiped his hands. "I feel like I'm being smothered in cotton. Can't breathe at all. I don't know how you do it."

"Breathing comes naturally to me."

"I hear good reports about the Pets and Prisoners program," Peter said.

"I doubt they'll cut it any time soon."

"You might not be here long enough to worry." Mel shoved his handkerchief in his pocket, then thought better of it. He took it out, folded it and shoved it in again.

"Christian, we've had some encouraging news." Peter put both hands on the table and leaned forward. "Very encouraging."

Christian, who had been wending his way through the appeals process for too long to be hopeful, waited. But even though he struggled not to feel anything, something inside him tightened, a spring coiling in anticipation.

"Bertha Petersen says she talked to you?"

"About Karl Zandoff? She did."

"It must have been on your mind ever since."

In truth, Christian had refused to let himself dwell on his conversation with Bertha. False hope was more dangerous than none, and "long shot" had been coined for coincidences like this one. "It hasn't been on my mind. Why should it be? Zandoff's about to fry, and the only thing we ever had in common was his brief residence in Virginia. If he ever lived here at all."

Mel waved his hand, directing the conversation like a hyperactive symphony conductor. "He seems to think you have more in common than that. You were convicted of Fidelity Sutherland's murder, but Zandoff was the one who calmly slit her throat."

For a moment Christian couldn't breathe. Then he shook his head. "You're telling me this is what you believe? What you hope for?"

"He's telling you what Zandoff told the authorities in Florida this morning. He confessed to killing Fidelity. He was there, at South Land, the afternoon Fidelity was killed. He caught her alone in the house. He killed her—"

"How does he say he got my knife?" The knife that had killed Fidelity, a specially designed horseman's knife with several blades and tools, had belonged to Christian.

"Found it in the Sutherlands' barn on a window ledge. You'd been there that week to ride, hadn't you? You probably used it to pick a hoof or trim a strap, then left it."

"What about the jewelry? I've read Zandoff's history. He only killed for pleasure."

"He always took trophies." Mel fanned himself with his hand. "And this time he says he needed money to get back to Florida. Nobody was at home, so afterward he took his time looking for something he could sell. She didn't keep her jewelry under lock and key. We knew that. He found it, pocketed it and went outside."

"That's when he saw you," Peter said. "You were calling Fidelity's name. He said you were on the way inside and you looked furious. He knew you would find her, and he started to worry that someone might catch and search him before he got far enough away to avoid suspicion. So he dug a hole and buried the jewelry."

Mel took over. "But not everything. After he heard your voice, he was in such a hurry that he dropped a necklace."

Christian stared at him.

"That's the necklace you found on the stairs," Peter said. "The one that put you in this prison."

"They're looking for the jewelry now." Mel took out his handkerchief again. "He's told the police where to look. When they find it, it will corroborate his story."

Christian sat forward. "And if they don't?"

"Why wouldn't they?"

"Because it's been nine years. Where does he say he hid it?"

Peter answered. "Along the fence line between South Land and Claymore Park."

"Do you know how many people come and go at South Land? Do you think there's really a chance that if any of the drifters who've worked for the Sutherlands found that jewelry they would have turned it in?"

"Zandoff says he was planning to go back for it," Peter said. "Only he never had the chance. He got scared and took off for Florida without it. But he claims he hid it well. We've got a good chance, Christian. A very good chance."

"And if they do find it?"

"Then we'll be back in court to have you released while the matter's investigated further."

Christian sat absolutely still, but his heart was speeding. He could school his appearance, even his thoughts, but his body remembered what it was like to be free.

Peter reached across the table and rested his hand on Christian's. "I know how you must feel. Believe me, I know, and so does Mel."

"How do I feel?" Christian wasn't even certain.

"Angry so much of your life has been wasted. Hopeful that the worst is almost over. Afraid that it isn't."

"Why would Zandoff confess?"

"He doesn't have anything to lose."

"He's got a wife, children...."

"Maybe he wants to do the right thing for once, to show his kids that he had some kind of morals."

"Maybe he just feels sorry for you," Mel said. "He knows another man is serving time for something he did."

Christian knew other men who had killed simply for the pleasure of it. Not a one of them would care if someone else took the rap.

"Maybe he's bragging." Peter removed his hand. "Maybe he just wants the world to know how good he was at what he did and how many times he did it."

"Or maybe he's hoping if he confesses to a few more murders, he can string the authorities along for a while and hold off his execution date." Mel put his arms on the table. "Who the hell cares, Christian? That's not your problem. In fact, as far as I can see, you don't have a problem right now. You just got to sit tight and wait. They're bringing metal detectors, and they're going to start digging holes along the fence line today. Zandoff's outlined the general area, but this may take a while. Nobody's exactly sure where or how deep he buried it. We don't want to miss it by inches."

Christian said nothing, but his mind was whirling.

"We wanted you to know," Peter said. "We didn't want to spring it on you. There's a chance this won't come to anything, but it's a small one. Even without the jewelry to back up Zandoff's story, we can still get back into court with this. It will take longer, and the outcome won't be as certain, but the odds are still in your favor."

"If we have to, we'll try to find somebody, anybody, who remembers Zandoff being in the area when Miss Sutherland was killed." Mel took out his handkerchief once more, this time to clean his glasses. "We'll search the records of local contractors, cheap hotels, ask at bars...."

Everything they described cost money, and lots of it. Every breath Mel took cost money. He had reduced his fees since the beginning, believing he would free Christian, and the resulting publicity would be worth the fees he lost. And to his credit, even after a devastating defeat, he had continued to reduce his fees during the appeals process. But even reduced, Christian's legal fees could put quadruplets through Ivy League colleges and send them to Europe after graduation.

The money had been paid by Peter Claymore.

Christian switched his gaze to Peter. "If something does happen, and they let me out of here, I'll find a way to pay you back."

"You were my son's best friend. You're like a son to me, Christian. Robby would have expected me to help you. You don't owe me a thing."

But Christian knew he owed Peter everything. Were it not for Peter, his life would be entirely without hope. And despite his better instincts, Christian could feel hope stirring. Despite a past that railed against it. Despite the friends who had deserted him and the detractors who had silently nodded their heads. Hope was light pouring through the broken pieces of his heart.

7

Maisy was a good cook, but Jake was a better one. Together they fixed a dinner that tempted Julia out of her self-imposed fast. She had Callie to think about, a vulnerable daughter who did not need another anorexic role model. Television already supplied too many.

She decided to address her own embarrassment up-front. "This is delicious. But I bet I'm making a mess."

Callie giggled. "You have gravy on your chin."

Julia felt a napkin dabbing around her mouth. She let her daughter take care of her, grateful that Callie seemed more interested in than frightened by her predicament.

"I'm going to try eating with my eyes closed," Callie said.

"One messy eater at a table, please." Julia smiled in her daughter's direction. "Poor Maisy will have enough to clean up as it is."

"Another biscuit?" Maisy spoke from across the table. "Julia?"

Julia shook her head. "This is more than I've eaten in a week. It's wonderful." And it really was. Maisy had always been an eclectic cook, quickly tiring of one cuisine and moving on to another. Thai lemon grass soup or Salvadoran pupusas had been as commonly served as country ham. Tonight she and Jake had prepared Southern classic. Fried chicken, biscuits and cream gravy, green beans cooked with salt pork and Jake's famous sweet potato pie for dessert. A heart attack on a plate.

"Pie after I clean up?" Maisy asked.

"I'll help," Julia said. "I can dry dishes."

Maisy didn't argue or fuss. "I'll help you find your way."

"I want to see Feather Foot." Callie's chair scraped the floor beside Julia. "He might be lonely."

"I'll take you." Jake's chair scraped, too. "Then we can close up for the night. I could use your help."

"Can I, Mommy?"

"You bet." Julia got to her feet and slid her hands along the table until it ended. Maisy took her arm, and, shuffling her feet so as not to trip, Julia followed her mother's lead.

The kitchen was large enough for a table of its own, enameled metal and cool to the touch. Julia rested her fingers on its edge. Whenever she had needed help she had done her homework here as a young girl, letting Maisy drill her on spelling words or Jake untangle math problems, step by step. She had abandoned this warm family center as she grew older, preferring her own company to theirs. Her room had become a haven, the telephone her lifeline.

Again she thought of Fidelity, and, inevitably, of Christian.

"You have the expression on your face you used to get as a little girl." Maisy released Julia's arm. "You're a million miles away. I used to wonder how to travel that far."

Julia was surprised. Maisy, for all her love, her sneak attacks into intimacy, rarely expressed what she was feeling. She decided to be honest. "I was just thinking about Fidelity."

"What brought her to mind?"

"Being here, I guess. I feel like a girl again."

"She was a big part of your childhood. Christian, too."

Julia couldn't touch that. "And Robby. So much sadness."

"You saw too much sadness."

"I've wondered if that's what this is about. If I'm blind because of that. If everything finally caught up with me. Fidelity's murder, Christian's conviction, Robby's accident."

"Did you ask the doctor?"

"Would you share the time of day with that man?"

"Julia, do you want me to see if I can find you a good therapist, somebody you'd feel comfortable talking to?"

Julia could imagine the sort of therapist her mother might choose. An escapee from Esalen, a guru who started each session with ancient Hindu chants or a fully orchestrated psychodrama.

Maisy laughed a little, low and somehow sad. "This is interesting, but I really can almost see your thoughts now. You've always been so good at hiding them, but that's changed."

"Maisy, I—"

"There's a woman in Warrenton who is supposed to be excellent. No fireworks or instant revelations. Just good listening skills and sound advice."

Julia wondered what choice she had. Did she want to call her own friends for recommendations and open her life to more gossip? Could she trust Bard to find someone more suitable?

"Why don't you give her a try? If you don't like her, we'll look for someone else." Maisy took her arm. "I'll wash in the dishpan, and I'll put the clean dishes in the other side of the sink to rinse. You can dry them and stack them on the counter."

Julia joined her mother at the sink, but the first dish she picked up slipped and fell back into the sink.

"Don't even say it." Maisy adjusted the water to a lighter flow. "I won't put you to drying the good china just yet."

Julia picked up the plate again and started to rub it with the towel Maisy had provided. "We did this when I was little. Remember? Of course, then I could see what I was doing."

"From the time we moved in here. When it was just you and me."

For Julia, those early days seemed like centuries ago. She remembered little before Jake joined their lives and almost nothing of living in the big house with her father. "Why did you move here, Maisy?" She had asked the question before, of course, but she hoped now she would get a more detailed answer.

"Truthfully? Ashbourne's too large to manage without help, and I thought we needed the time alone to heal after your daddy died."

"How about later?"

"By then I'd grown to love this place. I couldn't imagine the two of us rattling around the big house. Then Jake came along..."

Julia couldn't imagine Jake at the big house, either. Ashbourne had been built by and for people who assumed that they, too, were somehow larger than life. Jake had no such illusions.

Since the conversation was going well, Julia ventured further. "Ashbourne almost seems like a museum. A record of life on the day my father died."

"Ashbourne belongs to you. I never saw the point of changing things or selling the antiques. I like living here. It will be up to you to decide what to do with Ashbourne once you're ready."

"Bard would like to live there." Ashbourne was grander than Millcreek, although Millcreek had been in his family since the Revolutionary War.

"I always thought as much."

"But not until you open the property to the Mosby Hunt. It would be too embarrassing for him to live there if you didn't."

"And I won't." Maisy plunked more dishes on Julia's side of the sink. "Not as long as the land's in my name."

Maisy's objection to foxhunting at Ashbourne was legendary. Her determination to keep foxhunters off her land had made her the butt of many a local joke and the occasional prank. Julia, by default, had suffered, too.

"Speaking of Bard..." Maisy turned off the water. "I think that's his car."

Julia had been waiting all evening for the low purr of the BMW's engine. Now she heard it, too. "This should be a laugh a minute."

"Where would you like to talk to him?"

"Somewhere Callie can't overhear. How about the garden?"

"It's a little cool tonight."

"I have a sweater in the dining room."

"I'll get the door and the sweater."

Julia listened as Maisy's footsteps disappeared. She had steeled herself for this confrontation. Her marriage to Bard had always seemed simple and forthright. It had also been untested, and it was failing this one, as if the added weight of her blindness had tipped a precariously balanced scale.

Moments passed. She heard murmurs from the front of the house, a door close, then footsteps. She dried her hands and turned, leaning against the counter with her arms folded. When he crossed the threshold, she was ready.

"Hello, Bard."

"Julia." His voice was tight, as if his throat was closing around it.

"We expected you earlier. Maisy saved a place for you at the dinner table."

"I'd like to talk to you alone. If I'm allowed?"

She was annoyed by his tone. "You don't need to be rude. Maisy?"

"Right here. I brought the sweater."

Julia held out a hand, and Maisy placed the sweater in it. "Need help getting it on?"

"No, I'll manage."

Maisy must have turned, because her voice came from a different place. "Julia would like to have this conversation in the garden. Can you help her get there?"

"I can still escort my wife any place she needs to go."

Julia spoke without thinking. "And any place I don't need to go, as well."

"Now who's being rude?" Bard stepped forward to help her with her sweater.

She didn't apologize, although it had been a cheap shot. "Let's go out through this door. Callie's in the barn with Jake."

"I understand you sent for Feather Foot, too. Just how long do you intend to stay?"

"As long as I need to."

She heard the kitchen door open, then felt Bard's big hand on her upper arm. "Let's finish this outside."

He was a large man with a long stride. He did little to modify it as he propelled her to the garden. She stumbled once, and he slowed down, but she could tell he was annoyed by the way he continued to grip her arm.

"You should try this sometime." Julia came to a halt when he did. "Being dragged along by someone bigger than you. It's not a reassuring feeling."

"I didn't drag you." He hesitated. "Damn it, I'm sorry. Okay? I'm just so angry."

"Is this what happens when you don't get your way? Or hasn't that happened often enough for you to recognize the signs?"

"You're determined to be stupid about this, aren't you?"

"Stupid?"

"It was stupid for you to escape from the clinic. Do you have any idea how that made me look?"

"Let me guess. Like the husband of a stupid woman?"

"Damn it, Julia!"

She was silent, waiting for him to gain control. Although a large part of her wanted to have a screaming match, a larger part knew better. Not only would Callie hear, nothing would be accomplished.

He took a while to get hold of his temper. She imagined steam rising from a boiling kettle, then an unseen hand turning off the heat. The steam billowed, then puffed, and at last died away altogether. But the water was still hot enough to scald.

"Let's sit down," he said at last.

"Where are we?"

"There's a bench under a tree." He led her there. She could hear him brushing leaves from the wooden slats; then he repositioned her. She could feel the bench against the backs of her knees. She sat gingerly.

Julia knew enough of her mother's gardening style to visualize how this garden looked in moonlight. With fall in the air, Maisy would have planted gold and orange chrysanthemums. Purple asters bloomed here when the weather began to turn, perhaps there was flowering kale this year. Maisy's gardens were chaotically haphazard and more beautiful because of it, as if God Himself had randomly sprinkled all the colors of the world with a generous hand.

"I came here a lot as a teenager." Julia explored the bench with her fingertips. "You can see the road through those trees." She inclined her head. "Sometimes I'd see you riding by. Did you ever notice me?"

If he understood her attempt to take the conversation to a more conciliatory level, he gave no sign. "What were you thinking, Julia? Dr. Jeffers says you found your way downstairs by yourself. You could have been killed."

"I had help. Did he also tell you he threatened to have me committed?"

"He was trying to keep you there for your own good."

"Bard, I'm an amateur psychologist. I'll admit it. But doesn't it make sense that I won't get better unless I'm part of the cure?"

"Maybe you don't want to get better."

"Then there's no point to being at the clinic, is there? Think of all the money we're saving. I can wallow in my blindness for free."

He took her hand, swallowing it in his. "I don't mean consciously, Julia. I know you think you want to get better."

"Now who's playing amateur psychologist?"

"Well, if you wanted it badly enough, wouldn't you just see again?"

"Back to that."

"I don't know what to think." He squeezed her hand.

She let him, even though she really wanted him to disappear. *She wanted him to disappear.* The thought surprised her, and for a moment it choked off conversation.

"We won't talk about the clinic anymore," he said at last. "Maybe I was being too heavy-handed."

Concessions came with a price. She waited.

"I want you to come home."

She removed her hand from his. "I'm sorry, but for now I'm right where I need to be."

"I'm not going to work on you to go back to the clinic, if that's what you're afraid of. That chapter's over. We'll—"

"You're not listening again. Even if the clinic's never mentioned, I want to be here. I need to be here. It feels right."

"What are you really saying? That you need to be here—or you need to be away from me?"

Since she wasn't sure, she couldn't answer directly. "I need people I love around me. You work hard. You won't be home much, and Mrs. Taylor will end up taking care of me."

"I can take time off."

She tried to imagine Bard preparing meals and making certain utensils were in reach. Bard mopping up spills. Bard leading her to the bathroom, or picking her up if she stumbled.

"You would hate it," she said, and he didn't deny it.

"How long do you plan to stay?"

She had no plans. Her loss of sight was so mysterious, so precipitous, that it defied logic. She might wake up tomorrow, her vision as clear as crystal. She might spend the rest of her life in a world as dark as a starless winter night.

"I don't know how long I'll stay. As long as I need to."

"And what about me?"

"What about you?"

"I need my wife."

She waited for him to mention Callie. He didn't. "For what, exactly? I can't be much of a hostess right now. And the fox-hunting season will have to start without me." Bard often acted as honorary whipper-in for the Mosby Hunt, and the thrill of the chase was one of the primary joys they shared.

"You make me sound shallow."

"Then tell me why you want me there."

His angry tone intensified. "What's the point? You've obviously made up your mind. I'm the bad guy here. I tried to get help for you, and you rejected it. I asked you to come home, and now you want me to grovel."

She lowered her voice to counteract his. "I don't want you to grovel. I just want you to realize there's no point to my going back to Millcreek except to keep people from talking. You can visit me here anytime you want. You can visit Callie."

"That's not a marriage."

She wondered what exactly he would miss. Sex? She couldn't imagine Bard making love to a woman who was less than perfect. But even if she was wrong, sex was only a small part of their marriage. For all his masculinity, he was a man who seemed to need little, and she had never insisted on more.

"What is a marriage?" She was genuinely curious to know his answer.

"What's the point of this?"

"You have very little time for your family. If anything, this will give you an excuse to work longer hours."

"You never complained before. Is that what this is about? You're getting back at me for making money to support you?"

"Bard, you could support a harem. Already. Let's be honest. You work because you love it. You have to work. You have too much energy to sit still for more than a minute."

"And you never asked me to slow down. Maybe you liked it that way. You didn't have to put up with me as often. You didn't have to give up your dreams of another man!"

She was stunned as much by his words as his vehemence. "That's not true!"

"No? You think I haven't noticed how cold you are? You think I don't know why? And you think I don't know how much you hate it when I try to be a father to Callie? My name's on her birth certificate, but as far as you're concerned, I don't have any real right to put my stamp on her. She's your kid. Yours and a murderer's."

"Keep your voice down!"

"Oh, that's right. Nobody's supposed to know."

"I have never tried to keep you from spending time with Callie."

"As long as I spend it the way you want me to. You direct every facet of our lives, Julia. You have, right from the beginning. And you call me controlling!"

For a moment she felt dizzied by regrets. They had been married nearly nine years, and he had never expressed any of this. She had tried to be a good wife. She had not allowed herself to mourn for Christian Carver. She had believed her profound gratitude to Bard had quietly turned to affection. She knew his faults and limitations, but she knew her own, as well. She had believed that their marriage, even though it was built on a secret, was solid.

"She has *never* been my child." His tone was bitter. "You've never let her be my child. I'm as much your prisoner as Christian is the state's."

She was suffused with guilt, even though she didn't know if it was deserved. Her head was ringing with his words. "If you're trying to make me come back to Millcreek, you're your own worst enemy. We shouldn't be living together. Not with all this between us."

"We aren't going to fix anything with you living here. It's the next step toward a divorce. Is that what you want?"

She was saved from having to answer by Callie's voice floating up from the barn. She lowered hers again. "If you want to see Callie tonight, this is your chance. And we've said enough, don't you think?"

"Not nearly."

"She'll know you're here. She'll see your car. You can't ignore her."

"Fine, Julia. I'll go see her. But you stay here until Maisy comes to rescue you. For once, let me be her father without your help."

"Bard..."

"Save it."

A cool breeze fanned her side where he had been sitting, and leaves crackled under his feet. "Tell you what, if you can think of any reason to see me again, you know where to reach me. I'll wait for instructions."

She heard his footsteps on the cobblestone path. She lowered her chin and stared sightlessly at the ground.

Maisy watched her granddaughter run to her father, then stop several feet away, as if she was aware he might not want to see her.

"Hi, Daddy."

"Callie." He nodded his head. He didn't reach for her, but he didn't move away, either. "Your mother said you were checking on Feather Foot. She's doing all right in there?"

"It's so neat. Jake works there every day, and he can keep her company while I'm in school. She has everything she needs."

Bard looked at Maisy. "Sounds like you have my family all tucked in here."

Maisy didn't take the bait. "We're glad to lend a hand."

"I made a *B* on my history report." Callie moved a little closer. "The one about Mosby's Rangers."

"That's good." He sounded neither critical nor enthused. Clearly his mind wasn't on the conversation.

Callie tried again. "A *B* is good. It's better than last time, right?"

"That's not the way to look at it, Callie. A *B* is okay. An *A* would be better."

Callie didn't seem surprised. She made a face. "You mean I'm not supposed to be happy?"

"You can be happy." He seemed to focus on her. "A *B* is good enough to be happy about."

"Did you always get *A*s?"

"Pretty nearly all the time."

Her face fell. "Maybe I'm not that smart."

Maisy was angry enough at this exchange to intervene, but his next words stopped her. "You're smart enough to make *me* happy."

Callie giggled. He stepped forward and smoothed her hair. "Walk me to my car."

"Where's Mommy?"

Maisy frowned. Where was Julia?

Bard turned to her. "Julia's sitting in the garden. It's getting colder. She'll need some help getting back inside." He started toward the black BMW, which was parked near the barn, and Callie tagged along beside him.

"He looks like he ran into a hornet's nest," Maisy said when Jake joined her. "He left Julia in my garden."

"He's a man with a number of strengths. Dealing with feelings isn't one of them."

"I want to slap him when he makes Callie ashamed of herself."

"Maisy, he struggles. Anyone can see that."

She felt reprimanded, and it wasn't the first time. Lately she had felt the subtle sting of Jake's disapproval more and more. "She's just a little girl."

"She's a lot stronger than you give her credit for. They have to work out their own relationship."

"I know that." She sounded hurt, although she had hoped not to.

"Do you? You protect everyone you love. Some people would say you smother them."

"Do I smother you, Jake?" The hurt was still there.

"Only when I let you."

She knew there was nothing else she could say. He squeezed her arm, as if to comfort her. "I'll get Julia. I know you'll want to help Callie get ready for bed."

Maisy watched him walk away. Finally she drew a deep breath and realized it was the first she had taken since his answer.

8

"Mommy, when I shut my eyes, I can still see light. Can you see light?"

"I don't think so. Turn me toward the lamp."

From the noise she made, Callie thought that was funny. She stood on the bed and put her small hands on Julia's shoulders; then she guided her. "Can you see it?"

"When you close your eyes, you're still getting light through your eyelids. Whatever is wrong with my eyes, the light doesn't penetrate."

"Daddy says something's wrong with your head. But not because you hit it."

Julia was glad Bard had reassured Callie of that much, at least. "It's hard to understand."

"If you just try real hard, maybe you can see."

Julia heard Bard in her daughter's words. She positioned herself to sit on the bed. "Remember when you were learning to read, and no matter how hard you tried, you still couldn't make any sense out of all those letters? Remember how you had to have a special teacher who knew what your problem was and how to help you with it?"

"I'm not even nine yet, Mommy," Callie said with exaggerated patience. "I remember."

Julia put her arms around her daughter, or rather, she put her arms around empty space until Callie snuggled against her. "Well, it's the same way for me. No matter how hard I struggle to see, I can't. I'm going to need a special teacher to help me see again, somebody who knows what my problem is."

"A seeing teacher?"

Julia wished it were that easy. "A psychologist. A counselor."

"I'm learning to read. Maybe you'll learn to see, too."

"You're doing very well with your reading. And because it's harder for you, it'll mean more."

"I had to read out loud in class yesterday."

Julia had an agreement with Callie's teacher that this would never happen. "Why?"

"We had a substitute. Mrs. Quinn was at a meeting. I just told her it was hard for me, so she let me stop. But the other kids laughed."

"What did you do?"

"I didn't have time to do much. Leroy Spader got up to read and fell over somebody's foot. Then they laughed at *him,* instead." Callie paused. "But I didn't laugh. I helped him get back up."

"That was nice." Julia remembered Leroy. Usually when the class laughed at Callie, cocky little Leroy was the leader.

"Then I pushed him."

"You didn't!"

"Just back into his seat. That's all. So he wouldn't fall again."

Julia hugged her daughter harder. "No more pushing, Callie. I know Leroy provokes you, but that's not going to help anything."

"Why, because I'm supposed to be a lady?"

Bard's words again. "Not at all. Because it's the right thing to do. Girl or boy."

"Pickles!"

"Pickles?"

"That's what Tiffany says when she's mad."

"You'd better get under the covers now, sweetums."

"Can't. You have to stand up first. You're on my blanket."

Julia got to her feet. "I'm going to tuck you in. Just let me know if I succeed."

"I like your room. I'm glad I'm sleeping here."

Julia had always liked this room, too, and it hadn't surprised her that Callie chose it. The bedroom was large and airy, with windows on two sides and climbing trees just out of reach. At Callie's age, she had asked Maisy to paint it a sunny yellow, and it had remained that way until she was a teenager. Then Julia couldn't darken the walls enough to suit herself. In an uncharacteristic moment of parental defiance, Maisy had refused to let her paint them black, so she and her mother had compromised on navy blue.

Now the room was a soft lavender, or had been last time she'd been able to see it. "What color are the walls in here, Callie?"

"Purple."

"Light purple?"

"Uh-huh."

"I painted it this color my first year in college."

Christian had helped, and so had Fidelity. Julia felt a fresh stab of pain. Callie would never know her biological father had painted the ceiling just above her head. Or that her mother's best friend had painted the trim, carelessly slopping more on the walls than the window frames until they'd made her sit and supervise.

Callie wouldn't know that she had been conceived inside these very walls, just days before Christian was convicted of Fidelity's murder and sentenced to a life away from the daughter he didn't know he had.

"Purple makes me sleepy," Callie said. She sounded like a child drifting to the land of Nod.

"I can't read to you, but I could tell you a story."

"I don't think I can...stay awake."

Julia sat on the side of the bed again and felt for Callie's face. Then she landed a kiss on her daughter's forehead. "I'll tell you a longer one tomorrow to make up for it."

"You two ready for lights out?"

Julia hadn't heard her mother's approach. "This is one tired little girl."

Maisy's footsteps ringed the bed. "Good night, princess. We'll see you in the morning."

"Night... Leave the door open."

"We will." Julia felt Maisy take her hand.

In the hallway, Maisy put her arm around her daughter. "You're ready for bed, too, aren't you?"

"I am tired."

At the bottom of the stairs, after a long, slow descent, Maisy spoke again. "How did things go with Bard?"

Julia realized her mother needed to know at least part of what had occurred. "Bard's taking this personally. And I guess I antagonized him."

"I'm sorry."

"Are you?"

"I don't want your life to be any harder than it already is."

"He pulled out all the stops." And inside she was still trembling from the dissonant roar.

"Julia, whatever you decide, you know it'll be all right with me, don't you? I'm not trying to make you do anything."

Julia thought about that. Maisy had always been a permissive parent. Sometimes Julia thought the absence of rules had been a sneaky but useful form of control. With few parental limits, Julia had been forced to choose her own so carefully that when she'd erred, it had usually been on the side of caution.

"You're not forcing me to do anything I don't want to do, but you want me here, Maisy. You've made it clear."

"I won't lie. I love it."

"Am I imagining it, or have you been clearing out the hallway?"

"I've just been making paths. Lord knows, we've needed them for years."

Julia allowed herself to be steered slowly toward the downstairs bedroom. Since finding her way through the halls of Gandy Willson, she had grown more confident. She still shuffled, but no step was an anxiety attack.

"I've laid out a nightgown for you. All your bathroom things are in a row on the shelf above the radiator. Will you need help?"

"I'll manage."

"Then how about if I leave you in the bathroom first, then come back for you in a few minutes? Unless you're planning to take a bath?"

"I'll shower in the morning."

Julia found everything she needed and got ready for bed. Back in her room, she felt along the foot rail of the bed for her nightgown.

"I can leave you alone to undress and come back later," Maisy said.

"Thanks, but I think I'm going right to sleep."

"Actually, I need your help with something."

"Then stay while I change."

Julia heard the bedsprings creak. The bed, like nearly everything else in the house, was an antique, which Maisy had always called "preloved."

Maisy was silent while Julia undressed, until she got down to her bra and panties. "Honey, you're so thin."

"I'm at a disadvantage here. I can't see you, remember?"

"Trust me, thin is not what you'd see."

"I haven't been hungry since the accident. But I'll gain it back."

"It's very Audrey Hepburn."

Julia managed a smile. "Do you remember all the times we watched *My Fair Lady* when I was growing up?"

"It was one of the few things we agreed on."

Julia would have liked to be able to argue, but Maisy was right. They had shared so little, not just during the normal turbulence of adolescence, but throughout Julia's childhood. She had never quite understood it. They were very different people, but they loved each other. They loved Ashbourne, too, and, in their individual ways, the culture of Ridge's Race. But for all that, Julia had never felt they stood on common ground, or even that they could reach each other across the divide.

At Callie's birth, her first prayer had been that her own daughter wouldn't drift from her as she had drifted from Maisy.

"I've thought about this a lot." Maisy must have shifted, because the springs creaked once more. "Your hand slipped out of mine when you were little, and I never found it again."

Julia slid the nightgown over her head and felt its familiar swish against her hips. But the whisper of silk was the only familiar thing about the last moments.

"I love you, Maisy," she said tentatively. "You know I do."

"That's never been an issue."

"I don't know what else to say. We're very different. Maybe I'm more like my father?"

"In little ways, maybe. He wasn't a man to talk about his feelings."

"Neither are you," Julia said gently. "Although you will talk about any other subject under the sun."

"Harry had a way of drawing people to him that neither of us has mastered. He walked into a room and the light went on. Not because he worked at being charming, because he was so confident." She paused. "Powerful. He was powerful, and anyone who met him wanted to live in his sphere."

Julia found her way around the bed and sat on the edge. "I don't remember anything about him."

"I know. Jake was all the father you ever really knew."

"Enough father for anyone. The best."

Julia suspected that the window into her mother's feelings was closing. But it had been a beginning and something to ponder. "You said you needed my help?"

Maisy didn't answer immediately. When she did, she almost sounded embarrassed. "Julia, I'm writing a novel."

Julia supposed if any of the mothers of her friends had admitted such a thing, their daughters would have been stunned. The mothers of Ridge's Race gave charity teas and served on committees, they shepherded children and grandchildren to horse and pony shows and steeplechase events, entertained friends, oversaw the baking of ham and the assembly of salads for tailgate parties. They did not, for the most part, pursue their muse.

Maisy had always pursued hers with a vengeance.

Julia thought back to her mother's last creative attempts. "You got tired of sculpture?"

"I was a failure."

"Not so. I thought some of the things you did were interesting."

"Julia, we both know what interesting means in the art world. Spare me false praise."

"I liked the bust of Callie. I really did."

"You were the only person who knew it was Callie, and that's only because you let her pose for me."

"So you've moved to writing. Didn't you try your hand at poetry when I was in college?"

"No matter what I wrote, I rhymed. I shamed myself."

"Well, if you're telling me this because you want my approval, you know you have it. I think it's great."

"I'm glad to hear that. I want to read what I've written to you."

Julia sobered. "I'm not going to be much of an audience, Maisy."

"I know you have a lot on your mind."

Maisy had tried to be honest with her. Now Julia tried to be honest with her mother. "I feel like I'm putting my life back together, or taking it apart, I'm not sure which. I feel like I'm curled up in a hard little ball, the way a porcupine does when it's under attack. Everything that's happening inside me right now is centered around me and my life. I feel selfish, but there it is. I don't know if I even have the ability to think about anybody else."

"I understand."

"I'm glad."

"I still would appreciate it if you listened to my story. I'll tell you why," Maisy continued before Julia could object. "I think you *need* something outside yourself to think about. Just for a small part of each day. I understand what you're going through. I do, as well as anyone could. But I also know you need a break from the crisis, and it's going to be hard to get one. You can't read. You can't paint. You can't ride. You can listen to music or television, but I think while you do, you'll be worrying and digging away at the things inside you."

"That's all I'm good for right now."

"Your heart and soul need a resting place. You need to heal a little before you move on to the next thought. You need *time* to heal. Is this making any sense?"

To Julia, what made sense was that her mother, in her own confusing way, was trying to help her. Right at the beginning Maisy had offered her a home, solace, the use of Maisy's own eyes and hands as she cared for her. Now she was offering two things more. Respite and a piece of Maisy's own heart. Julia, as an artist, understood that every creative endeavor, even the most amateur, was a gift of self.

How could she refuse to listen?

"I don't think you'll find it *that* painful, Julia," Maisy said dryly. "You should see the look on your face. I swear."

"Okay, maybe you're right. I'd like to do something for you if I can, in return for everything you've done. But do you want me to give my opinion? Because that might be tough on both of us."

"Not really. Mostly I need a captive audience. Come here and get under the covers. It's cold, and you're not wearing enough." Maisy stood, and the mattress lifted.

"When did you want to start?" Julia pulled the covers back and got under them. She felt the way she had as a little girl, waiting for her mother to tuck her in. Only she was a mother now and her own daughter was sleeping upstairs.

"Right now suits me."

Julia's heart sank. The day had been long and difficult, and she'd hoped for a reprieve. "A bedtime story?"

"It's the quiet time of day. And maybe it will help you fall asleep."

Julia struggled to keep her voice light. "Maybe I'll fall asleep while you're reading. What will that tell you?"

"That you're tired. Only that you're tired."

"What kind of novel is it?"

"A romance, I think. At least that's how it seems to be shaping up. When it comes right down to it, though, that's what I like to read. I need a happy ending."

"You'll guarantee one?"

Maisy paused. "Can't. These characters have a mind of their own. It's going like gangbusters."

Julia was afraid to think what that said about quality. Maisy's pottery had always gone like gangbusters, too. "You used to read to me when I was little. Every night. It was one of the things I loved best about my childhood."

"I used to tell you to settle back and let the story take over. Do you remember?"

"Yes."

"Julia, settle back tonight and let the story take over. Forget everything else that happened. There'll be plenty of time to remember it all again in the morning."

"You have the book?"

"The first chapter's right here." The rustle of pages followed her words. Julia heard a chair scraping the floor, then the creak of a cane seat as Maisy lowered herself into it.

"Does Jake know about this?"

"Your stepfather doesn't ask questions. He knows he'll hear all the details eventually. More than he usually wants to know."

Julia settled back. Maisy had a soothing, melodious voice, and she was capable of putting a great deal of drama into whatever she read. She would do her best to make the book entertaining for Julia.

"Go ahead and close your eyes," Maisy said.

"Not that it makes much difference." But Julia did.

The sedate flow of Maisy's words began to wash over her.

From the unpublished novel *Fox River*, by Maisy Fletcher

My father had great hopes for me. I was to marry into New York society and advance the status of our family. My brothers, George and Henry, were, by my father's high standards, without significant potential. Lumpish and plain-spoken, they would do well enough managing the import and mercantile company that had brought our family to the brink of a better life. But I, Louisa, with my golden curls, my sea-green eyes, the anticipated extension of my considerable childish charm, was to carry all of us over the threshold.

My father died before he could see his plan to fruition, but my mother, lumpish and plain-spoken herself, made my father's mission her own. When she saw that my brothers could indeed manage the family's affairs, she focused her attention on me. Even though I was not yet ten, I was to be a memorial to my father's dreams.

Despite the fact that we—like our three-story brownstone—stood on the fringes of Fifth Avenue society, I was schooled by its finest masters. By the time I was eighteen and Cousin Annabelle Jones invited me to summer at her family estate in Middleburg, Virginia, my posture was perfection, my voice as musical as a canary's warblings. The fashionable girls' school I attended had only taught me the rudiments of history, geography and literature, but I could dance until dawn and ride with a proper seat. I had learned the fine art of flirtation and the more advanced art of conversation. I was ready, it seemed, to polish stepping-stones for generations of Schumachers still to come.

If I could not marry a man with a European title, as Astor, Guggenheim and Vanderbilt daughters had done, I could, at the very least, marry one who set us squarely in the middle of the Social Register.

I hesitate to say it now, but from the beginning I cooperated with all plans for our future. Not because I was spineless or without any thoughts on the subject. Born just after the turn of the century, I was the product of a new era, a willful child, high-spirited and fully capable of demanding my way when it suited me. But I was always certain a life of ease, a life of acceptance by people I admired, suited me best. When the Great War ended, I knew I had come into my own.

As I grew, I was seldom in my mother's presence without an etiquette tutor or a dressmaker in attendance. Mama filled her days overseeing my education or making overtures to women who thought her beneath them. Now, when I think of her, I see unsmiling lips and hazel eyes darting from face to face in a crowded room, searching for the next person who might advance her cause.

I remember little about the days just before I traveled to Virginia. My mother cried. I do remember that. She was plain-spoken, perhaps, but also, at heart, a sentimental woman. On my last evening at home, as I was preparing for bed, she told me that marriage was never quite what it seemed. Men did not marry for friendship but because they wanted their needs attended to. Once I was safely wed, I should use the skills we'd so carefully nurtured to better the life of my husband, but never to set myself above him.

I was to fade carefully into the background, making certain that my husband shone brightest in every setting. I was, in short, to become a more accomplished version of my mother.

I am certain I loved Mama. As colorless, as remote as she seemed, sometimes I glimpsed the woman beneath. I remember a cool hand on my feverish forehead, secret cups of hot chocolate when I'd undergone a disappointment, the flash of pride in her smile when I bested my brothers at some childish endeavor.

I am certain I loved her, but at that moment I couldn't remember why. I was stunned she understood so little about me.

Annabelle Jones, a distant cousin on Mama's side, was from a family several generations more advanced in society than our own. Her paternal grandfather, a Union officer from a New York family, had survived the War Between the States at a desk in New Orleans, where he busied himself performing clandestine favors for local businessmen. With an eye for the main chance, Colonel Jones had endeavored to make the wartime lives of those prominent New Orleanians as comfortable as possible. The fact that this sometimes involved smuggling and outright theft hadn't troubled him.

After Appomattox the colonel had gone on to use his connections to establish himself as a cotton exporter and, later, as an officer of the Southern Pacific Railroad. Now, despite their Yankee origins, the greater Jones family moved among the cream of Louisiana society, as well as that of other Southern cities. Josiah Jones, the Colonel's youngest son and Annie's father, had settled in Virginia to indulge his love of country life and horses.

Annie was a grave disappointment to her family. Vivacious and intelligent, she was also, sadly, not a pretty woman. She was as tall as a man, with broad shoulders and hands, and a lack of physical grace that arose from trying to fit herself into a world made for smaller women. Annie's face was long, and her lovely brown eyes were shaded by unfeminine black eyebrows. I'd seen first-hand the effect she had on eligible men. Each suitor carefully weighed the humiliation of being married to a homely woman against the enticement of her name and influence. As of yet, no one had found the latter to be enticing enough.

Annie was my closest friend. Never, and I can say this without reservation, did I love her because of the benefits our friendship might hold. Certainly I was young and self-centered, but never calculating. I loved Annie for her wit, her insights, her deeply rooted loyalty. I sensed, even as a child, that Annie would never hurt me.

On the morning that Annie and her parents ended their visit to New York and came to take me and my considerable wardrobe to the train station, I said goodbye to the stuffy, cheerless home of my childhood. My mother remained in the doorway as we pulled away from the curb in an autotaxi. She didn't wave, but she held a handkerchief to her lips, as if to block some latent protest. My last memory was of her tiny, dark-clad figure leaning against a pillar, the heavily draped windows of our house like eyelids squeezed tightly shut.

"You won't be sorry you came," Annie promised, taking my gloved hand in her own, as if she was afraid I already might be homesick. "We'll have such fun, Weezy. I promise we will."

"You'll have to stop calling me Weezy," I told her. "Or I won't have any fun at all."

Annie had a wonderful, unfettered laugh, a laugh that frightened men as much as her extraordinary height and masculine shoulders. I smiled at the sound of it and clasped her hand harder. I was absolutely certain that the best part of my life was about to unfold.

I remember, oh, I remember so very well, that ecstatic conviction that everything I'd ever dreamed of was finally within my reach.

9

An unfamiliar guard came for Christian just after breakfast. He had already eaten the requisite ounces of scrambled eggs and grits and a biscuit that was harder than Milk Bones. His second cup of coffee had been stronger than dishwater, and for once, more palatable. He hoped this was an omen for the day ahead.

"Carver..." The guard, a thin, furtive-looking man, jerked his head toward the door. "Warden wants to see you."

Since Peter and Mel's visit yesterday, Christian had thought of little besides the possibility of acquittal. Now, to his chagrin, his heart jumped in his chest, and not because the coffee had more than a wisp of caffeine in it.

He buttoned his work shirt as he walked half a step in front of the guard through the maze of corridors and checkpoints, making sure not to crowd the man or make him nervous. Prison life was a compromise between pride and common sense. A man gave up the parts of himself that didn't really matter and held on to everything else he could. Long ago Christian had given up trying to prove his manhood with the guards.

Last night he'd dreamed he was mounted on a massive white stallion that lifted him over the prison walls like Pegasus floating on air currents.

The warden's office was large and comfortable, a vivid contrast to the rest of the prison. One wall was lined with diplomas and books on psychology, law and enlightened penal systems. Christian and the guard waited in the doorway to be recognized.

At last the warden, an overweight man in his fifties, nodded to the guard. "You go on. I'll call somebody to take him back once we're finished here. Mr. Carver, come have a seat."

Christian was neither fooled nor encouraged by the warden's pleasant tone. His dealings with Warden Phil Sampsen had been mercifully brief and for the most part cordial. As long as the Pets and Prisoners program garnered positive publicity for Ludwell, Christian had little to fear. But the warden was a capricious as well as political man, filled with petty dislikes and an overblown sense of his own importance. He believed himself to be particularly insightful about the motivations of the men at Ludwell. He relished playing God with their lives and did so with alarming frequency.

"You had time for breakfast?" The warden was paging through a document on his desk and didn't look up as Christian took a seat.

"Yes, sir."

"Good. Good." The warden flipped another page.

Christian knew better than to ask why he'd been summoned. He would find out when it suited the warden.

The warden scanned and flipped in silence. Christian was careful not to fidget. Finally the warden looked up, removing wire-rimmed reading glasses and setting them beside the pile of papers. He rubbed the bridge of his nose, which, like everything about him, was a little too large, a little too prominent.

"I know what's going on with your case, Carver. I was just looking over your file."

Christian assumed Sampsen was talking about Karl Zandoff's confession. He wondered if the jewelry had been found. He tried not to show his impatience. "Yes, sir."

"Looks to me like you've enjoyed the full benefits of the law, young man. Would you say so?"

Christian would not say so. Had he enjoyed the full benefits of the law, he wouldn't have been brought to trial. By now he would be married to Julia Ashbourne, perhaps even be a father. Together he and Julia would be breeding and raising the best damned hunters in America.

The warden filled the silence. "Maybe you don't think so."

"I've had a good attorney. I've had help on the outside."

"That would be Peter Claymore, of Claymore Park?"

Christian nodded.

"And Karl Zandoff? Have you had help from him?"

For a moment Christian didn't know what to say. The warden's question seemed to have come entirely out of left field. "I don't know Zandoff, sir. I don't know anything more about him than what I've read in the newspapers."

"Well, he claims he worked in Virginia about the time Miss Sutherland was murdered. Claims he worked right down the road from her house. As I recall, you worked down the road, too, didn't you?"

Christian phrased his answer carefully. "I grew up at Claymore Park. We get a lot of drifters in the horse business. Most jobs don't pay that well. Men leave after a few months and move on."

"He claims he was working construction. You had construction going on at Claymore Park about then?"

"Peter Claymore's stables are the finest in Virginia. He's always improving on perfection."

"Then maybe Zandoff was one of the men working for Claymore."

"Men come and go in construction, too. If he was there, I don't remember him."

"Now, I'm just wondering, son, if that's really true." The warden made a tent with stubby, nicotine-stained fingers. "I'm wondering if there's something you've been wanting to get off your chest all these years."

Christian didn't think the warden was fishing for a critique of prison policy. "I'm sorry, sir. I'm not sure where you're going with this."

"Your family life wasn't exactly the best, was it now?"

Christian wondered about the file on the desk in front of the warden. He kept to the basics. "My mother died when I was six. My father died when I was twelve. Peter Claymore took me in after that."

"He's been like a father to you? Would you say?"

"He's been kinder than he needed to be."

"It says here your daddy burned down Claymore's stable."

"That was the conclusion after the investigation."

"He had a little drinking problem?"

"The report said my father set the stable on fire with a ciga-rette. They think he'd passed out."

"Not much of a role model, son. A drinking man with so little regard for the property of others."

Christian couldn't let that pass. "He knew every horse in that stable. He'd raised half of them and trained most of the rest. He talked to those horses. They were never property in his mind. They meant everything to him."

"So you're saying he didn't do it, is that it?"

"I'm saying he didn't do it out of a disregard for Mr. Claymore or the horses in that stable. But he did have a problem, and in the end, I guess it got the better of him."

"You guess?"

Christian rephrased. "In the end it got the better of him."

"See, I'm wondering here if I'm seeing a pattern. A man de-nies too much, I start to worry."

"And since I've said from the start that I didn't kill Fidelity Sutherland, you're wondering if this is all part of the same thing."

"You got it."

"I was twelve when my father died. He was a good man with a bad illness. The fire started in the tack room where he'd fallen asleep, and he was a chain smoker with poor judgment when he was drinking. There's not much to dispute."

"And Miss Sutherland?"

"The afternoon she died I was looking for her. I found her necklace on the stairs. I went up to her room—"

"You felt you had that right, huh? Just to go into her room like that?"

At the time anger had given him that right. "Fidelity and I were old friends. When I was searching for her, I thought it was odd that her necklace was just lying on the steps. I was certain she was home, so I picked up the necklace and went upstairs to find her. She was lying in a pool of blood."

"And when the law found *you,* you had her necklace in one hand and the knife that killed her in the other."

"I found the knife on the floor beside her. I picked it up. I guess I hadn't seen enough bad movies to know better."

"Says here it was your knife."

"Mine was the only one unaccounted for. Mr. Claymore had half a dozen made as Christmas presents that year, with Claymore Park's logo on the handle. They were special knives, with blades for trimming and picking hoofs, a thinning comb and a leather awl."

"And at least one sharp cutting blade."

Christian saw no need to answer that.

The warden looked up from the file. "You had a good lawyer, and the jury still voted to convict you. They thought you were guilty, son. So do I."

"Most of the world agrees with you, Warden."

"And how many of them are going to agree when Zandoff's confession makes the headlines?"

Again Christian wondered if the jewelry had been found. "I don't know what you mean."

The warden rested his chin on his fingertips. "I'm talking about people not trusting you, Christian."

Christian knew Sampsen had dropped the "Mr. Carver" on purpose. The warden had progressed to the point in the conversation when he wanted Christian to believe the two of them had overcome some hurdle, that they had become friends.

"May I speak frankly, sir?"

"You know that's what I want."

"Trust seems a poor second to freedom."

"Well, I guess I can understand that." The warden sat back in his chair. "There's not a man at Ludwell who'd want to stay, if he didn't have to. None except some old lifers, who'd be scared to go anywhere else. But it's like this. Some of my men, the best of the bunch, have thought about what they did to get in here and come to terms with it. I've had men confess to me, like I was their priest, men who screamed and yelled they were innocent right up until they walked through these doors."

Christian wondered what the warden had done to these so-called men. "I guess they needed to get it off their chests."

"I respect them for it, too. A man who can confess his sins is a man on his way to cleaning up his life."

Christian could almost hear the strains of "Rock of Ages" in the background. "If the cops find Fidelity's jewelry buried where Zandoff says he buried it, why would anyone continue to suspect me?"

"Because you were right there, Johnny on the spot with the murder weapon. You had the girl's blood on your hands, and you had the motive. Maybe you and Zandoff did it together."

Christian sat back. That scenario was so far-fetched, he wondered why the warden was bothering. But he supposed it was a taste of what he would face if he was released from prison. For all he'd done and all he'd confessed, Karl Zandoff was still a mystery man. He would leave more questions than answers after his execution. One of those questions would be the circumstances behind Fidelity's death.

The warden must have read something in his expression. "Me, I'm wondering why this Zandoff never went back and dug up the jewelry himself. Supposed to be some valuable pieces."

"Fidelity's jewelry was unique, very individual. It would have been impossible to sell off without detection."

"Report says you killed her because you were furious with her. There was talk maybe you were in love with her and she wasn't interested."

"I didn't kill Fidelity, and I was in love with her best friend. If I ever met Zandoff, ever even glimpsed the man, I don't remember him." There was nothing else to say.

"Well, I'm powerfully disappointed in you, son. I thought maybe, just maybe, we might take care of this right here and now. You see, you might get out for a while, but I'm betting you'll be back before long. That little girl's parents are important people. You don't think they're going to sit back and let you walk the streets of their town, knowing you might still be guilty. Me, I think it would be better to get it all out in the open now. Let Zandoff take credit for his share and you take credit for yours. You might get your sentence reduced. You could finish it with your head held high."

Christian couldn't keep the sarcasm from his voice. "Let's see. Sentence reduced. Total freedom. Which has the most appeal?"

Warden Sampsen shook his head. "You've got a good record here. You've done good work with our guide dog program. I'm giving you the chance to do the right thing."

"Warden, the right thing is to let me out of here."

The warden picked up the report and thumped the edges against his desk to straighten them. Then he turned the stack and closed the folder over it. "I'll give you some friendly advice, Mr. Carver. If some scumsucker in our legal system decides to let you out of here, don't ever go back to Ridge's Race. I'm already getting calls. Nobody wants you there. At best, you're a reminder of something they'd rather forget. Go somewhere—anywhere—else. The farther away the better. But just so you know, you'll never be able to go far enough. Because if the law finds a reason to catch back up with you, we will."

Sampsen looked up and smiled. "We surely will."

10

Jake passed the bread basket to Maisy. "There was some sort of commotion today over at South Land, or maybe it was Claymore Park. When I went to the hardware store, I saw half a dozen sheriff's department cars on the dirt road that runs between them."

The family was enjoying a late-night supper. Julia was halfway through a plate of lasagna, some portion of which had landed on her napkin. A long day had passed as she had struggled to reorient herself to the house that had once been home.

"What do you suppose that's about?" Maisy said, from the other end of the table. "I hope nobody's been hurt."

"If some kind of crime was committed, it'll be used as another argument against development," Jake said. "If it wasn't, somebody will point out how important it is to keep the county rural and safe."

Development was a hot topic in western Loudoun County. The picturesque country life they all enjoyed was constantly threatened by developers who wanted to break up the area's farms and estates and build mini-estates or, worse, town houses. There was fear that an entire way of life would vanish into suburban sprawl.

"You didn't hear anything when you were in town?" Julia used her index finger to scoop a bite of lasagna onto her fork.

"Kay Granville thought she glimpsed men digging a line along the fence," he said.

"That seems odd, doesn't it? If it was a water or power line that malfunctioned, they wouldn't send the sheriff, would they?"

"They might if everyone else was tied up and it was important enough."

"I could call the Sutherlands," Maisy said. "They expect me to call for odd reasons."

Julia's hand paused on the way to her mouth. "We'll find out soon enough. Flo and Frank have probably already fielded half a dozen calls."

"If something's wrong, we should know. So we can help."

"If something's wrong, we'll know soon enough," Jake said. "Bad news travels fast."

"How come?" Callie wiggled in the chair beside her mother and bumped Julia's arm. "Mrs. Quinn told us about the way sound travels in science class. How does sound know if news is good or bad?"

"It's just an expression," Julia lowered her fork and started scooping food on it again. "It means people like to tell each other bad news."

Callie's silverware clattered against her plate. "I know some bad news."

"The dinner table's probably not the best place for that," Julia said.

"Well, it was only bad news a long time ago. A bad man lived around here and he killed a girl."

Everyone fell silent. Julia realized she was holding her breath. She forced herself to speak. "This really isn't the right time to discuss that."

"How come?"

Maisy rescued Julia. "Because mealtime is a time for good thoughts."

"Are sheriff's cars good thoughts?"

"I shouldn't have brought that up," Jake said. "My fault."

"Oh." Callie was silent a moment.

Julia tried to think of a change of subject as she struggled not to show her distress.

"Too bad," Callie said. "'Cause I know why they're digging."

The child's words fell into empty space. The only sound in the room was the ticking of a Garfield the cat clock over the sink. Julia could envision the cat's tail swishing back and forth, back and forth.

"I think you'd like to tell us why, wouldn't you?" Maisy said at last.

Julia set down her fork. "Maisy—"

"Because when the bad man killed somebody, he buried her jewelry!" Callie said triumphantly. "And now he's told them where."

Even the clock seemed to stop ticking.

"How do you know this?" Maisy said.

Julia was stunned that her mother could ask the question as if it hardly mattered. Maisy was a better actress than Julia had guessed.

"Tiffany told me," Callie said.

"How does Tiffany know?" Julia felt for her water glass. Tiffany was Callie's best friend. Her mother Samantha trained horses at Claymore Park.

"Tiff said her mommy and a friend were talking about it."

"Well, now we know," Jake said. He didn't quite manage nonchalance.

"Tiff said the bad man's already in prison."

"Callie, I think it's time we moved on to another subject." Julia was almost desperate.

"But if he's in prison, there's nothing wrong, is there? He did something wrong, now he's helping. That's good news, isn't it?"

Julia could feel tears welling, tears that would be much too hard to explain to her daughter. For nine years she had believed in Christian Carver's innocence. Now his daughter was discussing his confession as offhandedly as if she was discussing a friend's birthday party.

Callie lowered her voice. "But Tiffany says he's going to die soon. Even though he's helping. I don't think that's fair, do you?"

"Enough!"

"Julia..." Maisy's warning was clear. "Callie, this is a sad story, and really not appropriate for the table. We can talk about it after dinner, okay?''

"I still don't think it's fair," Callie muttered. "Those men in Florida are mean."

"Florida?" Maisy said.

"Maisy, we can't tell Callie not to talk about this at the dinner table, then keep the conversation going." Jake was firm.

Julia had lost all appetite. "Callie, are you finished eating?"

"Yes," Callie said sullenly. "I don't like it when everybody yells at me."

"Nobody yelled at you except me," Julia said. "And I'm sorry. Let's go in the other room and finish this conversation, okay? We can let Maisy and Jake eat in peace."

"That's not necessary," Maisy began.

"No, Julia's right," Jake said. "She and Callie can talk in the living room. When we're done, we'll dish up pie for everybody. Your favorite," he told Callie. "Lemon meringue."

"Okay?" Julia said.

"I guess." Callie's chair scraped the floor. "But I want a big piece."

"You know it," Jake said.

Julia slid her chair back and gripped the table edge. She edged herself between her chair and Callie's before she relinquished it. Then she slid her chair back in place and turned. She allowed Callie to lead her through the doorway.

In the living room, she paused to get her bearings. "The sofa's over there?" She pointed.

"Uh-huh."

"Let's sit there."

Once they were settled, Julia put her arm over her daughter's shoulders. "I'm sorry I snapped at you."

Callie was obviously still pouting. "I was just telling you what Tiffany told me."

Julia didn't know exactly what to say. "I know you were. And *we* started the conversation, didn't we?"

"Uh-huh."

"Callie, the girl who died a long time ago was my best friend.

Her name was Fidelity. She was Flo and Frank Sutherland's daughter.''

"Really?" Callie sounded more fascinated than shocked.

Julia played with her daughter's pigtail. "That's why it's hard for me to hear about this."

"Oh... How come nobody ever told me?"

"Well, it's not something I like to talk about."

"Why did the man kill her?"

"Nobody really knows. Until now...until now he said he *didn't* kill her. I guess maybe he'll explain."

"You knew him?"

Julia had known Christian, yes. In all the ways one person could know another. "He was a friend of mine, too. And of Fidelity's. It's very, very hard to accept the fact that he murdered her."

"Tiff said he was driftwood."

"Driftwood?"

"Something like driftwood." She paused. "Drifter."

Julia was confused. "No, a drifter is somebody who moves around a lot. He lived at Claymore Park."

Callie lowered her voice. For the first time, the severity of what had happened seemed to sink in. "Tiff said he killed a lot of people. I'm glad he didn't kill you, Mommy."

"He didn't kill a lot of people, honey. I don't know what Tiff heard, but that's not true."

"Tiff said they're going to put him in a chair and kill *him* because he killed so many people in Florida."

Julia had a sudden vision of chasing a fox and having it go to ground. One moment the fox was in sight, body tensed, the next it simply vanished. "Florida? Callie, what did—"

The telephone rang, and she and Callie sat in silence as Maisy answered it. Then Maisy came into the room, telephone in hand. "It's Flo Sutherland, Julia. She needs to talk to you. It took her a while to track you here, but she says it's important."

Julia didn't reach for the telephone. In the past weeks her life had changed immeasurably. She knew it was about to change again.

"Julia?"

"Take Callie in the kitchen, would you, Maisy? I think she's ready for her pie."

"Come on, Callie."

Callie got up, and only then did Julia reach for the phone. She waited until Callie and her mother had gone before she brought it to her ear.

Maisy knew better than to ask Julia to listen to the next chapter of her novel that night. After Flo's telephone call, Julia had held up well enough to put Callie to bed and get ready herself, but Maisy knew that the one thing her daughter needed most was solitude.

The house was dark, the dishes finished, and the windows closed and latched before she went to look for Jake.

She had expected to find him in their bedroom, but when she found he wasn't, she went out the back door and made the trek to the barn. She heard him talking to Feather Foot before she even opened the door.

"What a good pony, a pretty pony."

She stood in the doorway and watched them, the hulking, gentle man and the flirtatious little paint. "Did you bring her sugar cubes? After telling Callie not to give her too many?"

"Carrots. Left over from dinner." Jake didn't turn.

"Guess I can't find fault, then."

"She's a pretty little thing. Feisty, but pretty. A lot like Callie."

"And you spoil her the same way."

He stroked the pony's nose a moment before he faced his wife. "I like to spoil the women in my care."

"It's been a tough evening."

"You want to talk about it, don't you?"

"I suppose. Do you?"

His mouth twisted wryly, neither a smile nor a frown. "I wish I had something to say. Something wise and all-knowing about the universe and the way things always come right in the end."

"They don't."

"That's why I don't have anything to say." He brushed his

hands together, then held out his arms. She crossed the floor and went into them.

"The phone call was a terrible shock for Julia."

"Terrible?" He tightened his grip, hugging her closer. "To discover that a man she loved isn't guilty of murder after all?"

"She's always known that."

Jake rested his cheek against Maisy's hair. "You want to believe that because you like to keep your eyes closed to certain realities."

"And what reality are we talking about this time?"

"That life is far more complex for your daughter than it is for you. That she has never developed your defenses."

She was hurt, but she tried for humor. "She's married to Bard Warwick. A defenseless woman couldn't survive that."

He kissed her hair. "No matter what you want to believe about her, Julia did doubt Christian's innocence, at least momentarily. And now she's going to have to face the fact that she didn't stand beside him when he needed her most."

"He wouldn't let her."

"Because she faltered on the witness stand."

Maisy shivered. The evening was cool, but Jake's arms were warm. She supposed the shiver had something to do with a chink in the defenses Jake had mentioned. "I'm so torn. If they find Fidelity's jewelry tomorrow, Christian will surely go free. I've prayed for that since the day he was sentenced, but Julia has so much to deal with. Having Christian come back now will make things that much harder, won't it?"

"It won't make things easier." He stepped back a little and rubbed his hands up and down the sleeves of her sweater, as if to warm her. "What makes you think he'll return?"

"Because Peter's been his champion. I'm sure he'll offer Christian a job at Claymore Park."

"Peter has contacts all over the horse world. He can help Christian find a job far away from the scene of the crime. Christian's been gone nine years. Will this still seem like home? When nearly all of Ridge's Race and beyond was sure he murdered Fidelity?"

"I think when you've lost everything and you're given a chance to find some part of it again, that's what you do."

Jake seemed to consider that. "You're a wise woman, Maisy."

"Do you think so?"

"I think you let it slip out now and then, when you don't think anyone's listening."

She frowned. "How *do* you put up with me?"

"Very easily."

"Sometimes lately I'm not so sure."

He didn't ask what she meant. "Time moves on and people change. Their lives change with it. Christian's life is changing again. Julia's life is changing, and she'll have to face it, whether she feels ready or not. Our lives are changing, too."

"How are they changing, Jake?"

"We're growing older. There's less time to say the things we need to."

"What things?"

"A lifetime of things that've gone unsaid."

She was sure he was being purposely obtuse. "Do you have things you need to say?"

He smiled a little. "I'm working my way toward them, I suppose. How about you?"

She thought of a thousand things she'd wanted to tell him or Julia and never had. She, who chattered continuously.

Instead she asked a question. "Jake, do you still love me?"

"Yes, I do."

She felt vulnerable, an unexpected and unwelcome sensation. "You've been critical lately."

"Have I?"

"You seem impatient with me and with the things I say."

"I guess it goes back to time moving too fast. I don't think you're saying the things you need to."

"This isn't making any sense."

"I don't know how to make sense of it. I feel like our life together's been about peeling off layers. I wonder sometimes if we'll ever succeed."

"I feel like I know you."

"As well as you let yourself know anyone."

"That would be a good example of the word 'critical'."

He shook his head. "That would be a good example of the word 'honesty'. Maybe there's too little of it in our marriage. Maybe that's what I'm feeling impatient about."

She felt they'd covered ground and gotten nowhere. She missed the man she'd married, the man who had accepted her unequivocally.

He gripped her shoulders. "Don't look at me that way. You haven't lost me. I don't love you any less. Maybe I'd just like more of you."

"How much more of me could anyone stand?" She patted her round belly. "How much more could there be?"

"I think we'd better check on things inside. If Callie needs something, Julia's in no shape to get it for her. Not tonight of all nights."

She realized he was putting her off, but she was relieved. She'd had enough to face that day. "You know, Jake, if you want more of me, that could be arranged tonight."

"Could it?"

"We've been slowing down a bit lately. Maybe we should pick up the pace?"

He put his arm around her and squeezed. But when they were finally in bed, holding each other tight, she still felt the distance between them.

11

Nine years had passed since Karl Zandoff buried Fidelity Sutherland's jewelry between fenceposts, between properties, between Christian's hope of exoneration and the reality of his imprisonment. At ten-thirty on Thursday morning, as autumn leaves began their annual spiral and one of the two digging crews stopped to raid a jug of steaming coffee, Pinky Stewart, shovel-wielding sheriff's deputy, struck a metal tin that had once held Reducine ointment.

Six hours later, and only because Peter Claymore had the political influence he did, Christian Carver walked out of Ludwell State Prison.

Mel Powers's forehead glistened, but not nearly as brightly as his eyes. He was an emotional man—an asset he played to the hilt in a courtroom—but never so emotional that he couldn't calculate his way to the next appeal. Since arriving at Ludwell that morning, he had routinely alternated tears of victory with a shit-eating grin.

Christian hadn't smiled or cried. He felt like a deer caught in headlights, unsure whether to stand or run, and unable to think quickly enough to make a decision. Years ago he had given up the dream of freedom, then reclaimed it with Zandoff's confession. Now that the dream had come true, he could think no further ahead.

He hadn't even had time to say goodbye to the men he had worked with, or to Landis or Timbo, who had depended on him for instruction and advice. One moment he was wearing his prison work shirt, the next he was in a suit bought for the occasion by Peter Claymore. He'd been handcuffed and transported in a prison van to the same courtroom where he had lost his freedom.

And he had found it again.

Standing at the top of the courthouse steps, he was dismayed at the sun beating down on his bare head. He'd been outside almost every day since his imprisonment, but the air and sun felt different here, as if he had entered an entirely new universe. For a moment he was filled with panic, afraid to breathe for fear his lungs would fill with poison, afraid to move for fear the sun, unadulterated by the shadows of prison walls and razor wire, might melt his skin.

He had refused to give a statement, but news crews were there anyway. The equipment aimed in his direction was an entirely new generation of technology than what he remembered. He felt a stronger stab of panic.

Peter edged Christian down the steps. "Son, you're out for good. They aren't going to find anything that will put you back behind bars. Now, let's make a run for my car."

Christian grimaced and wished he could strip off the tie. "Let's get it over with."

He was safely inside Peter's Lincoln before anyone spoke again. He was aware of leather seats against his palms, the purr of a perfectly tuned engine. He realized he was exhausted, sick with it, as if some unseen hand had robbed him of everything that kept a man moving and breathing.

"Where are we going?" he said at last.

Peter put a hand on his knee. "Where do you want to go?"

He nearly said home. But there was no such place, and probably never had been.

"A bar," Mel said, when Christian didn't respond. "The first one we see. Chris needs food, and he needs a good stiff drink. So do I."

Christian had sworn off liquor before he could have his first drink, the result of being Gabe Carver's son. Now he wondered if his father had understood something he hadn't.

"Christian?" Peter said.

"Yeah." Christian leaned back and closed his eyes. "The first bar we see."

Julia could find her way through the house with only the occasional stumble. Karen had organized her drawers and toiletries so that she could find the things she needed. Maisy had cleared the halls and rooms. Julia had even learned to make her way out to the garden, where Jake had leveled stones to be certain she didn't catch a toe and trip. Adjusting had taken time and concentration. Now that the basics were, for the most part, finished, she had little to occupy her mind.

But nothing would have emptied it of Christian Carver, anyway.

"Julia, I'm making a cake. Why don't you come stir it for me?"

Out of habit, Julia looked up at the sound of her mother's voice. Karen had gone to Millcreek just before three to pick up more of Julia's clothes and hadn't yet returned. Julia knew Maisy's cake was just an excuse to help her stay busy, but she was more than willing to go along with it. "Can I lick the bowl?"

"I won't tell the salmonella police if you don't."

"I don't know how helpful I'll be. You might end up with more on the counters than in your pans."

"I'll take that chance." Maisy hesitated. "See you in the kitchen, honey."

Julia was sure her mother wanted to take her by the hand and lead her, and it was a welcome surprise that she hadn't offered. Julia found her way through the hall with no problems and turned the corner into the kitchen, where her luck ran out. She felt for the edge of the counter to orient herself, and her hand brushed something cool and smooth. The contact was temporary. The item crashed to the floor.

"Damn!"

"It's okay, Julia. Just a bowl. I shouldn't have left it so close to the edge. It's my fault."

"No, it's not." Julia wanted to hit something or somebody.

And simply wanting to wasn't nearly good enough. "It's my fault for being blind."

"I'm cleaning up the pieces. Don't come in until I'm done."

"When is this going to end? If this is all in my mind, don't you think something would shake loose and I'd see again?"

"I think if it were that simple you wouldn't have lost your sight in the first place."

"How am I going to be able to take care of Callie if I can't see where I'm going? If I can't see who's coming?"

Maisy didn't answer right away. Julia could hear the sound of the broom brushing the floor, the clinking of pottery, the slide of the dustpan.

"That's what this is about, isn't it?" Maisy said at last. "It's one thing to be suddenly blind. That's terrible enough. But to be blind and afraid that Christian will come back—"

"This isn't about Christian."

"Isn't it?"

This time Julia fell silent. She wanted to deny the truth again, but how often had she done that over the years, and how much damage had it caused?

"Christian is part of the reason I wanted you to come in and help me," Maisy said.

"I don't see the point in talking about what's happened. Do you? I can't change a thing now. I can't go back nine years and say things I didn't say then."

"That's not what I'm talking about, honey. And you can come in the kitchen now. The mess is cleaned up, and there's nothing else perched on the countertops that you can knock over."

Julia took a tentative step. "There isn't going to be much left in this house when I'm finished with it."

"It's needed clearing out for a long time. Come over to the fridge and we'll work at the counter beside it."

"Do you have another bowl?"

"You're talking to the pottery queen."

Julia felt her way to the fridge, then shuffled right until she had positioned herself at the counter.

"I'm going to put the bowl in front of you with the cake mix inside it, then I'll start adding ingredients. You can start stirring in a moment. Here's a wooden spoon.''

Julia felt the handle against the back of her hand and reached around to take it. ''What were you talking about, then, if you weren't talking about the way I abandoned Christian?''

''You didn't abandon him. You were young, and you'd just lost your best friend. Almost everybody thought Christian killed Fidelity, and there was enough evidence to convince a jury. You were momentarily torn. That's all you ever were.''

''That was enough. I sat on the witness stand, and when the prosecutor asked if I was completely sure Christian didn't kill Fidelity, I couldn't answer.''

''Julia, Flo called a little while ago.''

Julia gripped the spoon harder. She heard her mother slide another bowl in front of her. She had the urge to send that one crashing to the floor, as well. ''What did she say?''

''They found Fidelity's jewelry where Karl Zandoff said it would be. That and the confession are enough to free Christian, at least until an investigation is completed and he can be pardoned. They scheduled an emergency hearing for this afternoon. Flo said it looks like Christian will be out of prison by nightfall, if not sooner.''

Julia closed her eyes, although there was little point. ''How's she taking this?''

''We didn't discuss that. She just wanted me to relay the message to you.''

''She knows I'm living here now?''

''I'm not sure. She seemed to think the news should come from me and not from Bard.''

Julia let that sink in. She had not told anyone she had moved home. For that matter, few people knew what had happened. Bard had told their friends that she'd been badly shaken by the fall and was under doctor's orders to rest. But the word would get out soon enough.

''You can start stirring anytime.''

Julia felt along the edges of the bowl until she knew its boundaries, then dipped her spoon in gingerly and began to slowly mix the liquid and dry ingredients. ''Where will he go?''

"I don't think anybody knows, but..."

Julia finished Maisy's sentence. "But Peter will offer to take him in. I doubt he's been on a horse since—" Her voice caught. She rested the spoon against the side of the bowl and stood with her back as straight as a wooden stake, trying not to cry.

If Maisy noticed, she gave no sign. "I bet he stayed in shape. He was always a very physical person. It might take him a while to get his legs back, but he'll catch up quickly."

Julia took a deep breath. "I don't want him here."

"I can think of a number of reasons why that might be true."

"No, there's only one. I don't want him near Callie."

"I can understand that."

"Can you?"

"You don't want Christian to find out that Callie is his daughter."

"I don't even want you saying that in this house."

"Honey, Callie's at Tiffany's. The house won't be echoing with anything we've said when she walks through the front door."

"You bring it up all the time. You tell me how much Callie looks like her father. You point out that Christian had the same learning disability when he was a boy. You talk about the way Callie cocks her head sometimes, just exactly the way Christian always did."

"She does."

"Are you planning to just blurt out the truth to her someday, Maisy? Sort of a pass the cookies, oh, by the way, that bastard Bard Warwick really isn't your father?"

"Julia, I'm not the problem."

Her mother was right, and Julia knew it. It was the final straw. The tears she'd tried so hard to subdue fell.

She heard Maisy push the bowl toward the back of the counter, then she felt her mother's arms closing around her. She was surrounded by the comforting fragrances of violets and devil's food cake mix. It made her cry harder.

"It's a fork in the road," Maisy said, stroking her daughter's hair. "And you don't even feel up to walking a straight line. But you will. You can. You'll get through this, honey, and make all the right choices. There's no question.''

For once Julia was profoundly grateful to be suffocated in her mother's soft arms. But as she sobbed, she wondered who was comforting Christian. Who would tell Christian that at this crucial fork in the road he would take the right path? Who would hold him and reassure him?

She knew, without a doubt, it should have been her.

12

The Horseshoe Bar and Grill wasn't known for its cuisine. The menu was limited, the cook indifferent. Christian had never eaten anything that tasted better than the steak sandwich and French fries Peter ordered for him.

He'd lost the fine art of ordering for himself. When confronted with even a limited menu, he'd frozen. After nearly nine years of having the Commonwealth of Virginia decide for him, the menu had seemed as incomprehensible as a neurosurgery textbook.

Sensing his dilemma, Peter had recommended the steak sandwich; then he had ordered a round of beer for everyone. Christian was on his second now while they waited for frozen cheesecake to defrost.

"Feeling any better?" Peter asked.

Christian drew rings in the condensation on his mug. "Yes. Thanks."

"Everything's happened too fast."

Christian tried to smile, but he was out of practice. "Or not fast enough."

"Nine years not fast enough," Mel said.

"It's going to take you a while to adjust, son," Peter said. "You have to give yourself time. Don't expect too much right away. Ease back in."

Mel polished his glasses, then held them up to the bare incandescent bulb hanging over their table. "Which brings up what you plan to do. You haven't had much time to think about it, but it must have crossed your mind."

"I need to get a job and start paying Peter back for everything he's done."

"You given any thought to what sort of job?"

"Bertha Petersen might help me find something. And I finished my degree while I was behind bars. Maybe there's a job out there for an ex-con with a degree in biology."

"I have a job for somebody like that." Peter, who seemed as at ease in the honky-tonk Horshoe Bar as he did astride a prize hunter, leaned forward and rested his arms on the table. "I want you to come home, Christian. I need you there."

Christian had been fairly certain Peter would offer him a job, and he had been just as certain he would refuse. But he hadn't expected Peter to say that he *needed* him. He was unprepared, and suddenly unable to answer.

"Christian, opening hunt is less than a month away, and the Mosby Hunt needs a huntsman. I've tried a couple of men but haven't found anyone who could do the kind of work I expect, and I'm getting too old to do the job myself. We need someone who knows how to breed and train and work with our vet and kennel staff. You'd have help, of course. My whole staff would be at your disposal. But—"

"I can't." For a man who couldn't choose between a steak sandwich and a chicken filet, those two words came easily.

Peter fell silent, but Mel took up the slack. "You've had so many offers, Chris, you've already settled on something better?"

Christian ignored Mel. "Peter, you don't need me. There must be a hundred men more qualified to be your huntsman than I am. I haven't even been on a horse since—"

"I'd be worried about that if you were anybody else, but you could ride before you could walk. Your daddy saw to that. And I taught you to hunt myself. I've never seen anyone with better instincts. You were whipping-in before you were fifteen, and half the time you were the one who kept track of the dogs when Samuel began to fail.''

Samuel Fincastle had been the club's huntsman for almost twenty years. Samuel had died when Christian was in prison, and Christian hadn't even been able to pay his respects. It had been one more bad moment among many.

"Everything will come back quickly, and you'll feel right at home," Peter continued. "Until you do, I'll cast the hounds myself. You ride along for the rest of cubbing season until you're feeling comfortable enough to take over." Peter smiled a little. "I will say I'd hate to have your legs after that first long ride or two."

"Even if I could toughen up fast enough, what do I know anymore? Why go back in time?"

"You want to know why?" Peter sat back. "Because you taught my son to ride, Christian, when nobody else had the patience. And you sat up more nights than I can count with mares we might have lost if it hadn't been for you. You were the one who persuaded me to concentrate on American foxhounds to strengthen the bloodlines in our kennel, and you were right, even though nobody else could see it."

Christian held up his hand. "I was a kid, and that was another life."

"And since then, and despite everything, you've gone on to finish your college degree and administer a successful guide dog program. With all that, you can't see why I might want you? Why I know I can trust you to work hard, work fair, and help an old man hold on to everything he's worked for?"

"I don't see an old man."

Peter's expression was strained. "I'm sixty-two going on a hundred. I'm slowing down, and I need somebody I can count on."

Christian had never heard Peter ask for help. Peter was always the one who offered a hand. Christian still wasn't sure this wasn't a ploy to get him to accept more assistance.

"Maybe you don't want to go back to Ridge's Race?" Mel said. "Maybe that's too close to what happened? Too scary?"

"Trust you to put all the cards right out on the table," Peter said dryly.

"What's the point of bullshitting around about this? Christian wasn't exactly a local hero, was he? It takes time for people to change their minds after something like this. People don't want to believe they could have been that wrong."

"I'm still sitting here," Christian told the two men. "I might not be able to order a sandwich without breaking a sweat, but I can speak."

"Well, am I right?" Mel demanded.

"Yes and no."

"I've always said diplomacy was a lost art. Maybe not." Peter made room at the table for the cheesecake that a man with hairy arms slid across to them.

Christian caught his before it sailed to the floor. He tried to remember when he'd last had a dessert that overlapped the edges of an ordinary saucer.

"Christian?" Mel glanced pointedly at his watch.

"I've gotten pretty good at watching my back and even better at ignoring things that don't concern me. I can think of another reason to go back to Ridge's Race."

"If you're thinking you can pick up your life where you left it..." Mel warned.

"Nothing like that." Christian knew better than to think that anything in Ridge's Race would be the same, or even that he might want it to be.

"Then what?" Mel dug into his cheesecake.

"I want to know exactly what happened to Fidelity."

Mel's mouth was full. "We know what happened to Fidelity. Karl Zandoff killed her. What else do you have to know?"

"Nobody's actually placed him at the scene."

"He placed himself there," Peter said. "Which is all that really matters now. What's the point of looking further?"

"Until somebody else can put him there, people will still wonder, won't they?"

"Who cares?" Mel said.

"Because I'm wondering. I want to know what happened to her." His voice rose. "I want to know how Zandoff managed to do this when nobody even remembers him being in Loudoun County. I want to know how he chose Fidelity, how he knew when she would be alone, how he caught her unaware." Christian slapped his palm against the table. "I want to put it completely to rest. It's all I've thought about. I have to know so I can move on."

The other two men were silent. Finally Peter spoke. "Christian, this is a matter best left to the authorities. The Florida cops aren't going to let you anywhere near Zandoff. And no one here is going to appreciate you poking around in police business. The fact that they put you in prison when you weren't guilty will be enough for them to live down. Let them gather the details in their own way."

"At least I have what's left of the rest of my life. Fidelity doesn't have that. We were friends. She was the first girl I kissed. Maybe she was spoiled rotten, but she had a good heart. She didn't deserve to die, and now she deserves to be put to rest. Really put to rest."

Peter put his hand on Christian's arm. "Not by you."

Even though Christian knew Peter was right, he also knew he couldn't sit back and let the rest of the story unfold without him. He just wouldn't rub Peter's nose in it.

"I want you at Claymore Park," Peter said. "But not if it's going to make things worse for you or anyone else in Ridge's Race. I want you to heal. I don't want you reopening wounds." He paused. "Come home with me, son. I lost my boy, and you lost nine years of your life. Let's see if we can help each other a little."

Christian was not Peter's son, but something in Peter's eyes told him that Peter hoped Christian might be able to fill a little of the hole left by Robby's death. Peter had stood beside him through his nightmare, and now it was time for Christian to stand beside Peter.

He gave just enough of a nod to get the job done. "I'll come, but I won't guarantee I'll be exercising anything except your most docile mares until I've got my legs back."

Peter clasped Christian's arm, then picked up his glass. "A toast to a new life and the new huntsman of Mosby Hunt."

Christian and Mel lifted theirs in answer. The resulting tinkle of glass against glass reminded Christian of Fidelity Sutherland's laughter.

"It's been a difficult night," Jake said as he and Maisy finished up the dishes.

Christian's freedom hadn't remained a secret for long. Bard had come by just as they finished supper to demand once again that Julia return to Millcreek where he could keep her safe.

Maisy wondered exactly what Bard wanted to protect her from.

"What a welcome for Christian." Maisy dried the last plate and set it in the cupboard.

"Not the best," Jake agreed. When Julia refused yet again to go back to Millcreek, Bard had made it clear he intended to warn Christian to stay away from his family. Nothing any of them said had made an impact on him.

"He's been unfairly imprisoned for nine years, and now he has to come home to Bard Warwick at his worst," Maisy said.

"That's not all he'll come home to, is it?"

"I don't know what you mean."

"He has Peter Claymore. He has *you*."

She didn't answer.

"You've written him every month since he was sent away."

"How do you know that?"

"I live with you, remember?"

"You've never said anything."

"What was there to say? Except that you're a wonderful, warmhearted woman."

"I don't mind hearing it."

"I don't mind saying it." He kissed the top of her head. "You'll be going to see him, won't you?"

"You know me so well."

"Maisy, just be careful. You can't make everything right."

"I know that."

He patted her ample behind and left the room.

Maisy joined Julia in her bedroom once she was sure her daughter was settled for the night.

"Doing all right?"

Julia grimaced. "I've just been thinking about Bard. He feels threatened by the whole scenario. He's only comfortable if he knows exactly what's going to happen next. And no one knows that, do they?"

Privately Maisy thought Bard was unhappy because he didn't have complete control over the situation. "I hope you realize he can't keep Christian away from the two of you no matter what he does. Callie will run into him. It's inevitable."

"I have to take this one step at a time."

"Are you up for another chapter?"

Julia's real answer was clear in her expression, but it was a testimony to her love for her mother that she nodded. "I guess I could use something else to think about right now."

"I'm happy to oblige." Maisy settled herself in a chair while Julia got into bed. "Are you enjoying the story so far? I didn't go on too long about Louisa's trip to Virginia, did I?"

"As a matter of fact..."

"You're not enjoying it?"

"No, actually, I'm, well, surprised."

Maisy laughed. "Why?"

"It's interesting. You haven't written anything else, have you?"

"Oh, I've been dabbling for years."

"You never told me."

Maisy considered that. "I suppose it's because writing means more to me than anything else ever did. Maybe the things that mean the most are the things we don't talk about."

"Are we talking about you now, or me?"

Maisy shuffled her pages. "Let's talk about Louisa and her introduction to hunt country. Just lie back and forget about everything else for a little while."

"You never ask for too much, do you?" Julia closed her eyes.

From the unpublished novel *Fox River*, by Maisy Fletcher

My first glimpse of Sweetwater was across a pond shaded by weeping willows. Azaleas in every shade of pink lined the brick driveway to the house, and rhododendrons in bud peeked from the lush canopy of an evergreen forest. The house, of the same maroon brick, sat on a gentle rise, held proudly erect by columns as thick as the trunks of the magnolias and maples gracing the sweep of emerald lawn.

Annie had prepared me. As we traveled, she had told me tales of the men and women on nearby estates. They were far more interesting than most people of our class, vital, exuberant and sometimes overwhelmingly rich. We would visit them, Annie had promised, each and every one. There were teas, yes, and dances, but we would also go to races and horse shows, and take long companionable canters through the woods. Fox hunting was an autumn sport, but we might help walk the Fox River hounds, if we were so inclined. The pack was housed at Fox River Farm, the personal property of a man named Ian Sebastian, who was the finest horseman in Virginia. We would ride there after we rested.

Although I didn't have Annie's zest for horses, the social whirl seemed to be made expressly for high-spirited young ladies. As we disembarked from the carriage and started toward the house, I could feel the mantle of expectations that had been laid on my young shoulders slipping away.

Sweetwater's stables were a revelation to me, well scrubbed and marvelously efficient. The head groom, a man called Major, prided himself on producing the finest overall mounts in the county. For champion hunters, though, Annie explained, a rider had to look toward Fox River Farm. "Our horses go the distance, but Fox River horses win the prizes and the fox."

As we rode toward Fox River Farm she explained. The difference between Fox River and Sweetwater horses, it seemed, was temperament. Ian Sebastian was fearless, a man who could master even the most recalcitrant stallion. He bred for conformation, beauty and intelligence, but Fox River mounts were not for the faint of heart. They ran faster, jumped higher and threw more riders than any others in Virginia. It took a man like Ian Sebastian to master them, and men like Ian were rare. Fox River hunters were in demand worldwide, but only by the most stalwart of riders.

The ride was glorious. The woods were carpeted with trillium and Virginia bluebells, and each hillside promised a new, more spectacular vista. Always, in the distance, the mountains stretched to the sky, but the moment we crossed a creek bed to Fox River, it was as if the world was suddenly under magnification, the sky bluer, the grass as lush as a prairie, the looming mountains taller and more majestic.

"It's the most beautiful setting in the county," Annie said. "The air seems purer here. Much of the forest is still virgin, and I've often wondered if that's the difference."

"Have you ridden through the forest?"

"The hunt comes through the edges. Ian is Master of Foxhounds and knows every tree and creek bed. Without his guidance, a rider might be lost for days."

We rode for what seemed a long time, and secretly I was growing weary. When we reached a wide stream, bordered on the other side by deep woods, Annie pulled her horse to a halt. "This is Fox River."

I was disappointed. "It hardly seems like a river."

"It never was, not like the James or the Mississippi. Most of the water was diverted some time ago into irrigation for nearby farms. This is all that's left of it. Just a stream now, sadly enough."

"Is the house far?"

"We still have a ride ahead of us. Would you like to eat here?"

I rejoiced at the chance. The Sweetwater cook had packed a leather pouch that Annie had strapped to her saddle. Inside we found ham biscuits and deviled eggs, dried apples with pecans, and slices of lemon cake, which we dove into with the appetite of healthy youth.

"Where would the stream lead if I followed it?" I was wading by the time I asked the question, my green riding habit hiked to my knees, my boots on the bank above me. Annie was yards away, leading our horses to a patch of pasture just beyond a low rise so they could graze.

"Into the woods."

That was perfectly clear. Annie had already told me that we would follow the edge of the woods until we saw the house. "Does it stop there?"

"No. It continues through Fox River Farm proper and on into the mountains." Annie disappeared over the ridge.

A butterfly landed on a wild daffodil at the water's edge, and as it continued its flight I followed, stepping from stone to stone along the bottom. At its deepest the water came to my calves, and the river stones were round and easy on my bare feet.

I had no fear of getting lost, despite Annie's warning. There was only one stream, and it would be easy enough to follow it back. The afternoon was warm and the water a pleasant contrast. I was in the woods before I gave the matter much thought.

The forest canopy above my head was a parasol of the most amazing green. Once I'd left the sunshine behind, the air cooled, becoming moist and fragrant with the scents of pine and spruce. Virginia creeper and wild grape vines twined over oaks and maples that were older than our country, and birds rustled in the undergrowth.

The stream diverged, still easy enough to follow, and I chose the right fork.

I don't know how long I waded. It was a lazy day, and I was grateful to be on my feet again. By summer's end I would be used to riding for long hours every day, but for now it was spring.

When I heard a crashing sound in front of me, I thought little of it. Noise is amplified in a forest. A mockingbird hopping on a pine needle bed can sound like a horse clip-clopping on a country road. I stopped and waited, but when all was silent, I continued on.

The second time I heard the noise I thought better of going forward. I could no longer see the forest edge or glimpses of sunshine to lead me back. The time had come to turn around and follow the stream to find my horse and Annie. I was preparing to do just that when the tall undergrowth at the streamside parted, and a black bear and two half-grown cubs appeared.

I froze. The day had been enchanted, and I hadn't given a single thought to danger. Fox River seemed like a kingdom in a fairy tale, and until that moment, I'd felt like a princess.

Water would not deter a bear. I knew this. And even

had I been able to get a leg up into one of the huge trees at the other side, I knew that bears also climbed. Black bears were not the most dangerous of beasts, but mother bears with cubs in tow were a different matter.

At first the mother seemed not to notice me. Her children were rowdy, as children often are, and she cuffed one as I'd often seen children cuffed when misbehaving. Then, as I watched with horror, she spotted me for the first time. She rose to her hind legs and roared, a sound I hope never to hear again.

I had no plan. Plans are for people who are capable of thought. I did the worst thing I could have. I ran. Not through the water, but out of the water and into the woods, where the ground was smoother and some speed possible. I dodged trees and crashed through the undergrowth, making much more noise than the three bears had.

I was afraid to look behind me, sure I'd see her gaining and lose my ability to move. I lost my hat, and my habit caught and tore, but it didn't slow my progress. The forest grew cooler, damper, more redolent with decaying foliage as I ran deeper into it. Finally, as I was sure my lungs had already burst, I peeked behind me to find that I was alone. The bear had stayed with her cubs.

I crouched behind a stump and waited, too winded to go farther. At last my breath came easier and my heart slowed. I could hear the sounds of the forest around me, but nothing of bears.

I waited there for perhaps an hour. I knew that Annie would be frantic and certain I was lost. At last I stood and gauged my position. I was sure I knew which way I had come, and once I found the water again, I could follow it back to the clearing.

I made several false starts until I remembered to look for signs of my own flight. I had not run as far as I'd thought. With care and in time I was able to find a path back to the creek, pausing for minutes as I listened for the bears before I waded back into the water.

I realized then that my feet were scratched and bleeding. It hadn't mattered as I tried to escape, but now the stones were hard against them and the water stung. I walked slowly, staying to the far side so I could abandon the stream again if necessary. The first strong rays of sunlight through the forest canopy were like paintings I'd seen of heaven opening. I wanted to drop to my knees in a grateful prayer.

I came out of the forest to find Annie and my boots gone, and the horses nowhere in sight. I called her name, but my only answer was birdsong and the music of the stream.

"Annie!"

The baying of hounds greeted my second shout. Over the rise where Annie had taken our horses four foxhounds appeared, and then a strange black horse. On the horse's back was a man so magnificent, so perfectly wedded to his mount, that for a moment I believed I was in a fairy tale after all.

His hair was as black as the horse beneath him. His shoulders were broad, but his body was perfectly suited for riding, long, lean, and graceful in a way that had nothing to do with femininity. He examined me in my torn habit, my hair straggling around my shoulders and laden with twigs and dead leaves, my face and arms scratched and dirty. Then he gave a mocking bow.

"Miss Louisa Schumacher?"

I drew myself up to my full height, straightening what was left of my skirt. "Who else?"

He laughed, a deep booming noise that somehow reminded me of the black bear's roar.

"Have you had an adventure, Miss Schumacher?"

I thought perhaps I was about to have an even greater one. "Will your horse carry two?"

"My horse could carry an army. Can you ride a real

horse, Miss Schumacher, not one of those insipid Sweetwater nags?''

"If I can face down a bear, I believe I can ride your ostentatious horse." I paused and put my hands on my hips. "But not unless I know your name."

I knew it, of course. I had heard Annie's stories, and I knew whose property we were on. I examined Ian Sebastian as he introduced himself, then I started toward him.

"My hat and boots seem to have disappeared, my dress is torn and wet, and I smell like the forest floor."

"Your friend is at my house, gathering reinforcements to search for you. Shall we find her before anyone else has to view this particularly terrifying sight?''

I laughed. I couldn't help myself. I was young. I was free from my mother's strict surveillance, and I had survived. I was about to climb on the back of a great black stallion and ride away with the most remarkable man I had ever seen.

Ian Sebastian leaned down to help me up on the saddle in back of him. I'm not certain why, but it seemed perfectly rational that he didn't dismount and lead me to his house as most gentlemen would have done.

I lifted my arms, then a foot to his stirrup, and in a moment I was floating on air.

13

The house at Claymore Park was unabashedly Prairie style in a region more apt to celebrate Colonial or Classical architecture. Asymmetrical hipped roofs with wide overhangs sheltered courtyards and terraces outlined by square brick pillars and horizontal planters. Inside, ceilings soared whimsically or snuggled low, and turning any corner was an invitation to be surprised.

The original home, an antebellum Greek Revival mansion, had burned down at the same time that Frank Lloyd Wright's designs were beginning to take hold. Peter's grandfather had commissioned a friend at the University of Chicago to design a replacement, and the result had been the talk of Ridge's Race—and sometimes still was.

When Peter inherited the family home he had opted for an eclectic decor. As a career naval officer he had traveled the world and shipped home furniture and art from every port. By the time he came back to stay, the house was a museum to his travels and a showplace in demand for charity house tours.

As a full moon rose higher, Christian stood looking at the silvered cedar siding, the narrow windows that Robby had described as holes where the soul of the house had leaked away after his mother's death. For Robby Claymore, this house had ceased to be a home that day.

"It's too big." Peter stood beside Christian, gazing up at his home. "People still needed large homes when this one was built.

Families were bigger, and guests came to stay for weeks. The house this one replaced had twenty-five bedrooms.''

As a boy, Christian had counted the bedrooms at Claymore Park. There were eleven. There were also two guest cottages and workers' quarters on the property, and a smaller house of compatible design for the property manager.

Peter turned away. "Now that both Edith and Robby are gone, the only things I hear in the evenings are my own footsteps."

After nine years of listening to sobs and belches, to coughs and demented laughter, Christian tried to imagine that sort of peace. One night, before the guards could intervene, he had listened helplessly as a man murdered his cellmate.

"Has it changed very much?" Peter asked.

Christian had changed, and everything he looked at was viewed through that filter. "It's hard to imagine the house without Robby inside."

"He never for a second believed you were guilty, you know. He died your best friend."

Robby had never written or visited Christian in prison, but Christian had understood. Some things were too painful to talk about.

"Where would you like me to bunk?" Christian said. He had little enough with him. A razor and comb, a couple of T-shirts, a blue work shirt, two pairs of jeans. He needed a bed and a drawer, and even the stable offered those.

"I had Rosalita prepare a room upstairs for you. We're renovating the property manager's house. It's yours when the renovations are finished next month."

"An entire house?"

"I'll want you to furnish it at my expense. The last family nearly destroyed it. I'll feel better about having you in there. I know you'll—"

"That's too generous."

Peter faced him. "Christian, what did you expect? A pile of straw and an old saddle blanket? You'll be running this place for me when I can't do it anymore. And that's all the thanks I'll need."

"I don't—"

"I've grown tired of this subject. I'm not in line for sainthood, even if we Baptists did that sort of thing. Claymore Park needs a young man who feels a connection to it. I expect you to take on more and more of the management of the place after you've rested and readjusted to life on the outside again. And I'll compensate you fairly for your hard work."

"You've already compensated me."

"Everything I've done was for your daddy. Gabe was a good man, a talented man with a terrible disease. I should have helped him more. I should have insisted he get medical help. Lord knows the signs were easy enough to read. The only way I've been able to live with turning my back on him was to help you."

"I don't know why. One of the first things I learned in prison was to watch out for myself and not worry about anybody else."

Peter smiled a little. "Did you now?"

Christian saw his skepticism. "I'm not the man you think I am. Not anymore."

"We'll see. Meantime, let's take your bag upstairs and get you settled. These first few weeks I want you to take things easy. Get acquainted with open space again. Ride. Exercise the hounds, if you like, and get to know the rest of the staff. Then you can launch into a full work schedule."

The sound of a car coming up the gravel driveway stopped them both. Christian turned as Peter did and watched a black BMW pull to a stop fifty yards away in a lighted parking space.

"It's Bard Warwick," Peter said. "Do you feel up to this?"

"Up to what?" Christian watched Warwick launch himself from the car. Lombard Warwick had never been a friend. Now he was the husband of the woman Christian had hoped to marry.

"There are two types of conversations one can have with Bard," Peter said. "One's dull as dirt. The other's an argument."

"I guess we'll be having the latter." The way Bard had slammed his door was proof enough.

Peter lowered his voice. "This is a man who looks like a gentleman, quacks like a gentleman, and doesn't have one true quality of a gentleman. At least none I've ever observed."

Bard strode toward them. "Carver, I want a word with you."

"More than one, I imagine." Christian folded his arms and waited.

Bard gave Peter the barest nod. "I'd like to speak to him in private, if that's all right, Peter."

"I resent being dismissed on my own property. So I'm going to stay and make sure you don't cause this young man any more trouble than he's already had today."

"The way I hear it, today was sort of a celebration. He's out. He's standing here while the moon rises, and he's not exactly in chains."

"I can't even imagine what we have to talk about," Christian said. "But get it off your chest, Warwick."

Bard looked pointedly at Peter, who didn't move, except to tilt his head in question.

"All right," Bard said. "I didn't want to involve you, Peter, but I guess you've earned this. I know some bleeding heart judge let him out of prison today, and I know why. Because you've pushed and prodded and all around shoved the legal system to its max. But that doesn't make it right."

Peter shook his head as if to rid himself of a pesky fly. "Did you somehow miss the fact that another man confessed to killing Fidelity Sutherland?"

Bard was dressed as if he'd just come from the office, but his shirt was wrinkled and his tie was unknotted. Christian thought Bard wasn't aging particularly well. He was beginning to resemble his father, a humorless, heavy-handed man with nineteenth-century ideas about self-worth and social class. In his earliest days in prison Christian had tortured himself with pictures of Julia married to a very different Bard, an urbane, intelligent Renaissance man who would give her everything she deserved and quickly take Christian's place in her heart.

Now he revised that picture.

"I've heard the entire story," Bard said. "It's as full of holes as a fishnet."

Peter was beginning to look angry. "We're lucky a judge sees this more clearly than you do."

"Are you finished yet?" Christian said. "Now that we've had your expert legal opinion?"

"I came to warn you," Bard said, turning toward him and shutting Peter out of the conversation. "The judge may have let you go, but the people of Ridge's Race can take care of their own. My property borders Claymore Park, and I don't want to see you step foot on it. Not ever. You will never be welcome there, and furthermore, I want you to leave my family alone. You might have been friends with my wife once upon a time—"

Christian raised one brow. "Friends?"

Bard flushed. "But don't you so much as speak to her or to my daughter. You'll join Zandoff in hell if I discover you've laid a hand on either one of them."

Peter stepped forward and put *his* hand on Bard's arm. "You've said just about enough. Go home."

Bard shook him off. "What's the matter with you, Peter? Can't you see what he is?"

"I can, which is exactly why I want him here and I don't want you. Go home."

"If he comes near Millcreek—"

"You'll have to close the farm to Mosby Hunt, then," Peter said. "As of this afternoon, Christian is our new huntsman. And as such, he'll be riding everywhere we have permission to hunt. Is that what you want?"

"You have to be kidding."

"I'm not."

Bard forced a laugh. "You think anybody, any member of Mosby Hunt, will allow this man to be huntsman?"

"I'll resign as Master of Foxhounds if the board decides against me."

Christian wanted to protest, but he knew better than to do it in front of Bard. "You've said what you have to say, Warwick, and I've had a long day. I'd like to go inside and get settled."

"Jesus, maybe you *should* resign," Bard told Peter. He shook his head as if he was sure that Peter was the bloodiest fool east of the Mississippi. Then he strode back to his car.

"Let's get you installed in the guest room," Peter said, as the sound of Bard's engine died away.

"That's just a sample of what you'll be facing if I stay here," Christian said. "Do you really want to do this?"

"Christian, I'm curious. What did you see?"

"I saw a man, probably one among many, who doesn't want me here."

"You really have been away too long, son. What you saw was a man trying to protect something he's lost a grip on." Peter shook his head wearily. "Bard Warwick doesn't speak for this community. He speaks for himself, too loudly at that. He's worried, all right, and not that you're a homicidal maniac."

In silence they walked up the path to the front terrace.

It seemed the height of irony that by midnight Christian still wasn't asleep, despite a soft bed and quiet house. He didn't miss Ludwell, although he found his mind wandering back to his cell as he stared at moonlight dancing on the ceiling. He was sorry he hadn't had a chance to say goodbye to Landis and wondered if he should try to contact the young man's family now that he was on the outside. He wondered if Javier would look for him when he was paroled, and if Timbo Baines would stay with the guide dog program now that Christian wasn't there to supervise him.

He wondered if Bertha had been told about his release. Would she travel to Ludwell to make certain the program continued to run smoothly?

He wondered if he was losing his mind.

He was free. He had a new job doing what he loved best, for as long as he wanted it. Next month he would have a real house he could call his own. He had the best horses in Virginia at his fingertips, some of the state's most beautiful property and a clear conscience. And still, his heart was back at Ludwell.

He didn't trust fate. A large part of him was waiting for someone to snatch away his freedom, for someone to say, "You know, it's the funniest thing. We made an error and you belong in jail for the rest of your life after all." Perhaps he was cushioning himself against that eventuality.

Or perhaps he was thinking about prison because he was unwilling to delve further back into his memories, to remember the life he'd led here at Claymore Park once upon a time.

Facing memories was an inexorable slide into the past, the veritable floodgate opening. For a moment he felt physically ill, the victim of vertigo and nausea. He sat up to stave off both and realized his skin was clammy. A cavern would have seemed smaller than this bedroom. A crypt would have been noisier.

He threw off his covers and swung his feet over the side, resting his head in his hands.

He was a grown man, but he felt like he was ten again. The second the nausea passed he got to his feet and made his way to the window. Stretched in front of him was one of the most remarkable tableaus in the state. Myriad acres of prime horse country divided by picturesque stone and wood rail fences, the occasional ancient tree anchoring the rolling hills for shade, state-of-the-art barns and stable designed by the same architect who had built the house, and out of sight right now but always presiding over the landscape, the Blue Ridge Mountains.

He remembered the first time he had seen Claymore Park. And he realized that if he stayed, he was doomed to remember every single moment.

"I'm hot, Daddy. We been driving since dawn almost."

Gabe Carver looked down at his son, his eyes not quite focused. "You don't think I'm hot, too, boy?"

"We've been driving in circles for a while now. You don't know where this Claymore Park is, do you?"

"I've got me a map." Gabe tapped the side of his head and grinned. "Don't need anything more than that."

Christian knew it was a lie. At ten he knew a lot more than most boys his age. He knew that his father needed to be taken care of, that he was good with horses and terrible with everyday life, that he had started drinking heavily right after Christian's mother died and now he only stopped long enough to find the next in a series of low paying stable jobs.

"We gotta stop and ask somebody. We're already late."

"No such thing as late in horse country. I was on time, they'd wonder about me."

Christian kept a careful eye on his father's driving. He knew Gabe had sneaked a few drinks before he got behind the wheel of their prehistoric pickup that morning, but there'd been none since. If they did find Claymore Park, Gabe had a chance at a job. For as long as he could keep it.

Christian wished he had a real map. He vowed to wheedle one out of an attendant at the next service station. And from the looks of the gas gauge, that should be soon.

"There's the road. You think you're so smart." Gabe made a wide turn onto a gravel lane and downshifted as they started to climb a low hill.

Christian had no illusions that they were really nearing their destination, but he bit his bottom lip and waited until they reached the top, just in case. He was glad he hadn't said anything when his father finally pulled to a temporary halt and pointed. "Claymore Park. Read the sign."

Christian already had. "How'd you know?"

"Told you." Gabe tapped his head again. "And we're hardly late at all."

Christian looked down at the magnificent estate spread out in front of them, and his heart sank. For the past four years he and Gabe had made their way east from the small Wyoming ranch Gabe had sold to finance his wife's final hospital stay. At the beginning the jobs had been decent enough, but as Gabe's reputation as a drinking man preceded him, they had grown progressively worse. Now, one look at Claymore Park told Christian that any job here would be a long shot. This was no hardscrabble ranch, and the horses grazing down below them had never carried a cowboy.

"Just look at this place, boy." Gabe shook his head. His eyes filled with tears. "Just look at it. Can you believe it?"

Christian hoped his father wouldn't cry. Sometimes Gabe's crying jags lasted for hours. "It's just a horse farm, Daddy. And you know more about horses than anybody in the whole world."

Gabe sighed and pulled his straw hat lower on his forehead. "Let's go see if I can convince them." But he already sounded defeated.

Christian had seen enough of America to suit him, and his head wasn't turned by grass or mountains. He'd passed through the Rockies and lived, at least temporarily, in Kentucky's famed bluegrass country. From the side of the road he'd seen farms to rival this one, but none set quite so perfectly. Even at ten, he recognized quality.

Mares with new foals dotted the paddocks, sleek Thoroughbred mares with legs as long as a racetrack homestretch. Buildings harmonized with the landscape and their neighbors, all of the same gray cedar and brick as the house peeking through the trees up ahead. He heard the peculiar yelping of hunting dogs, and somewhere below he heard men shouting.

The main barn loomed like a castle and might well have cost as much, at least in Christian's mind. They parked beside a row of sleek pickups with Claymore Park's logo—a horse soaring between heaven and earth—stenciled on the sides. Gabe slicked back his hair with his palm and reangled his straw hat on top of his head.

"You got a clean shirt in the suitcase," Christian told him. Christian knew, because he'd done the laundry at their last campground.

"Won't matter one bit." Gabe sounded sad, but at least he wasn't crying.

Christian got out and brushed off his jeans. He was glad it was late May and nobody would ask Gabe why his son wasn't in school. He wasn't good at school, and he didn't see why it mattered if he went regularly. He was never going to be anybody. He could hardly read.

"You ready?" he asked Gabe when his father came around the truck.

"Shoot, yeah." Gabe put on a big grin. "Let's go tell 'em how to run this place."

Inside the barn Christian felt his jaw go slack. He'd seen some pretty slick operations, but nothing quite like this one. The horses behind the half doors were magnificent, and the facility itself was as clean as an old lady's kitchen.

"Well, would you look at that?" Gabe said. "Looks like they had one of those interior decorators. About as much like our place in Douglas as a mule and a racehorse."

Christian didn't like to think of Wyoming, where he'd had a mother who loved him and a father who had held himself together. "Where is everybody?"

"Dunno. Maybe they're out looking for us. Maybe they figured we was a little lost." Gabe punched Christian on the arm.

Christian doubted that the stable staff even remembered Gabe was coming. "We'd better look around."

They walked down the center aisle toward the opposite door. Christian felt the way he did every time he walked through the door of a new school. Afraid to touch anything, afraid to be noticed.

Outside again, they looked over a confusing array of outbuildings, barns and pasture. A weatherbeaten man in a blue polo shirt emblazoned with the Claymore Park logo came out of one of the outbuildings and started past them.

Gabe stepped in front of him. "We're looking for Jinx Callahan. Know where he is?"

The man managed to look Gabe over without appearing to move his eyes. He shrugged and started around Gabe.

Christian blocked his exit. "I bet Mr. Callahan doesn't like to wait around."

The man grimaced. "The breeding shed." He jerked his head to the right, then hustled down the path.

"That's probably the breeding shed," Gabe said, gesturing toward one of the smaller low-slung brick buildings in the distance. "Let's try there."

Despite his long legs, Christian had to lope to keep up with his father. Gabe seemed determined to get this over with and move on.

Judging from the noise as they neared the building, they had discovered the right place. "Noisy bastard, that one," Gabe said. "Sounds like he's enjoying himself, don't it?"

Christian, as used to the sounds of horses breeding as he was to the smell of manure, wasn't paying attention. He'd spotted a boy his own age peeking through the open doorway. The dark-haired boy was smaller than he was, wearing shorts with about a hundred pockets and a black-and-white striped shirt that made Christian dizzy just to look at it.

The boy turned at their approach, just as all hell broke loose inside the shed.

"What the—" Gabe stopped in his tracks.

Gabe was quick to see the problem, but Christian was quicker. Stallions were notoriously excitable beasts, and the stallion in the breeding shed had gotten completely out of control after covering the mare. The two men who'd been supervising had dropped the loosely held twitch and were scurrying to get out of the way of his hoofs. The mare, whose back legs were hobbled together, was flailing from side to side as if she, too, had a point to make. With the two horses thrashing inside the pen, it was only a moment before their combined weight and lethal hoofs brought down one side.

As Christian watched, the stallion, a great chestnut brute, reared and turned, starting directly toward the boy in the doorway.

"Christ in an inner tube!" Gabe sprang forward, but Christian had seen the danger first. He was already on his way toward the mesmerized boy, reaching him just a heartbeat before the stallion ran him down. Christian threw himself against the boy's slight body, just knocking him to the ground and out of the way as the horse thundered past.

He waited for hoofs to strike, for the snapping of bones or the searing of flesh, but his timing had been good enough.

"No, you don't!" Gabe shouted.

Christian looked up to see his father swinging on the horse's halter. In horror, he watched as the stallion dragged Gabe fifty yards or more. Finally he came to a restless halt, with Gabe still holding firm.

"Who the hell is this guy?" Somebody ran past the prostrate Christian, and another man followed.

Christian got up slowly, then held out his hand to the boy, who was still on the ground. "Hey, come on. Let's see what happened."

"Who are you?" The boy got gingerly to his feet. He had a narrow face, with thin features and dark brown eyes that were too big for both.

"Christian Carver. My daddy's looking for a job here."

Tears filled the boy's eyes. "You tried to kill me!"

Christian frowned. "No, your horse did that. You just stood there. Who are you, anyway?"

The boy stuck out a trembling lower lip. "Robby!"

"Didn't anybody ever tell you to get out of the way of a charging horse?"

"I just wanted to see!"

One of the men left the stallion in the care of the other man and Gabe and came back to the boys. He was as old as the mountains and every bit as rugged. "Robby Claymore. I swear, you weren't the boss's kid, I'd whack your fuckin' behind. You been told to stay away from the stallions before." He turned to Christian. "You saved his lily-livered ass. Who are you?"

"Christian." Christian looked over at his father. "Gabe's son."

"Never saw nobody grab a charging horse and hang on the way your daddy did, boy. About as stupid a thing as I ever did see. He could have lost both arms." Clearly he was impressed. "You got some of the old man inside you, looks like."

It had been a long time since Christian had felt proud of his father. "Yes, sir."

"D'you say thank you?" the man asked Robby. "We'd be scraping pieces of you out of the dirt back there if this kid hadn't saved your hide."

Robby clamped his lips together.

"Jinx?"

Christian looked up to see a handsome middle-aged man with salt-and-pepper hair bearing down on them.

"Look, boss, I told you once, I told you a dozen times, Gypsy's Son needs a longer break between mares. You push him too hard and he goes crazy. I—"

"What happened?" The man addressed Robby in a soft voice that still held notes of steel. "I want to know exactly what happened, son, and I want to know now."

"I...I..." The boy couldn't seem to get past that one vowel. Christian realized he was about to dissolve into tears.

"It was my fault," he said quickly. "I think I scared Gypsy's Son. Robby here tried to get out of the way, but I tripped over him. If it hadn't been for me—"

"Robby?" The man waved Christian to silence.

"It—it—it happened real fast," Robby said.

"I think this young man just tried to save your neck for the *second* time today."

"I'm—I'm—sorry, Daddy."

"Who are you?" The man turned to Christian. "I'm Peter Claymore, owner of Claymore Park."

Christian wiped his hand on his jeans before he extended it. "Pleased to meet you, sir. I'm Christian Carver. That's my dad over there."

"You and your daddy are going to be working here?" Peter raised a brow and looked directly at Jinx.

"Looks like he's got any job he wants." Jinx grinned. "Him and his dad."

"Put them on the payroll as of last Monday." Peter smiled. The smile died when he looked at his own son. He shook his head and walked away.

Jinx drifted back to the stallion who, under Gabe's expert touch, was behaving as docilely as a lamb.

"Why'd—why'd you try to help me?" Robby demanded.

Christian thought about that. "Because, well, just because. And besides, I know about fathers." He nodded at his own wisdom.

"Yours, too?"

Christian rolled his eyes. "Mine for sure."

"You're going to be—be staying here?"

"Looks like it." For as long as Gabe could hold the job, anyway.

"I could show you stuff."

Christian liked the sound of that. "What kind of stuff?"

"I have a fort. Want to see?"

"A fort?" His own childhood had disappeared so long before that he felt like Robby's grandfather. "Sure. I'd like that."

Gabe came to join them. Gypsy's Son was under Jinx Callahan's control now. "Well, I got the job. And they're going to pay you to help feed and exercise the mares, if you want. Looks like we're in fat city, boy."

Robby didn't seem impressed with the Carvers' good fortune. "We're going to see my fort."

"Can I?" Christian asked Gabe.

"Yeah, you go on. You two kids get acquainted. Maybe you can be friends."

Christian wondered exactly what that meant, but he was more than willing to give this new life, every bit of it, a try.

Robby grabbed his arm. "Let's go."

And they had gone everywhere together after that. The two boys had been like pieces of a puzzle that was easiest to decipher when they were together. Robby had been good in school, and the moment he realized Christian couldn't read, he set about changing that. Neither boy knew the meaning of "learning disability," but Robby, inventive and highly intelligent, found new ways to help Christian put sounds together in his head so that reading finally began to make sense and an entire world of knowledge opened up to him.

In exchange, Christian taught Robby how to handle horses. Although Peter Claymore had hired the best riding instructors, only Christian realized that Robby, with his expansive, questioning mind, needed to "think" his way on horseback. As they worked on Christian's reading skills, they studied breeds and conformation, saddles and tack, theories of horsemanship and equine history. Robby, who was only comfortable with what he thoroughly understood, became a competent rider.

Now Christian looked out on the acres he and Robby had explored so thoroughly together. The automobile accident that had taken his friend's life seemed particularly unjust. Robby must have been disheartened after Christian's conviction. Although Robby had grown from a scrawny, narrow-faced boy into an attractive man, he had never found it easy to make friends. With Christian's imprisonment and Fidelity's death, he had lost two of the three people he felt most comfortable with.

With Julia's marriage to Bard, he had probably lost the third.

Christian knew that if his friend were alive now, he, more than anyone, would be overjoyed that Christian had been freed.

It was just one more tragic irony.

14

"Tell me again what you know about this woman." Julia scooped her hair back from her face and wished she had brought a barrette. She had forgotten that the air conditioner in Maisy and Jake's pickup had died, and Jake, Mr. Fix-it to the rich and influential, had never quite gotten around to replacing it. Despite autumn's arrival, the day was surprisingly warm.

"You're shouting," Maisy shouted.

"That's the only way I can make myself heard with the windows open!"

"I think that's why Jake never fixed the air conditioner. He has an excuse not to listen to me when we travel together."

Julia smiled at what might well be the truth. "Slow down, Maisy. You'll get another ticket."

"How do you know how fast I'm going?"

"By the speed of the wind rushing past me. Slow down."

Julia was thrown forward, and the wind decreased a little, but just a little. "Nobody wants to give me a ticket. The last patrolman who tried ended up begging me to go away. And all because I tried, very nicely, to explain about Cora Falworth and the Amazon rain forest."

"Please don't tell me what that had to do with you speeding."

"*He* didn't want to hear my story, either."

"You were going to tell me what you know about this woman?" Julia and Maisy were on the way to Warrenton for Julia's first visit to her new therapist, and Julia knew she was being childish. But after her experience with Dr. Jeffers, she wanted reassurance.

"Her name is Yvonne Claxton. She's somewhere between my age and yours. She has a Ph.D. from a school in California and postgraduate training from someplace in New York."

"That's not very specific."

"I'm not a specific kind of gal, honey. I don't remember useless details. I'm more impressed with what people have said about her. She's insightful, kind, and more than willing to take her time getting to the bottom of things. She visited the gallery a time or two when I was there. I liked her enormously."

The gallery in the Ashbourne stables was Maisy's biggest triumph, and although now it was run by a board of directors, Maisy was still very much on the scene. She was friends with all the artists and craftsmen who exhibited there, and drew heavily on them for counsel.

"You're afraid she can't help, aren't you?" Maisy said.

"Well, I don't expect to come out of her office commenting on how blue the sky is, if that's what you mean."

If Maisy noted the frost in Julia's voice, she didn't comment. "What I mean is that you're wondering if there's any point to this."

Julia fell silent, but guilt finally motivated her to speak. "I didn't mean to snap at you."

"We're almost at her office. Just hang in there."

By the time they parked, Julia was feeling even more certain that this was a bad idea. Maisy opened her door and put her hand on Julia's arm. "You ready?"

"How far to the door?"

"About ten yards."

"I hate this."

"It's your first time out in public. Of course it feels strange."

"I feel like a little kid playing Blind Man's Bluff."

"I could carry you."

For some reason that broke the tension. Julia laughed. "You're a pain in the patootie, you know that, don't you?"

"I try my darnedest. I won't lead you into anything, and I'll tell you if you have to duck."

Once inside, Julia felt better. The office was cool, and the waiting room sofa was comfortable. Maisy had told her no one else was there. Julia shifted in her seat. "I'd ask for a magazine, if there was any point to it."

A door opened and a woman spoke. "You must be Julia."

Julia got to her feet. "I guess it's pretty obvious."

"Sure. Maisy said you looked exactly like her." Yvonne moved toward Julia. "I'm going to put my hand on your arm and lead you into my office. Game?"

"Game." Julia appreciated the warning. She chalked up points for the therapist. She said goodbye to her mother, and Yvonne guided her through a short hallway and into her office. She helped Julia into a chair and seated herself nearby.

"I'm going to describe myself," Yvonne said. "Unless Maisy already did?"

"Not physically."

"I'm African-American, almost six feet tall, thin, but not thin enough to model. I wear my hair short and my dresses long, and my eyes are a peculiar shade of blue, thanks to some slave owner in my background. I have big feet and hands, and perfect little ears studded with gold until the day I can afford diamonds." Yvonne paused. "Why don't you describe yourself?"

Julia was still assembling the picture of Yvonne in her mind. "Why? You can see me."

"I'm interested in how you see yourself."

"I'm blind."

"Uh-huh."

Julia bit off her words. "That's how I see myself."

"Then I'd say you're blind in more ways than one."

Julia let that sink in. "I have a serious face, features I've never had to agonize over, a widow's peak that caused me no end of torment as a teenager, a thin body growing thinner since most of my meals end up in my lap. Small feet, blue eyes some slave owner probably bequeathed *me,* and ears no one with a brain would want to accentuate."

"Come on, let me see them."

Julia pulled her hair back and grimaced. "Big ears."

"Normal ears, but not nearly as wonderful as mine."

Julia gave a little smile.

"And not such a serious face when you smile," Yvonne said.

Julia sobered. "It's odd to know you're looking at me and I can't see you. It makes me feel like I'm under examination."

"You are."

"I don't want to be here. I don't want anyone else examining me."

"Had your fill of that already, did you?"

"They couldn't find a thing wrong with me. Not one blessed thing. This is all in my head."

"Uh-huh. But I'll let you in on a little secret. The people who come here all have that problem. There's a lot of that 'head' thing going around."

"Have you ever treated anybody with hysterical blindness?"

"Nope. It's not all that common, particularly not with symptoms lasting as long as yours. We could search a long time and still not find you a therapist who's treated your condition before. And if we did find someone, he'd tell you what I'm going to. Every case is different. Every person is different. Every precipitating event is different."

"Precipitating event? I fell off a horse."

"And that triggered it. Yes, I know."

"I've fallen off horses before."

"Tell me how it feels."

Julia sat back. She was aware of a ceiling fan spinning overhead. Somewhere in the distance she heard a car start. "Do you think you can help me?"

"I'm hoping you'll help yourself. Tell me how it felt to fall off that horse, Julia. I don't ride, so start from the moment you mounted."

Julia closed her eyes and began to describe the day she lost her eyesight.

Christian had heard stories of famine victims who survived for months with little food, only to die when well-meaning relief workers fed them too much, too quickly. After his first day back at Claymore Park, he understood that better. He had been inundated with sensations whose existence he'd nearly forgotten. He felt bloated and drained simultaneously. He was aware of each breath he took, as if even the simplest things about his body were under siege.

Now, as the sun sank over the mountains, he sat on one of Claymore Park's numerous terraces and tried to get a grip on his emotions. He had survived imprisonment. He would survive freedom.

"It has to be hard." Peter came out on the terrace and handed Christian a glass of iced tea. "Every day will seem easier."

"It's that obvious, huh?" Christian took the glass but couldn't drink. He was sure if he put one more thing inside his body, it would explode.

"You were raised with more physical freedom than most young men. Prison must have been particularly difficult."

Christian dredged up a smile. "I don't want to go back, if it's all the same to you."

"That would have been my guess." Peter took a chair near his. "Did you ride today?"

"No." Christian had acquainted himself with the horses, but he had felt too explosive to mount any of them. He was afraid that once he got on horseback, he would imitate his cowboy ancestors and simply ride off into the sunset.

"What do you think of my hounds?"

Dogs were something Christian still felt at home with, and he latched on to the topic. "I think you've been doing some brilliant breeding."

"Do you?" Peter sounded genuinely pleased.

"How are they doing in the field?"

"Well enough. Of course, you know we have successes and failures. Luckily we've had more of the former, but a couple of the new puppies are real disappointments. I don't know if they can be trained or not. That's one of the first things I want you to look at for me when you're rested."

"Which ones?"

"Clover and Balsam. Clover in particular. I bought her to breed down the road a piece, and she's a pretty thing. She's got impeccable lines. Her mother was a Champion American Bitch Hound, and her father was the Best Stallion Hound at the Bryn

Mawr show two years ago. I paid a small fortune, because I thought we could use the new blood. But from all reports she has the brains of a flea, not a trait I want to pass on."

"I'll look for her."

"Do you want to walk down there now for a little introduction?"

"Okay." It sounded like a good idea to Christian. There was less chance he would fly apart if he kept moving.

Peter clapped him on the back. "Good. Let me grab a jacket."

The kennel was far enough from the house to cushion the noise and close enough for easy access. The kennel, like everything else at Claymore Park, was state of the art.

There were three large, airy rooms holding anywhere from one to two dozen couple of hounds—hounds were sometimes coupled together for training, and were usually counted that way instead of individually. The bitches had a room to themselves, and the dog hounds had two, since bitches also had a separate facility to themselves when they were whelping. Each room had platforms that folded down for sleeping and stayed that way except in the early morning, when the room underwent a thorough cleaning. It wasn't unusual to walk into one of the rooms and see the hounds piled happily on top of each other, snoozing away.

Each room ended with a chain-link fence looking over an outdoor run, and all of them butted against a roomy feeding area where twice a day the hounds feasted on kibble. Just beyond was an acre of fenced grass for exercise and play.

Peter greeted each dog fondly, naming them as he went and explaining their strengths and weaknesses. "Darth, short for Darth Vader here—"

"Darth Vader?"

Peter looked up. "It was a 'D' litter. Robby named him just before the accident. He had an unfortunate tendency to snap at the weaker dogs, and at Robby, for that matter. He's a bit more even-tempered now that he's older and neutered."

"I don't remember Robby being interested in the hounds."

"Darth stood out from the crowd, I guess."

Christian fondled Darth's ears. "We know his weakness. What's his strength?"

"He has more drive per pound than any dog in the pack, and a voice that can be heard all the way to Leesburg."

"He's a good-looking guy." Darth had all the physical characteristics a breeder looked for. A neck long enough for him to easily lower his head to the ground to follow a fox's line. Feet and legs designed to cover a multitude of miles, a deep chest and widespread ribs that provided plenty of room for his heart and lungs.

"And who's this?" In the "ladies" room Christian turned to a bitch with a lolling tongue.

"That's Lizzie. She could find a needle in a haystack."

"As long as she can find a fox." Christian tried to imagine himself controlling this pack. Each animal was an individual with unique talents. Some dogs led, some followed. Some dogs caught every scent but lost interest quickly, while others were tenacious to a fault. For the first time he felt a brief stab of enthusiasm for his new job.

Peter started through the kennel to the yard beyond. "Let's find Clover and Balsam."

The younger dogs had their own quarters. Christian had spent only a moment or two here earlier in the day. The confines of the smaller kennel had reminded him too sharply of his cell. This second trip was going better.

In the puppy house, which was similar to the larger quarters, Peter introduced Christian to Balsam, a long-bodied male who growled when Christian approached.

"Not real sociable," Christian said, wiggling his fingers in the dog's direction until Balsam finally sniffed them and gave Christian a tentative canine okay.

"Something must have happened to him before he came to us," Peter said. "I hope we can overcome it. I'd hoped to breed him."

Christian rubbed the puppy's ears, and the dog sidled closer. "I've seen this before. I'll give him some extra attention, and we'll see if we can build his confidence."

"Come here, Clover." Peter squatted and held out his hand to a group of puppies several yards away. Three of the four came to investigate. One stayed where she was, scratching idly and losing her balance after two haphazard strokes.

"I'm guessing this one's Clover." Christian moved closer to the puppy, who instead of righting herself had taken to wiggling back and forth on her back, all four legs waving ecstatically.

"Either she's the dumbest animal ever bred in Virginia or she's too smart to subjugate herself to a human."

"I wouldn't bet on the latter." Christian scratched the puppy's belly, and she quivered in ecstasy. She was a pretty thing, tri-colored like the others, with prominent brown markings and, from what he could tell at this angle, well formed. "How old is she?"

"Over a year."

"Has she been out with the others?"

"Uh-huh, and I'm afraid she's particularly fond of horses. Fond enough to put herself directly in their path whenever she gets the chance. I coupled her with an older hound every day for two weeks to see what would happen, and she tripped him up every time he tried to move. He couldn't do anything with her. I don't know how long she'll last on a quiet walk, much less a hunt."

"I'll watch her for a while and see what I come up with."

"Do whatever you think best. I spent a lot on her, but I don't want to fool with a dog that has no real future with the pack."

Christian gave the puppy one last scratch before he got to his feet.

Peter stood, too, and joined him. "You look good here, son. Right, somehow. And more relaxed."

"I understand dogs better than I understand people."

"And trust them more."

"Maybe."

"You can count on a dog to stand by you."

Christian had spent a fair portion of the day thinking about the two people who had stood beside him during his years in prison. He had thanked Peter for his support, but he hadn't said a word to Maisy Fletcher. He realized now that part of coming home and beginning a new life was setting that right. He was never going to feel comfortable in his own skin again unless he made amends and moved on.

"I'm going to stay here for a while, but don't let me keep you if you have plans for the evening," Peter said.

Christian shoved his hands into his pockets. "I thought I'd go see Maisy tonight."

"Maisy?"

"She wrote me every month while I was in Ludwell. I never answered her."

"Maisy's a real piece of work, but of all people, she would understand why you didn't write back."

"Couldn't," Christian said. "There was nothing I could say."

"You're sure you feel up to seeing her?"

"I don't feel up to sitting around tonight. And I owe her a thank you."

"Well, you know you have the use of any vehicle on the property."

"I appreciate it. But I'm going to walk over. I guess my license has expired."

"I could drive you. You're sure you want to walk to the Fletchers'?"

"It'll do me good."

"Then give Jake and Maisy my regards."

"I'll do that."

They parted at the kennel door. Peter stayed to tend to the watering system, and Christian left for the hike to Ashbourne.

He had made this trip a thousand times with Robby on bikes or horseback, or on foot with fishing rods so they could stop at their favorite fishing hole on Jeb Stuart Creek. Christian had mapped out shortcuts for rainy days, the prettiest routes for lazy days when he just wanted to think. The best paths if he wanted to ride his horse hard or take the highest jumps.

Now he felt a moment of panic as he looked for the straightest route, the one he'd used as a young man who couldn't bear to be separated from the young woman he loved. He had forgotten his way, or the landmarks had changed so drastically that what should have been an easy, straightforward trip now seemed like a maze.

Twilight was deepening, and for a moment he stood absolutely still, his body tense and his breath coming in short spurts. Then, little by little, he forced himself to look around and plot another, foolproof course. What did it matter if he had forgotten his favorite path to Julia's house? After tonight, he doubted he would need it again.

In the end, with a dozen possible routes to Ashbourne, he gave up and chose the road.

"When I was a little girl I came out here to catch fireflies." Julia had her arm around Callie, who was snuggled close against the evening chill. They were in Maisy's garden, and Callie had just finished describing every flower.

"Did you put them in jars? I think that's mean."

"I put them in jars, but I always let them go before I went inside for the night. I had a party here once. My girlfriend and I caught dozens and made lanterns out of them to light the garden. Then the boys came and let them go and chased us in the dark."

"Was that the girl who died?"

Julia understood her daughter's fascination with this subject, although she wished it weren't so. "Uh-huh. Fidelity."

"Who were the boys?"

Julia wondered what had made her tell Callie this story.

"You don't remember their names, do you?" Callie sounded as if she couldn't imagine such a thing.

"One of the boys was named Robby. He was Peter Claymore's son. I'm afraid he's dead, too. He died in an automobile accident just after you were born."

"You have bad luck with friends."

Julia didn't know whether to laugh or cry at that. "I guess I do."

"Who else came to the party? Did Daddy come?"

For one stunned moment Julia didn't know how to answer, then she pulled herself together. "Not your daddy. Just a boy named Christian. He lived at Claymore Park, too. His daddy worked there."

"Did he die, too?"

Julia considered how to answer. Callie had been the one to tell the family that Karl Zandoff had confessed to Fidelity's murder.

If she hadn't heard Christian's name, she would soon. Soon all of Ridge's Race would be discussing his release from prison.

"Callie, do you remember how confused I was when you told me about the bad man who killed Fidelity?"

"Uh-huh."

"Well, that's because, for a long time, everybody believed that Christian had killed her."

"They thought a boy killed her?"

"No, he was a man by then, honey. And he went to jail for it, even though now we know he didn't do it."

"He was in jail and he didn't kill anybody? That's not fair."

"Well, no. It's not."

"Did you try to get him out?"

Julia was silent.

"Somebody should have tried," Callie said when her mother didn't answer. "I would have."

"Most people really thought he'd done it."

"Did you think so?"

Julia considered lying, but in the end she thought it might come back to haunt her. "I didn't, but I wasn't always sure."

"Is he mad?"

"Mad?"

"Mad that he went to jail when he didn't kill anybody."

"I'm sure he's very mad."

"I would be."

Julia figured the time had come to end this conversation. "I think it's probably time for you to go to bed. You have school tomorrow."

"How are you going to get inside? It's dark."

"That doesn't matter to me. Remember?"

"You might fall."

"Tell you what, you go on in and get your nightgown on, and if I'm not in the house by the time you've brushed your teeth and washed your face, you can come out and look for me."

"Don't I have to take a bath?"

"Not if you promise you'll take a shower before school tomorrow."

"Yes!"

Julia felt her daughter leap to her feet, then a brief childish hug. Finally she heard the tapping of Callie's shoes on the flagstone path.

She was grateful for the silence. The day had seemed one hundred hours long. The trip to Warrenton and her session with Yvonne Claxton had taken a surprising amount of energy. She had described the day of the accident and its aftermath. She had explained why she left the clinic and Dr. Jeffers' care, and her reasons for moving back in with Maisy and Jake.

"Do you think your marriage is a good one?" Yvonne had asked.

"I don't think about it one way or the other." Julia had realized how elusive she sounded.

"You've been married nine years, you say?"

"That's right."

"Then would you say that for nine years you haven't noticed what state your marriage is in?" Yvonne's voice was gentle.

"It's a marriage. I signed on the dotted line. There are things about Bard I like and things I don't, just like anybody else."

"And how do you cope with the things you don't?"

"By not thinking about them."

"Julia, can you see that what you're describing is another type of blindness?"

Julia pulled herself back to the present. She didn't want to think about the therapy session or the problems Yvonne seemed intent on uncovering. She liked Yvonne, and she thought if anyone could help, it might be her. But she knew that the process was going to be painful, no matter how patient or gentle Yvonne chose to be.

The evening was growing cooler. She was wearing a sweater, but it wasn't going to keep her warm for long. She supposed she ought to start inside, but the sounds and smells here were enticing. Fireflies had gone for the season, but crickets continued to chirp, and somewhere in the distance she heard a bullfrog's croaks and the occasional lowing of Ashbourne's shaggy Highland cattle. The air smelled sweetly of autumn clematis and fragrant olive, as it had every autumn of her life.

In a short time she would put her daughter to bed, then go to bed herself. Maisy would read another excerpt from her book, and afterward Julia would try to fall asleep. But she wondered what voices Yvonne had released that day and whether they would keep her awake.

Then she heard a voice she had never expected to hear again.

"Hello, Julia."

Julia spun around and followed the voice with sightless eyes. "Christian?"

"That's right."

She heard panic in her own voice. "What are you doing here?"

He gave a harsh laugh. "Don't worry. I'm sorry I scared you. I'm not here to slit your throat."

"I didn't mean—"

"You'll have to forgive me. Gallows humor is the only kind I seem comfortable with anymore."

"You startled me. That's all."

When he spoke, his voice was still coming from a distance. "Are you out here alone? Or is your husband liable to corner me at any moment?"

"Bard? What would Bard want with you?"

"We had a welcome home chat."

"And you came anyway?"

"I wouldn't have, if I'd known you were here. I came to see your mother."

For the first time Julia realized that Callie was inside, and that soon enough she would be coming out to look for her. Panic rose higher. "I didn't mean that the way it sounded. I'm sorry he bothered you. If he told you he didn't want you to see me—"

"It was a waste of his time. I didn't have any plans to seek you out."

"I just meant that I don't like him...anyone making threats in my name."

"You prefer to make your own?"

"Is it possible to start this conversation again?"

"How, exactly?"

Silence fell. Julia had never regretted her blindness more. She felt as if she was floating in darkest space. When he wasn't speaking, she had no idea where Christian was or what he was doing.

Worse, she couldn't *see* him. After nine years away from him, after wondering—at her most vulnerable moments—how he had changed, she couldn't see him to catalog the differences.

She wondered exactly what he thought of her, a blind woman sitting alone in the darkness.

"I didn't hear a car," she said.

"I walked."

"You came the back way?"

"Not at first. I came by the road until I recognized the turn-off."

"The farmer who rents the land made some changes. Took down some old trees, planted windbreaks, rerouted—"

He cut her off. "Nine years is a long time. Everything's changed."

"Christian, I—"

"Don't say it, Julia." He sounded closer now.

"How do you know what I'm going to say?"

"I can't think of anything you *could* say that I'd want to hear. Not that you're glad I got out. Not that you always believed I was innocent. Not even the truth, that you believed I killed Fidelity. If you're willing to admit that by now."

Not that you married another man just one month after they sent me to prison.

The last phrase was unspoken, and Julia had never been more grateful for silence.

She had followed the sound of his voice, turning as he moved in front of her. "That doesn't leave us much room for a conversation, does it?"

"I came to talk to your mother." He paused. "My timing's always been bad, hasn't it? Take the day I found Fidelity lying in a pool of blood. Half an hour later, and no one would have accused me of murdering her. I wouldn't have been found holding my own knife. Somebody else would have found her necklace on the stairs...."

"Christian—" Her voice broke.

"Julia, good God, you can't even look at me, can you? Have I changed that much, or are you really afraid of me?"

"I—"

"Mommy!"

Julia stiffened. Callie's summons had come from the house, but Julia knew that in a moment her daughter would be coming to find her.

Their daughter.

He had heard the summons, too. "Is that your little girl?"

She ignored him, hoping to stave off Callie's arrival. "I'll be inside in a minute, sweetheart!" she called. "Stay there."

Christian was just in front of her now. She could hear leaves crunching under his feet, a heel scraping stone. "Don't worry. I'm leaving. You don't have to protect her from me. I'll see Maisy another time."

She couldn't let him leave this way. No matter how afraid she was for Callie or how humiliated she was that her own eyesight had betrayed her—a fact he obviously hadn't discovered because of the darkness. She had loved this man. They had created a child together. In a million ways he had lived in her heart ever since.

"You're always welcome here, Christian," she said, although her voice was no louder than a whisper. "Whether I'm here or not. And as bitter as you are, I still hope someday you'll forgive us all."

"So do I."

She thought she heard a trace of the young man she had loved. He had always been the most honest person she knew, the one who found it impossible to lie.

And yet when he had needed her to believe in him most, she had doubted him.

Her voice was so soft she could hardly hear her own words. "I know you don't want to hear this. But I am so terribly sorry..."

"You're right. I don't want to hear it."

She heard the crunching of leaves again, but this time farther away. Bushes rustled behind her. Then silence fell, and he was gone.

Callie was not about to give up. "Mommy, are you coming?"

Julia rose and stumbled forward, toward the house and what were becoming the normal rituals of bedtime. But she knew that when Callie was in bed, when Maisy's chapter was finished and the house was silent at last, she would still hear Christian's words.

Over and over again.

From the unpublished novel *Fox River*, by Maisy Fletcher

A month into my stay at Sweetwater, it was obvious that Ian Sebastian was courting me. He was almost twenty years my senior, a widower since the age of twenty-three, and the man Virginia mothers had been training daughters to charm for more than a decade.

"I never expected Ian to marry again," Annie told me. "Some men seem beyond it, as if a woman is no competition for horses and hunting."

"Ian seems to find me at least as attractive as a horse," I said.

Annie's laughter was never feigned. It started at her toes and swept away everything in its path. I laughed, too, just at her exuberance. I laughed a great deal that month.

I had never been so happy. At home I had been admired by strangers but never cherished by anyone. I felt cherished in Ian's presence. He treated me like a porcelain doll, but never the sort that was displayed on a shelf. I was that most beloved of playthings, the doll who went on all adventures, who was introduced to all friends, who was petted and cosseted and only relinquished at bedtime.

"Do you suppose he'll wait until summer's end to ask your brothers for your hand in marriage?" Annie asked.

If Ian waited that long, it would only be because he'd taken his time making up his mind. I told Annie this, and she agreed. "Then do you think he might ask for it soon? For instance tonight, at the ball?"

The first truly formal party of the summer was that night. Fox River Hunt was holding a starlight dance in the clubhouse to raise funds for the upcoming season.

"I have no idea what Ian Sebastian will do," I told her. "We spend more time riding together than we do anything else. He's always tutoring me on my posture, my hands, the placement of my heels. Perhaps he wants to show me, like one of his prized mares."

"Being tutored by the greatest horseman of the countryside is hardly a chore, Weezy."

As a matter of fact, I found it a bit of one. As thrilled as I was to be the focus of Ian's considerable attention, I was not as thrilled to have my entire world centered on how to distribute my weight when taking a jump or whether I should wear a bowler or a cork-lined velvet cap.

"I always thought there was something primitive about Ian Sebastian," Annie said. "Something elemental that all his money and success have never touched."

"Have you fancied him for yourself?" I asked bluntly.

"Me? Not at all," she answered just as bluntly. "He frightens me a little."

"Ian?" I couldn't imagine it.

"He's a passionate man, a powerful man who's used to getting his way. I've never been quite sure what he might do if someone refused to give it to him."

Since I'd seen no signs of that, I discounted what Annie had said. I wanted a man who lived his life on a broad canvas. A man who swept through life and left a whirlwind in his wake.

We dressed carefully that evening, Annie in a deep gold that set off the tan her mother called a disgrace. I dressed in pale green, a dress my mother had chosen for its lace overlay. Since neither of us had yet made the decision to bob our hair, we swept it over "rats," and I wore pearl and emerald earrings that had been a gift to Mama from my father. I hoped they might bring me good luck.

On the trip to the Fox River clubhouse, Mrs. Jones lectured us about proper behavior. Things might be more informal out here in the country, but we were not to walk the grounds with any man unless we were chaperoned. We were to divide our attentions and not allow anyone to monopolize us.

I wondered if Mrs. Jones had spent the past month with her head in the sand. Surely someone had pointed out Ian's interest in her young houseguest.

When we stepped out of the carriage, the party was already under way. Although a fair percentage of the membership lived in the north and only came south for the foxhunting season, the club had spared no expense. They had hired a small orchestra all the way from Richmond, and the soaring of violins filled the summer air. Servants took our wraps, and members of the board of governors escorted us inside as Mr. and Mrs. Jones trailed behind.

The clubhouse, a lovely converted farmhouse, was the center of social activities. The country for miles around us was in flux, moving from a bucolic culture into one that was much more fast-paced. The wealthy from places like New York and Detroit had discovered the nearly perfect terrain for foxhunting and had begun an invasion destined to change the old ways forever. From the beginning of my stay I had recognized the names of some of the nation's wealthiest and most influential families.

Ian's family had been landowners in Virginia since the War for Independence. After the War Between the States, the Sebastians held on to their property by making compromises more principled men refused. Fox

River Farm was nearly sold at auction before an ancestor of Ian's discovered letters from Thomas Jefferson in the attic and hawked them to pay the property's back taxes. Years later the letters were declared forgeries, but by then, Fox River Farm was no longer in jeopardy.

Once inside I looked for Ian, making certain my search wasn't obvious. As a friend of Annie's father came to claim her for the next dance, I joined a group of young women gossiping in a corner. I knew them all and liked some of them. We exclaimed over each other's dresses and jewelry until, one by one, they were claimed for the dance. I turned down a man I didn't know, explaining that I had just arrived, and chatted with a man much too old to lead me around the floor. We were in the midst of a conversation about the merits of growing winter rye or soy—a subject as foreign to me as the table etiquette of New Guinea cannibals—when Ian appeared.

I have rarely seen a man as handsome as Ian was that night. He wore a black morning coat, and his white shirt set off his bronzed features.

"You're not dancing," he said, by way of introduction.

I looked down. "I seem to be standing absolutely still."

"You were made to dance, Louisa. It seems almost criminal for the music to be playing."

"Rather than take action against the orchestra, I could dance. If a certain gentleman decided to ask me."

He considered. "Have you been lectured on proper behavior tonight?"

"Lectured?"

"By Mrs. Jones? She seems to be the sort for lectures."

"Don't tell me she's gone after you, as well?"

He laughed, flashing even white teeth. "No chance of

that. But she has passed a severe look or two in my direction."

"I think she's secretly afraid of Annie, and Annie will back us up."

"Where is the perennial cousin?"

"Dancing."

He held out his arm. "Then, by all means, you must join her."

I had imagined how it might feel to be in Ian Sebastian's arms. As we had ridden to his house that first day, the feel of his muscular body against my breasts had taken my breath away as seriously as my encounter with the bears. Since that day, though, he had kept his distance as he pursued me. Mrs. Jones, for all her stabs at propriety, had nothing whatsoever to worry about.

Now I was entranced by the feel of him. Not that he took liberties and held me too close. But the narrow space between our bodies was as tantalizing as the whisper of his breath against my cheek. He danced as well as he rode.

"Plan to take a walk with me after supper," he said, just before we parted.

"We'll have to sneak away."

"I'll meet you under the sycamores at the north of the building just after the music starts again."

Before the meal was served I danced with others, then had one more glorious turn around the floor with Ian. I was escorted to the buffet, then to our table, by Mr. Jones, where I encountered Annie for the first time since our arrival.

"I'm having a marvelous time," she said in a low voice, when her mother turned away to speak to a matron at the next table.

I had noticed the way her eyes sparkled and the unusual blush on her cheeks. She looked almost pretty. "Have you met someone?"

"Not exactly. I've known him forever. His family lives here part of each year, but he's been in Europe, then he finished out his military service in Boston, and he's only just come home."

"Who? Where?"

"Paul Symington." She inclined her head toward the left without looking in the same direction. "He's sitting with Lillian Albright and her family."

I looked to her left and saw a portly young man with rounded shoulders. He seemed nothing special until he smiled at Mrs. Albright, and suddenly I saw why Annie was so entranced. I guessed that he could be that rarest of all creatures, a man with whom a woman could be friends.

"He looks like someone who might just possibly be good enough for you," I told her.

"I've loved him since I was ten and he found me crying over a trapped rabbit. He set the poor thing free."

"You never told me."

"I'd put him out of my mind. I thought he was going to marry Helen Faraday once he came home, but he says no, that the war showed him what was really important."

"And what's that?"

"The pleasures of a woman's soul."

I thought quite possibly I was going to fall in love with Paul Symington.

For the rest of the meal I wasn't sure whether I should be happier for Annie or myself. Ian caught my eye twice. He was seated with the other governors and their families at the head table, the youngest and by far the handsomest of the men. As the meal ended, he was called on to give a speech, which he did with no reluctance. Since only a portion of the club was in attendance that night, he kept it short and funny. He was greeted with loud applause, and my heart swelled with pride until I remembered I had no reason to be proud. Ian Sebastian hadn't yet declared any intentions toward me. One day I might awaken and find his interest had been transferred to another.

I realized how disappointed I would be if that transpired. In my imagination I had installed myself at Fox River Farm, borne Ian's children and settled into a life of casual wealth and great respect. I had little desire to return to Fifth Avenue society with its pretensions and limitations. I was enchanted by the freedom I experienced here.

In those moments of panic it never once occurred to me that marriage to Ian might curtail my freedom in unexpected ways.

The meal ended, and the orchestra, now well fed and rested, began to play again.

I took my cue and excused myself. As I was leaving, Annie caught my arm and introduced me to Paul Symington. I stopped for a few moments to chat, then, as Paul led a starry-eyed Annie to the dance floor, I made my way outside, making certain that Mrs. Jones missed my exit.

Outside, I skirted the clubhouse, avoiding several gentlemen smoking near the front, and slipped around to the north side of the building to look for Ian. It was dark outside, with only a wispy crescent moon, and although light spilled from the windows, the sycamores were farther than I remembered. Horses whinnied to each other in the darkness, and somewhere a nightbird trilled a nocturne. I felt my way for the last twenty yards, tiptoeing carefully so I didn't sprawl at Ian's feet.

"There you are." Ian stepped out from behind the largest tree and held out his arms.

I was well-bred. I knew what a lady did and didn't do, but I threw myself into his embrace with all the fervor of youth. And when he kissed me, my last shred of reserve disappeared.

We parted at last, my lips bruised from the force of his, the taste of local corn liquor on my tongue.

"This can't go on, you know." Ian settled his hands on my hips as if to keep me from running away, although that was the last thing on my mind. "I had a wife and confess to not liking it very well. I never planned to take another."

Although I wanted to ask him about the woman who'd died bearing his child—for I'd learned that much from Annie—I knew there were more important things to settle. "And now?"

"And now I find myself thinking of taking another anyway."

"Really? And have you someone in mind?"

"A wily young vixen who might very well serve the purpose."

I supposed that for a foxhunter, comparing a woman to a vixen was the rarest of compliments.

I rested my fingertips on his shoulders. "Suppose you asked your young vixen. What do you think she might say?"

"I think she might well throw herself into my arms."

"What a foolish, foolish girl. Everyone knows a man should be kept guessing until the moment he proposes."

He laughed. "I want more than her hand. I want her warm body in my bed. I want her womb filled with my sons."

"Sons only?"

His expression darkened, but only for an instant. "I lost a son before he could take his first breath. I want another."

I had never wanted anything as much as I wanted, at that moment, to give Ian a son. And I knew that I could. I was young and healthy, filled with vitality. I was sure I could give him everything he yearned for.

The sadness—for that's what I thought it was—disappeared, and he smiled down at me. "Will you marry me, Louisa Elsabeth Schumacher? Will you become the mistress of Fox River Farm and the mother of my children?"

I thought briefly of the other men I'd known. They were all paler imitations of this one, doomed to suffer in his shadow. I was eighteen, and Ian was a man of thirty-seven, but at that moment we were only two people, equal in every way, considering our future.

"Yes, I'll marry you," I said.

"At the end of July. When your family comes to visit." It was not a question.

"So soon?" I wondered if I could prepare that quickly. I wondered what my mother would say.

"We'll have time for a wedding trip if we do it then. But I have to be back in the fall. I can't miss the season."

"Not even for me?"

He stroked my cheek. "I'm Master of Foxhounds. This is something you'll have to understand."

And I did. I was marrying a way of life, not simply a man.

"A small wedding or a large one?" I said.

"Shall we marry at Fox River? Outdoors in the gardens?"

"In the evening, when it's starting to cool. Then we can ask as many people as we like."

"Done." Only then did he pull me close again. "We'll go to Italy. I'll show you Venice."

I had always dreamed of a wedding trip to England, but he sounded so pleased with himself that I gave up that dream on the spot. Where we went wouldn't matter, anyway, because we would have each other. And besides, surely no one in Venice chased foxes. For the trip, at least, I would be the only "vixen" in Ian's little world.

When he kissed me this time, I melted against him.

Later, inside and in the presence of the Joneses, Ian gave me an emerald ring that matched, almost perfectly, the earrings my father had given my mother. I was certain it was a sign that our marriage was written in the stars.

15

Christian chose to walk home from Ashbourne along an unfamiliar path. He knew he wouldn't get lost, but there was no reason to hurry, no real life yet to rush back to.

He found his way without incident. At the swimming hole on Jeb Stuart Creek, where he'd often spent summer afternoons, he sat on a rock and listened to an owl hooting somewhere in the distance. It was better than thinking about Julia.

An owl had hooted the night before his father died. He hadn't thought about it for years, but he remembered now. The owl, who must have roosted close to the Carvers's quarters, had awakened him. He had gotten out of bed to look for it and stumbled over his father's unconscious body. Gabe had collapsed on the floor, too drunk that particular night to make it to bed.

Gabe wasn't a mean drunk. Most of the time he simply passed out. The next morning he was gruff but never abusive. This time, awakened too soon, he was angry. Without realizing who was sprawled on top of him, he lashed out with a fist. Then he lapsed back into a drunken stupor.

Christian hadn't been quick enough to avoid his father's attack. He cried out, but Gabe was already unconscious again. Christian dragged himself to the window, sobbing more from anger than pain, and the owl had continued to hoot.

The next day he had a black eye and a swollen cheek, which he'd explained away as a stable accident, but Robby knew better. At eleven, Robby, immature about some things, was wise in the way of adults. He knew how much Gabe's drinking embarrassed Christian.

Gabe was the finest trainer ever to set foot on Claymore Park. He was funny, intelligent, nearly as charming with people as with horses—but only when he was sober. He wasn't sober often, except when he was on the job. When he needed to be alert and focused to work with the horses he loved, he could be. But when he needed to be sober for his son, he couldn't.

Gabe had embarrassed Christian in front of Robby more than once, lurching drunkenly, stammering on about people Robby had never known, crying about his dead wife. Robby, who had his own problems with his father, had recognized Christian's humiliation and expressed sympathy. The two boys had grown closer.

The day that Christian showed up with the black eye was different. Robby threatened to tell his father what Gabe had done, and the two boys fought. Christian understood what Robby didn't. Because Gabe was so talented, Peter Claymore managed to look the other way when it came to his drinking, but if Robby brought it to his attention, he would have to do something. And the something might well be to fire Gabe.

"Things have a way of working out," Christian told his friend. "Maybe he won't drink as much now that he knows what he's like when he's drunk." He convinced Robby not to tell Peter, but years later, he still wondered if silence had doomed Gabe to a fiery death. By covering up the depth of Gabe's illness, had Christian lit the match that burned down the barn? Because that very night Gabe had overindulged again, probably from sorrow for giving his son a black eye. And perhaps to protect him, he had fallen asleep on a cot in the tack room. With a cigarette in his hand.

The rules at Claymore Park were clear. No one smoked near the barns, not within fifty yards. And anyone caught was sent on his way. Gabe smoked the way he drank, in uncontrolled binges. After a day at work, he came home and smoked a whole pack, one cigarette after the other as he fumbled over his first six-pack of the day. Christian had never seen his father smoke in the barn, but Gabe *always* smoked when he drank. And clearly he had been drinking that night. Found along with the remains of his body were the scorched remnants of aluminum cans.

Gabe's final six-pack.

By the time the fire was detected, Gabe was dead and the barn well on its way to incineration. Jinx and the other stable staff got most of the horses out, but they lost a prize stallion and a mare who had foaled that morning. Peter's extensive trophy collection, elaborate scrapbooks, priceless records and ledgers, all went up in smoke. So did Christian's past and present, and for a while he was afraid his future had, as well.

Then Peter Claymore had stepped forward to say that Christian could stay at Claymore Park as long as he wanted. Forever, if he chose. Christian had been profoundly grateful.

Although Robby wanted him to live at the house, Christian had elected to share Jinx Callahan's quarters. Jinx reminded Christian of his father, and the Callahan lifestyle was nearly as casual. The old man, never married, had taken Christian under his wing.

Had he moved away, Christian would never have become close to Julia or Fidelity, certainly never been blamed for a murder he hadn't committed. Perhaps without the turmoil of the trial and Christian's conviction, Robby might not have driven his car into a tree.

The lives of the four friends had been woven together as densely as the fibers of a blanket. Nothing could be picked loose or undone without eventual disintegration.

Now, staring at moonlight on the still water of the creek, the owl hooting somewhere above him, he thought about the day Fidelity and Julia had really entered his life. He had been preparing for the Middleburg Spring Races, and suddenly his whole future had changed.

"You're sure you want to do this?" Robby watched Christian brushing Night Ranger, a dapple gray colt with a white mane and tail who was the pride of Claymore Park.

"Why do you keep asking?" Christian stepped back to look at his handiwork. The colt's coat was gleaming, but he wasn't yet satisfied.

"I don't understand the point of these events." Robby stood

and stretched his six-foot-two body. In the years that Christian had known him, Robby had grown into a young man who usually got a second look from young women. Neither Christian nor Robby had completely filled out their lanky frames, but now, as they entered adulthood, the promise of fulfillment was there. Even though eighteen-year-old Robby spent more time hunched over a desk than riding or playing tennis, he still had the look of a young athlete.

Nineteen-year-old Christian, on the other hand, had always been rail-thin and lightweight enough to race for Claymore Park, although clearly that time was ending. He still turned plenty of heads, though. Between working for Peter and attending community college part-time, he had little time for dating, but women interested him more than he let on.

"You've never understood the point of any horse events," Christian said. "You have to love horses, which you don't. You have to love competition, which you don't—"

"I have to love Claymore Park, which I don't."

"Don't say that."

Robby picked at a splinter sticking out of the wall. "I don't, not the way you do. If I thought I had to live there forever, I'd go crazy."

Robby's relationship with his father wasn't an easy one. Peter had high expectations where his son was concerned. Robby wanted to study physics next year at one of the Ivy League colleges. Peter was proud of his son's considerable academic achievements, but he still expected Robby to come home once he'd finished and stake a claim at Claymore Park. Christian was afraid that just wasn't going to happen.

"There are half a dozen top-notch universities in driving distance," Christian said. "American, George Washington, Georgetown..."

"I know the list."

"You can get a job at one of them once you've finished graduate school, or in D.C. at some agency doing research. You can still live at Claymore Park."

"Only if you promise to stay on and run the place."

Christian liked the sound of that. He looked up to say so, and over the stall door he stared into the most beautiful pair of blue eyes he'd ever seen.

"Hello, boys. Remember me?"

Robby turned. He didn't say a word.

"Oh my, have I changed that much?" The blonde unlatched the door and slipped inside.

Robby found his voice. "Fidelity?"

"Well, it's not exactly like I had plastic surgery, Robert Claymore. I'm the same old me."

Christian recognized her now. The Sutherland family was a fixture in Ridge's Race, and South Land was a neighbor of Claymore Park. As boys, he and Robby had often played with Fidelity and her girlfriend Julia Ashbourne on lazy summer afternoons. In the days before adolescence had complicated the simplest things.

Now he remembered a party at Ashbourne with fireflies in old Mason jars and two giggly preteen girls. Fidelity, mouth filled with braces, had waylaid him behind an ancient catalpa tree and kissed him until his bottom lip bled.

He was grinning when he spoke. "You're hardly the same old anything," Christian said, admiring her. He calculated that Fidelity was seventeen and in glorious bloom—somewhere between bud and full flower. Her blond hair fell below her shoulders in luminous waves; her complexion was pale and perfect, her body... Well, her body filled out a pink sweater and designer jeans in a way that left him feeling as if he'd already run his race.

"You missed me, Chris?" She smiled, flashing tiny perfect—and very expensive—teeth. "I've just been up the road at Foxcroft." Foxcroft was a pricey school for the horsey set. Debutantes in jodhpurs and breeches.

"Where's your friend Julia?" he said. "Don't you two go everywhere together?"

Fidelity gazed down at her nails. Apparently she didn't like what she saw, because she polished them against her sweater. "Not to school, we don't. Her mother sends her to public school, even though they could afford better." She looked up again, as if she realized what she'd said. "Oh, I'm sorry. You probably went to public school."

He grinned. "Yeah. I even l'arned to read and write a little."

She laughed, the tinkling of a brook. "You always were a funny boy. And Julia's here somewhere. She stays away from the stable."

"She doesn't like horses?"

Fidelity shrugged. "She's afraid of them. She doesn't ride."

Christian thought that odd, since Ashbourne had some of the finest pasture land in the county.

Fidelity, who obviously wasn't afraid, stepped closer and casually stroked Night Ranger's muzzle, as if he wasn't worth as much as her father's Mercedes. Her Scarlett O'Hara drawl was as exaggerated as everything else about her, and worked every bit as well. "I hear you're going to ride this old nag today."

"You heard right."

She turned to Robby. "How come you're not riding, Robert?"

Robby shrugged. "Because I don't care who wins. Chris does."

"I like a man who doesn't have to prove himself."

Christian watched his friend turn red at the compliment. She turned back to Christian. "And I like a man who does."

"In other words, you like men, period."

"Oh, you're clever, aren't you?"

"Fidelity?"

Christian looked up and saw a dark-haired beauty in a royal-blue jacket outside the stall and knew immediately who she was. He had seen her around high school, although she had been too young to be in any of his classes. "Hey. Julia Ashbourne. Long time no see."

"Christian." She smiled shyly. "And Robby. Hi to both of you."

"There's room for you," Fidelity told her friend.

"I'd rather stay out here. I don't want to spook him," Julia said.

"Good thinking." Christian realized he hadn't quite finished pulling Ranger's mane, and he still had to polish his boots before weighing in and donning Claymore Park's green and gold silks.

But he wasn't ready to take his eyes off either girl. They were Snow White and Rose Red, a visual fairy tale.

"What a gorgeous horse," Julia said. "But he's so big."

"He has to be to get over those jumps." Reluctantly Christian went back to work.

"You really don't ride?" Robby asked her. "No kidding?"

"I... Well, we didn't keep horses. My mother didn't want them on the property. Didn't you ever notice?"

"Julia's mommy is a little touched in the head." Fidelity didn't say the words unkindly.

Julia defended her mother. "Horses are a lot of work, Fidelity. You know they are. And Maisy didn't ride. What was the point?"

"Who's Maisy?" Christian asked.

"My mother."

"You call your mother Maisy?"

"Everyone calls her Maisy."

Christian remembered a warmhearted, friendly woman who looked like a rock band groupie. He supposed that he had called her Maisy, too.

Another voice joined the chorus. "How's it going, Christian?"

Christian saw that Peter had come up beside Julia in the doorway. "I'm almost finished, sir."

"I could finish for you, if you'd like. Or I could send your audience away to improve your concentration."

"Better eject them. I still have to change."

"You work Chris too hard," Fidelity told Peter in her magnolia blossom drawl. "A man has to have time for fun."

The way she said it sounded like an invitation. Christian realized he was smiling.

Peter laughed. "Miss Sutherland, do your parents stay up at nights worrying about you?"

"You want the truth, Mr. Claymore? They haven't had a bit of sleep since I turned thirteen."

"And where have you boys been since that momentous day?" Peter asked Robby and Christian.

"Apparently not where we should have been," Christian said.

"Good luck, Christian," Julia said as the others cleared out of the stall. "We'll be rooting for you and Night Ranger."

Fidelity flashed him one final smile. "That's right, Chris, we'll be rooting for you. Just don't take your eyes off the course. We wouldn't want to be responsible for an accident."

He was still smiling ten minutes later when he swiped his boots one last time. An hour later, he wasn't smiling. The sport of steeplechasing was serious business. Nationwide, the industry gave away millions in purses. The Middleburg Spring Race Meeting was well established, and even if it wasn't the Kentucky Derby or even the Virginia Cup, it was still an important event. At the Derby the horses ran a flat track, but in Virginia, the best races were steeplechases, with a series of hurdles to clear. Thoroughbreds had been racing in Middleburg since 1911, and some of the best hurdle horses in the state participated.

Night Ranger was a four-year-old with potential. He had started on the flat track, then competed in a novice steeplechase race or two, but this maiden race—for horses who had yet to win—was his first real trial. The purse was relatively small, but the prestige was substantial.

Peter himself had supervised Ranger's training, but Jinx Callahan and Christian had done most of the work. Christian didn't consider any of Claymore Park's horses his, but if he'd been asked to choose the one he was most attached to, it would have been Ranger.

He and Ranger were entered in the third race of the day, and it was almost time to mount.

Although it was late enough in the spring to hope for good weather, the day was cold and cloudy, and the grassy hills in the shadow of the Blue Ridge were muddy from yesterday's rain. That hadn't stopped people from attending. The town of Middleburg, described by one observer as a Rolls-Royce with a trailer hitch, loved everything about horses. The race was a social occasion, an excuse for gourmet tailgate parties, complete with lace tablecloths and exotic flower arrangements. Vendors sold everything from hot dogs to Wellingtons. Businesses entertained loyal customers, families reunited, horse people in worn jeans or designer duds compared notes and made deals while horses thundered over waving grass sprinkled with dandelions and buttercups.

Christian, an apprentice jockey, figured this season was probably his last chance to compete. He had grown slowly, fueling hopes for a real career in racing, but in his late teens he'd begun to shoot up, until now he was six foot and rapidly filling out, as well. Although jump jockeys were larger than flat track, by next season he probably would weigh substantially more than the average 140 pounds. He would have to content himself with amateur events and whipping-in for the Mosby Hunt. As long as he was on horseback, though, he would be okay.

"You set?" Peter joined him in the jockey tent after he and his saddle had been weighed and the proper weights attached. Jinx Callahan, now in his seventies, was in the paddock walking Ranger, stylishly attired in a green blanket with gold braid that matched Christian's silks.

Christian donned his helmet and strapped it under his chin as they went to join Jinx. "Any last-minute instructions?" he asked both men.

Jinx spat on the ground. "Stay away from Samson's Pillar. I don't trust that horse. He doesn't have the temperament for racing. And watch out for Jenny's Idea. She's your stiffest competition."

"Just listen to Jinx. He knows," Peter said. "I'm heading for the stands." He didn't wish Christian luck, his way of not putting undue pressure on him.

Jinx saddled Ranger, then held him while Christian mounted. "*Don't* break a leg," Jinx said. "Especially his."

Christian took the reins and started around the ring, watching out, as Jinx had warned, for Samson's Pillar, a sleek bay with a white blaze ridden by a jockey in red and white. Jenny's Idea, a dark bay filly, was prancing ahead as if she could hardly wait to take the field. Christian knew Ranger was in for a race.

He caught a flash of blue out of the corner of his eye and looked over to see Julia Ashbourne smiling at him. In the barn he had been so blinded by Fidelity that he hadn't registered much more than Julia's hair color and height. Now, in the sunshine, he saw how pretty she was, rosy-cheeked, with an oval face and wide-set eyes that gave patrician features a hint of nobility. Out of Fidelity's shadow, she was a knockout.

She held up two fingers in a V for victory. He grinned, then reluctantly turned his concentration back to Ranger. Looking away took self-discipline, but he couldn't afford to be distracted now. Too much was at stake.

This particular race was two and a half miles over national fences—synthetic fencing used at most U.S. courses so it could be moved with ease. Claymore Park had devoted considerable acreage to training its steeplechasers and to being certain the sight of the jumps was familiar. Night Ranger should be at home with the fifty-two-inch jumps, if not at home racing in a crowded field. He was powerful and fleet-footed, but he wasn't experienced. Anything could happen today.

They circled the paddock over and over, and Christian stole one more peek at the spectators, but Julia had disappeared, probably to find a place at the fence. Undoubtedly the Sutherlands had rented prime space near the judging stands for their private party, and Julia would have a good view of the homestretch.

The horses filed out of the paddock to head toward the starting area, and once they were on the course the bugler blew the familiar call to post. There were no gates. The horses were grouped by number in a common area at the start, and when the flag was lifted they took most of the course three times. Christian made a point of staying away from Samson on the trip to the starting area, rewarded for his care a moment later when Samson backed into another Thoroughbred, and the jockey—a trainer from nearby Upperville—let loose with a torrent of abuse.

As eight horses and jockeys settled warily into place, Christian flexed his fingers. "Just do your best, Ranger," he murmured to the horse. "And I'll do mine."

The flags were lifted and the horses shot forward. Peter, Jinx and Christian had discussed strategy, taking into account everything from the condition of the field to the records of the other horses. Night Ranger, for all his youth, was cautious, only picking up speed as his confidence grew. With this in mind they had decided to let him stay back until he was confident enough to make a surge. Christian might urge him on, but he wasn't going to interfere.

They were halfway toward the first hurdle before Christian had a moment to consider his position. There were four horses grouped to take the first fence. The white rail wings extending at angles from the sides beckoned like a mother's welcoming arms. The horses sailed over the fence, and Christian readied himself for his own chance at it. Ranger sailed, too, with Gone for Good, a chestnut gelding, beside him. Ranger pulled ahead of Gone as he galloped toward the next jump, moving up on the inside until he was close to the group of four. One of those horses dropped back, and Christian guided Ranger into the opening.

He saw immediately that the bay beside him was Samson, but there was nothing he could do about that except avoid erratic movements. At this speed, though, that was too much like trying to outrun an eighteen-wheeler speeding downhill.

He took the next hurdle with the other horses, and once on the other side, began to pull ahead of Samson. Jenny's Idea was in the lead by nearly a length, but he was surprised she wasn't farther. Jenny, unlike Ranger, was reputed to do her best work at the beginning of a race. He had done nothing to urge Ranger on, but his horse was running as if his life depended on it.

He debated whether he should hold Ranger back, then decided against it. Ranger deserved a chance to show what he was made of, and even if mistakes were made today, Peter and Jinx could use the information to plan strategy for the next race. Ranger had a long career ahead of him.

Ranger remained in third position for the next four hurdles, behind Jenny's Idea and a roan named Somebody's Baby. Samson stayed on his heels but caused no trouble. By the time they were taking the course the second time he was neck and neck with Somebody's Baby, pulling ahead at one hurdle, dropping back a bit at the next. Jenny's Idea was only half a length in front and seemed to be tiring. At the third and final assault on the hurdles he heard hoofbeats behind him and glimpsed Samson's Pillar coming up on the outside.

Ranger had pulled ahead of Somebody's Baby again, and he was closing the gap between himself and Jenny's Idea when Christian sensed, rather than saw, Samson swerving toward him. Instinct saved him. He swerved, too, despite pulling himself slightly off course for the next-to-the-last jump, and flicked

Ranger with his whip. Ranger surged ahead. Christian heard a commotion behind him but knew better than to investigate. He was riding for his life now, guiding Ranger back into position while trying to make up for lost steps. The jump loomed, and he took it right beside Jenny's Idea.

They were neck and neck in the backstretch now, with one jump to go, and Ranger, spurred on by Christian, was hellbent for leather. Jenny's Idea was struggling and took the last jump a beat or two after him. From that point on, the race was Night Ranger's. At Christian's urging the horse streaked down the final stretch and finished three lengths ahead of Jenny's Idea.

Eventually Christian slowed Night Ranger to a walk. Jinx was waiting by the time he came back around, and so was Peter.

"Do you know what happened?" Jinx shouted.

Christian, winded, shook his head.

"That goddamned Samson rode right into Somebody's Baby. Like to have killed them both."

"Did it?"

"Nah. But I can tell you neither of them'll be racing again this season. Samson better not race again, period. Not against Claymore horses."

"That was a splendid ride," Peter told him. "Quick thinking all the way. You averted a catastrophe. You've got all the right instincts. What'd you have to go and grow for, son?"

It was the first time Christian ever remembered Peter calling him that. He grinned. "I held it off as long as I could, sir."

"He grew for me," another, feminine, voice chimed in. Christian looked over to see Fidelity Sutherland and Julia Ashbourne coming toward them. He wasn't sure how they had gotten down to the course, but he supposed in horse country, when your names were Sutherland and Ashbourne, you went anywhere you darned well pleased.

"I don't like little men," Fidelity said. "I like them long, tall and strapping. Cowboys, like our Christian." She smiled up at him. He noticed she had dimples, and he supposed he should have expected it.

His heart was still speeding. From the corner of his eye he noticed Julia Ashbourne, smiling as if she was really glad he'd triumphed. Fidelity Sutherland was throwing herself at him, but suddenly, mysteriously, he only had eyes for her friend.

"There's a party tonight," Fidelity told him. "You'll come with me—us?"

"You'll be there?" he asked Julia.

"Sure. We can make it a celebration." Her smile, subtler than Fidelity's, was every bit as lovely.

"Go ahead," Peter told him. "You've earned it. You and Robby go along. Somebody else will take care of Ranger tonight."

Christian wasn't sure exactly what he'd won that day, but he was sure the race had been worth it.

16

So many nights at Ludwell, Christian had awakened from dreams that he was riding. He had promised himself that if a miracle happened and he got out of prison before he died, the first thing he would do was saddle up and ride away. Despite that, he hadn't been on a horse since his release.

"Christian, I've got something to show you." Peter came into the kitchen where Christian was finishing supper. Christian had spent the past three days in the kennel getting acquainted with the hounds and learning to work with the staff, Fisher and Gorda, who rightfully resented his sudden appearance and authority. He thought he'd made inroads with both, but no opportunity had presented itself to ride.

Or he'd made no opportunity. He wasn't sure which.

Now he looked up at Peter, who had an uncharacteristically broad smile on his face. "What is it?"

"Come see for yourself. You're finished there, aren't you?"

Peter had been gone most of the day. Now Christian figured he was about to find out why. He carried his plate to the counter. Peter's housekeeper, Rosalita, had made it clear he was not to lift a finger around the house.

"You had a good day?" Peter asked on the way outside.

"Productive. I think I'll get along fine with Fish and Gorda."

"Fish will get used to you quickly enough. Gorda is happy as long as she doesn't have to do all the dirty work by herself. Fish's been known to wiggle out of it."

"I'll make sure we share it."

"I know you'll do your share, but remember, son, you have bigger fish to fry. Your first responsibility is to the kennel and the staff horses, but I want you to save time for working with some of our steeplechasers. You were on your way to being a top-notch trainer before you went..."

"You can say it, Peter. I haven't forgotten where I've been."

"I hate to say the word prison. I hate that it happened."

"We share that."

Peter laughed, and tension drained out of the conversation as they made their way toward the stable.

"Okay, get ready to meet an old friend," Peter said.

Christian could think of a number of old friends he did not want to meet just yet. And one he'd surprised in the dark at Ashbourne, the one he had wanted to meet least of all.

Peter flipped a switch, and more lights came on overhead. They started down the center aisle, paved in an intricate herringbone pattern. The fir walls were stained a golden-brown and varnished to a high gloss; there was enough brass over stall doors to keep the stable hands busy for hours. After the fire, Peter had reconstructed the barn using the original plans. It was the same layout Christian remembered from his boyhood. Only the central tack room had been replaced by two rooms on the end of each wing. Christian wondered if Peter had done this so he wouldn't think of Gabe Carver every time he stepped foot inside.

Peter motioned Christian to a stall nearly at the end of the row. "Seen this fellow before?"

Night Ranger whinnied a welcome.

"I don't believe it." Christian stepped forward and ran his hand along the horse's muzzle. "Where'd he come from?"

"Remember I sold him to a farm in Kentucky?"

Christian remembered. The sale had come three months after Fidelity's death, and the offer had been too good for Peter to pass up. Christian had still been free on bail to bid farewell to his favorite mount, but it hadn't been a particularly good day. "What happened to him afterward?"

"They raced him for a while. He did well, but he damaged a knee. It healed, but they lost interest and sold him to a smaller operation, who sold him to a smaller operation...." Peter grimaced. "The last place was a two-bit horse barn in Maryland. He wasn't getting much care and not doing particularly well. Our old friend here was on his way to becoming dog food."

Christian winced. "Hey, fellow," he said, continuing to stroke the horse, who didn't seem inclined to move away. "You're home now."

"I don't think it'll take that long to get him back in shape. Good feed and pasture, the right kind of exercise and care. I wish I'd never sold him. I know he was your favorite."

"I wouldn't have been around to ride him, anyway."

"Well, I have the chance to make it up to both of you now. He's yours. Your name was on the bill of sale."

Christian stepped back. "I can't accept him."

"Why not?"

"He's a valuable horse."

"Not anymore, except to you and me, maybe. But he's still got some good years ahead of him. And even at his age he'll make quite a hunter. As huntsman, you'll need a mount you can count on. Here he is."

Night Ranger snorted, as if he agreed.

Now Christian knew why he hadn't ridden. He had been waiting for this horse, as big a piece of his past as almost anything living.

"I'm going for a ride," he told Peter. "Want to come?"

"I think not. You two have some catching up to do." Peter clapped him on the back before he left.

Christian stared at the horse in front of him. "We've both been in some pretty awful places, huh, guy?"

Night Ranger nuzzled him, as if he really did understand and agree—or at least wanted an apple.

Christian laughed. "Okay, let's go see if we can get some of it out of our systems."

Julia liked quiet evenings. Bard often had night meetings, and once Callie was in bed she had usually taken advantage of them to paint. With that diversion gone, she had too much time to think, her hands stilled and useless, her mind wandering places she wished it wouldn't go.

Tonight she sat on the front porch and listened to the sounds of evening. The family had just finished supper, and Callie was riding Feather Foot under Jake's watchful eye. Julia was still thinking of her session with Yvonne that morning. Christian and Fidelity had been the topics of conversation. She had told Yvonne that Christian was Callie's father, and that he didn't have any idea he had a child.

"Keeping your daughter away from him must have been a hard decision," Yvonne had said. "You must have been very angry."

"No, I loved him." Julia cleared her throat. "And he loved me." She thought of the man who had confronted her in the darkness, and tears filled her eyes. "But that was a long time ago."

"Would you like to talk about this?"

"You must read the papers."

"I do."

"Then you know he was accused of a murder he didn't commit."

"I have read about it."

"Fidelity, the woman who died, was my best friend. We were closer than sisters."

"And Christian?"

"It's a long story. A complicated story."

Yvonne's voice was louder, as if she had leaned forward. "I get paid to listen to complicated stories. Life's messy."

"Mine certainly is."

"Then you have a lot to tell me. Why don't you start with Fidelity?"

So Julia had begun when they were six.

She and Fidelity had become friends in the first grade. That winter they had attended the same afternoon story hour at the local library, where they had been forced to dress up like autumn leaves and fir trees, living illustrations of the librarian's favorite book. Then and there they had made a pact that they would be princesses or fairies, but never again forest vegetation.

Although South Land was one of Ashbourne's closest neighbors, Harry's death had removed Maisy from the Ridge's Race social whirl, and Julia had vanished with her. But once reintroduced, the two little girls became inseparable.

Fidelity went to private school and Julia to public, but in their free time they swam in the Sutherlands' pool or Jeb Stuart Creek, played tennis or Barbie dolls or went to movies. They picked Ashbourne apples and grapes, giggled at everything, slept at each other's houses and refused to be separated, until Fidelity was as much a fixture at Ashbourne as Julia was at South Land.

When Maisy met and married Jake, both girls were bridesmaids. When Flo took thirteen-year-old Fidelity to Paris, Julia ate snails and truffles and prowled the Latin Quarter right along with them.

The time demands of adolescence changed the number of hours the girls could spend together, but they remained fast friends. Fidelity went to art shows to see Julia's entries and posed when Julia needed a model. For Fidelity's sixteenth birthday, Julia painted an oil portrait that was so well received she was commissioned to do others for local families.

In turn, Julia went to horse shows to watch her friend compete. Fidelity wanted a spot on the Olympic equestrian team, and the Sutherlands spent a small fortune on horses and special training. When places on the team went to older girls, Julia's shoulder was the one Fidelity cried on.

Then Christian Carver came into their lives, and nothing was ever quite the same.

The porch creaked, followed by Maisy's voice. "You are too alone out here."

Julia put her hand on her chest. "You startled me."

"I didn't mean to," Maisy said. "I thought you heard me coming."

"I should have. I was a million miles away." Or ten terrible years.

"I have another place where you can do your thinking, if you'd like."

"Where?"

"Come with me and I'll show you."

Julia rose. She was glad for the interruption. "Let me put my hand on your arm."

A few minutes later Maisy sat her on a chair in the enclosed porch behind the kitchen. The room had been a studio, an exercise room, even a warm spot to hatch baby chickens the year Maisy decided they needed fresh eggs. The last time Julia had been in there the room was used for storage, but clearly it had been emptied and spruced up since then.

"I'd tell you not to peek, but I guess that's not necessary," Maisy said.

Julia figured they had come a long way if her mother could joke about her blindness. "I'm going to counter every one of those little quips with a joke about your diets."

"I've heard them all. If Y2K had panned out the way it was supposed to, I would have had my own personal storehouse."

"I'd give a lot to see every single pound of it."

"You will."

"What are we doing here, Maisy?"

"You're about to get a surprise."

Maisy was the mistress of surprises. Julia had been treated to them throughout her childhood. Her favorite desserts, doll clothes patterned after her own, wildflowers in cut-glass vases on her dresser.

"Growing up here was good," Julia said, as she waited. "I was spoiled nearly as badly as Fidelity."

"Not even close. I loved old Fiddle-dee-dee, but Flo and Frank loved her so much they never gave that girl a chance to develop an ounce of character. She was always swimming against the tide."

"She did pretty well anyway."

"You still miss her, don't you?"

"The clouds never seemed to reach me when Fidelity was around."

"Clouds?"

Julia was still thinking about the session with Yvonne. "What do you remember about my childhood, Maisy? Was I a happy little girl?"

Maisy was silent so long Julia wasn't sure she planned to answer.

"You weren't unhappy," Maisy said at last.

"That's how I remember it, too. Never unhappy, exactly. But always searching for something. Needing something I didn't have."

"Sunshine."

"Maybe. And Fidelity brought that with her. Sometimes we were all blinded by it. I know that now. But I'd rather have too much than too little."

"I never really knew what to do for you. I guess I still don't."

"You don't have to do anything. This is my battle."

"Well, here's something that might help. Put out your hand."

Julia extended her hand and touched something cool and damp. She pressed her fingers into it, and a pungent odor arose. "What? Clay?"

"Jake and I have set up a little studio for you. It's not much. But there are three kinds of clay, brayers, wooden tools for shaping, even hand cleaner. Enough to keep you busy for hours if you like. You might not be able to see what you're sketching, but you can certainly feel whatever you sculpt."

Julia dug deeper, and the clay gave slightly. It needed working to soften it, a job she looked forward to. "This is a great idea. What made you think of it?"

"I've spent a lot of hours with clay. I know how therapeutic it can be."

"Therapeutic?"

"Here, let me slide the table in front of you. It's not much more than a card table, but it holds everything you need."

"What do you mean therapeutic?"

"Dealing with my life and your father's death. Who I am, where I was going. The things we all deal with." Maisy hesitated. "The things you *weren't* dealing with until you lost your sight."

"Maisy..." Julia warned.

"Am I wrong?"

"You're treading where you shouldn't."

"I ran into Peter Claymore in town this afternoon."

"And?"

"He told me Christian came over a couple of nights ago to see me."

Julia wanted to throw the clay at something. Instead she picked it up and began to slap it from hand to hand.

"Did you see him?" Maisy asked.

"He was here. Did I see him?"

"I'm sorry. I didn't mean—"

"We spoke. I was sitting outside in the dark. Not that it mattered to me. He came up behind me. He said he'd come to see you."

"Where was Callie?"

"Inside."

"You must have been afraid she'd come out and look for you."

"She nearly did."

"He's going to see her soon, Julia. You'd better decide how you plan to handle it when he does."

"He won't be back, Maisy. He was...resentful and angry. He hates me. He won't take a chance on seeing me again."

"He knows you're living here?"

"I don't know what he knows!" Julia drew a deep breath. "I'm sorry."

"For what? For being angry that I won't let this alone? Well, I can't. Callie is my granddaughter, and Christian is her father."

"Bard Warwick's name is on the birth certificate. And that's all anyone ever has to know."

"Don't you realize half the town has figured out who that child's father is? The rumors began before she was born. She's going to hear them one day. Christian will very soon."

Julia felt a scream creeping up her throat. "Maisy, stop this. I don't want to talk about it anymore."

"She's growing more like him every day."

"Stop it!"

"No, darn it. You stop it. You can't make things go away because you don't want to see them!"

The silence that followed was broken only by the sound of a mockingbird in a tree outside the window.

"Call me if you need something," Maisy said at last. "Or call Jake. He should be in soon. I'm going out for a while."

"Where are you going?"

"I'm going to find Christian. I can buy you a little time, but that's the best I can do. He wants to see me, he can see me on his turf. But sooner or later he and Callie are going to be in the same place at the same time. And then we'll all see how long it takes him to figure out she's his daughter."

"I won't forgive you if you tell him."

"Your father used to say things like that when he was angry. I hated it then, and I hate it now."

Julia was too angry to apologize.

"Well, at least it's clear whose daughter *you* are," Maisy said.

Julia was left in the darkness with her mind darting in a thousand different directions. She slammed the clay on the table in front of her. Then she began to knead.

Maisy calmed down a little by the time she reached the front gate. But she wasn't going to apologize. She loved her daughter, and, like every mother, she blamed herself for everything that went wrong in her child's life. But there were things Julia simply had to face, and who better to tell her so?

She was afraid she might run into Callie and Jake on her way to the pickup, but they were nowhere in sight. She got in and turned the key. For once it started without a hitch.

Maisy took that as a good sign, a sign that the pickup was aching to be driven somewhere far away. Tomorrow she was going into town and trading the sucker in. She didn't care what Jake thought. She had spent far too much of her life worrying about everything she did.

She was halfway to Claymore Park before she was calm enough to think straight.

She couldn't tell Christian about Callie, nor had she ever had any intention of doing so. But neither was she going to warn him away from Ashbourne. She and Jake had not been blessed with children, but if they had been, she would have wanted a son like Christian. He was a strong, decent man who had been dealt a bad hand in the game of life. Now she wondered if he had finally succumbed to fate and become embittered and angry.

Who needed friends more than Christian?

Despite the evidence, the press coverage and local opinion, Maisy had never doubted Christian's innocence. Her letters to him in prison had confirmed it again and again. She had met with Peter Claymore regularly to see how the appeals were progressing and offered Ashbourne money to help defray legal costs. Peter had refused her help, but he had kept her abreast of every development. She had done what little she could for Christian. But now there was nothing left to do except offer support.

She took the turnoff to Claymore Park and pulled into a spot near the stable, but she sat behind the wheel for several minutes, trying to think about what she could say and how she could let Christian know she cared. What could she tell him that wasn't a lie?

She got out at last and smoothed her dress over her substantial hips.

"Maisy?"

Peter Claymore was coming out of the stable and seemed surprised to see her.

"Peter." She held out her hand, and he took it and kissed her cheek.

"What are you doing here?"

"I came to see Christian. Is he around?"

"He's riding, but he should be back soon. I'm glad you came. It's a lonely time for him."

"I was just sorry I missed him the other night."

"If you walk over that hill a little ways, you might see him."

"I'll do that." Maisy patted her belly. "I need the exercise."

"I remember when you were skinny as a rail. I like you this way just fine."

"That's the best thing about old friends. They'll take you any way they can get you."

"Have a nice walk."

Peter started up to the house and Maisy up the hill. She was puffing by the time she got to the top. She did need exercise, and she did need to diet. She resolved to think about both if she survived this hike.

She could have waited there, but she hated standing still. Her life was a whirlwind of her own choosing. She understood why and how it had happened, but not quite how to set it right. Now she kept walking until she'd climbed another hill.

Not far in the distance, on the back of an enormous gray horse, a man was riding toward her, his back to a rosy horizon. Her breath caught in her throat. For a moment she simply stared as the ghost of Harry Ashbourne rode toward her in the twilight. Then she realized the man on the horse's back was Christian.

Christian slowed as he saw her; then he sped up until he was only a few feet away. He dismounted, holding his horse's reins, and his lips curved into a smile. "Maisy Fletcher."

"Christian." She moved toward him and stood on tiptoe to kiss his cheek before she stepped back. "There are no words to tell you how glad I am to see you."

He nodded. "Weren't you expecting me?"

"That's why I'm here."

"You look, I don't know...stunned. Have I changed that much?"

"To be honest, it was déjà vu. My first husband owned a horse that looked almost exactly like this one. For a moment I thought I was looking at his ghost."

"You never met Night Ranger, did you? Ranger, this is Maisy Fletcher. My good friend." He swept his hand toward Maisy as if he were really introducing them.

"So, this is the famous Night Ranger. Julia talked..."

He filled in the silence. "Yeah, she would have. But I guess I never rode him to your place. He wasn't a pleasure horse. He was too valuable."

"You look like you belong together."

"I guess he's mine now. Peter found him and bought him back for me. We've both been away too long, though. My legs feel like spaghetti, and he's hesitant, like he's not quite sure what to do."

"You'll find your way together."

"Let's walk back." He led Ranger along the path she'd followed, and Maisy walked beside him.

"I hear you came by a few nights ago," she said.

"I didn't know Julia would be there."

"She's staying with us for a while."

"Oh." He sounded surprised.

"It seemed best. She needs a lot of help, and I have the time. We've had to do a lot of adjusting. You never realize how much you depend on your eyes until you have someone living with you who can't see." Maisy realized she was babbling, saying more than she needed because she didn't really know what to say.

"What do you mean, can't see?"

"Didn't you realize? She didn't tell you?"

"Tell me what?"

"She's blind."

She heard him draw a breath. "She fell off a horse a couple of weeks ago while she and her daughter were out riding together. She took a jump, the horse didn't. She wasn't injured, but when she came to, her eyesight was gone."

He was silent, as if he was taking it in.

"No one seems to understand why it happened," she went on. "They did test after test. There's no reason why she shouldn't see, except that she doesn't. So now they think..."

"Think what?"

"That it's psychological."

"What do you think?"

"Our bodies can play tricks on us."

"You don't think this is some sort of medical mumbo jumbo? That they don't know what happened, so they're taking the easy way out?"

"She got excellent care, and the best specialists looked at her. There just doesn't seem to be any other explanation."

"I'm sorry," he said at last. "I can't imagine what that's like."

"Sometimes things happen that don't make any sense. Like you going to prison."

He stopped. "I came over a few nights ago just to tell you how much I appreciated your letters." He hesitated. "And to say I'm sorry I never wrote back."

"Did you read them?"

"At first." They started walking again. "Then I couldn't read them. It's hard to explain."

"You don't need to. I sent them because I wanted you to know I cared. I never said anything important. I probably don't even have anything important to say."

"They reminded me of a lot of things."

"Julia..."

He grunted.

She knew he didn't want to continue that line of discussion, but she'd already alienated her daughter tonight. She figured she might as well go for broke. "You can't understand why Julia married Bard so soon after the trial, can you?"

"It's not my place to understand. That was a long time ago."

"She was shattered, Christian. Surely that makes sense to you. She lost Fidelity, then she lost you. Bard held her together, and in the end, he seemed like a refuge from all the pain."

"This isn't my business anymore. I'm sorry she's blind. I really am. But none of it's my concern."

"You've never forgiven her for doubting you."

She didn't think he was going to answer, but he did after a long silence. "No, I never have. You didn't doubt me. Peter never did. Robby knew I didn't kill Fidelity. But Julia..."

"Julia wasn't even twenty. She was young, but she stood by you, and she only wavered once—"

"Yeah. On the witness stand in front of God and country."

"She'd been badgered by the prosecutor, Christian. She was under oath."

"So she told the jury how angry I was at Fidelity that afternoon. And when the D.A. asked if I'd been mad enough to kill her, she didn't deny it."

"She was distraught. She didn't know what to say or how to say it."

"Maisy, some part of your daughter wondered if I had killed her best friend."

"If you expected blind faith, then you chose the wrong woman. Julia always shakes the truth like a puppy shaking a rag doll, until all the stuffing comes flying out of it. The evidence was all on the prosecutor's side. You were right there with the weapon in your hand. In his mind you had motive—"

"There is no motive good enough to kill another human being."

"I could dispute that, but I won't. The real miracle was that after all the pain she suffered, after all the facts had been laid out in front of her, Julia believed in you as strongly as she did."

They reached the barn before he spoke again. "What happened to you in the last nine years, Maisy? You never used to speak your mind this way."

"I'm making up for lost time." Maisy put her hand on his arm. "I always thought of you as the son I couldn't have. Don't let bitterness destroy you, Christian. You've had a terrible chunk ripped out of your life, and you'll never get it back. But let go of that as quickly as you can."

"I just want to be left alone. I'm glad you came over tonight. You've been a good friend to me, and I'll always be grateful. But right now I'm just going to try to get on with my life. I hope Julia gets on with hers. I hope her eyesight returns, but nothing about her is really my concern anymore."

Maisy wondered how many hours Christian had lain awake in prison convincing himself of that.

And tonight, after Maisy had read to her and left Julia alone in the darkness, how many hours would Julia lie awake wondering how she was going to tell Christian that her life and her daughter *were* his concerns after all.

From the unpublished novel *Fox River,*
by Maisy Fletcher

As I'd expected, my mother wasn't pleased about my marriage. In Virginia Ian Sebastian might pass for nobility, but on Fifth Avenue he was no one of importance. In New York he was a farmer, nothing more. My brothers, practical to the bone, discreetly checked Ian's financial standing and reputation, then attempted to persuade her that the match was a good one. But Mama could not be consoled. I would never be one of New York's Four Hundred. She had failed in her mission.

The wedding went forth as planned, without her genuine blessing. At six o'clock, in a break with tradition, both George and Henry walked me down the aisle, and Annie, newly engaged to Paul Symington, was my only attendant. I wore a white lace gown that revealed a scandalous length of leg and a train that trailed well below it. My bridal cap was trimmed with orange blossoms and hundreds of seed pearls, which swirled down the veil like a waterfall. My bouquet, a gift from Ian, was so heavy with orchids, roses and hothouse gardenias that my arms tired before I reached him.

Fox River Farm had never looked more glorious. I had fallen in love with it on the day Ian swept me onto his horse and into his life. The house, a two-story Georgian with a centered gable, was built of rose-colored brick with soft gray trim and a recessed portico that provided us with porches on both levels. The Sebastian who had built it had relished multipaned windows, and the original handblown glass remained, distorting all views of the countryside.

Ian wore his morning coat with striped trousers, although he had threatened to wear his formal Master of Foxhounds attire and announce my presence with a hunting horn. The minister beamed at both of us as we repeated our vows and Ian slipped a gold band on my finger. The minister harrumphed a moment later when our wedding kiss lasted too long to suit him.

"We'll have to make a sizable donation to the church," Ian told me on our way down the aisle as man and wife.

I laughed, happier than I'd known I could be. My fairy-tale life was proceeding on schedule.

The reception lasted for hours. In my stay at Sweet-water I'd learned that Virginians believe having fun is a sacred duty. Even my mother, who tried to find fault, had a difficult time. And when a great aunt of Ian's, a dear woman of more than ninety years, recited the family's lineage all the way back to a manor house in Leicestershire and an obscure title bestowed by Charles II, my mother was mollified enough to invite us to visit before our ship sailed for Europe.

It was nearly midnight when the last guest departed. My family and our out-of-town guests went to Sweet-water to spend the night with the Joneses or to the Red Fox or Colonial Inns in Middleburg. I was almost sorry when the house was finally empty and even the servants had tactfully vanished. Until that moment the wedding and everything that had come before had seemed dreamlike, the culmination of all my childhood schemes. Now I was married and a new life was beginning with a man I hardly knew.

I hadn't thought about the latter very often in the past months. How well does a woman ever know a man? We move in different spheres, think different thoughts, have different interests. When our paths cross, we are polite, even kind to each other. But friendship, like the one I shared with Annie, is unlikely. A woman can hope that a man will appreciate her strengths and forgive her weaknesses, but true understanding is something else indeed.

Now I wondered if I had made a wise choice. Until that moment I had never really questioned my upbringing. I had cooperated fully in Mama's plan to find a rich, well-connected husband, and despite her misgivings, I had found one and married him. But had I allowed pride to overtake my good sense and bound myself to a mystery man?

Ian strolled into the room just as that final thought occurred to me. He took one look at my face and burst into laughter. "It's perfectly natural, darling, to be a little worried right now."

"Is it?"

"After all, you've just taken a big step, and we're about to take another."

I had looked forward to this next step with a mixture of curiosity and longing. I knew the mechanics, if not the finer points, and thought it all sounded quite extraordinary. "You would certainly know about that," I said. "Having had a wedding night once before."

He took a moment to light a cigarette, waving the match to extinguish it as he asked, "Would you like to know about Frances? You've never asked."

I wasn't certain, but I nodded.

He drew a deep puff of smoke into his lungs. "We were the same age, Frances and I. She was from Virginia. Her family settled Clarke County, and her roots were as deep as mine."

"A good match."

"We were compatible. At least sometimes. But

Frances was fond of having her own way, and whenever she was displeased she left for the bosom of her family. I spent the years of our marriage enticing her to come home again. That final time, she was pregnant and refused to stay at Fox River, despite the fact that we had arranged for the best medical care. She wanted to be with her mother. Our son was born a month early, and the delivery was fatal for both of them. The midwife in attendance knew little about modern medicine."

I was dismayed. "Ian, I'm so sorry. That's a terrible story."

"I wouldn't have burdened you with it tonight, but there shouldn't be secrets between us."

"I'm glad you told me."

"You can see why another marriage held no appeal until now."

I felt honored to have changed his mind—which might well have been the intent of telling his story. I placed my hand on his arm. "I'm not Frances. I married you for better or worse today, and I'll stay with you through both."

His expression softened. "We'll hope there's very little of the worse to live through."

"I've heard that tonight could be part of the better, if we stop telling each other sad stories and go upstairs."

"You're a forward little vixen, aren't you?"

"I don't know. We could find out together."

He stubbed out the cigarette and pulled me close. And as I'd hoped, what followed was part of the better.

What I didn't know was that there was so much worse to come.

17

Julia had only half listened to Maisy's novel. Louisa's story, with all its happily-ever-after and romantic flourishes, seemed too unrealistic tonight. And even though Louisa herself had hinted there was worse to come, Julia couldn't get involved in another woman's life. Not when her own was in such disarray.

Julia had apologized to Maisy. Although she wished her mother wouldn't interfere, she knew Maisy was right. Christian was a free man, and his daughter was living down the road. Their paths would collide, and soon. How long before Christian realized the truth?

There were no happily-ever-afters in this story. Christian had been cheated of so much, and every day that passed without knowing about Callie was more undeserved punishment.

She threaded her fingers behind her head and stared sightlessly at the ceiling. How could something that had held such promise end so tragically? She wondered if, by writing the fictitious Louisa's story, Maisy was trying to tell Julia to keep hope alive. Was *Fox River* Maisy's well-intentioned but slightly demented way of trying to show Julia the way back to Christian?

She squeezed her eyes shut. She was being unfair, and she knew it. Whatever Maisy's intentions, she was not engineering a reunion. She simply wanted Julia to do what was right, to tell Christian he had a daughter.

Julia remembered a time when she had told Christian everything, when most of the time he had known what she was thinking before she said the words. That wonderful intimacy had begun at the Middleburg Spring Races and ended in a courtroom.

But it still lived in her memories.

At the party after the race, Christian Carver had been friendly to both girls, carefully not paying attention to one more than the other. But Julia was certain he had his eye on Fidelity.

After the party, an exhausted Julia, her defenses down and her hormones charged, followed Fidelity into her bedroom at South Land. She tossed her own shoes beside her friend's and joined her on the bed. Like Fidelity, she had changed into something dressier, but unlike her, she smoothed her skirt before she lay down. Fidelity could simply drop her clothes on the floor when she undressed, and tomorrow someone would whisk them away to the laundry or dry cleaner. At Julia's house anything she left on the floor stayed there until she picked it up.

"Okay, so I really like Christian," Julia admitted. She curled her knees and propped her head on her elbow to see Fidelity. "He's real, if you know what I mean."

"Too real. I mean, he's an orphan, and his daddy burned down Claymore Park's stable. That's about as real as it gets."

"Well, he's not the son of a millionaire, if that's what you mean."

"Robby sure is." Fidelity propped herself up. "What do you think of Robby Claymore?"

"I've always liked Robby, too."

"He's practically tongue-tied around me." Fidelity giggled. "For a rich boy who's as smart as he's supposed to be, he sure doesn't have any confidence. He needs confidence. Too bad I'll be too busy with his best friend to give it to him."

Fidelity was always on the prowl, sampling life, taking what she liked and discarding whatever she didn't. She wasn't cruel; in fact, she had a generous heart. But losing a place on the Olympic team was the first time she'd been denied anything she wanted. Fidelity still thought it was a fluke.

"I don't think Christian is the kind of man you should mess with," Julia said. "He's not like you, Fidelity. He's serious. He's had a lot of setbacks, and he had to grow up fast. I don't think he knows how to play games.''

"Games?'' Fidelity dimpled. "Do tell, Julie boo, what games am I playing?''

"You don't want a boyfriend without money.''

"Well, he could pass. He has the look. He's been around the Claymores so much he has excellent manners. Didn't you notice he was perfectly at home tonight? Oh, and he rides with Mosby Hunt. Daddy says he's the best whipper-in they've had in years.''

"He was a hero tonight. Tomorrow he'll be mucking out stalls at Claymore Park.''

"So? I muck out stalls, too.''

"You've never done a lick of work in your life.''

"Well, I know how to muck out a stall, if it ever comes to that. And I do care for my own horses, but you wouldn't know, because you won't come near them.''

"I just think you should go easy on Christian. Don't you get tired of breaking hearts?''

"Oh, go on. I never break hearts. I just bend them a little. Wrinkle them. You know. If I get tired of Christian—''

"*When* you get tired of Christian—''

"He'll be a big boy about it. He's an adult. He'll act like one.''

Julia lost her temper. "Maybe you should act like one for a change.''

Fidelity raised one perfectly plucked brow. "So...you want him? That's what this is about? If you want him, I might reconsider.''

"Forget it. I don't want your cast-offs.''

Fidelity lay back and stared at the canopy. "Okay, here's the thing. You've really got to develop a backbone, Julie boo. You're letting me run you over.''

"What?''

"You never wanted anything before, but now you want Christian. And you're still handing him over to me on a silver platter.''

"What do you want me to do? Scratch out your eyes?''

"Didn't you notice who he spent his time looking at tonight?''

"I don't seem to have your sixth sense.''

"*You*, doofus. Even when presented with my dimples and baby blues, it was you he was watching."

Julia didn't know what to think.

"Do you know how I get every single man I want?" Fidelity said.

"By flaunting every single cell of your perfect body?"

"By choosing carefully. I only go after what I *know* I can have. Period. Why bother with anything else? The one time I set my sights on something out of my reach, I lost. He has his eye on you. I know what it looks like."

"And you're not mad?"

"It's a big ocean out there. There are a million champion bass just waiting to be hooked."

Julia didn't know what to do after that. She was afraid Fidelity was wrong; then she was afraid Christian might be hesitant to single her out, since the girls were close friends. One day, before she could do anything, she came home from school to find him waiting on her porch, with Maisy dancing attendance.

She parked her Escort beside his Claymore Park pickup and walked up the front path, trying to look nonchalant. Maisy, in an embroidered Mexican sundress paired with hiking boots, greeted her, then disappeared into the house. Julia wasn't sure which surprised her most, Christian's presence or Maisy's discretion.

"What a neighborly thing to do," Julia said. "Dropping by like this to see my mother."

"I thought you'd be home earlier."

She would have been, if she'd known who was waiting. She sat down on the step beside him, glad she was wearing something besides jeans today. She smoothed her knit skirt over her knees. "Won any more races lately?"

"Nope. How about you?"

"Nope."

He stood. "I hate to say it, but I have to go. I've stayed too long already."

Disappointment was a slap in the face. "Oh..."

"I should have called. I've been here an hour. I've got a class tonight, and I have to get ready. Walk me to the truck?"

They walked in silence up the path. He stepped through the

gate, latching it behind them, then leaned against it. "Why don't you ride?"

For a moment she couldn't think.

He smiled, as if encouraged. "It's not really because you don't keep horses here, is it? You could always ride at South Land."

"What does Fidelity say about it?"

He hesitated. "She says you're just not a horse person."

"I *thought* you'd talked to her. You're here because Fidelity told you to come!"

"I'm here because she gave me the right excuse."

"And why did you need one?"

"Because..." His grin was charming. "Because I didn't want to make any mistakes with you."

Her oxygen supply dwindled. She had to take a deep breath. "Okay, I'm afraid of horses. I don't know why, but they terrify me."

"Well, they're pretty big. Everyone's a little anxious at first."

"We aren't talking a little anxious. I break out in a cold sweat. I tremble so hard I can't hold the reins. I get sick to my stomach."

"But other than that?"

She tried to laugh. "Fidelity tried to teach me. Believe me. I wanted to learn, I really did. But she can't understand my reaction. Nobody can, including me. I'm just..." She paused. "Why were you talking to Fidelity about me?"

"I... Well, I wanted to make sure I wasn't poaching on somebody else's territory."

Relief filled her, followed by elation. "I'm not afraid of anything else. I've done mountain climbing, whitewater rafting. Heck, I've even been brave enough to be Fidelity's best friend all these years. That should count for something."

He smiled at her, a smile that sent the oxygen rushing through her veins again. "Julia, why don't I teach you to ride? Can you trust me? I can be patient. I know how to move slowly. We can take *everything* one step at a time."

She wondered exactly what they were talking about.

"Will you give it a try?" he said.

She thought of herself on the back of a horse, high above the ground, slipping from side to side as the horse moved recklessly beneath her.... She thought of Christian right beside her.

Could you teach someone to ride without touching them? She didn't think so.

"I like the way you think things through," Christian said.

"You have a horse that's tame enough? You're not going to start me on Night Ranger, are you?"

He took her hand over the gate and squeezed it. "How about tomorrow? Before you have a chance to lose your nerve. Come early. It's Saturday."

"What's early?"

He dropped her hand. "Seven. I'm scheduled to walk hounds at eight. That will give us plenty of time to sneak in your first lesson."

She watched him saunter away. He had a loose, swinging stride, a young Wyatt Earp on his way to Tombstone. Only when he'd disappeared did she realize what love had gotten her into. By then, it was too late to change her mind.

In the next weeks, Robby, Christian, Fidelity and Julia seemed to find a million excuses to be together, in any combination they could manage. The roots of friendship had been dormant; now the friendship blossomed again. They swam, ate and listened to music. They watched movies and had cookouts, growing comfortable with each other again as only old friends can.

Julia was anything but comfortable with Christian, though. She had never before encountered this rush of emotion, the sweaty palms, weak-in-the-knees, pulse-pounding glories of sexual attraction. Every time she was with him the sensations intensified.

She found herself noticing the smallest things. The golden hair sprinkled along his tanned forearms. The strong line of his jaw and ridged slope of his nose. The slight hesitation before he spoke his mind, as if he couldn't be careless, even in the heat of argument. When she let herself dwell, even for moments, on her feelings, she realized her attraction was not purely physical. Christian was a totally genuine man. He said what he thought, then stood by it. He was strong in all the ways that mattered.

Although she was the most pathetic riding pupil imaginable,

he refused to give up on her. His patience was extraordinary. Unfortunately so was his self-control.

A full month of riding lessons passed before Julia felt courageous enough to walk her mount around Claymore Park's riding ring without Christian on a horse beside her. She had no idea why she was so terrified, except that fear seemed a sensible emotion under the circumstances. Horses were huge, erratic and oversensitive creatures. They startled at noises or paper blowing across the ground. They nipped, trampled and reared.

They also, once the fear began to disappear, made her feel twenty feet tall when she was sitting on one.

By mid-June, six weeks into her training, she could post a trot and gracefully sit a canter. She looked forward to mounting and only rarely wanted to dismount at lesson's end. Learning to ride had meant close contact nearly every day with Christian. He had been patient, comforting and demanding enough to make her want to overcome her fears. Once the worst was over, she had spent twenty-three hours of every day waiting for the hour they would spend together.

"You have all the right instincts on horseback," Christian told her at the end of two months. It was evening, but the summer sun was sinking slowly. "You're not Harry Ashbourne's daughter for nothing."

Julia glowed from the compliment—made sweeter since it was coming from him. Until that moment she had been isolated from the horse world that surrounded her. Now, not only did she ride, but she was part of the aristocracy, the daughter of a legend.

He led Night Ranger over to Whitey, the reliable old mare she had learned on. "So before you swell from pride and get too big for your horse, we're going to try something more challenging."

She cocked her head and smiled down at him. From this angle she could see every sunbleached strand of hair peeking from under his cowboy hat. His jeans were faded and dusty, his T-shirt the color of winter grass. He was, in a word, gorgeous.

"You might not be smiling when we've finished," he warned.

"I feel like I can do anything."

He grinned, pushing his hat farther back as he did. "Some men would take that as an invitation."

"Well, some men are bolder than others. They grab whatever they want."

"And is that the way you like your men?"

She pretended to consider, then she smiled. "What challenge do you have for me today?"

"We're going for a trail ride. You need some practice outside the ring."

She was surprised and pleased. "Really? You trust me?"

"I'd trust a five-year-old on Whitey. But yeah, I trust you. Let's go." He swung up into the saddle. "Ranger hasn't had any exercise today. Normally I don't take him riding for the fun of it, but we'll make an exception. This is a celebration."

As a child she had dreamed of riding across pastures, through forests, over hills. Fear had made that impossible, but now Christian had paved the way. She was anxious at first, but once she got used to the easy rhythm, she relaxed. He rode ahead, then circled back at a gallop, to take the edge off the Thoroughbred's energy. They cantered together through rolling pasture; then, at a walk again, he rode beside her in companionable silence.

"What do you think?" he asked at last.

"I love it. This must be what it's like to hunt. At least a little."

"Except we're not wearing funny clothes."

She laughed. "I have photographs of my father, dressed as master. He was...dashing. That's the only word for it. I like those funny clothes."

"Do you want to hunt?"

"No."

"Why not? You've come this far."

"Well, I'd have to jump fences. There's no chance of that."

"No? That's too bad, because that's your next lesson."

Her smile disappeared. "I don't think so."

"It's the next thing you need to learn."

"I don't care if I learn to jump. I just wanted to be comfortable on a horse."

"You know you'd be welcomed by Mosby. Now that Fidelity's riding with us, you're the only holdout. Robby rides, too, when he's not trying to make his father angry."

"People haven't forgiven my mother for posting Ashbourne."

"But you're not your mother. And your father was master. That's what people will think about when you ride with us."

"I'm not good enough to foxhunt."

"But do you want to be?"

Whitey moved restlessly beneath her, and Julia steadied her without thinking about it. "I don't know. I used to hear the hounds early in the morning, off at Claymore Park or South Land, and... I don't know if I have the courage to do this."

"You've come so far. Come a little further. We'll take it slow. You'll feel like you're flying. Like you have wings."

If anyone else had suggested this, she would have refused immediately and permanently. But she was beginning to think Christian could persuade her to do anything.

"How do we start?"

"There's an easy jump coming up. It's pretty basic. You won't even know you've done it."

Her heart began to pound simply at the thought. "I don't know...."

"We'll look at it, then you can decide."

They turned into the woods that bordered the pasture and picked their way downhill and over an old stone bridge. Ten minutes later Christian pointed. "Over there."

Against the darkening sky Julia saw an uneven split rail fence. One section was lower than the rest.

"For us," Christian said. "Easy as sin."

"For you, maybe."

They stopped at the edge of the field. "Want me to show you how it's done?"

She bought time. "Sure."

He urged Night Ranger into a canter, and before her heart could climb into her throat, the big gray was sailing effortlessly over the rails. Christian and the horse disappeared into the woods beyond, then came out and took the fence again. He rode up beside her. "What do you think?"

"I think I'd better go home now. It's past my curfew."

He must have seen the fear. Lord knew, she couldn't cover up something that enveloping. He looked thoughtful.

"I don't want to fall off," she admitted. "Falling terrifies me."

"You are going to fall off. If you ride, you're going to fall eventually. That's just the way it is. But that's why I'm giving you lessons. So you'll develop the right habits and fall infrequently. If you fall off during a hunt, you'll have to help throw a party at season's end. You and half a dozen other perfectly healthy people who made an involuntary dismount or two. It's all good fun." He paused. "We'll go over together."

"I don't think so."

"You're safe with me."

"There's not enough room for both horses to take it."

"No, I mean *together*. On Night Ranger."

"How?"

"I'll show you." He dismounted and held Night Ranger's reins. "Just tie a knot and loop Whitey's reins over that stump." He nodded to one side. "She'll wait."

She silently debated.

"Have I steered you wrong, Jules?"

She smiled at the nickname. He had begun calling her Jules at their first lesson, although no one else ever had. "No."

"I won't. I promise. Get down. It's going to be dark soon."

She did. She settled Whitey at the stump, then walked slowly back toward Christian. "I'm used to Whitey. Night Ranger scares me."

"I'll be with you. Nothing will happen. I'll hold the reins while you mount."

She almost refused. He must have seen it in her eyes, because he put his arms around her, and before she could blink, he kissed her.

The ground fell away at her feet. The sky descended. Her arms crept around him, and she kissed him back with no hesitation whatsoever.

He finally stepped away, but only after kissing her cheeks, her chin, her forehead.

"Christian, my father broke his neck and died when he fell off a horse."

"From what I know of your father, that was the way he wanted to go. From all accounts he was as reckless as the devil. Harry

Ashbourne chose to take chances. You don't have to take as many. Do you understand what I'm saying?''

Life was filled with risks, but none so personal as this. Even though Julia remembered little about her father, she did remember a powerful man who had scoffed at weakness. Now she could almost hear him tell her not to give in to fear.

''By the way, did you notice I just kissed you?'' Christian said.

''Can we take that up later?''

''Just tell me if you might want me to do it again sometime.''

She put her hands on his cheeks and kissed him hard. ''Christian, we've got to do this now, before the kiss wears off and the sun sets.''

He grinned. ''Up you go.''

She was seated on Night Ranger before she had time to reconsider. ''What about you?''

''Here I come.'' He swung up behind her. Despite her petite size, the saddle wasn't really big enough for two, but that seemed to be the least of her worries. ''Hook your feet over my legs. I've got the stirrups. And sit back against me.''

That last part was easy—and thrilling. He circled her with his arms, reins in each hand. ''We're going to fly, Jules. Don't do a thing. Just enjoy it.''

She bit her lip, so recently and thoroughly kissed.

He didn't ask if she was ready. He probably knew she wasn't and wouldn't be. He urged Night Ranger into a canter. ''Okay, when we lift off, just lean forward and grip with your knees. I've got you. You can't fall. Don't close your eyes.''

She was terrified. The fence was coming toward them at an alarming rate. At first she was sure they weren't going over, then she was afraid they were.

Then they had.

Christian reined Ranger in on the other side. ''Still there?''

She thought she'd probably left some part of herself on the other side of the fence. ''Am I?''

''How do you feel?''

She wasn't quite sure.

He coaxed Ranger forward, circling until they were heading

back across. This time she was ready, and when they lifted high, she crouched and squeezed her knees.

"Good. Much better." He circled again. Then again.

Finally he pulled the big horse to a halt and swung down. But he didn't hold out his hand to Julia. "Okay, Jules. Your turn. You do it alone this time."

She hadn't been frightened enough to ignore the way his hard body had moved along her back, the strength in his arms. "I can't. This is Night Ranger."

"Who better?"

"Will he listen to me?"

"We'll see." He grinned. The answer was there.

A challenge had been issued. She straightened her shoulders and waited while he shortened the stirrups. Her hands were trembling, and she was sure the horse would respond badly to her fear. But he stood perfectly still, waiting for her command. It was now or never. She knew if she turned away, she would never get this far again. A door would stay closed in her life.

And Christian would think she was a coward.

"Just remember not to pull up as you reach the jump or while you're going over," Christian said. "That's the worst thing you could do. Commit yourself, then go for it. Night Ranger will do the rest."

"See you," she said. She gathered the reins and squeezed Ranger lightly. He started toward the fence, as game as he had been the first time. They rose together, flying. She didn't even bounce as they came back to earth. She circled him and took it from the other side.

Christian was waiting near Whitey, his arms outstretched. Night Ranger had hardly stopped before she leaped to the ground and threw herself into his arms.

He swung her around. "I knew you'd do it!"

"It was wonderful! Wonderful!"

"I'm so proud of you." He cupped her face in his hands. "If you did that, you can do anything."

Her eyes were shining. She didn't close them when he kissed her again. She wrapped her arms around him and pulled him as close as she could. Triumph changed to something else. She pulled away a little.

"Did you kiss me before just to give me courage?" Her breath was coming fast, and so was his.

"I kissed you because I couldn't wait another minute." He unhooked her barrette and twisted her hair in his hands. He kissed her neck. "The teacher isn't supposed to take advantage of the pupil."

"What if she wants to be taken advantage of?"

"Does she?"

She kissed him in answer.

He groaned. "Then here's how we'll play it. We'll take it slowly for a while. I'll give you time to get used to this, in case you change your mind. Then it's no holds barred."

She gripped his shoulders. "It's no-holds-barred right now. We've taken it slowly enough, don't you think?"

"Do you know what you're saying?"

"I'm saying I fell in love with you at the Middleburg Races. Then I had to learn how to ride just to get your attention. I've waited long enough."

"Jules, you always had my attention." He gathered her against him, and they sank to the soft grass. Ranger wandered away to inspect the pasture near Whitey, and the sky darkened into night. The ground was damp against her back once Christian had undressed her. She didn't care. He was warm against her, young and strong and nearly as inexperienced as she. Nothing mattered. They touched and kissed and laughed, and when he was finally inside her, they moved together with rash enthusiasm as their horses grazed contentedly nearby.

18

Both Mel and Peter had told Christian not to investigate Fidelity's death. He understood their qualms. He had some of his own. But nobody else had his investment in discovering all the facts.

In Christian's mind, too much didn't add up. Although Zandoff claimed to have been working in Middleburg when Fidelity was murdered, no one had remembered him. Since Zandoff claimed that the man he had worked for had never reported his wages, his employment was still a question mark.

Then there was the matter of Zandoff's other crimes. Zandoff strangled his victims. He had not, to anyone's knowledge, used a knife or committed robbery, although he had always taken some token to remember the experience. He had carefully removed the bodies afterward and buried them. And he had attacked his victims sexually before killing them. There hadn't been any sign that Fidelity had been sexually assaulted, just murdered, without even a sign of struggle.

As long as questions remained, Christian knew that some people would believe he'd been involved. His own freedom might still be taken away, and having that threat hanging over his future was unbearable.

Almost more unbearable was not knowing exactly what had happened to Fidelity and why. She deserved to be at rest, the beloved daughter of Flo and Frank Sutherland and nothing more.

At breakfast the next morning Christian reluctantly asked Peter for a ride into Leesburg so he could get a driver's license. Peter left him at the driver's license bureau with the keys to his Lincoln. Peter was going to lunch with a friend, and he planned to have her drop him off at home.

Paperwork and driver's test completed, Christian got behind the wheel and considered his alternatives. He felt none of the exhilaration that he'd felt at sixteen, celebrating his first license. He was glad, though, to have the freedom to pursue his quest. And he knew where he wanted to start.

Half an hour later he was at McDonald's, sitting across the table from Pinky Stewart, the sheriff's deputy who had found Fidelity's jewelry.

As a sophomore in high school, Pinky had moved to Northern Virginia from South Carolina, and Christian had befriended him. As seniors they had been on the baseball team that had taken state honors, Christian the pitcher, Pinky at first base. He was pink-cheeked—hence the nickname—and round-faced, balding now, but still boyishly cheerful. He had been thrilled to see Christian, despite dark looks from his colleagues, and he had agreed to have coffee with him when it would have been in his professional interest not to.

"You don't look half bad, considering," Pinky drawled. "I was glad it was me that found the jewelry. I couldn't do a damned thing for you when you were on trial, but I dug extra hard when I heard what we were looking for."

Despite the knot in his stomach, Christian had to smile a little. He obviously had one supporter in local law enforcement. "Were you surprised to find it?"

"Maybe a little. There wasn't a lot of reason to think you didn't kill her. Just that I knew you didn't have murder in you. At least I didn't think you did."

Christian thought maybe he had "murder in him" now if he discovered that someone in addition to Zandoff had helped kill Fidelity and stolen nearly nine years of his life.

"There are still some unanswered questions," Christian said. "Too many for my taste."

"Not enough to keep you in prison."

"I want to know exactly what happened." Christian explained why.

Pinky listened, tapping his fingers to the rhythm of Christian's words. "What are you telling me for?" he asked, when Christian had finished.

"I need help. I wasn't there during the investigation. I don't know what they found and what they didn't. Were there other leads they didn't pursue because they thought they had me cold? And how far have they gotten trying to prove that Zandoff was in town? Exactly what do they know that I don't?"

"Those records are confidential, Chris. You know I can't tell you anything."

"Hasn't the legal system screwed me one time too many?"

Pinky was silent, but his fingers continued to drum. "You know, I'm not very good at what I do. I don't have the killer instinct, if you know what I mean."

"For nine years I saw the killer instinct firsthand."

"Yeah, well, Sheriff Gordon's not all that pleased with my work. He'd fire me given one little chance. He's got a nephew who wants my job worse than he wants the neighbor girl's soft little pussy."

"That bad, huh?"

Pinky grinned. "I'm looking at the fire department."

"What are your chances?"

"Good enough to take some risks." Pinky leaned closer. "I'd love to rub Sheriff Gordon's ugly old face in this. You know? I'll see what I can do. Just don't expect anything right away, and don't come around again. Call me at home." Pinky reached for his wallet and pulled out a business card. "You remember Wanda Swensen?"

Christian thought he'd better try if he was going to keep Pinky's friendship. He pictured his schoolmates and was rewarded with the vision of a delicate blond with an unfortunate nose. "I do."

"We been married four years. Here's our little boy." He handed Christian a photograph. Christian had been right about Wanda's nose. "He looks like a little stinker."

"He is. Keeps us hopping. Wanda's pregnant with number two. We're hoping for something quiet this time. Either sex. Just quiet."

Christian gave him back the photograph. "You're a good friend, Pinky."

"Come over sometime. We'll throw a few balls. Hell, who knows, we might start another team."

Yvonne had asked Julia to come every day for the first week, and Maisy had been more than willing to make the trip. Today she was making a detour, so they left early.

"You're not going to tell me where we're going?" Julia said.

"I'm not. It's a surprise."

"Like the clay."

"Did you like it?"

As a matter of fact, Julia had liked it a lot. After she'd taken out weeks of disappointment by slamming it around, she had begun to pinch off little bits, using her fingers to sculpt human figures, trees, horses. She wasn't sure anyone else would have been able to tell what she was doing—Callie had asked why her mother was making circus animals—but the vision in Julia's head, the vision of a quiet forest, had begun to take shape and clarify as she'd worked.

She told her mother as much. "I'm glad you thought of it," she finished.

"Well, this isn't the same kind of surprise. This one's about me."

"Good for you. I can't wait to see..." She grimaced. "Truer words were never spoken, huh?"

"Well, even if you don't *see* this, you'll feel it. Big time."

Julia fell silent. Talking in the truck was difficult. And even though it was cooler today, the windows were half open and wind rushed through. She leaned her head back and closed her eyes. When she awoke, they were just pulling to a stop.

"I don't think this will take long. I've done most of the preliminaries by telephone," Maisy said.

"Where are we?"

"At the Ford dealer. I'm picking up a new truck. Jake would drive this turkey until it dissolved into a pool of motor oil."

"Does he know?"

"No, he does not."

"Good Lord. What's he going to say?"

"Jake will love it once he's used to it," Maisy said. "But this isn't about Jake. It's about me. I'm tired of making do when we don't have to. We need a new vehicle, and we're getting one today."

"I've never seen you like this."

"You ain't seen nothing yet."

Julia laughed a little. "Well, that's true enough."

"I'm sorry. We haven't gone through all the sight clichés quite yet, have we?"

"Not even close."

"If they're as good as their word, I'll just sign on the dotted line, hand them a check, drive the new truck over here and make the switch. I've already cleaned everything out of this one. That will be Jake's first clue. When he sees a pile of maps, water bottles and jumper cables on the front lawn."

"Go get 'em, tiger."

To Julia's surprise, Maisy was back in about ten minutes. She warned Julia before she opened her door, but Julia had heard the soothing purr of a vehicle drawing up beside the old pickup.

"Okay, it's a done deal. I'll help you down."

Julia took her mother's arm and stepped carefully down to the running board, then the ground.

"Two steps. You got it."

Julia climbed up into the new pickup. The smell of plastic, leather, rubber and polish overwhelmed her. "Oooh, this is comfortable." She bounced on the seat a little.

Maisy climbed in after a brief conversation, probably with the salesperson. "We're off. Lord, listen to this thing purr. Your seat belt's hanging down on the right. And we're turning on the air conditioner."

Julia fumbled for the belt. "Do we really need it?"

"I'm going to run it all winter long just because it's there." Maisy pulled out of the parking lot, squealing her tires the way Robby and Fidelity had every time they pulled away from Ashbourne. Julia experienced a moment of pure nostalgia.

"On to Yvonne's," Maisy said. "Oh, does this baby feel good."

"Don't speed."

"Me?"

"Maisy, don't speed."

"You sure do know how to take the fun out of life."

"And how to keep you alive."

Maisy slowed down.

"Describe it."

"Ford Ranger. Fire engine red, black leather interior. Every single add-on they had. This thing will cook dinner, milk the cows and dress up in a negligee for a little late-night nookie."

"Jake is going to *have* a cow."

"Let him."

Julia couldn't let that pass. "Okay, what's going on? Are you two falling apart because Callie and I are there? Are we putting too much strain on you?"

"Get that idea out of your head right now."

"Then what is it?"

"I'm not sure. We're fine. It's nothing for you to worry about. But we're just having trouble communicating."

"How?"

"We just seem to talk past each other. Whenever Jake and I have a conversation it's like sonar, bouncing off objects and ping-ponging in all directions. Have you had that experience with Bard?"

"No."

Maisy was silent.

Julia continued after a moment. "I think what you're describing is a lapse in communication between two people who have always been extraordinarily close. You notice when you're not communicating well because normally you do."

"That's probably true."

"Bard and I say what needs to be said, and each of us understands the other."

"Well, that's good." Maisy said the words, but she didn't sound as if she believed them.

"Maybe not so good," Julia said honestly. "Because we don't even try to say the little things. The feelings, the funny little things that happen to us. We don't report conversations we've had or hopes that got dashed or nightmares or fantasies or—"

"Did you expect to?"

On the surface the question seemed odd, but Julia thought it was a good one. "No, Maisy. Is that what you wanted to hear?"

"I wanted to hear that my daughter was madly in love with her husband, always had been and planned to be forever. Barring that, I wanted the truth."

"I don't know if Bard would have had that kind of relationship with anybody, but I know he won't have it with me."

"What does that mean?"

Julia wasn't sure of everything it meant, but some of it was clear. "Do you believe in soul mates?"

"Absolutely not."

"Well, that surprises me. Your book is so, well, romantic."

"It's a book. Just a book."

"Then Ian isn't Louisa's soul mate?"

"You'll have to be the judge."

"Isn't Jake yours? Wasn't my father?"

"No to both. They are...were two very different men. I loved them both. I felt connected to them in different ways. But did I feel either of them was the only man I was supposed to be with?"

"Did you?"

"Fate has a way of intervening in the best laid plans."

"You were young when my father died."

"Uh-huh."

"You seem to have coped by dropping out of your world and finding another."

"That's a fair assessment."

"Wasn't there support to be found here? Neighbors and friends? From what I can tell, my father was a popular figure in the community."

"He surely was."

"And after his death, people didn't rally around?"

"They were kind and concerned. But in one moment my life changed so dramatically, I only wanted to forget the world Harry had loved so well."

"So you posted Ashbourne, withdrew from the social whirl—"

"And concentrated on raising you and, eventually, on loving Jake."

"If Bard was killed, my reaction wouldn't be so extreme." As soon as the words were out, Julia wished she had censored them.

"You believe in soul mates, and he's not yours. Is that what you've been trying to say?"

"I don't know what I believe. But I believe you're lucky. Even if you and Jake aren't communicating well right now, you have in the past. You have something to fix."

"And you don't?"

"You've hated Bard Warwick since the day I told you I was going to marry him."

"No, I hated the fact that you felt you had to marry to preserve Callie's future. I hated that he played on your despair and offered you what a good man couldn't. I hated the fact that he expected you to fit into his world and did nothing to accommodate himself to yours." Maisy hesitated. "I won't go on. That's a bad enough start to the day, isn't it?"

Julia knew if she'd been looking at her mother, Maisy would be gripping the wheel. Her voice was tight with anger. And Julia knew the anger wasn't aimed at her.

"Not a bad start," Julia said at last. "An honest one."

"He has good qualities," Maisy said reluctantly. "I can see those, too."

"I married him. Don't I owe him my loyalty and devotion?"

"Not if he doesn't deserve it. And that's part of your mission right now, isn't it? To determine who's owed what?"

"I'm getting therapy on the way to see Yvonne. Am I going to get it on the way home, as well?"

"I'm going to drive my new truck and keep my mouth shut."

"That would be an interesting change."

Yvonne brought Julia into her office and made her comfortable, as always. Then she dropped a bombshell. "I'd like to try something completely new today."

"And what's that?"

"Hypnosis."

"You're kidding."

"Not even close."

"Don't I have to be able to see so you can swing something in front of me?"

"You watch too many old movies."

"What's the point?"

"To help you get in touch with whatever you don't want to see. To help you see it in a different way."

"I can't be hypnotized."

"How do you know?"

"It's something girls do at sleepovers. I never even got close."

"This isn't the same thing at all."

"Somebody discussed this with me at the hospital, Yvonne."

"People with this particular problem are often easy to hypnotize."

"Hysterics, you mean."

"Do you think of yourself as a hysteric?"

"Before this, that would have been the last word I used."

"I don't think of you that way. I think of you as a woman who has a secret she's keeping from herself, a creative, talented, insightful woman, an artist who could be more in touch with what's inside her than most people are, although she doesn't allow it. A woman who, when she is out of touch with something, tries desperate measures to avoid it."

Julia immediately thought of Christian and Callie and all she had done and was still doing to avoid the inevitable. Shame filled her.

"Julia?" Yvonne asked gently.

"The psychologist at the hospital suggested hypnosis. I told him no. I'm telling you the same thing."

"Why?"

Julia realized she was wringing her hands. "I don't... I don't want to relive anything that's happened to me. I've lost a lot. I don't want to feel those feelings all over again."

"We can make it easier to bear. You can describe events as if you were watching them happen to someone else."

"No."

"When you're ready, then."

"I won't be ready."

"Let's talk about this desire to avoid pain. Okay? Let's start with something very small. Have you ever lost a pet?"

"No."

"What about an opportunity? Something small. Something you wanted and didn't get?"

"I had a chance for an art scholarship in high school, but I missed the deadline."

"Well, that's small enough. Let's begin there. Tell me about the day you realized you'd blown your chance."

19

Julia didn't know when she had the idea to go riding. At some point between telling Yvonne about losing an unimportant scholarship and explaining how she had almost let her fears keep her from learning to ride, she'd realized how much she missed being on horseback. Once aware of it, the ache had almost stopped the flow of words.

At home she closed herself in the downstairs bedroom and called Millcreek Farm, asking Mrs. Taylor to transfer the call to the barn. She spoke to Ramon, the same groom who had delivered Feather Foot for Callie, and told him what she wanted. Then she went to find her mother.

"You're not going to like this," she warned Maisy.

"Try me."

"I'm going riding. I'm taking Callie when she gets home from school."

"How are you going to accomplish this?"

"Ramon is riding over with Sandman. He's the gentlest horse Bard owns. Ramon will come with us to make sure we're all right. Please don't worry."

"Julia..."

"I have to do it, Maisy. I need to be on horseback again. You know what they say about being thrown and getting right back on? I'll be safe. We'll just go for a trail ride."

"There's nothing I can say to stop you, is there?"

"Not a thing."

"Do you need help finding something to wear?"

Karen, who had turned out to be invaluable, was off for the day, but Julia had arranged her own clothing in the drawers. "I have a pair of jeans. I'll be ready by the time you bring Callie home from school."

Although she was a little nervous, excitement was her main emotion. She was waiting in the yard when Ramon rode up. He called to her, and she waved. "Who are you riding?"

"Moondrop Morning."

"Why?" She knew Morning, of course. He was Bard's newest hunter, a high-spirited bay gelding with a ridiculously romantic name Bard hadn't given him.

"He needed the exercise. And he behaves these days. Mr. Warwick, he's been working with him every evening."

Julia wished Bard was as patient with Callie. Or that Callie interested him as much.

"Mrs. Warwick, I don't like to question you. But you're sure you're ready to do this?"

Julia had always liked Ramon, a young man from El Salvador who had seen more bloodshed and terror in his brief years than a career soldier. Ramon, who had been studying to become a veterinarian before he was forced to flee, was polite, great with horses and able to tolerate Bard's officious behavior.

She winced inwardly at that thought, but the truth was undeniable. Bard, prince in his family in the same way that Fidelity had been a princess in hers, had a way of treating his employees as if they were inanimate objects. Fidelity, for all her faults and money, had treated everyone who worked for the Sutherlands as if they were cherished friends.

"You're right to ask," she assured him. "But I'll be fine as long as you come along. We're not pulling you away from something you had to do?"

"I had to exercise this horse. Do I have to tell Mr. Warwick where I did it?"

She could see his smile in her mind, a white flash against caramel-colored skin. She smiled back. "Not as far as I'm concerned. In fact, I'd like it better if you didn't."

"Mommy!"

Julia hadn't noticed the gentle purr of Maisy's new pickup or the door slamming. A small body barreled into her, and she wrapped her arms around Callie. "Hey, sweetums. How was school?"

"I hate school. Are we really going to ride?"

"We sure are."

"Hey, Ramon!" Callie pulled away from Julia. "Want to see me saddle Feather Foot?"

"It's a sight I wouldn't miss."

Julia heard footsteps, then her mother's voice. "You know, if I were twenty years younger..."

"You have good taste, but of course, you married Jake."

"We'll see how good my taste is when Jake gets his first glimpse of the new truck."

Jake had gone on a fishing trip and wouldn't be back until dinnertime. "Maybe he'll come back while we're riding," Julia said. "Then you can have it out with him without witnesses."

"I might *need* witnesses."

Julia laughed. "Callie's got to change, then we'll be ready. Do me a favor, okay? Lead me to Sandman so I can mount."

"I don't think so."

"What do you mean?"

"There are two horses standing there. One looks as mean as the other."

Julia heard Callie. "Thanks, Ramon!" She ran past, shouting as she did. "Ramon's-going-to-finish-so-I-can-change-I'll-see-you-when-I—" The door slammed.

"Do you think she's looking forward to this?" Julia asked.

"I think I'm going inside. Come and get me when you're back. If Jake's home and you can't find me, look for a freshly dug grave in the Ashbourne plot."

Julia heard her mother leave and, only minutes later, the door slamming again. "I'm ready! I'm ready!"

"Boots on? Hat?"

"Got 'em. Can we go now? Ramon's coming. Hey, Feather Foot!" Callie raced off.

Julia waited until she heard Ramon's steadier steps. "Are you ready, Mrs. Warwick?"

"All set. Lead the way, would you?"

He took her arm, and they started across the grass. It was an odd sensation to be so close to two huge beasts without her sight. "Almost there?"

"Almost. Sandman's holding still." Ramon took her hand and placed it on Sandman's saddle. She pictured Sandman, a dark bay with quarter horse blood and the sturdy conformation that went with it. The leather was slick beneath her fingers, and she realized she was perspiring. "Here are the reins," he said. She felt the leather straps slide beneath her palm, and she lifted it farther to accommodate them.

On her own, she felt for the stirrup with her right hand. Then, as Ramon steadied her, she placed her left foot in it and, with a slight boost from Ramon, lifted herself into the saddle.

"Thanks." Astride now, she gathered the reins into the correct position and made certain both feet were firmly in the stirrups. "Everything feels good."

"Miss Callie's ready, too."

"Then we'll wait for you."

The next time she heard his voice, he was ahead of her. "Miss Callie, would you lead the way? I'll follow behind."

Julia realized this was sound reasoning. Callie knew the paths around Ashbourne, and this way Ramon could keep them both in sight.

"Oh, boy!"

"You go ahead," Julia said. "I'll just give Sandman his head and he'll follow. But no funny stuff, Cal. Remember, I can't see what you're doing."

"Hey, I'm the mommy!"

"You still have to eat vegetables."

"Let's go!"

Julia heard the thud of horseshoes on turf, then Sandman started forward. She was riding again.

"Just relax and enjoy," Ramon said, falling in behind her. "You'll be safe. I'll see to it."

Christian hadn't needed to spend significant time with the puppy hounds before he realized that Clover, despite impeccable bloodlines, was the stereotypical "dumb blonde" of the dog world. She was pretty to look at, fun to cuddle, and so brainless she hadn't yet realized there was more to life than either.

After stumbling over her every single morning, Gorda, a matronly woman in her fifties, was ready to toss the puppy out of the kennel. Fish, irascible and "car'ful with his energy," had even volunteered to make a trip back to Pennsylvania in his free time to return Clover to her breeder.

"You're convinced she's worthless?" Christian had asked that morning, and both had answered an unequivocal "yes."

Christian wasn't as sure. Dogs, like people, matured at different rates. He had a soft spot for late bloomers. On the other hand, he had trained enough dogs both in and out of prison to know that, under most circumstances, intelligent, trainable dogs didn't come from puppies like Clover.

"I called Clover's breeder," Peter told Christian late in the afternoon. "He says there hasn't been a single complaint about any of the other puppies in her litter."

"She wasn't the runt?"

"Far from it." Peter looked sheepish. "I chose her myself. I had first pick. Blinded by a pretty face, I guess."

"Well, she has everything but brains."

"Upshot is, he doesn't want her back. Won't take her, in fact. But he's promised me the pick of the next litter for free, although after this, I'm not sure I want to try this line again."

"I'd say go ahead and take him up on his offer. Just think twice before breeding whatever you get, even if you're lucky the next time."

Christian clapped Peter on the back. "I'm going to take her out alone for a while. Night Ranger and I have a lot of work to do if we're going to the opening hunt. We'll take the puppy and see how she does."

"We can't afford to feed and house her if she doesn't shape up, Christian. She'll have to be culled."

"Let's see what I can do."

Christian went to saddle Night Ranger. Every time he went to the barn the horse appeared to be waiting for him, or, more probably, for the carrot in Christian's pocket. In the day since he had come home to Claymore Park, Ranger seemed to have developed more interest in life. He was still a long way from the confident, clever horse he once had been, but Christian had faith he would improve. "You, me and Clover. What a team, huh, guy? Misfits all."

Christian patted Ranger's neck as he saddled him. When they were both ready, he led him outside and launched himself into the saddle for the short ride to the kennel. The puppies greeted him like an old friend, jumping on each other and tumbling to the ground in warm, soft puppy piles. Clover stared sleepily at him from a corner, and only after coaxing did she amble over to investigate. He wondered if she felt the way he had in elementary school, aware that the other kids knew some marvelous secret he didn't. If she did, then she was also learning that the secret might never be divulged.

He picked her up, fairly certain the afternoon would be shot before he could snag her attention long enough to get her out the door. Outside, he deposited her on the ground not far from Ranger. Then, Ranger's reins in one hand, he started away from the kennel, calling to Clover as he went.

She sat sleepily at first; then she brightened as she realized she was supposed to come along. Tail wagging and ears perked, she walked directly into Ranger's path, flopped to the ground and rolled onto her back to have her belly scratched.

"It's going to be a long afternoon," Christian said. "Come on, dumb dog, I'm trying to save your life here. Put a little effort into this, will you?"

She wriggled happily until he nudged her with the toe of his boot. Then she sprang to her feet and began to yap at Ranger. It wasn't a sound foxhounds usually made. There was no throat-warbling music to it, no trumpeting medley. Clover barked like a particularly obnoxious poodle. Christian was reminded of a silent film star forced to appear in her first talkie. Clover's career was going up in smoke, as well.

"Haven't you been listening to the other hounds?" he chided. Ranger, to his credit, was ignoring the yapping puppy. "Maybe we should turn you loose with the other bitches and see if you can be taught?"

Clover wagged her entire body, and he had to smile. She was trotting along beside him now, satisfied she had subdued Ranger all by herself.

Once they were safely away from the kennel he mounted Ranger, satisfied the horse would avoid stepping on Clover if at all possible. "We won't go too far," he promised Ranger. "Because something tells me we'll be coming back with the puppy in the saddle. But let's give it a try."

About twenty minutes into the ride Julia was sure she'd made a terrific decision. The air was cool, but the sun warmed her shoulders and arms. Callie was obviously proud to be in the lead and excited to be riding with Julia again.

"So, where are we?" Julia asked.

"You know where Mr. Greely keeps his bull?"

"Callie!"

Callie giggled. "Well, we aren't there!"

Julia laughed. "Don't scare me like that."

"I don't know where we are. Just riding. But I know how to get home."

"Ramon?" Julia asked.

"Do you know where the woods dip down to the fence line between Claymore Park and Ashbourne?"

Julia knew exactly where they were now. They were riding along the edge of the woods, where a trail of sorts existed. "Okay. I didn't have any idea. No landmarks for me these days."

"It's a good farm. Good land. Good pasture. The creek for water. Too bad no horses."

"At least the Highland cattle are fun to look at."

"When you learned to ride, did you have a horse here, Mommy?"

Julia had told Callie that she'd learned to ride late, but not how it had come about. "No. I learned to ride at Claymore Park, and I had permission to ride their horses anytime I wanted."

"With your friends?"

"Yes."

"Tiffany's mommy works at Claymore Park, and she says I can ride there sometimes, too!"

Julia gripped her reins tighter. "Did she?"

"Then I'll be like you."

"We'll have to see what Mr. Claymore says about that. They're his horses."

"There's somebody riding over there now. I can see somebody."

Julia wondered who had wandered so far from the training track or the rings where the horses were usually exercised. She listened carefully, but the only sound to greet her was the yapping of a dog. "Ramon?"

"Callie, hold tight," Ramon said. "The puppy's coming this way."

"What puppy?" Julia said. She heard a shout in the distance, and the yapping changed subtly, more the cry of a foxhound. "Ramon, does Peter have the hounds out?"

"Just one. A little one. It's not Mr. Claymore."

"Who is it, can you tell?"

"No one I've seen."

Julia knew exactly who it was. "A young man? Blond?"

"Yes."

"This would be a good place to turn around. We've come far—"

"Hold hard, Callie," Ramon shouted. A torrent of Spanish followed.

Julia heard her daughter's surprised cry. From behind her, she heard more profane Spanish intertwined with the trampling of hoofs. Sandman seemed unaffected, but she knew both her companions were having trouble subduing their horses. The puppy was closer now. Much closer, judging by the baying, and she knew, with a sinking heart, it had gotten through the fence.

"Ramon! Feather Foot doesn't like—" Her words were interrupted by her daughter's shriek and the sound of hoofs. "Callie! Are you all right? Callie?"

"Mommy!"

Julia had never needed her sight more than now, but even though fear was roiling inside her, the day was as black as a starless midnight.

"What's happening?" she cried. "Callie!"

She heard hoofbeats coming toward her, then swerving. "I've got her," said a familiar voice. "Circle, honey. Circle her! Big circles."

"I can't!"

"Circle. Now!"

Julia knew Christian had come to Callie's rescue, but before she had time to even consider what that meant, Sandman began to sidle uneasily beneath her. She gathered her reins and spoke soothing words, but she was grateful when Ramon spoke from the ground below. "I've got him."

"Callie! Where's Callie?"

"She's circling Feather Foot. She's in control. The man is helping her."

"Why didn't you—"

"Morning, he spooked. I would have made things worse."

"Is she okay?"

"She's a good little rider. She's fine. He has the pony's reins now."

Julia swallowed the lump in her throat. "And the puppy?"

"At your feet. Sleeping."

She wanted to cry. The need nearly overwhelmed her. She told herself to stay calm, that this moment would end quickly, but as she heard her daughter's excited chatter, she knew it was just beginning.

"You jumped that fence. I saw you! That's a tall fence!"

"How did you see me?" Christian said. "Your pony was running away."

"Not running away. I had him. I just couldn't...couldn't get him to stop."

Christian chuckled. "And that's different. I can see that now."

"Is that your foxhound? Mommy, I got rescued!"

Julia didn't know what to say.

"Hello, Julia." Christian sounded close by.

She followed the sound of his voice with her eyes. "Christian? Thank you so much."

"He jumped the fence. His horse is beautiful, Mommy. What's his name?"

"This is Night Ranger. Your mommy used to know him when he was just a colt."

"Night Ranger?" Julia was shocked.

"Uh-huh. Peter found him in Maryland and brought him home."

"He can jump so high!" Callie was obviously thrilled. "I never saw a horse jump that high. Can I ride him?"

"No!" Julia and Christian said together.

Julia realized how vehement she had sounded. "Callie, your pony just ran away, for goodness' sake. You're not quite ready for Night Ranger." She paused. "Christian, is she all right?"

"Looks all right to me. Looks very excited, as a matter of fact."

"Are you the Christian who went to jail?" Callie said.

"I'm afraid so."

"I think that's so mean. They should pay you a lot of money for making you do that. He didn't do anything, Ramon, and they sent him to jail," Callie said.

"That happens a lot in my country," Ramon said. "I'm Ramon Lopez."

"Christian Carver."

Julia pictured the two men shaking hands without dismounting. "Is that dog still under my horse?" She was desperate to leave.

"Oh, look!" Callie was practically cooing. "Oh, can I pet him?"

"Her," Christian said. "Just a minute. Let me get your pony. We don't want a repeat."

"Callie, I think we'd better go—" Julia was interrupted by the sound of feet striking the ground, then her daughter's voice at her side.

"Oh, look. She's so pretty. You're so pretty, aren't you? And what a silly little dog. Don't you know how little you are and how big a horse is?"

Julia stared straight ahead. "Will someone please tell me what's happening?"

"Your daughter is falling in love with my dog," Christian said.

"She's always loved dogs." It seemed inane, ridiculous, to be having this conversation. She wanted to scream; she wanted to sob.

"She has a few, I guess."

"Well, no." Bard hadn't wanted them.

"She should," Ramon said. "Maybe Moondrop Morning, he would behave if he was used to dogs."

"She's kissing me, Mommy!"

"I knew this dog was good for something," Christian said.

Both men laughed. Julia didn't know what to say or do. The situation was so impossible it defied convention.

"She's a cutie," Christian said, and Julia knew he wasn't talking about the puppy.

She tried to sound grateful. "Thank you."

"I thought she'd look like you, though."

"She does. Through the eyes."

"Look at me, Callie."

Julia's heart seemed to pause.

"Maybe a little," Christian said at last.

She closed her eyes and tried not to cry.

Christian lowered his voice. "Julia, the other night..."

"It's all right, Christian."

"I didn't know...."

She assumed he was talking about her loss of sight. "Of course you didn't. How could you?"

"I'm sorry."

"I've never been sorrier than when my daughter's pony ran away...." She drew a deep, shaky breath. "And I couldn't—"

"It's all right. Nothing happened."

"Aren't you going to ask why a blind woman's riding when she can't take care of herself, much less her daughter?"

"It sounds like a question you expect to hear from somebody."

"I think we'd better go."

"If I can tear my puppy away."

"Thank you again."

"No problem. I found out Ranger and I can still make it over a fence. That was a real bonus."

In her mind she saw the young Christian Carver sailing over hurdles on his glorious gray. If she had known what was in store for her that long-ago spring day, would she have left Claymore Park and never looked back?

She heard her daughter's delighted squeal as Callie continued to play with the puppy.

The answer was clear.

20

When Christian got back to Claymore Park with Clover, Peter was in the stables talking to a remarkably lovely woman with cropped strawberry-blond hair and a nose dotted with freckles. She was dressed in jeans and a green-and-yellow Claymore Park sweatshirt. "How'd she do?" he called, as Christian dismounted.

"By she, you mean Clover? I have a solution for you."

Peter looked down at the puppy. "All the pistols are locked up in the house."

"She spooked Callie Warwick's pony."

The young woman seemed concerned. "Is Callie all right?"

Peter interrupted to introduce them. "Christian, this is Samantha Fields, one of our trainers. She's been on vacation for the past week."

"I've been cleaning house and doing laundry," Samantha said. "A year's worth. Hello, Christian." She held out her hand. "Callie is my daughter Tiffany's best friend."

He extended his own. Until that moment he'd nearly forgotten what it felt like to hold, even briefly, a woman's hand. Samantha's was anything but soft, but compared to his it was narrow and small-boned. Long repressed desires reasserted themselves.

"So, you were telling us about Callie?" she said.

"She's fine. She was leading a trail ride of sorts with her mother and a man named Ramon."

"Ramon Lopez. He works at Millcreek Farm," Peter said.

Christian continued. "The pony took off thanks to Clover. I had to help her stop him."

"Julia's okay?" Samantha said.

"Seems to be."

"She's pretty daring to be riding now that she's blind."

"What?" Peter interrupted. "What are you talking about?"

"You hadn't heard?" Samantha asked.

"I know she took a fall and went to the hospital, but I thought she was fine."

Samantha shook her head. "I hate to think about it. She's one of the nicest people I know and the only nice adult at Millcreek."

"Sa-man-tha," Peter warned, but he was smiling.

"Sorry, but it's true. That husband of hers—" She paused. "Whoops, tell me he's not a friend of yours?" she asked Christian.

"No." Christian knew he should be salivating over this long-legged dynamo; instead he was hanging on every word about Julia.

"Bard Warwick doesn't deserve a daughter like Callie," Samantha said. "He wouldn't be happy with her if she was perfect. He'd find something to criticize."

Christian found that hard to imagine, since in his brief encounter with Callie he had found nothing to criticize whatsoever.

"So what about the puppy?" Peter said.

Christian addressed his question to Samantha. "Callie doesn't have a dog?"

"No, I don't think she has any pet besides Feather Foot. Old Bard probably wouldn't allow it. Small friendly creatures of any species seem to be on his hit list."

"She and Clover hit it off. I think we should make one little girl very happy."

"Give Clover to Callie?" Peter said. "Will Julia let you?"

"I thought I'd ask Maisy," Christian said. He had no intention of getting close enough to Julia again for a conversation.

"I don't think Julia would be the problem," Samantha said. "But you know, Julia's living with her parents now. Maybe Bard Warwick doesn't have that much to say about what she does and doesn't do for Callie these days."

"She is? Julia's staying at Ashbourne?" Peter sounded surprised again. "Why don't I know anything?"

"Because you're not the least bit interested in gossip unless it affects who's hunting with you and who's not," Samantha said.

Christian cut to the chase. "Shall we give the puppy to Callie?"

"If they promise to have her spayed," Peter said. "I don't want any accidents with the pack."

"I'm sure that won't be a problem."

"Then why not? It's a humane solution." Peter lifted a hand in farewell and started toward the house.

"We've met before," Samantha told Christian when Peter was gone.

"I can't believe I wouldn't remember."

"I was a friend of Fidelity Sutherland's."

He was searching his memory, but she made it easier. "My ex-husband, Tiffany's father, was one of Fidelity's conquests, a polo player named Joachim Hernandez. Is this sounding familiar?"

He shook his head. "I'm sorry. Which came first, your friendship with Fidelity or Fidelity going after your husband?"

"Unfortunately she set her sights on him *after* we were married. I was away on a shoot, and he told her we were separated. She didn't bother to check her facts."

"I'm getting sorrier."

"It doesn't matter now. Both of them are dead. Joachim was killed in a bar brawl a couple of years after our divorce. In a way, Fidelity did me a favor. That was the first time I realized Joachim was lower on the evolutionary scale than a salamander. It took a few extra years and a kid to get up my courage to leave him, but Fidelity started me down the road."

Christian had a sudden vision of a sleek, handsome Argentinian and a rail-thin model with long, red hair. "You were on the cover of...*Vogue?*"

"Never, unfortunately, or I'd be a rich woman. "But I was inside a time or two. In the days when eating once a week was a treat."

"You look better now."

"I'm so sorry about everything that happened to you. And to Fidelity. I wanted to hate her, but I never could. She wasn't mean-spirited, just careless. No one ever taught her not to grab for everything she wanted."

"How did you end up here?"

"I think I married Joachim because I loved horses."

Christian smiled, and she smiled with him. "Once I was single again, I realized I'd rather ride than simper at a camera. And I had Tiffany to think about. I didn't want to jet off to shabbier and shabbier shoots and leave her with God knows who. So I came here about six years ago. Started as assistant to the manager, took his job, then worked my way up to trainer once Peter saw what I could do in my free time."

"How well did you know Fidelity at the end of her life?"

"As well as anybody did, I suppose. We had Joachim in common by then."

"You know about Karl Zandoff."

"Uh-huh."

"Does he look familiar to you at all? Did you ever see him or anyone like him hanging around Fidelity?"

"That was a long time ago. She was nice to everybody. It was part of her charm. But she surrounded herself with the wealthy and the popular. It's hard to imagine a man like that anywhere near her."

"What about others? I'm trying to put it all together. I'm the only person in the world who knows for sure that I didn't have anything to do with her death."

"Then who better to find out who did?" She squatted to ruffle Clover's ears. "Before and after Joachim there was a steady stream of men in and out of her bed."

"Do you remember any names?"

"Get out the phone book."

He must have looked shocked. "I'm serious, Christian. I remember thinking that Fidelity was living her life like a racehorse galloping to the finish line. Did she know she was going to die, do you think? Was she trying to grab everything before she did?"

"What else was she trying to grab?"

"That whole crowd was into drugs."

"Including you?"

"Nothing like them to keep weight off. But I was too smart to do anything more than abuse a few prescriptions. Fidelity was into the expensive designer stuff."

"Do you have names you'd share with me?"

"I'll do anything I can for you." She smiled again, not a blatant, come-hither smile, just a healthy, outdoorsy, all-American come-on.

He thought of Julia Ashbourne Warwick, with her sightless eyes, expressive features and tension-racked body. He thought of his own, traitorous reaction to her today. He had wanted, more than anything and despite everything, to scoop her off her horse and carry her away on his.

"The names will do for now," he said tightly.

She didn't seem offended. "Then I'll see what I can remember. Just be careful. These guys can play for keeps."

"Somebody already did. I mean to find out who."

"It's been a long time since we've had fresh fish," Maisy told Jake, kissing his cheek. Jake's fishing buddy tooted his horn as he raced down the driveway, and both of them waved.

"I had a good day," he said, holding up a stringer with tomorrow night's dinner. "How about you?"

"Terrific. Of course, that's about to end."

"Is it?" Moonlight cast a glow over his white head, something just short of a halo.

She was sorry he looked so beatific. Standing up to an angel was tough. "Yep. We're about to fight."

"You don't say."

"A rip-snortin', no-holds-barred, rootin'-tootin'—"

"Why?" Jake asked.

"Well, far be it from me to create a reason, but—"

"Maisy, what's going on? And whose truck is that in our driveway?"

"Funny you should ask those two questions at the very same time."

Jake was good at waiting. He waited now, knowing he would get his answer when her patience gave out.

"Why don't we take a little moonlight stroll and look at it together?" She tucked her arm through his.

"I'm sweaty, and I smell like fish."

"Sexy smells, both of them."

"Are we going to do more than stroll in the moonlight?"

"Would you like to?"

"I thought I'd already caught my share of fish today. Maybe not."

He hung the stringer over the fence, and they strolled toward the barn where the new truck was parked. "Jake, a very wise man has been telling me recently that I don't communicate the things that are important to me. At least I think that's what he's been saying."

"I would listen, if I were you. Wise men are hard to come by."

She tightened her grip. "There are a lot of things I need to say. I don't have a clue how to say most of them. Or when. Or even why."

"You're doing pretty well right now."

"Well, here's the thing. One of them just hopped up and popped me in the head yesterday."

"One of those things you needed to say?"

"Yes, well. And needed to do. One of those things I needed to do."

"So you did it? Or you're about to?"

"Well, both. I did it, and now I'm about to show it to you."

He stopped about twenty feet from the truck. "It's a very beautiful pickup, Maisy. And don't you think it's about time? I was repairing the repairs on the old one. There wasn't one piece left of the original."

She stood very still. "You old coot! Why didn't you tell me you wanted another one?"

"You have to be at least seventy to be a coot."

"I have hinted and whined and wheedled for years to get a new truck."

"That's right."

"Well, why didn't you do something?"

"I did."

"What!"

"I waited for you to take the matter into your own hands. You look pleased. Are you pleased?"

"As punch!"

"This truck's too good to waste on Loudoun County. We could buy a camper top and take it across country, over mountains, drive right straight through rivers. Nothing can stop us. We can lie in bed at night and look out at the stars. You can cuddle close. I can cuddle closer."

She was so happy she wanted to sing. "Are you sure coot's reserved for seventy and above?"

"It's a beautiful truck, Maisy. Let's climb inside."

"Well, inside's good. But I tossed a couple of bales of hay in the bed and spread them around. There are a couple of old blankets on top of it. You'll see. We could lie down and look at the stars tonight...."

"Just at the stars?"

"I do have to read to Julia...."

"There's still plenty of evening left, isn't there?"

"Have I told you lately that I love you?"

"There should be music with that." He put his arms around her and pulled her close. "I think I hear some about to be made."

From the unpublished novel *Fox River*, by Maisy Fletcher

Our ship sailed a week through peaceful waters, but I am not a sailor. I was wretchedly ill for the whole voyage, never quite getting my sea legs. Ian, though annoyed, was relatively good-natured about it, particularly after he discovered several other horse enthusiasts on board.

On arrival in Southampton we traveled to London, rested one night, then started for Italy by train. I hadn't realized how tired I still was or how much the wedding and now the trip had depleted me. By the time we left the station I was still speechless with fatigue, wishing only to sleep until we arrived.

Ian, who had shown some sympathy for my *mal de mer*, could not understand my exhaustion. He insisted that I keep him company, sitting in our compartment rather than taking to my bed again. He had married me, he said, for conversation, not for how lovely I looked asleep.

Guilt assailed me. Surely I had neglected him, perhaps worse than I'd been aware of. This was our wedding trip, and I suspected there would be few trips in our future.

I sat with him, struggling to keep my eyes open and my conversation witty. He drank whiskey throughout the day, nearly half a bottle, then in the evening ordered dinner to be brought to us. The courses went on and on, and by the meal's end I wondered if he had forced me to eat them just to see how long I would obey him and stay awake.

But I was being silly. This was our wedding trip, and the food was remarkable.

We retired at last, and Ian took me in his arms. Because of my illness on the ship, this was the first time he had approached me since New York. I resisted as he stripped off my nightgown, but if he realized it, he gave no sign.

"Ian, I still don't feel well," I cautioned him.

"You'll feel better when we've finished."

He was determined, and I was chagrined that I had denied him my favors on our voyage. He was a newly married man, and I was the woman he had chosen after years of solitude. I hoped he would be quick and that I might go to sleep at last when he'd finished.

But if he knew what I hoped for, he gave no sign. He took his pleasure slowly, then, just as I was finally falling asleep, he took it again for good measure. When he fell asleep at last, I lay awake, tense and unhappy, wondering if I had any reason to be either.

He apologized the next morning, or at least attempted to. I, of course, interrupted to tell him it was my fault. I should not have been a seasick bride, and if his patience had run out, it was more than understandable.

I vowed to put his behavior behind me, and as our train crossed into Italy we snuggled together like the newlyweds we were.

It was nearly evening of a long, hot day by the time we reached Venice, and we disembarked at the station to find that my fairy tale had resumed. Never had I seen anything as exotic, as lovely, as Venice, even in July, when the summer heat steamed up from the canals, and tourists crowded and befouled the waterways. We traveled to our hotel in a private gondola, although the vaporetti were a less lavish way to make the journey. The hotel, a white marble palazzo, had been highly recommended to Ian. It was directly on the Grand Canal and within an easy walk of Piazza San Marco with its glorious basilica, clock tower and flocks of pigeons.

Our rooms were lovely, with views of the water from three windows temporarily shuttered against the sun, and graceful old furniture that had been crafted during the rise and fall of centuries of Venetian doges. I was enchanted, but Ian was not.

"The damn city smells like a sewer."

"I'm afraid it is, more or less, darling. Particularly with these crowds and this heat."

He faced me. His cheeks were ruddy and his forehead damp with sweat. I was sure I looked no better. "Are you complaining, Louisa?"

"Explaining." I smiled. "But it was silly. Because you already knew that, didn't you?"

He didn't smile in return. "It will cool off when the sun sets."

"And we can throw open our shutters and peer out at the Grand Canal. Surely this is the most romantic place in the world."

As our trunks were delivered he went to take a cool bath, and I supervised the unpacking. He seemed happier when he returned, and I followed his lead, taking my time to wash off the grime of travel.

In the tub I was roused from a near stupor by the sound of angry voices in our sitting room.

I heard the door slam, then silence.

I was unsure what to do. Question him? Comfort him? But before I could decide, he stormed into the bath. "Did you cancel the food I ordered?"

I hadn't realized he'd asked for a meal to be sent up

to our room, and I told him so. But by then he was sitting on the edge of the tub and his eyes were blazing.

"He said the *signora* asked for the things he just brought."

He was so angry that for a moment I felt afraid. "He must have the wrong parties, Ian. He's mixed up the rooms. I didn't even think to order anything. I thought you'd want to dine downstairs."

"I am a patient man, a good enough man, I think, and I ask very little. But I will not have you or anyone else making changes without consulting me. Do you understand?"

I was growing angry now. I had already explained myself, but I was afraid to argue with him. I was undressed, and he was fully clothed, and I wasn't yet accustomed to being naked in front of him. "I'll always consult you," I promised, in clipped tones. "There's simply been a mistake."

He leaned toward me. "Honesty is very important to me. Do you understand that?"

"Ian, who are you going to believe? An employee of the hotel or your wife?"

I don't know what he might have said or done next. But there was a knock at our door, and Ian got up to answer it. I fled the tub, toweling myself dry and slipping into a silk wrapper.

He was sitting at the small table overlooking the Grand Canal when I entered the room. The shutters had been opened, and the sky was blazing with all the colors of sunset. It was still sweltering, but at least a breeze trailed through the windows now.

He looked up at my appearance. "Our food has arrived."

"I see it has."

"Come and enjoy it."

"I hope he told you there had been a mistake."

Ian frowned. "I said come and eat."

I joined him across the narrow table, but I didn't pick up my fork.

"He said he'd made a mistake," Ian said at last. He clearly wasn't pleased he had to admit it.

My anger disappeared. "It's been a long dusty day." I leaned across the table and put my hand over his. "But the night will be cooler and just as long."

"There are some things that drive me to distraction," he said, in a gruff voice.

"We're all that way."

"I won't have anyone going behind my back and making changes."

"I'll be sure to remember that."

"And I won't allow anyone to lie to me."

"Ian, you've married the right woman. I have no reason to lie to you."

And I didn't.

At least not at that moment.

21

Maisy hummed her way through breakfast and cleanup. Jake was gone already, but Julia hadn't yet come down. Karen was dropping Callie off at school on her way to do the grocery shopping. Maisy scraped plates and stacked them in the sink to soak, then she scrubbed counters, moving from "Baby, I Need Your Loving" to "Unchained Melody" without so much as a breath.

"Somebody sounds happy this morning."

Maisy turned to find her daughter in the doorway. "It's a beautiful day. Did you sleep well?"

Julia was silent.

"I guess not," Maisy said. Julia looked as if she hadn't closed her eyes.

"I had a lot running through my mind. Your story for one. It bothered me. I lay awake trying to figure out why. Then I realized."

Maisy waited.

"You're trying to tell me something, aren't you?"

Maisy rinsed and squeezed her sponge before she answered. "I'm reading you my first novel. I guess I'm trying to tell you I want to be a writer."

"You *are* a writer. A good enough writer to keep me awake last night."

"I suppose that's good news for me."

"Maisy, I know what you're doing."

"Do you?"

"This isn't a simple romance, is it? You've patterned Ian after somebody."

Maisy attacked the smudges on the refrigerator door. "They say that every character a novelist invents is based on people she's known, even if she doesn't realize it."

"Darn it, stop evading the truth. You've patterned him on Bard."

"What makes you think so?"

"I don't have to go into this. You know the similarities are there." Julia moved to the table, finding the edge and feeling her way to a seat. "Louisa marries a man who can give her an easy life. She convinces herself she's in love with him, then she begins to see another side of his personality. He's demanding, controlling and given to fits if things don't please him."

"That's my story so far. But you're the only one who would know if it's your story, too."

"You've never liked Bard. You still don't like Bard. You never will like Bard."

Maisy put down her sponge. "You don't like Bard yourself these days. Don't put your feelings on me, kiddo. I have enough of my own to worry about."

Julia looked in her direction. Maisy was still disconcerted whenever her daughter's stare was off target. Julia lowered her gaze. "You know, I think I've apologized more in the last week than I ever have before. What's wrong with me?"

"More than usual."

Julia gave an unladylike snort.

Maisy filled the coffeepot with fresh water, then went for the Folgers. "I know things aren't going well with Bard. That's obvious."

"I was so young when I married him. Like your Louisa."

"Louisa wasn't pregnant, and she hadn't just seen the man she loved sentenced to life in prison."

"When I married Bard I made a commitment I had every intention of keeping."

"'Had,' Julia?"

"I guess I don't want to face the truth, but here it is. I'm not getting any closer to going back to Millcreek, Maisy. If my sight came back with the first sip of coffee, I still wouldn't pack and head straight home.''

''Then this really is a separation? Not a convenience?''

''I wish I could see your face right now. Are you smiling?''

''Gloating, you mean? No. Your marriage is breaking up. How could that make me happy?''

Julia lowered her voice. ''Just saying it makes *me* happy. A part of me feels devastated, but a part of me feels like I've opened a window and fresh air is sweeping into my life.''

Maisy didn't know what to say.

Julia stretched her hands out in front of her. ''I don't know how this will end. But I don't see how I can go home to a man who is only happy when I do exactly what he wants.'' She paused. ''A man you're portraying in your book.''

''Julia, you can read anything you want into my story. That's your prerogative. But it's a story.''

''Nothing more,'' Julia said. ''So you say.''

Maisy flipped on the coffeemaker. ''I made scrambled eggs for everyone else. What would you like?''

Christian hadn't thought through the difficulties of cornering Maisy alone to ask about the puppy. A foolproof plan to avoid Julia, which had seemed simple enough on the surface, was turning out to be difficult. In the long run it was going to be easier and more effective to simply ask Julia if her daughter could adopt Clover.

He and Julia were going to be thrown together through the years. That was inevitable. It was better to inoculate himself now with small doses.

The hounds were taking a well-deserved rest from a long morning walk when he finally went to saddle Ranger for a ride. He was waylaid, though, by a call from Pinky Stewart.

''I don't know much yet,'' Pinky told him quietly and without preliminary, as if he were afraid of being overheard. ''But Davey Myers Construction out of Warrenton seems to be the outfit that was doing most of the building around Ridge's Race and Middleburg back in the early nineties.''

Christian thanked him, and Pinky hung up.

"Did you tell me you had to pick up some supplies over at Horse Country in Warrenton?" Christian asked Samantha, who was grooming one of Claymore Park's famous broodmares.

She flashed him a smile, and despite the freckles and the boyishly cut hair he saw a glimpse of the glamour girl he remembered. "Somebody does. You volunteering?"

"They'll have the order ready?"

"All ready. Should be a load of..." She counted on her fingers silently. "Eight boxes. Nine, tops."

"I'll be a while."

"Want me to ride that horse of yours? Looks like he was expecting a little exercise."

"No, I'll do it as soon as I get back."

"See ya."

He thought about questions to ask as he whizzed past other estates dedicated to the good life of horsemanship, fresh air and enough surplus cash to pay off the national debt. He picked up the order first, then followed the directions he'd gotten at Horse Country to the headquarters of Davey Myers Construction. The office was in a small, dilapidated warehouse with a fleet of aging trucks in the driveway. Once past a bored receptionist, he waited in an office cluttered with papers and rusting file cabinets. Once Myers might have been successful, but despite the building boom of the past few years, the company didn't seem to be prospering now.

"What can I do for you?" A man of about seventy strolled into the office. He had a bulldog face and a body that reminded Christian of a clown's, oversize feet in shiny white shoes, pants stretched over a hula hoop-size belly.

"You're Davey Myers?"

"Used to be. Now I'm just an old man trying to keep up in a young man's world." He said it cheerfully.

"I understand you were the top contractor in the area back in the early nineties."

"Yeah. Then I had a stroke and my foreman ran off with half my crew *and* my third wife—what a looker she was, and only forty-five."

Christian whistled softly.

Myers looked pleased. "To add insult to injury, the government decided to take a close look at my bookkeeping." He motioned Christian to a seat.

Christian removed a stack of papers and set them carefully on the floor. He lowered himself to the chair and watched Davey Myers do the same. "But you're still in business."

"If you call this business. Licenses and insurance here, taxes there. I got the federal government, the state of Virginia, the city of Warrenton." He waved his hands in the air. "Don't get me started."

"I'm hoping you can help me a little, Davey."

"I know who you are. I still see good enough to read the papers."

"Then you've probably guessed what I'm doing here."

"Let's see if I'm right."

Christian told him about his search for all the facts behind Fidelity's murder. "I was told you might have been the one who hired Zandoff," he concluded. "That's why I'm here."

"And you think I might tell you something I didn't tell the cops?"

"No. I just hoped you'd tell me whatever you told them."

"You caught a bad break, kid. I know how it feels."

"Sounds like you do."

"So here's what I told them. I don't remember this Karl Zandoff creep. He's a nobody, nohow, as far as I'm concerned. And I never paid nobody under the table. I don't care what kind of crap they came up with, they went through my records. I had a bad accountant, a real bozo, you know? He couldn't add two and two without a calculator."

Christian imagined Myers was telling the truth about one thing, at least. This probably *was* what he'd told the cops.

"If I went out on one of your jobs today," Christian said, "how many immigrants would I find working for you?"

"Hell, they're the only people you can hire anymore. Everybody else wants to work with computers, wants to be a millionaire without getting dirt under their fingernails."

"And if I asked, every single one of your men would have a legitimate green card, right? Every paper would be in order."

Myers grinned. "I'm not so good at catching men in a lie anymore, you know? They tell me they have a green card, they show me something green..." He shrugged.

"Maybe you remember Zandoff, but you're afraid the cops will find out your accountant screwed up Zandoff's records, or maybe you're afraid that foreman of yours did something he wasn't supposed to and you'll be left holding the bag."

Myers leaned forward, knocking another stack of papers to the floor. "You know what? I'd tell you if I did. Just between us. But I've stared at photographs ever since the police told me I might have hired this guy. I mean, what a creepy thought, you know? Here's Zandoff, up on one of my roofs, checking out the pretty girls walking by." He made a face. "I had nightmares."

"Nightmares but no memories?"

"I've hired hundreds of men in my day. If he was one of them, I just don't remember." He tapped his head. "Stroke took a lot with it."

Christian wished him well and stood to leave. At the door, Myers told him the names of a couple of other construction companies to try. "I thought for a while..." Myers scratched his nearly bald head. "I did a lot of work over that way. Got promised a lot more, too, not far from where the girl was murdered. So I asked what men I got left that used to be with me back then. Nobody remembered the guy. Nobody. Nohow."

"I don't remember a lot of new construction going up. Some barns, a house or two. Is that the kind of stuff you did?"

"Nah, we did one of those prissy, upscale developments. Fancy schmancy houses. Take a hundred acres and put ten houses on it. City people think they're living in the wilds of Alaska. Expect to see grizzly bears. I made money on that project."

"Near Ridge's Race?"

"Just west."

Christian thought he knew the development in question. At the time he hadn't thought anything of it, but an old estate had been subdivided, and the locals hadn't been happy. "There was talk of a lawsuit to stop it, wasn't there?"

Myers waved his hand. "Nothing to it. We had our permits. We got the land fair and square. Course afterward, the town of

Ridge's Race—if you can call that pissing little dot on the map a town—passed every ordinance they could to stop us. Didn't even matter by then. The land we wanted wasn't for sale."

"What land, do you remember?"

Myers looked as if he was trying, but he shook his head. "Can't. Sorry."

"I don't suppose you'd have records?"

Davey Myers just grinned.

Evening seemed to fall earlier every day, and it was twilight when Christian finally rode to Ashbourne. He'd thought about stopping on his way home from Warrenton, but by the time he had spoken—unsuccessfully—to two other builders Myers had suggested, the afternoon had slipped by. He'd had supplies to unload and a hound who had just come home from the vet. It was after dinner before he could saddle Night Ranger.

He stepped down from the saddle several hundred yards from the stone house and led Ranger the rest of the way. He and the horse were already doing better. His legs were stronger, and Ranger seemed to be enjoying life. He shoved Christian now with his nose, as if to propel him along.

Christian laughed and moved a little faster.

He tied Ranger a distance from the house, near an old stone watering trough that Maisy had planted with chrysanthemums. He heard laughter from inside, a sound that would probably always remind him of years spent without it. Light spilled from the windows. He smelled wood smoke. Jake always liked a fire, even when the weather didn't warrant one.

He didn't have to knock. Callie, with a child's finely tuned ears, had heard him approach. Or so she told him as she barreled out the door right into him.

"I heard you coming. Where's your horse?"

He squatted to speak to her eye to eye. "If I tell you, will you promise to stay a safe distance away from him? He's a good horse, no mistaking it. But I don't know if he's used to children."

"I won't get close. I promise. Oh, I see him!" She dashed down the steps.

"Christian, what a nice surprise." Maisy stood in the doorway wiping her hands on a dish towel. Today she was dressed in a Hawaiian muumuu. Bare toes with fuchsia toenails peeked out from under the hem.

He couldn't believe his luck. "I came to talk to you about something."

"We're about to sit down to dinner. Have you eaten?"

He had assumed they would eat earlier. He didn't know much about children, but he knew they hated to wait. "I ate already, thanks."

"That's too bad. We have fresh trout. You always liked the way I cooked them. I remember."

He remembered family meals when he and Julia played footsie under the Fletchers' table, exchanged torrid glances—and kisses when everyone else left the room. He remembered one meal, just before he was sent to prison, when he and Julia went upstairs after her parents left for the evening and made sad, desperate love. Their last time together.

"It's about Callie," he said. "That's why I came."

Maisy seemed to stiffen. "You really ought to be having this conversation with Julia, honey."

"Well, I probably should. But I'd rather talk to you."

Maisy stepped down so they were level. "Where's Callie?"

"I sent her off to talk to Night Ranger. She promised to stay back. Will she?"

"She's a good child, but horses are a temptation."

"He's big enough to intimidate her a little."

"Christian, I really think you should be having this conversation with my daughter."

"Julia told you what happened yesterday?"

"I heard all about it. I'm so glad you came along when you did."

"I didn't want to say anything then..."

Maisy looked upset. "Christian, I—"

He cut her off. "I had to talk to Peter first, anyway. But he's in agreement. Callie was taken with the puppy. And we can't keep her. Will you talk to Julia and see if she'd let Callie have Clover? I think she'll be a good pet, just not any good with the pack." He grinned wryly. "She's not the brightest bulb in the chandelier."

"That's what you came for? You want to give Callie a puppy?"

Christian frowned. From the surprised expression on Maisy's face, he could only guess she thought that was inappropriate.

And perhaps it was, considering their history. Perhaps it sounded like he was trying to wiggle back into the life he'd been torn from. Perhaps she thought he was trying to make another man's child love him. After all, he had once loved the child's mother.

He stepped backward. "Look, I'm sorry. I guess it was a stupid idea. Forget it. Don't even bother Julia with—"

"Bother me with what?"

He looked up and saw Julia standing on the porch. He felt as trapped as he had the first day a cell door had closed behind him.

"It doesn't matter." He turned to go.

"Christian has a wonderful idea," Maisy said quickly. "He wants to give Callie the puppy who caused all the problems yesterday. He said the two of them got along so well, it just seemed natural."

Christian turned around to see that Julia looked surprised. "That's why you're here?" she said.

"We can't keep the pup. She's the worst excuse for a fox-hound I've ever seen. But she'll make a great little pet. I just thought Callie might like to have her."

"I'll let you two decide." Maisy hitched up her muumuu and scurried back up the stairs. "You can do it inside, if you'd rather," she called over her shoulder.

"No," Julia and Christian said together. Julia felt for the porch rail and descended. "For somebody who told me you never want to see me again, you sure are showing up a lot."

He examined her before he spoke. She was a woman who would age well. Good bones, classic features. She had never depended on clothes or makeup to cover up who she was. She was too thin, a little haggard, and the blank stare disconcerted him.

But to him, sadly, she was still beautiful.

"This was a mistake," he said. "I just thought..."

"You thought what?"

"I don't know."

"Christian..." She shook her head. "Do you know how often I've wished the past nine years never happened?"

He had not expected this conversation. He had not expected Julia to dive straight into his heart. "Not as often as I did, I bet."

"You were my whole world."

"Some part of that whole world thought I'd murdered Fidelity."

"You'll never forgive me for that, will you?"

"How important could I have been to you? You married another man before we could even talk about it."

"You were too hurt to talk about it. You wouldn't call and I couldn't call you. You told me you wouldn't read any letter I sent."

"Tell me now. How could you have believed I'd cut your best friend's throat?"

"I didn't believe it. But that whole world I was talking about came tumbling down around me. Can't you understand that? Of course it was worse for you, but it was terrible for me, too. Fidelity was gone, they were trying to take you away. And they caught you with the knife that killed her. Your knife."

He could feel some of his bitterness seeping away. Julia had hardly slept after Fidelity's death. He remembered that now. During the trial she had told him that every time she closed her eyes she saw Fidelity in a pool of blood. She'd hardly eaten. He remembered the last time they'd made love, and how frighteningly thin she had been. Thin enough to take his mind off his own growing fear that the truth would not be discovered in time to save him.

She spoke softly. "On the witness stand I remember feeling like I was completely alone. That you were a million miles away and I couldn't reach you. That I was alone with a million lights and cameras focused on me, and people shouting at me to see reason."

"That's not the way it was, Julia."

"That's how it felt. Like I was a bug under a microscope, that all those people knew something I didn't. Just for a moment. The worst moment." Tears filled her eyes. "I have relived it every single day. I tried to forget, but I couldn't. I felt like I'd put you in prison, Christian. One moment of doubt had turned the final key."

He wanted to be glad that all the years he'd suffered, she had suffered, too. Perhaps he could have gloated if the woman he had demonized for nine years had ever really existed. But he saw now that she hadn't. This was the woman he had loved. Older, sadder and racked with guilt over one moment's betrayal. Too thin, still. Probably not sleeping well. Still. Blind now, because her body had turned against her.

He touched her cheek. She jumped, obviously not expecting it. He rubbed his thumb along the trail of a tear. Her skin was as soft as rose petals. A woman's skin. Rose petals. Both had been in such short supply in his life.

He dropped his hand. "Why did you marry Bard Warwick?"

"I fell apart. He put me back together."

"Are you happy? Were you happy? Before..."

"Before I stopped seeing the world around me?" She shook her head. "No."

"I'm sorry." He wasn't. He supposed his selfishness was to be expected. He had spent so many nights imagining her happy in Warwick's arms. He was glad she hadn't been, even though he thought less of himself for his own reaction.

"I had Callie," she said. "That seemed like enough."

He remembered why he had come. Not to settle the past, but simply to give this woman's child a gift. "Will you think about the puppy? Not because it comes from me. If you think it would make her happy. If it's not too much trouble right now to have a pet."

"I'll ask Maisy and Jake. If I go back to Millcreek—"

"*If?*"

"Bard doesn't really like dogs. We'd have to leave the puppy here. But Callie could come every day and visit."

"Then you'll think about it?" he said.

"I'll think about a lot of things, Christian. I can't stop thinking."

He closed his eyes, and the world was dark. He wondered how

she stood it. Did she will herself to see again, failing every moment? But he understood what it meant to be blind. Hadn't he been blind for years where this woman was concerned? She had loved him, and he had let a moment of indecision kindle the worst kind of hatred.

Wasn't hating the person you loved most the greatest of sins?

"Call me when you decide," he said.

"Christian, thank you. It's a wonderful offer."

"She seems like a wonderful little girl."

"You have no idea." She stretched out her hand. He hesitated. "Squeeze it," she whispered.

He couldn't refuse.

"Maisy?" Jake came up behind Maisy in the kitchen and put his arms around her waist. "What's wrong?"

Maisy wiped her eyes. "Do you remember just before Fidelity was killed? I woke up every night for a week feeling like the breath was being squeezed from my lungs. And it got worse afterward."

"Premonitions?"

"I don't see the future. But I feel other people's distress. I can feel things happening around me, things pushing in all around us. I learned to do that when I was young."

"And you feel it now?"

"Don't you?"

"Julia has to live her own life."

"I'm her mother. I needed to warn her to be careful. Instead I tried to keep her safe. Now she can't see."

"You were a good mother. The best."

She faced him. "Things will get worse before they get better, Jake."

"They often do."

Maisy heard a noise in the front hall and knew her daughter and granddaughter were coming. She would eat Jake's trout, perhaps help put Callie to bed, then she would read another chapter to Julia. Afterward, with Jake sleeping beside her, she would lie awake and fight for every breath.

"Just don't leave us, no matter what happens around here," she said. "Stand by us, Jake."

He smiled gently. "Haven't I always?"

From the unpublished novel *Fox River*, by Maisy Fletcher

Our welcome home after our wedding trip was enthusiastic. Annie and her parents had a party in our honor, and Ian slipped effortlessly back into his roles as respected community member, Master of Foxhounds and owner of Fox River Farm.

I had more trouble finding my footing. The house had run well without me, and few changes needed to be made now that I was in residence. With the exception of Annie, none of our neighbors, who were few and far between to begin with, were close to my age. Ian, almost twenty years my senior, was the youngest landowner for miles. The children of our neighbors had married and scattered to the four winds. Although the local dowagers were welcoming, there was no one besides Annie with whom I could be friends. Then, one afternoon in September, while we were off on a ride together, Annie gave me unwelcome news.

"I have a secret." We had stopped to rest under century-old maples, our habits pulled above our knees and fanned out around us. "I haven't told Mother and Father yet."

"I love secrets." So far I had kept my own, too embarrassed to share stories of Ian's behavior on our wedding trip. Venice, sinking, decaying monument to a visionary people, had only disgusted my new husband. The scene at our hotel had been one of many. I comforted myself with the hope that Ian was a man happiest and best behaved in his own domain.

"Paul has taken a job as a stockbroker in Chicago. We'll move right after the wedding."

The wedding was in October, and Annie's news was unwelcome. I had hoped, even expected, Paul and Annie to settle near their parents. Land was still cheap enough, and someday they would inherit their parents' property.

"You'll hate the city," I said. "Where will you ride?"

"We've already found a house and a nice piece of land not too far away. Large enough to keep a few horses. I'll be the farmer, and Paul will travel into the city every morning to earn our bread and butter."

"What will your parents do without you?"

Annie looked sad. "My father is thinking of selling Sweetwater. So many people are looking for property in the Fox River Hunt, and he could get a fair price. He claims he has little enthusiasm left for the hard work of raising horses."

"And your mother?"

"She complains of the day-to-day isolation here. They have friends in Chicago and would find more quickly. I hope they'll consider moving there. If Paul and I give them grandchildren, they'll want to be nearby."

Although the Joneses were only distant cousins, they were family—the only family I had outside of New York. Annie's leaving would be devastating enough, but if her parents left, I would be truly alone.

"I don't know what to say." And I didn't. I was realizing for the first time how vital Annie's friendship was to me.

"You and Ian will come and visit, of course. And we'll come and visit you."

"You'll want to see Paul's parents." But she didn't need to remind me that the Symingtons were only residents of Virginia for part of the year. At best we would see each other infrequently.

I resolved to find a way to fit myself more firmly into place here. That evening at supper I approached Ian about having the opening hunt breakfast at Fox River Farm. I knew the governors were in the process of making up fixture cards for the season that announced the date and place for every hunt. The schedule would soon be set.

"Annie tells me it's traditional for the master to give the first hunt breakfast. I wondered if you would like me to see to it?"

He studied me, as he often did. At those times I had no idea what he was thinking, and I'd grown to be wary of them. I was never sure what he might say when he was finished.

"You're young, and you've never organized an event like this one. What makes you think you could pull it off, Louisa?"

"I spent years training to be a proper hostess. It was Mama's life mission."

"And you think study did the trick?"

"You've assembled a good staff here. Lettie is the finest cook for a hundred miles, and she promises she'll turn out a memorable feast. It's just that I want to do something to make you proud of me."

He studied me some more. "And why else?"

I was beginning to fear he might read every passing thought and accuse me again. "I want people to see that I'm more than just a pretty girl who caught your eye."

He smiled warmly, and I relaxed under the unexpected rays.

"Are you feeling lonely?" he said.

"I have you." I returned his smile. "But you have a farm to run, and your duties with the club. This is something I can do to help and still get to know people better at the same time. Unless you'd rather I didn't try."

"Will you be able to give the breakfast and ride the same day?"

"I don't see how. I'll want to be here to make certain everything's perfect. But people will understand, won't they? They'll forgive me this one lapse?"

He considered. "There'll be other hunts."

In truth, there would be far too many for my taste, but I didn't dare spoil his good mood. "Then I'll go ahead with it?"

"I'm glad I have a wife who thinks about what's best for everyone."

The unexpected compliment made my spirits blossom extravagantly. If I could please Ian Sebastian, a stern taskmaster indeed, then I would surely find my place.

I spent the bulk of the next month making preparations. I called on members who had given breakfasts in the past and sought their advice. The women, who were without exception excellent riders and hostesses, were happy to oblige me. Since people would drift in as they finished their day's ride, I needed hearty, simple fare. I settled on a menu that included Brunswick stew, ham with Lettie's buttermilk biscuits, icy bowls of ambrosia, spicy baked beans and, for dessert, apple and pecan pies. Despite Prohibition, the bar would be well stocked. Foxhunters worked up a terrific thirst.

The cubbing season, a training period for green hunters and puppy hounds, was already a success. Ian arose at dawn each morning a hunt was scheduled, and most of the time I went with him to learn what I could. When it was time for my first real hunt, I didn't want to shame him.

In the intimacy of early morning, participating together in the sport that was Ian's life, we seemed to grow closer. Ian was even tempered and considerate, and I began to believe the incidents I'd witnessed in

Italy had been the reactions of a vital, active man who was simply out of his element. He cut a handsome figure, a brilliant rider taking all challenges, but never any so great he couldn't defeat them. On horseback he was the man I had married, the powerful, passionate man in complete control of his environment.

I was determined that the breakfast would be a success. I saw to the preparation of bootlegged rum punch for the men while they waited for the hounds to be cast. I made arrangements for two of the stable boys to come to the house in the morning and relocate the dining-room hunt table that had come from England with Ian's family. They were to place it just off our front veranda so that the punch could be served, as was the custom, without anyone needing to dismount. Once they were off, the real work of setting up for the breakfast would begin. I had decided to arrange the flowers for the tables myself, choosing gold and white spider chrysanthemums, cut from the lovingly maintained flower borders of Ian's longtime gardener Seth.

Ian rose well before dawn. The cubbing season was a time for training and exercising horses and hounds. The dress was less formal, the pace less strenuous. But with the opening hunt of the season, formal attire and protocol were required. When I came downstairs, Ian was already in buff-colored breeches and the traditional scarlet coat—which I had learned to call pink, as tradition demanded. His stock was tied and anchored with the requisite pin, his boots polished and glowing. Men in good standing with the Fox River Hunt wore jackets with forest-green collars, our official color, and sterling buttons etched with a fox's "mask" or head. I straightened Ian's lapels and leaned in for a good morning kiss, but he hadn't the patience nor time.

He moved past me. "I have to see to the horses."

Our groom and the stableboys would do most of the work, but I knew that today, of all days, the horses, Ian's own and those of the huntsman and the whippers-in, had to be perfectly groomed, their manes intricately braided, their coats gleaming. Ian would supervise every detail.

"Then I'll see you when the others begin to arrive." I planned to put out rolls, steaming coffee, fruit and, of course, the rum punch, just in case anyone needed a bite to sustain them before the fun began.

He gave me just a moment, his face unsmiling. "It's an important day, Louisa."

"Yes, of course it is, darling." I knew his job wasn't easy. It was up to Ian to make certain everyone had a good experience while adhering to stringent safety rules and etiquette. "But it'll be a good day. You'll see to it."

"You see to it, as well."

"Everything will come off. I promise. I'll do you proud."

He left without another word, and I went into the kitchen to find Lettie. She was a rail-thin woman in her fifties who had been born a Fox River slave but had been freed before she had memories of slavery. I had listened in fascination for many an afternoon as she described her childhood at Fox River. Occasionally, just to be certain she kept my interest, she would drop tidbits about Ian, but never if I asked for them.

As I expected, Lettie was just taking the first rolls from the oven. "You'll have one yourself and don't tell me no," she said when I found her.

I obliged, although my stomach protested. I hadn't wanted to eat the night before, either, a product, I was sure, of my high expectations for the day.

The rolls were light and flaky, and the butter, from a neighboring farm, was as rich as King Midas. I swallowed the last big bite without chewing. "Seth promised he'd cut flowers for me bright and early, so if there's nothing I have to do here, I'd best go down to the gardener's shed and make the arrangements."

"You tell Seth I said to wash down the walkways," Lettie said. Since she and Seth had been married for almost forty years, she never missed a chance to tell him what to do.

"Anything else, Lettie?"

"You getting scared, Miss Louisa?"

"That's probably silly, isn't it?"

She shook her head. "Mr. Ian can be hard, and you want to please him. I know you do."

"He's my husband."

"Miss Frances tried so hard it wore her out. Just about wore me out, too, watching her."

Her words made me uneasy. "She went home to her family a lot, didn't she?"

"Easy enough to do, they living just over the mountain."

"I imagine that didn't please Ian."

She seemed to think better of the subject. "You run on now. Mary comes in, she and I'll start on the ham biscuits. You just do those flowers and make them pretty as you can."

I put Lettie's words out of my head when I reached the gardener's shed. Seth, older than his wife and fifty pounds heavier, had already cut armloads of gold and white chrysanthemums, black-eyed Susans and Queen Anne's lace, and placed them in jugs of water, along with feathery greens and fern fronds. In a short time I had filled several containers, one to adorn the hunt table and several to grace the porch, where Lettie planned to set up the early-morning fare. When the fox-hunters rode off in search of their prey, I intended to return to the shed and finish arrangements for the table.

Seth helped me carry them up to the house, and it wasn't an instant too soon. Neighbors began to arrive, some from properties close by, some far enough away that they had been forced to rise well before the light to make their way. Some had left home yesterday and stayed overnight with families closer to Fox River Farm, or sent their grooms ahead so they could take the rutted roads this morning in their Mercedes or Packards without encumbrance.

I had known what to expect, but as the scene grew, my heart swelled with the drama of it. The men in their scarlet or black Melton coats and white jodhpurs, some with formal top hats, some with velvet hunting caps. The women in their dark habits, bowlers or caps perched jauntily on upswept hair, skirts draped evenly above their ankles. Then there were the horses, gleaming bays and polished chestnuts, all as perfect as if they had just stepped out of their stable doors. Some of the horses had bits of red ribbon woven into their tails to tactfully point out that they kicked and were best avoided. Some wore colorful blankets that were replaced with stark white saddle blankets by excited grooms brought along for the occasion.

I was greeted with gratitude and enthusiasm. The crowd was varied, as I had expected. The older, more established families were joined by newcomers. Annie and Paul had come, and with them some of the other local young people, back from school or jobs for the festivities. The exodus from the north had begun some weeks ago, and foxhunters had arrived for the season, settling into newly purchased farms or hunting "boxes" they had rented in the area.

I had been bred for this moment, and breeding will show. I took to playing hostess the way a Thoroughbred takes to jumping fences. I chatted, extolled and sympathized, all the while making certain that no one's needs were ignored. I supervised the placement of food and the quantities of rum in the punch, and I glowed at the compliments I received over both.

Until the moment Ian took me aside, eyes blazing and hands clenching his riding crop.

"Do you know what you've done?"

He was so obviously furious that quiet speech was something of a miracle.

I tried to defuse him. "Have I forgotten something?"

"You little idiot. You don't know anything, do you? You've chosen flowers in the colors of the Piedmont and Orange County Hunts!"

I might be a newcomer, but I did know that the two nearby hunts were our rivals. And the rivalry wasn't particularly friendly, since both funds and land were limited. "I didn't know." I was genuinely dismayed. "Nobody ever told me their colors."

"Piedmont is old gold. Orange County is white. You should have known! I thought this was too much for you to manage. You've humiliated me, Louisa."

"How can you think I did it on purpose? It was an honest mistake."

"You should have asked."

"How could I ask if I never thought about the question?"

He stared at me as if I'd grown a new head, but I lifted the only one I had and narrowed my eyes. "There's only one way to salvage an error," I said. "Pretend it isn't an error at all. Ignore it completely. It's all you can do."

"Tell me, does that go for our marriage, too?" His voice was thick with recrimination. "Do I ignore the fact I've married a thoughtless ninny?"

I blinked back tears. "I only wanted to please you."

"You have failed miserably." He was clenching the riding crop so hard that his knuckles paled.

As Ian strolled off to mount his horse for the rum punch toast, I thought of Frances, and Lettie's reminiscences in the kitchen that morning.

I swallowed hard, then again, following far behind him to see the ceremonial send off. Annie, who was riding with Paul and both sets of parents, stopped me. She was mounted on a chestnut mare named Lulabelle that I had ridden happily in my carefree days at Sweetwater. She spoke loudly enough that it was clear she wanted others to overhear.

"Louisa, you are such a brilliant girl. Who else would have thought to combine the colors of the neighboring hunts in her flower arrangements along with our Fox River green? It's a splendid tribute to the comradeship of Virginia foxhunting. Just exactly the kind of reminder we all need at our first hunt of the season.''

"We've set the right example, haven't we?" I said as loudly, holding my chin high in the air.

Someone applauded gaily; then the moment was over. Annie, the soul of diplomacy, had done her best. I wondered if she had overheard anything of my exchange with Ian, or if she had simply heard criticism of me and come up with this solution on her own. Whatever the answer, I was profoundly grateful.

The toast was appropriately jovial. Fifteen couple of hounds had been brought out by the huntsman, and all the riders had finished their last-minute preparations. The horn was lifted and the opening notes sounded. In a flurry of dust and the flicking of equine tails, the Fox River Hunt was off to find a fox.

I stood rooted until the last rider was out of sight. I knew Ian intended to have the hounds cast on the west bank of Fox River, in a valley known simply as "The Dip." He had spotted foxes there during cubbing season, and it seemed the natural place to begin. I hoped they would be successful, but I also hoped they would give me time to make doubly certain nothing else went wrong.

For a moment the injustice of it incensed me. Wasn't it a husband's duty to protect his wife? To smooth over difficulties? To cherish her even if she made an error? Was this the way our marriage would proceed? He would watch and wait, then pounce when my judgment lapsed?

"I hope the poor fox stays in his den," I murmured. Then I went to ask Seth to find more flowers of different colors to add to the table arrangements.

As expected, the hunt began to straggle in about one. The field, made up of all the riders with the exception of the Master of Foxhounds and his staff, invariably consisted of "first flight," the gamest and best riders, and hilltoppers, those who were new to the sport or too old or awkward to excel at it. Additionally, there were foot followers. All had been invited to the breakfast, along with landowners whose property would be used during the season.

Riders arrived according to their skill, the best starting to filter in about four. Annie and Paul arrived and made excuses for the Joneses, who had gone straight to Sweetwater. Mr. Jones had injured a leg on one jump, and Mrs. Jones had insisted they go home before removing his boot. In the meantime, I had fed dozens of people, some who remained and others who started home after a little rest and camaraderie. I heard tales of the fox they had chased, a big red, always thought to be more exciting than the native gray foxes. This fox was much admired for his wily prowess and his ability to stay just ahead of the pack.

I heard the hunting horn sometime later and the hounds "giving tongue" as they made their way back home. I was feeling more charitable toward Ian by then, since I had heard nothing except the most glowing reports about him that day. I was certain that when he'd rested and the field was gone at last, he would be contrite.

I had not expected what awaited me.

I heard the hounds enter the yard and the clatter of horses following close behind. I turned from helping an older neighbor to a more comfortable chair and saw Ian wheel into the yard on Equator, the same black stallion he had ridden the day we met.

I lifted my hand in greeting until he dismounted, then pressed it to my chest in horror. Ian strode toward me, the bloody mask of a large red fox hanging from his right hand. He held it out to me and spoke for all to hear. "For my wife and gracious hostess, who wasn't able to attend the first hunt because of her consideration for the rest of us. We've brought the hunt to you, Louisa, with our gratitude.''

I looked at what was left of an accommodating, clever animal, then up at the man I had married. The satisfaction in Ian's eyes was the last thing I saw before I collapsed in a faint.

22

Since the Mosby hounds belonged to the club, members were expected to participate in their care and given the opportunity to "walk hounds" twice a week. Before hunting season, this was usually done on foot, tramping miles through fields and along country roads. The huntsman and kennel staff always went along, watching out for the hounds and helping members identify and get to know each hound's personality.

The first morning he exercised the hounds with members of the club, Christian steeled himself for trouble. He knew Peter's decision to make him huntsman was unpopular. Peter had been frank about some of the conversations making the rounds and the protest being organized by Bard Warwick. But Peter had held firm, and Christian hadn't experienced anything more than a certain curt civility.

The first big event of the fall, however, was the hunter's pace, and Christian knew if there was going to be trouble, this would be the place for it. He wasn't afraid what people might say or do, but he wasn't looking forward to the experience. He supposed he'd had his fill of being an outcast.

The hunter's pace was a fund-raiser and icebreaker for the season, as well as a chance to introduce the public to the sport of foxhunting. A course was mapped out that was similar to one that might be used during a real hunt. Entrants, riding in teams, rode the course as if they were following hounds. Teams were released every three minutes, and at day's end, the teams who had finished closest to the ideal time agreed on by the judges were the winners. No team consulted a watch nor knew the deadline they were supposed to meet.

The afternoon before the hunter's pace, Christian and Peter mapped out the course, which meandered over Claymore Park, South Land and a corner of Millcreek Farm. "Damn shame Maisy Fletcher closed off Ashbourne," Peter grumbled as they made elaborate detours to avoid Ashbourne's boundaries. "Harry Ashbourne is spinning in his grave."

Christian had always thought it gutsy of Maisy to resist her neighbors. He thought he understood her loathing of the sport. Personally he sympathized with the fox. He knew what it was like to have all the hounds of hell running after you. As huntsman, he planned to make sure no fox died on his watch.

After he and Peter had mapped the course, they carefully calculated the distance with a rolling measure and found it to be just a fraction over ten miles. They had assigned speeds of eight miles per hour for the hunters and six miles per hour for the hilltoppers—children and beginners. This allowed time for several breaks, just as there might be in a real hunt when the hounds "checked" or lost the fox's scent. Volunteers would man tables at those points and offer drinks to the riders, who had to hold on to their cups as proof they'd followed the course.

They spent the rest of the afternoon and evening preparing, until it was time for Peter to go into town for a meeting. Christian checked with Rosalita to see if anyone from Ashbourne had called about Clover, but there were no messages.

He had spent two weary nights thinking about his conversation with Julia and his out-of-bounds reaction to the feel of her tear-dampened skin. He had been celibate for almost nine years. It made sense that touching a woman, any part of a woman, would make him want to crawl out of his own skin with desire. But touching Julia had been like going home.

He wasn't sure he had forgiven her. Forgiveness was a concept left over from a different life. People who'd never lost anything could forgive easily.

What mattered was whether he understood, whether he could put himself in her shoes and believe that, under the same circumstances, he might have had doubts, as well. And in the early hours of that morning, after waking in a cold sweat with no memory of what he'd been dreaming, he knew that he did understand. He could put it behind him at last.

But it would be harder to put Julia behind him. He knew this when Rosalita shook her head and said that no one had called. Loneliness, a companion he'd thought he'd tamed for good, had its icy hands at his throat.

He shook his head and went to heat up the supper Rosalita had left him. The big house seemed unbearably empty, and he hoped the house that workmen were painstakingly renovating for him would be ready sometime that century.

He was halfway through chicken enchiladas when Rosalita popped her head into the kitchen. She was a supremely competent Texan without a drop of Hispanic blood. In his youth her daddy had been in love with a gorgeous *señorita* and had named his baby daughter for her—although he had never told the baby's mother why. Rosalita was white-haired and withered, but she had the stamina of a ten-year-old.

"The neighbors are here to see you."

He wondered if a lynch mob had gathered. "Neighbors?"

"From Ashbourne. Maisy Fletcher, her daughter and grand-daughter."

"Julia's here?" He was glad to see Julia venturing away from Ashbourne. He was just glad he was going to see her, period.

"They wanted to wait outside. It's a pretty night."

"Would you mind—"

"Go ahead. I'll wrap and save it for you."

"You're the best."

"Oh, I know," she drawled.

He strode to the front door, but no one was in sight. Then, from the porch, he saw Maisy and Callie examining a water garden that had been installed in the spring. "We're over here," Maisy called.

He saw Julia then. Standing to the side, straight and slender and sightless. He went to her first. "Julia?"

"Oh, Christian." Her face lit up. "I'm glad you were home."

She was married. She had a child. But suddenly he felt like a kid himself. "I'm glad, too," he said gruffly. "You must have decided something."

"We'd love to have the puppy. You're sure it's okay with Peter?"

"One hundred percent."

"May we pay the club for her?"

"It would be impossible to set a price. We might end up having to pay you. Consider her a gift."

"Then we will, with thanks."

"Does Callie know?"

Julia was silent for a moment. "I thought *you* ought to tell her. I think you two are going to be friends."

As if Callie was taking cues, she scrambled off her knees and launched herself in his direction. "Christian! You've got fish! As big as Jake's trout!"

"Jake's trout were the size of koi?" he asked Julia.

"Not much bigger by the time he cleaned them."

Callie skidded to a stop in front of him. "Can I see Ranger? Can I see that puppy? Mommy used to ride here when she was little. Can I ride here someday?"

"Your mommy wasn't all that little," Christian said, ruffling Callie's hair until he remembered this was Bard Warwick's daughter, Bard who had threatened Christian if he went anywhere near his wife or child. He dropped his hand, reining in his enthusiasm. "Come back when you're grown and we'll see."

Her face fell. "Tiffany rides here sometimes."

"We'll think about it, okay?"

"People always say that and never do. I wish I could make people think when they're supposed to."

He grinned. He remembered Julia as a child, and she had been nothing like her daughter. She'd been quiet, sensitive, thoughtful. Callie, who didn't look like her mother, either, was fresh air in a crowded room. Oddly, she reminded him of Fidelity.

"I *will* think," he promised. "Long and hard. Besides, I know something better than riding. You know what it is?"

"What?"

"A trip to see the foxhounds. Want to come?"

"Can I see Clover?"

"First stop." He suspected it would be the last stop, as well.

"I've been here. I know where the kennel is!"

Maisy, who had been unusually quiet, grabbed Callie's hand before she could run off. "You show me. Let Christian help your mother."

"Mommy, could you just not be blind right now?" Callie said. "Could you just see so we can get there quicker?"

Christian thought Julia might be hurt, but she laughed. "From your mouth to God's ear, sweetums."

"What does that mean?"

Maisy tucked Callie's hand under her arm. "I'll tell you. Let's go."

Even with Maisy as an anchor, they were out of earshot quickly. Christian took Julia's hand and placed it on his arm. "Can you walk this way? Will you feel comfortable?"

"Uh-huh."

They started off, and he was surprised she moved with such confidence. He was so busy looking for obstacles, bumps in the path, tree roots or loose stones, that he didn't speak until she did.

"She likes you."

He knew she meant Callie. "I like her, too. She reminded me of someone, but I didn't put my finger on it until a moment ago."

"Who?" She sounded breathless, and he slowed his pace.

"Fidelity."

"Really?"

"She has the same energy, the same charming honesty. And she's going to be every bit as beautiful, I'm afraid."

"I hope she has all Fidelity's good qualities and none of her bad."

"Even the best people get careless when nobody tells them no. You'll tell Callie no, I'm sure. She'll learn to set boundaries."

"I don't need to. Her father tells her no all the time." Julia paused. "I'm sorry. That was out of line and not your business, was it?"

"Bard made Callie my business when he told me to stay away from her. And you, for that matter."

"Bard has said a lot of things to a lot of people. Christian, a couple of friends called me today. They tracked me down at

Ashbourne. They wanted to know if I'd be at the hunter's pace tomorrow. They wanted to know if I agreed with Bard.''

''About what?''

''He started a petition. He wants the board to veto your selection as huntsman.''

Christian was only surprised that Bard's wife was the one who was telling him. ''I knew it might be unpleasant tomorrow. I'm prepared.''

''What will you do if Bard gets his way?''

''I'll train horses. Peter's the real problem. This is important to him. He'll withdraw as master and have the kennel moved. I think he might even close off Claymore Park.''

''Bard's attitude actually has very little to do with you and everything to do with me. I'm sorry.'' She hesitated. ''I keep saying that, don't I?''

''Well, the reasons vary.''

They walked on in silence until she spoke again. ''Do you know why I named her Callie?'' She went on, since it was obviously a rhetorical question. ''It's short for Callinda.''

''That's an unusual name.''

''When Fidelity and I were little, she told me she was going to name her daughter Callinda. I don't know where she got it, or why. But she was adamant. She had her whole life planned. First she would compete in the Olympics and win a gold medal, then she'd graduate from college and move to Kentucky and work for a racing stable for a while doing promotion and publicity, until she met the right billionaire.''

''Never a small thinker, our Fidelity.''

''They would have a daughter—only one, because she didn't want to ruin her figure—and she would name her Callinda Julia.''

''So is Julia Callie's middle name?''

''No. It's Fidelity.''

He shouldn't have been surprised, but this revelation moved him. He put his hand over hers and pressed it tightly against his arm. Only for a moment, but he knew his message had been received.

''I couldn't call her Callinda, though. It was so, oh, I don't know, flirty? Sassy? It seemed a lot to saddle her with, so I settled on Callie.''

He heard all the "I's" and none of the "we's" he might have expected. But he didn't ask her what Bard had said. He didn't give a hoot.

"Fidelity would be pleased," he said.

"Maybe she's watching over Callie. It would be like her, wouldn't it? She never learned the meaning of no. Why would death stop her from doing anything she wanted?''

"Do you really believe that?''

"I used to want to. I was so lonely for her...for you.''

He knew better than to take that at more than simple face value. "Robby must have been lonely, too. Did you spend much time with him? Before he died?''

"Robby closed himself off. After you went to prison, he disappeared into his books and research. I tried to stay in contact, but it was painful for both of us. He drank too much, I think. I know he'd been drinking when his car smashed into the tree. Robby was never one who could ask for help.''

"We're almost there. There's a gate into the yard, but it's open. I'll go through. Take my hand and I'll guide you.'' She did and got through without mishap.

Callie and Maisy were waiting in the yard, and together they strolled to the puppy quarters. "All of you can come, or you can wait out here and we'll bring Clover out to play," Christian said.

"Oh, I think we'll stay here," Maisy said. "You two run on.''

Christian opened the door and ushered Callie through, flipping on the light. Their entrance was greeted by a dozen wiggling bodies, thrilled with this interruption of the routine.

"So many puppies!'' Callie's eyes were as big as Frisbees. Some children might feel overwhelmed, but not this one. She obviously adored animals. She threw herself into the midst of them, petting, scolding, squatting so they could lick her face. "Clover, where are you?''

Christian saw Clover but wisely said nothing. To his surprise, Clover joined the fray, wiggling as if she knew she'd been paged. It might be the only time in her life she'd listened to a command.

"Clover!'' Even in a sea of tricolored foxhounds, Callie recognized the puppy. She dove for her and lifted her high, not an easy feat, since the puppy, like all foxhounds, was destined to be a good-size dog. "There you are. Do you want to come out and play?"

The other puppies demanded attention, but Callie only had eyes for this one. Clover licked her face. "Oh, she likes me!" Callie said.

"I think she likes you enough to go home with you. What do you think?"

Callie looked up at him. "I can take her home?"

"She's yours. Mr. Claymore is giving her to you. Your mommy and grandma said you could have her."

"I can have her? Forever?"

"She's all yours."

Callie zoomed toward him, the puppy sagging under one arm. She threw her free arm around his hips and hugged him hard. "You did this, didn't you? It wasn't Mr. Claymore. It was you."

He smoothed her hair. The ice around his heart was melting faster than he could clean up the mess.

"Don't take her, Mommy. I'll make sure she doesn't chew anything or pee on the floor. I promise!" The good news: Clover seemed to be housebroken. The bad news: Callie refused to be parted from her for the night.

Julia knew how hard those rules would be to enforce, but Maisy had already promised she and Jake wouldn't be upset if Callie had the puppy in bed with her.

"I can guarantee that compared with who she'll want in her bed later in life, this is a big fat nothing," Maisy said wryly.

Now Julia tucked them both in. Clover gave her a sloppy good-night kiss, along with Callie. Julia left the bedroom smiling.

The smile didn't stay in place long. She found her mother in the kitchen. "I think she's happy, don't you?"

"Thrilled's more like it."

"And you won't mind keeping Clover here if we go back to Millcreek?"

"No. I'll see more of Callie that way."

Julia found a chair. "You left me alone with Christian at Claymore Park."

"More like Callie dragged me off."

"Were you hoping I'd tell him?" Julia knew she didn't have to spell out what she meant.

"I hope you'll tell him, yes. I'm sure that wasn't the time or place for it."

Julia drummed her fingers on the table. "Maisy, I have another favor. It's a big one."

"I'm not telling him for you, if that's what you want."

"I want to go to the hunter's pace tomorrow. I'm going to let Callie enter with Tiffany."

"Are you sure?" Maisy sounded worried.

"Samantha promised to ride along with them, and the jumps are optional for everybody. The children have a shorter course. They'll have the time of their lives."

"It sounds like fun, I guess. But you want to be there?"

"I do."

Maisy was silent. Julia knew why. Until now, Julia had played along with Bard's desire to keep her "condition" a closely guarded secret. Now she would be exposing it to everyone.

"I don't care what people think," Julia said. "I'm not ashamed of what's happened to me. I'm blind, and as far as I know, it's not contagious."

Maisy snorted. "You'll need help."

"Will you stay with me? Make sure I don't walk into trees and stumble down hills?"

"Do you know how long it's been since I went to a Mosby Hunt activity?"

"Since my father died. If you don't want to do it, I can ask Karen to work an extra day."

"No. It's time I showed up for something. But I will not wear denim or tweed, not for you or anyone."

"You can wear whatever you want. Feathers and sequins. I don't care."

"Bard will."

"Bard is making trouble for Christian. He's circulating a petition to keep Christian from becoming huntsman."

"Pushing paper is a lawyer's greatest pleasure."

"I'm going tomorrow to make sure that people know I don't support him."

"Are you sure that's a good idea?"

"About nine years ago I sat on the witness stand and let a jury think I had doubts about the man I loved. If I don't stand up for Christian now, it's almost as bad. Maybe I'm blind, but I'm not so worn down by it that I can't stand up for what's right and for someone I care about."

"I'm proud of you."

Julia got to her feet. "I guess I'd better get a good night's sleep. It's going to be an exhausting day."

"Do you want to hear another chapter?"

"Sure. Compared to what poor Louisa is dealing with, my life is a bowl of cherries. Even if Ian does have a mysterious resemblance to Lombard Warwick the third."

"It's a story, Julia."

"Only a story. But maybe it will give me some backbone to face tomorrow."

From the unpublished novel *Fox River*, by Maisy Fletcher

What makes a man expect perfection of a woman when he is far from perfect himself? I tried to be a good wife, but my efforts, which would have pleased any reasonable person, didn't please Ian, and he made sure I knew. Had he known how deeply rooted was my flightiness, my poor judgment, he would have chosen another woman to wed. But since our marriage had to continue, I would learn the things I needed. He would make certain of it.

He mellowed, of course. After several days he graciously excused me for my mistakes, admitting that I was young, after all, and couldn't be expected to know everything quite so soon. Perhaps he'd even had a hand in my failures. Had he supervised me more closely, I might have measured up.

I was torn by this new concession to my youth. After experiencing the dark clouds of his wrath, I was so overcome with gratitude that I tried to forget the injustice of it. But at odd moments I still found myself growing angry.

The anger dwindled as Ian and I settled into new roles. He instructed me at length on every aspect of being a good wife, and I, anxious to avoid strife, took his lessons to heart. After several hunts when I stayed at the back of the field on Jubilee, a gentle bay that Annie and her parents had given me for a wedding present, Ian determined that I needed a more spirited Thoroughbred and some advanced riding lessons. I demurred, but when it was clear Ian would not let this go without another scene, I agreed to learn to ride the four-year-old Crossfire.

I was frightened of Crossfire from the beginning. A stunning white gelding, Crossfire was larger and longer of leg than any horse I'd ridden, nearly seventeen hands. His sire was Cuban Sunset, the renowned hunter who had also sired Ian's stallion, Equator. Ian had intended Crossfire for himself, but the horse had been too predictable to keep his interest. Equator, a horse for only the most courageous rider, was more to his taste.

I found Crossfire to be predictably challenging, a horse with a mind of his own and the will to follow it. He knew I was half Ian's size and not even half as strong. He sensed my fear and exploited every one of my inconsistencies.

At first Ian was in his element instructing me. He was surprisingly patient, only growing restless with my struggles as the Thanksgiving meet approached. Thanksgiving was a special occasion for the Fox River Hunt, to be followed by a feast at the clubhouse. The field would be one of the largest of the season, and Ian was determined I would make my debut on Crossfire. Some part of this was because we would look handsome as we rode together, Ian with his black hair and black stallion, I with my blond hair and white gelding. I knew that Ian wanted to plant a new image in the minds of his cohorts. Stunning Louisa on her powerful horse. Perhaps then I would be the wife he deserved.

I rode Crossfire every day, jumping and taking the

expected falls. But I persevered, and eventually Ian's dream became mine.

That's the problem with dreams. They are rarely one's own. They seep from one soul to another, and if two people share a bed and the hours between dusk and dawn, then their dreams become one. Or at least the dream of the stronger becomes the dream of the weaker.

Ian was the stronger, of course. Older, physically superior, assured that he always knew best. I believed him when he said I could master Crossfire, and I did improve. If Crossfire didn't always take me seriously, he did listen when it suited him. In exchange I became more accustomed to the way his huge body bunched as we approached a jump, the fierce speed at which he thundered through a field, his uncompromising desire to be first.

Thanksgiving Day arrived, and we arose before dawn to ride to the clubhouse, where the meet was to begin and end. The hounds were to be transported by our huntsman and stable staff, and Ian and I had that final hour to go over everything he'd taught me.

"We'll cast the hounds down by Soldier's Bluff," he told me. "We're sure to scare up a fox or two in the first hour. The day's nearly perfect."

I knew what a perfect day entailed. Clear weather and cool. Since a fox's scent hovered near the ground and rose as the ground heated, the warmer our weather, the earlier our meets. Late November had been crisp and cool, however, and today was no exception. A light frost still clung to the ground guaranteeing that the scent would not float above the foxhounds' heads.

"The fences are well-maintained. John Higby has erected a new fence line, but carefully, so we'll have a new in and out to conquer. I've ridden it, and none of our riders should have any trouble. Certainly not you on Crossfire."

I wanted to share his confidence, but I was already

tired from holding Crossfire to a reasonable pace. He sensed the day's excitement and seemed ready to create his own at a moment's notice.

"I'm going to do my best," I promised, "but if Crossfire and I don't get along, I may have to drop back with the hilltoppers. You'll understand?"

"I'll understand that you've given up, not something I expect from you, Louisa. I married you because of your gumption."

I don't know what came over me, but I couldn't let that pass. "Is that so? Because sometimes, darling, it seems as if you're trying to bleed it out of me, one drop at a time."

No sooner were the words out of my mouth than I knew I'd ruined the day. Ian didn't take well to criticism. I waited for his explosion, but when it came, it was surprisingly mild. "Perhaps it seems that way at times, but I only want you to be the best you can be. Isn't that a husband's task?"

I had braved enough and knew his limitations. "I'm sorry. Of course you're only trying to help me."

"I suspect you don't think that at all."

"I'm only scared about today, Ian. Crossfire is just so much for me to handle...."

"Well, perhaps someone's little girl will bring a nice gentle pony for you to ride instead." He kicked Equator into a trot, then a canter, and before long Crossfire and I had been left in their dust.

I considered it a victory of sorts that I kept Crossfire from following at Equator's heels, but by the time we arrived at the clubhouse, I was already exhausted from trying to hold him in check. He wanted to run, and the sight of the hounds made his ears spring forward in anticipation.

I was greeted cordially. Annie and Paul were on their honeymoon after a wedding at a local church. The Joneses were unhappy that she and Paul were moving away, but they had adjusted. There was talk of their going to Chicago, too, and every time I heard it, I felt more alone.

The clubhouse was decorated with pumpkins and Indian corn, and inside, the fragrance of roasting turkeys was just beginning to scent the air. I chatted with some of the ladies as we waited for everyone to arrive. Mrs. Jones joined us, and after we'd asked what she'd heard from Annie, we began to talk about our mounts.

"That gelding of yours seems like a handful," Mrs. Jones said. "He's a bit large for a small woman, wouldn't you say?"

"Ian's determined I can ride him." I smiled but she must have seen the truth.

"Louisa, dear, if you're not comfortable with the horse, perhaps you shouldn't try him in a hunt quite so soon..."

"Ian would be very disappointed if I didn't."

Another woman, a Mrs. Rutherford from a farm close to Middleburg, chimed in. "He's a stern taskmaster, isn't he? Just the man to be our Master of Foxhounds..." She didn't finish her sentence, but the rest was clear from her tone. *"But not necessarily as good for a husband."*

The other women wandered off to see to their horses, but Mrs. Jones held me back. "You are getting on all right with Ian, aren't you?"

I'd thought her too frivolous to notice anything more than six feet from view. "Ian can be difficult." I was grateful to say the words out loud.

"I married Mr. Jones with the notion we would live in the city. I was particularly fond of the theater and missed it so terribly when we moved to Sweetwater. Now it seems we'll have the city for our declining years."

She was telling me things would improve with time. I had been telling myself the same thing for so many months that the platitude was almost a relief.

"I'll miss you if you move," I said. "You are the only family I have in Virginia."

She patted my hand. "Sometimes it's best not to have anyone to run to. You must make your own way with Ian, without interference."

Outside again, I found our groom and Crossfire, and mounted with his assistance. I knew immediately that we were in for trouble. He danced under me in expectation. He had hunted during cubbing season, but apparently it hadn't settled him. He knew what was coming and planned to be in the forefront.

The field was larger than usual. We gathered around Ian, who explained his plan. There were several places to be particularly careful. A newly plowed cornfield that we were to avoid, a section of forest where timber was being harvested, a portion of Fox River downstream from a beaver dam that had swollen with unusual rainfall and would be more difficult than usual to cross.

He ignored me, and I knew he was still angry. Our huntsman blew several notes on his horn and, with his twenty or more couple of hounds, started away from the clubhouse. The whippers-in, with whips that only seldom touched a hound, flanked them, their job to keep members of the pack from straying.

Ian followed well behind, and we rode behind him, as the field was supposed to do. It was the worst possible etiquette to pass the master, and nearly as bad to crowd him.

I hadn't taken to foxhunting with enthusiasm, particularly not after Ian had presented me with the fox's mask. The shock had stayed with me, and riding at the back of the field had been a way to cushion myself against witnessing the occasional fox's death. Clearly, though, if I was to make a success of my marriage, I had to develop the sporting spirit. Now I vowed to do my best, to make Ian proud, to relish the hunt as much as he did.

We reached the rough road below Soldier's Bluff after

a nearly perfect ride through meadow and forest. Later we would need to be silent so not to disturb the hounds. For now, riders chatted and caught up on local gossip.

When the field had assembled, the huntsman, using staccato signals on his horn, cast his hounds. Nothing happened for minutes as we sat quietly and waited for the hounds to pick up a scent. Then the pack's bitch strike hound opened, and in moments the entire pack was in full cry.

There was little to remember at the beginning of our chase. I struggled with Crossfire, but managed to hold him back as we took the first jump. Since it was a narrow path leading over the fence, we had to wait our turns, and I was elated when I was able to hold Crossfire in line before we had our chance to clear it. I kept my eyes up, my heels and hands low, and we sailed over the rails as if we were bound for heaven.

With my confidence growing, I concentrated on staying a safe distance from Ian. We were too close to the front for comfort, but I vowed not to retreat. I wanted Ian to see I was attempting to please him. If I rode well enough, he might forgive me.

The line of scent was strong and the hounds were enthusiastic. We rode hard for nearly an hour, checking twice to let the hounds reestablish the line. When we started up after the second rest, I realized immediately how sore my arms were from holding Crossfire and how exhausted I was. I admitted this just as a man and woman in their final years sailed merrily past me, and suddenly I was ashamed.

I struck out with hope that Crossfire might be tiring, too. But that was foolish. My horse was only warming up, and the battle to keep him firmly in the field continued. We took two more jumps, picked our way through the forest and crossed Fox River at a shallow spot away from the dam. The hounds were far ahead of us, and the field was straggling behind me now. The fieldmaster, whose job was to keep us together, rode far behind, helping those at the rear find their way across the river.

What happened next will live in my memory always. The hounds had grown silent, and I only knew which direction to go by glimpses of scarlet through the forest ahead of me. I turned Crossfire to follow, and we slowed our pace. I loosened my grip on the reins to conserve my strength, and at that same moment a sleek red fox with a brush—or tail—as thick as a tree limb streaked past us. The hounds were on him immediately, and before I could gather my strength to hold Crossfire back, he took the bit and started after them.

I fought my horse with no success. I was no more annoying to Crossfire than an ant, and he stretched out his great legs and ran like a racehorse. Ian was somewhere behind me, our huntsman well behind him. I heard Ian yell for me to hold hard, but he might as well have asked me to stand on my hands in the saddle. Crossfire continued his flight.

I heard Ian coming up behind me, but the pounding of Equator's hoofs spurred Crossfire forward.

"Hold hard, damn it!"

I sawed at the reins, forgetting everything I'd learned, but nothing would stop Crossfire. Ian gained on us only because of Equator's superior strength. In horror I saw the hounds leaping a fallen tree just ahead of us, flanked on two sides by forest and only wide enough for one horse to clear. I couldn't see the other side, indicating a drop, always a difficult jump, and even in my panic, I knew that Ian and I could not clear the jump together.

"Hold hard!" he shouted again.

"I can't!"

"You'd damned well better!"

I knew he saw the danger. He was in control of his horse. I was sure he would pull up at the last moment and let me take it first, even though it was a horrid breach of protocol to jump before the master. I readied myself to sail over it, trying desperately to get myself into proper position. Then Ian and Equator were beside us, and he was striking Crossfire with his crop.

The rest passed in a blur. Crossfire stumbled and veered into the brush, and I sailed over his head to land in the bushes. Later I was told that Ian made the jump effortlessly without impediment and continued on, leaving me to the care of the fieldmaster, who arrived in a few minutes.

"It's a good thing Ian stopped you!" the fieldmaster, a young man named Calvin, exclaimed, after he'd asked whether I was injured. "That horse of yours was completely out of control! He's too much for you, Louisa. I'd think you might have realized that by now. I'm surprised Ian allows it. He certainly must be in love with you."

I was scratched and bruised, but not seriously hurt. In utter humiliation, I was forced to walk out to the nearest road and wait until my horse was returned to me or someone going back to the clubhouse stopped to give me a ride.

I waited only a few minutes before a farmer passed in a hay wagon drawn by two mules, and I rode with him. Since he was going nearly as far as Fox River Farm, I continued home on foot instead of going to the clubhouse, too sore and upset to enjoy Thanksgiving with the others. I telephoned when I arrived so that no one would go out to comb the woods for me. Then I waited for Ian.

He was later than I expected. Our staff had already returned, leading a subdued Crossfire. The hounds were in their kennel, checked for injury, well fed and sleeping off the hunt when Ian finally arrived on Equator. I had spent the remainder of the day trying to anticipate what he would do and say.

Ian wouldn't admit that Crossfire was too much horse for me after all, because then he would have to admit that he had been wrong. Nor could I expect him to be sorry that he'd risked my safety simply to get across a jump before me. By now Ian might even believe he had whipped Crossfire simply to stop the horse's unimpeded dash after the foxhounds and prevent greater harm.

I, of course, knew differently. And although I'd grown adept at rearranging facts in my head, I couldn't change this one. I remembered clearly the fury on Ian's face as he raised his whip. In that moment, if Ian could have gotten away with whipping me instead of my horse, he would have gladly done so.

I was upstairs in my suite when Ian finally found me. It was too early to go to bed, but I had changed for the night anyway. Despite a warm bath and Lettie's chamomile tea, I was exhausted and aching. I wanted only to read a while and fall asleep. Ian would never issue an apology, but perhaps in the morning he might accept mine. In my rebellious heart I knew I owed him nothing, but in my head I'd realized an apology was the only path back into his good graces.

"So you made it home." He came into my bedroom and closed the door behind him.

I had hoped to avoid a conversation until tomorrow, certain he would simply sleep in his own room as he often did when he came in late. I put down my novel. "I phoned when I arrived. I hope you got the message?"

"It was delivered in front of three of the other governors. My wife in a farmer's hay cart. Quite a joke for the rest of the day."

"I'm sorry. I did ask them to tell you privately."

"I was chastised for allowing you to be so headstrong, Louisa. For allowing you to ride Crossfire today when clearly you aren't experienced enough."

I knew better than to appear angry, although inside I was seething. "I'm sorry about that, too. It must have been difficult to explain."

"Difficult?" Until that moment he had stood beside the door. Now he strode to the bedside. "I am the master. If they don't respect me, what will happen? How long will they allow me to serve, do you suppose?"

"You're the best master in Virginia, Ian. They'll—"

"If I can't control my own wife, how can I control the hunt?" Before I realized what he was about to do, he stripped off the spread covering me. "Tell me that, will you?"

Apprehension, which had become a subtle part of every day, expanded into something more threatening. "Ian, I tried as hard as I could. I really did. But Crossfire is too much for me. The others are right. I wish it were different—"

He hauled me to my feet, his hands like iron bands on my bruised arms. "What made you think you could ride him?"

As afraid as I was, I was still astounded. "But I told you, over and over again—"

He slapped me. Hard. "You told me? You told me? You whined a little, that's all. Had you been honest..."

I was gasping. No one had ever slapped me. Not my parents, not my teachers, not even my older brothers during play as children. My head spun round to the side with the force of his palm. "Ian, stop it!"

"Stop what? Stop you from making a fool of me? Gladly!" He slapped me again, and my head careened in the opposite direction.

I struggled in his grip, trying to get away. He landed two more blows, this time with his fist to my neck and shoulders, another to my breastbone that was so hard it forced the breath from my lungs. Then he shoved me back to the bed.

"You are a disgrace," he shouted. "And a menace in the field."

I was horrified. My hands crept to my burning cheeks. I could still feel the impact of his palms.

"Stop looking at me like that. This was nothing—

nothing—like what you really deserve!" He looked as if he was considering whether to continue his demonstration. I cowered back against the pillows.

"Tomorrow you'll ride all afternoon and practice controlling your horse. You'll do the same every single day, do you understand? You're a worthless powderpuff, Louisa. But your work will begin tomorrow, and until you've reached the standards I set for you, you'll stay at Fox River. You won't go anywhere, you won't do anything, you won't see anyone, until I'm satisfied."

He meant to keep me prisoner here until my bruises disappeared. I understood that, even in my terrified state.

"What do you have to say for yourself?" he demanded.

"I'm...I'm sorry." I managed to get the words out, although they threatened to stick in my throat.

He debated whether to accept the apology. I could see his struggle in his eyes. Some part of him, a hideous, overwhelming beast that had risen inside him, wanted to hit me again, perhaps until I fainted from his abuse.

Another part of him, a somewhat better man, seemed to gain control. He shook his head, then he turned on his heel and left the room.

23

Since the hunter's pace was open to the public and strictly for fun, Mosby Hunt members weren't expected to dress in their traditional clothes. Today it didn't matter what color coats or collars were. "Ratcatcher" or informal clothing was the order of the day for everyone. Except staff.

Christian tied and adjusted his stock and pinned it firmly in place with the plainest stockpin he'd found. He had been lucky enough to find clothes that fit without having to make a special order. Between Middleburg and Warrenton he had outfitted himself as huntsman—at Peter's expense. Dark canary breeches, scarlet coat, white vest, shirt and stock, gloves and braided belt, black velvet cap. The extravagant custom-made boots were a pair that Peter had given him without ceremony. "Robby's," he had said. "Please, if they fit, wear them. He'd want you to."

They had fit.

After swiping the boots one more time, he joined Peter in the stable. Peter gave him the once-over, then nodded his approval. "I've decided to bring Gorda and Fish for the morning, and some of the older hounds. People always want to see them. We'll pen them near the front gate. You'll be stationed there at first to give directions and check Coggins."

There were few rules for entry in the hunter's pace, but one was a negative Coggins, a blood test for equine infectious anemia.

Christian wondered if Peter had stationed him so prominently in his huntsman's uniform to make a statement. He supposed it was better to get the unpleasantness over with right at the start.

"Are you taking Night Ranger?" Peter said.

"I'd planned to. I got up early and washed him within an inch of his life and painted his hoofs. It took me a few tries to braid his mane and tail. He was not amused."

"Haven't done that for a while, have you?"

"Rampaging Ralph and Murdering Marvin got a little ticked when I practiced on them."

Peter laughed. "You're settling in, aren't you, son?"

"Well enough, thanks."

"Whatever happens today, I'll make this right. I promise."

"Don't jeopardize your own standing for me. I'd like to be huntsman, but it's not worth a fight."

"It's worth one to me. Especially if it's Bard Warwick I'm up against."

Christian remembered the few things Julia had said about her husband. "You don't like him, do you?"

"Never did."

"Do you mind telling me why?"

"Because he's a man with only one passion. Bard is like a champion racehorse bred to win and only win. Everything he does, everything he is, exists to accomplish that goal."

"He's already won, hasn't he? He has Millcreek Farm, he has Julia and Callie. He's respected in the community."

"Yes, and he's making money hand over fist, but it will never be enough. As soon as he wins one race, he enters another. I'm not even sure he makes a stop at the winner's circle. He's off and running again."

"An interesting analogy."

"The Warwick name is respected here, although, for the record, his father wasn't the best example of it himself. I just hope Bard doesn't do anything to sully it for his own children."

Christian wondered why there weren't more children. Julia was clearly a devoted mother, and Bard seemed like a man who might want a son to carry on his name—as archaic as that was by the standards of the day.

"He's an upstanding member of the club," Peter said. "He's

gotten close to stepping on toes, but never trod quite hard enough to wound anyone. I'm ready for the fight.''

Christian thought Peter was more than ready. He was looking forward to it.

''Okay, how do I look?'' Julia held her arms open so her daughter could do an inspection. ''Is my shirt buttoned evenly? Tucked in all the way around?'' She twirled slowly. ''Are my jeans stained or wrinkled?''

''You look pretty.''

Julia decided she'd better ask Maisy, just to be sure. She was wearing good jeans and a blue-and-green plaid shirt with a spruce-green cashmere pullover tied around her shoulders. She had fastened her hair with a silver clip. Small silver horse heads adorned her earlobes, a gift from Fidelity on the day Julia had proudly ridden through the South Land gates to show her friend she had conquered her fear of horses.

She heard Maisy coming downstairs, and she stationed herself at the bottom, repeating the twirl so Maisy could pronounce her dressed.

Maisy approved. ''You look great.''

''How about Callie?''

Maisy checked her granddaughter, too. ''Terrific. Callie, the pink elephant shirt's a perfect match with the zebra print shorts.''

''Maisy!'' Julia laughed. ''Oh Lord, you'd better be kidding.''

''I'm wearing jeans!'' Callie said. ''And my Harry Potter sweatshirt!''

''And she washed behind her ears,'' Maisy said. ''She's all ready. Time to go.''

''What's Maisy wearing?'' Julia asked her daughter.

''Grandmother clothes.''

''I'm wearing navy-blue pants and a matching shirt,'' Maisy said. ''I do look like a grandmother, at that. And before you say anything, I had my hair trimmed yesterday and most of the permanent's gone now. I am presentable.''

''Maisy's hair is brown,'' Callie said.

''Maisy, what color is your hair? Really?''

''I'll never tell.'' Maisy took her arm. ''Ready?''

Julia straightened her spine. The day was going to be a trial, but she was determined to get through it. "I can't wait to ride in the new truck."

The trip to Claymore Park only took a few minutes by road. Samantha had swung by with a horse trailer earlier in the morning to pick up Feather Foot. She and Tiffany planned to meet them at Claymore Park. They followed carefully made signs and parked in a meadow behind the house. As instructed, Callie hopped out and stood by the pickup while Maisy came around to help Julia down.

Some hunt clubs staged gala events with entrants who traveled hundreds of miles with champion horses, but Mosby's goals were different. Peter wanted to introduce the locals to the sport. Keeping property open for foxhunting was always a concern, and the hunter's pace was a chance to curry community goodwill. Local businesses sold food and crafts in a tent near the gate. At the end of the day there would be pony races and a costumed rider parade, as well as gag gifts for the worst riders in each division.

Julia slid sunglasses up her nose, then stepped down and put her fingertips on Maisy's arm. "Will you be my eyes and tell me what you see? Callie can help." Julia felt her daughter come up beside her, and she slung her arm over Callie's shoulder.

"There are lots of cars," Callie said.

Julia pictured brand-new sports utility wagons and trucks. "Horse trailers?"

"Boo-coo," Maisy told her. "The gate's about sixty yards ahead of us. And it looks like Christian is there with some other men talking to people and directing foot and horse traffic. He's in hunting clothes."

"How does Christian look? Older, obviously. But..."

"He looks a lot the same, as a matter of fact. Just tougher. Like he's forgotten what it's like to be young."

"He has." Julia could hear voices and birdsong. Somewhere to her left a dog was barking, and somewhere else a horse whinnied anxiously.

"He looks good in a pink coat. Your father did, too. Not every man does. Some look plain silly."

"It's not pink. It's red," Callie said.

"But that's what they call it," Maisy told her. "Just one of the silliest traditions in the world."

"I like those traditions," Julia said. "They hearken back to a more gracious time. When manners and chivalry meant something."

"You mean the days when they were still locking people in dungeons and sewage flowed on public streets?"

"Ask Christian about dungeons," Julia said. "And don't be so uppity." She patted her mother's arm. "Flo Sutherland told me once that you used to be a great rider. Is that why you quit foxhunting? Because the traditions are silly?"

"No, because I knew I would never be able to ride again without looking for the master on his great gray horse."

Julia was ashamed. "I'm sorry. I guess I didn't understand."

Maisy patted her hand. "I saw Christian the other day on Night Ranger. For a moment, just a moment…"

"He looks like my father?"

"Not up close. Not at all. But he sits that horse of his the way Harry sat his. Like they're one organism."

"I want to go ahead." Callie pulled away from her mother. "Can I?"

"Maisy?" Julia couldn't see to give permission.

"Callie, do you know enough to stay away from every single horse's behind?" Maisy said.

Julia laughed.

"Of course I do! Pickles!"

"Tiffany's favorite expletive," Julia explained.

"Then go ahead," Maisy said, "but be careful. And find Samantha right away. We'll pay your fee at the table."

They took the rest of the walk in silence.

"Christian's coming," Maisy said.

"Maisy, Julia." Christian's voice was strong and not too far away. "I didn't know you planned to come."

"I wouldn't miss it," Julia said, head held high. She put out her hand, and he took it for a moment, dropping it, she was sure, to take her mother's.

"Getting a good registration?" Maisy asked.

"Higher than expected."

"They've all come for the show."

"It's not the best one around. Most of the course is hidden from view."

"That's not the show I was referring to."

Christian gave a short laugh.

"Christian, you know how glad I am to have you as our new huntsman," Julia said loudly enough to be overheard, if anyone was nearby to listen.

"I'm glad to hear it."

"Well, it's a job you're eminently qualified for," Maisy said. "And you certainly look the part."

Julia wished more than ever that she could see him.

"We'll leave you to do your job," Maisy said.

"I'll be off riding the course. But I'll keep an eye out for Callie, although if she's with Samantha she'll be fine."

"She's as comfortable on a horse as I was off one at that age."

"Well, she's got the genes for it."

Julia swallowed a sudden lump in her throat. "Have a good day."

"I plan to. Thanks."

"He's gone now," Maisy said quietly. "But you are the center of attention. Watch it, they're descending."

Julia steeled herself to explain to the unseen horde why she was leaning on her mother's arm, why she could no longer see, and why she was living at Ashbourne with her parents and Callie until she had recovered.

Bard Warwick, with his horse Moondrop Morning, was the forty-third entrant in the Mosby Hunt's hunter's pace. Christian stood at the gate, as he had for every other rider, and asked Bard for proof his horse had a negative Coggins.

"I shouldn't have to show *you* anything, Carver," Bard said in a low voice. Grudgingly he handed over the paper.

Christian scanned it and nodded. "Thank you. If you'd like to take your horse over there and write a check, they'll issue you a packet of information and a starting time. If you preregistered, you'll be among the first to go."

"I hope you didn't spend a lot on the clothes."

Christian stared steadily at him. "Is there anything else I can help you with?"

"Sure, it would be a big help if you'd simply quit as huntsman."

Christian looked past him and saw Frank and Flo Sutherland approaching. Nine years had passed, but he easily recognized Fidelity's parents, although they had both aged two years for every one since. He had been tense to start with; now his body felt like an iron rod. "We have other people waiting to get through the gate," he said.

Bard glanced behind him. When he turned back to Christian, his expression was expectant. "I wasn't sure they'd come. Under the circumstances." He led his horse toward the table Christian had indicated, but Christian was sure he would turn, once he got there, to watch the fireworks.

"Mrs. Sutherland. Mr. Sutherland." Christian nodded. He did not tell them it was good to see them. It wasn't. They had been among the earliest to turn against him. He'd never really blamed them. Their grief was immeasurable. Whatever their faults as parents, they had worshiped their daughter, and he was sure that every day seemed impossible to face without her.

They were both stunned to see him. Their expressions were identical. Horrified. He wondered how Bard had missed the opportunity to let them know he would be here. Perhaps he'd thought the shock value would be worth more.

"Christian..." Flo spoke first. Fidelity had looked like her mother, although Flo's features were coarser, and she was taller than her daughter had been.

"I wish we weren't meeting like this," Christian said. "I'm sorry. I thought you knew I'd be here."

"No. No." Flo shook her head. Then she lifted her chin. "How are you?"

He was so stunned, he couldn't find the words to answer.

"Flo, this isn't the right time," Frank said, taking her arm. But Flo shook him off.

"I want to know how he is. It's a simple question. He went through nine years of torture, Frank. Don't I deserve to know how he came through it?"

Frank looked down at the ground. He was a handsome dark-haired man of about sixty. Now his cheeks were red with humiliation.

"I'm fine, Mrs. Sutherland," Christian said quickly. "I'd like to know how you are."

"I am sorry." She began to cry quietly, and it took all her determination to get the next words out. "I am so terribly sorry that we ever thought it was you. We knew you. We knew—"

Frank put his arms around his wife. When he looked up, Christian saw the same pleading expression in his eyes. "I... She's right, Chris. I—we thought... We shouldn't have. We just—" He shook his head.

Christian swallowed. For nine years he'd wondered how it would feel to have people crawling to him, begging for his forgiveness. Now he knew.

It felt like hell.

"You just believed what seemed most believable," he said.

"Fidelity loved you like a brother," Flo said.

"I loved her, too. Everyone did. I wish...I could have saved her. That I'd gotten there in time."

"If there's anything we can do. Ever." Frank stuck out his hand. "You have our support in your new job. I'm glad Peter chose you. His instincts are always exactly right."

"Peter understands honor," Flo said, wiping her eyes. "You'll make us proud, I know."

Frank took two certificates from his jacket pocket. "We're going to ride the course together. Our groom's bringing the horses in the back way."

Christian scanned the vet certificates, but they could have been in Greek. He handed them back and told them how to register.

"Have a successful ride," he said.

Then Flo Sutherland did the most surprising thing of the day. She leaned forward and kissed Christian's cheek. "Have a successful *life,* Christian. No one deserves it more."

"Julia."

Julia heard her husband's voice before Maisy could alert her that Bard had arrived. She stood quietly in the shade of a mulberry, well out of the path of horse and foot traffic, and waited for him. Not surprisingly, Maisy's story played through her head. She understood a bit of what Louisa must have felt at the Thanksgiving hunt.

And afterward.

"I'm surprised to see you here," he said pleasantly.

She kept her voice low. From Bard's tone, she supposed people were nearby. Somebody or other had been nearby all morning, offering help, digging for gossip, describing in a loud, slow-motion voice what she couldn't see, as if she might have gone deaf as well as blind. "Callie's competing with Tiffany. I wanted her to know I was here."

"It will be particularly boring, since you can't see the action."

"Maisy will describe it for me."

"Hello, Maisy," he said, clearly as an afterthought.

"You're looking fit, Bard. Will you be riding?"

"I'm teamed with Sarah McGuffey, of McGuffey Farms. Our horses are well matched."

Julia knew Sarah, a predatory divorcée of the prime time soap opera variety. She felt not a trace of jealousy.

"Which horse are you riding?" she asked.

"Moondrop Morning. Sarah's got a dark bay."

"You'll do well. Will you look for Callie and wish her luck?"

"I'm surprised you agreed to this."

"Why? She's a good rider. Samantha will be with her the whole way."

"Because of who's running it."

Julia didn't respond.

Callie must have caught sight of them, because the next voice Julia heard was her daughter's. "Daddy!"

"Callie." He sounded as if he was speaking to an adult. "I hear you're going to be riding."

"Daddy, I got a dog! A puppy named Clover! Christian gave her to me."

Julia tried to head her off. "She wasn't Christian's to give, sweetums. Mr. Claymore gave her to you. She belonged to the club."

"What is she talking about?" Bard said, obviously not addressing his daughter.

"One of the puppy hounds wasn't working out, and Peter agreed to let Callie have her."

"You got a puppy without consulting me?"

"I did."

"The puppy ran toward Feather Foot and Feather Foot ran away," Callie explained.

Julia now understood the full meaning of the expression "from bad to worse."

"What is she talking about?" Bard asked for the second time.

"She'll tell you, if you ask her."

"I'd like to hear it from you." Bard kept his voice light.

"There's nothing much to it. We went riding, and the puppy got loose and spooked Feather Foot."

"You went riding?"

She was surprised he didn't know. "Ramon brought Sandman and accompanied us."

He exploded. "What do you call a blind woman who takes a child riding?"

"Foolish, at worst. Hopeful, at best."

"It's okay. Christian saved me," Callie interrupted. "Like in a movie."

"He had the dog out for a walk at Claymore Park," Julia explained. "We were riding near the border. When he saw that Callie was in trouble, he jumped the fence and helped her get Feather Foot under control. Moondrop Morning was acting up, and Ramon had his hands full."

Bard was silent.

"Good luck, Daddy," Callie said. "I've gotta go."

Julia noted that her husband didn't return the good wishes.

"Now I understand why you didn't want to come home," Bard said after Callie had gone.

"You don't understand because you don't listen. My reasons haven't changed. I left you before Christian got out of prison."

"Left me?"

"It's not an overstatement."

"You don't sound like you plan to come back."

"This isn't the time or place to discuss that."

"Julia," Maisy said, taking her arm. "Flo Sutherland is on her way over here, and she looks upset."

Julia wondered what else could go wrong. Clearly, coming today wasn't going to make things better. She should have left Christian to fight his own battles.

"Julia."

Julia felt someone take her hands. "Flo... How are you?"

"No, how are you?"

"I'm doing well. I can't see, but I expect to get better."

"Not that she's doing anything she should to make that happen," Bard said.

"Bard," Flo greeted him frostily. "Maisy..." Her tone warmed. "What a pleasure it is to see you at a club event after all these years. And you look wonderful."

"I see you've had words with our new huntsman," Bard said. "I imagine seeing him at the gate was quite a shock."

"Bard," Julia warned.

He ignored her. "I've drawn up a petition to have Christian fired, and I'm hoping Flo and Frank will put their names in a prominent spot."

"I'm sorry to dash your hopes." Flo used the same tone she'd used earlier. "But Christian has my full support, and Frank's, too. We intend to convince the others who have signed to remove their names. Julia, you don't support Bard in this, do you? I would like to know."

Julia kept it simple. "Christian isn't a murderer. The courts have agreed, and it's time for all of us to help him set his life back in motion."

"I can't believe you, Flo," Bard said. Clearly he was furious. "There are a dozen unanswered questions. That man was standing over your daughter—"

"Enough," Maisy said, surprising Julia, who had started to interrupt herself. "You will keep that thought to yourself. Flo has suffered enough, and so has Christian. We don't need descriptions."

Flo lowered her already soft voice. "Bard, everybody knows your concerns. And most of us suspect why."

Julia tried to interrupt again. "Flo—"

"Julia, I'm sorry, but it's time you both realized that half the town has figured out who Callie's biological father is."

Julia drew a quick, audible breath.

Flo continued. "I'm sure you feel threatened, Bard. It's understandable. But I will not allow you to use my daughter's murder as a hedge against your insecurities. You will not make my life harder—or Christian's, either—just because you're afraid you can't hang on to what you stole from another man."

"How dare you!" he said.

"How dare *you?*" she countered.

Julia waved her hands to stop them both. "No more. Hasn't enough been said here? What if Callie overhears?"

"There's no one nearby," Maisy assured her.

"Julia, I will do almost anything for you," Flo said, "but I won't lynch a good man for the second time. Not to keep harmony between neighbors, not even to keep your secret."

"She's gone," Maisy said before Julia could reply.

"Leave us alone, Maisy," Bard said. "Please," he added after a pause.

"Julia?" Maisy asked.

"Just stay nearby, please," Julia said. She heard her mother walking away. Then she and Bard were alone.

"So, you've been telling people the truth," he said.

"I haven't told anyone. Don't you understand? People can count and they can see. She looks like Christian. Now that he's back, people have noted the resemblance."

"And so it all works out for you in the end, doesn't it? Your child's legitimate, thanks to me, and now that he's been sanitized, your lover's back on the scene. How long before you take up with him again? Or have you already?"

Strangely she wasn't angry, because she knew Bard was in pain. He had rescued her when she thought she needed it, even though now she saw she had been a swimmer drowning in a shallow pool. All she'd ever had to do was stand up and walk out on her own, but she had been too young, too distraught, too worried about her child's future, to get to her feet.

She didn't want him to suffer. She reached out to him but

couldn't find him, and he did nothing to help. She wondered if, on some level, he was glad she was struggling.

She dropped her hand reluctantly. "Nothing that's between you and me has anything to do with Christian. I've tried to be the wife I thought you wanted, but it hasn't made either of us happy. And there's Callie..."

"Yes, there's always been Callie. A living reminder of the man you love."

"Is that why you can't be the father she needs? Because she reminds you of Christian?"

He didn't answer.

"All you ever had to do to make Callie completely yours was love her," Julia said. "I know, because that's all Jake ever had to do. He's all the father I wanted."

"Really? And was Maisy still in love with Harry Ashbourne when she married Jake?"

"When I married you, I made a commitment. I wanted our marriage to work. I tried. But you don't want a partnership. You want to control me."

"I have to get ready to ride."

"Bard, Yvonne says you can come to one of my sessions. Maybe she can help us both come to terms with this."

"Terms? Here are the *terms,* Julia. You move back to Millcreek Farm, and you let me take care of you my way. You stay away from Claymore Park and Christian Carver. Leave the puppy, while you're at it. If Callie needs a dog, I'll select one."

She knew he was defensive. His strategy to rid Mosby Hunt of Christian's presence had failed, very publicly. Now that the Sutherlands had made their stand, no one was going to sign his petition. She knew when he was secure he was a kinder more thoughtful human being than the one standing before her now.

But did a woman live for the occasional golden moment? She thought of Louisa again, Louisa who'd had such hopes for her union with the mercurial Ian Sebastian.

Louisa, a fictional character whose life was the dark side of Julia's own.

"I won't meet those terms," she said wearily. "I'm finding my feet, Bard. And if you keep pushing me, I'll walk away."

"If you think I'll be weeping on the sidelines, think again."

She heard the sound of riding boots retreating. But she and Bard had parted company so many years before that his absence now meant very little.

24

Three mornings after the hunter's pace, Samantha found Christian in the kennel with the vet, who was checking the pack for heartworms.

"Got a minute?" she asked.

Fish stepped in to help, and Christian followed Samantha outside.

"You'd have to love dogs to love that place." Samantha waved her hand in front of her nose.

"Hey, we keep it clean, and the smell is no worse than the stables. Just dogs instead of horses."

"The kids have a day off for teachers' meetings, so I took Tiffany to spend the day with Callie. She showed me Clover."

"Did Clover park herself right under your feet?"

"Hard to believe she's a pedigreed foxhound."

Christian admired her. She wore khakis and a knit shirt in some shade of orange women probably had a name for. He liked her, and he found her healthy, exuberant beauty right up his alley. He knew she found him attractive, as well. He supposed if he asked her out, she would say yes.

Somehow he hadn't quite made the effort.

"Look, I know you have to get back to work," she said.

"We're making sure the pack's ready for the season."

"Have you been out with them yet?"

He hadn't, except for exercise. It was cubbing season, and Peter had asked Christian to wait until he was introduced at the hunter's pace. Peter himself had continued to hunt the hounds with the help of volunteer whippers-in, including Bard Warwick.

But now that Christian's job was official, he would begin going out with Peter, starting tomorrow. He wasn't sure he would be ready to be huntsman by the time the opening hunt rolled around, but he would be on his way.

"Tomorrow's my first day," he told her. "I hope I don't fall off my horse."

"Are you going to ride Ranger?"

"Probably. They take it easier than they will when the season begins in earnest. It will give me a chance to see how he does."

"He's a good old boy. He won't let you down." Samantha pulled something out of the pocket of her khakis and offered it to him. "I haven't forgotten our conversation. I made a list of people Fidelity hung out with when I knew her. Naturally our relationship was a bit strained after I discovered she'd been sleeping with my husband, but we still ran with the same crowd. These are people who knew her well. In the biblical sense, for some of the men."

Christian scanned the list. There weren't as many names as he'd feared.

"I only included people who are still around the area," Samantha said. "But the ones who've drifted away were minor players."

"Did you know Julia back then?"

"I think Fidelity kept the different parts of her life very separate. She could compartmentalize like mad. I don't know if Julia ever realized how wild Fidelity was."

"She didn't. She would have told me."

"You and Julia were close." It wasn't a question.

"We were going to get married as soon as we finished school."

"Tough breaks all around. I'm sorry."

He folded the paper and slipped it into the pocket of the coverall he wore when he worked in the kennel. "Thanks for the list."

"Christian, far be it from me to be pushy, but if you want to get together some time, I'd like it. You're one of the last of the nice guys. We'd have fun."

"I haven't been a nice guy for a long time, Samantha."

"A nice tough guy." She smiled.

He smiled back, but he didn't accept her offer.

The first name on Samantha's list was a young woman who worked in a Middleburg antique shop. Her eyes widened when Christian introduced himself, but she seemed willing to help. She told him the police had interviewed her after Fidelity's death, and in all the intervening years she hadn't thought of one important detail she'd missed.

"I knew her," she said as she dusted shelves of Depression glass. "I liked her, although at the time I hated the way she went after any man who caught her eye. But I always thought she'd settle down eventually, and I never knew anyone who really wished her harm."

When he asked about drugs or angry ex-lovers, she only shrugged. "Everyone did drugs, and any man who got involved with Fidelity had to know, didn't he, that the relationship was going to be short-term? If someone had gotten serious, she would have cut him off right away. That's just the way she was."

The next two people on the list hadn't seemed to know Fidelity well.

The fourth person was a girl who had gone to Foxcroft School with Fidelity. They had trained together for the Olympic team, and both had lost out. The loss seemed to have created a bond, although Caroline, a pretty brunette, said they hadn't spent much time together the last summer of Fidelity's life.

Caroline juggled twin girls as they talked at the restaurant she and her husband had just opened up in The Plains, another neighboring town. "Fidelity was flying a little high for me," she told him. "I was studying hard and making plans for my life, and she was trying to decide what to wear to which party and who to go home with afterward."

"Is there anything you can tell me? Anything she told you? Anyone who seemed out of place in her life?"

"She was doing drugs. Cocaine, mostly. Some of the designer

stuff, too. There was one guy, a polo player named Joachim, who supplied her and half the people she knew. I think he died a few years later in a fight. He always seemed to be hanging around, like he had stock in her or something.''

Christian was surprised. "Did you know Joachim's wife?''

"The model? I know she was away all the time on jobs. She probably didn't know what he was up to while she was gone. Maybe she thought all that money came from polo. Anyway, that was one of the reasons I stopped seeing so much of Fidelity. It was just getting too scary. Drugs scared me.''

He thanked her for talking to him and headed back to Claymore Park. Christian doubted Samantha would have helped him unearth Fidelity's past if she'd known he was going to turn up even more bad news about her ex-husband. He decided he had to tell her, to see what she could add. But not tonight.

He had promised Callie he would stop by to see Clover and help her begin training the pup. By now they'd had a chance to see what they'd gotten themselves into.

He decided to ride Night Ranger to the house. He could view the driveway from the last hill before Ashbourne and see if the Fletchers had visitors, notably Bard. If so, he could turn around. But when he reached the hill, the only vehicle in sight was the new red pickup.

At the house, he turned Night Ranger loose in the small, empty paddock closest to the barn and removed his bridle, hanging it on the rusty gate latch so Ranger could graze. Leaving a horse in the paddock was a ritual left over from his youth. He felt like a man who hadn't been to mass in years but finds himself standing and kneeling and crossing himself without missing a beat.

He walked up to the house, where he was greeted by one ecstatic foxhound puppy. "Hey, girl.'' He stooped in the grass and rubbed her neck. "How're you doing?''

"Christian!'' Callie stampeded out of the house as if she'd been waiting. "Christian!''

"Hey, Callie.'' Before he knew it, she had thrown herself at him and knocked him to the ground.

"I got you!''

"You flattened me,'' he agreed. "I'm your prisoner.''

"Callie!" Julia's horrified voice floated down the steps.

Christian was laughing, nailed by the child and the puppy, who was now standing on top of him, licking his face. "It's all right. She just caught me off balance."

Callie was giggling, too. He ruffled her hair before he pushed Clover away and sat up. Callie sat up, too. "Did you come to see Clover or me?"

Her enthusiasm surprised him. "Both of you, of course."

"Really?"

"Uh-huh. You're a team these days, right?"

"We are! Clover's the best dog in the whole world!"

"Is she?" He was relieved. He'd half expected Julia to throw the puppy at him as soon as he arrived. "What do you think, Julia?"

"I think my daughter has abysmal manners. Tell Christian you're sorry, Callie."

"I'm sorry." Callie's eyes were shining.

"I can see you are," he said.

He watched Julia descend the steps, feeling her way. She seemed to go about being blind the way she did everything. Carefully and intelligently. Some women would have let this sudden loss of sight defeat them.

"About this puppy..." Julia said.

Christian grimaced. "I don't think I want to hear this."

"She's absolutely terrific," Julia said. "Callie adores her. Maisy adores her. Jake puts up with her."

"And you?"

"I just try to keep her from getting under my feet."

He hadn't given that a moment's thought, but moving was tricky enough for Julia as it was. "Is she making it impossible to get around?"

"We keep her outside except at night," Callie said. "And I'm training her."

He wished Callie luck.

"Callie's actually making some progress," Julia said, holding on to the post at the bottom of the stairs. "Show Christian, Callie."

Callie stood and ran to her mother. Then she called for the puppy. "Clover...Clover... Here, girl."

Clover cocked her head, as if canine thoughts might possibly be passing through it. Then she abandoned Christian and rocketed toward her new owner, who squealed with delight. "See?" she shouted. "See?"

"Hey, that's terrific. Good job." He began to believe in miracles.

"I'm going to teach her to sit and stay and heel and all that stuff. Maisy got me a book with pictures in it."

"Just don't go too fast. You'll confuse her. I'd concentrate on one thing at a time until you're sure she has it down pat." At that rate he guessed Callie would be training Clover until Callie was married with children of her own.

"I'm going to teach her to lead Mommy around, like an eye dog."

"Seeing eye dog," Julia said.

"I trained guide dogs," Christian said. "It's a great job. But you'll have better luck trying to teach this one how to find foxes."

"That won't help Mommy."

Christian got to his feet, dusting himself off as he did. "Not unless she needs a fox coat."

"Yuck," Julia and Callie said together.

Christian laughed. "Callie, I wanted to tell you how well you rode in the hunter's pace. You and Feather Foot had a great time. Very close to the winners."

"We didn't win, though."

"Did you have fun?"

"Yes."

"That's what you were there for."

Callie scratched Clover's head. "My daddy won. He said I fooled around too much. I should have tried harder."

Christian didn't know what to say to that. She was what, seven? Didn't seven-year-olds fool around routinely?

Callie brightened. "Do you want to see Feather Foot up close? You can feed her an apple."

"It would be an honor. Julia? Is that all right?"

Julia looked unhappy. She probably thought he was spending too much time with her daughter. "You know, it's getting dark," he said, when Julia didn't answer. "Maybe I'd better just—"

"Please!" Callie pleaded.

"Go ahead, you two," Julia said. "I'll wait for you on the porch."

"Come on," Callie swooped down on him, hand extended. All Christian could do was take it and be pulled along by her enthusiasm.

"What are you doing out here alone?" Maisy's voice was followed by steps. The screen door slammed in confirmation.

"Christian and Callie are in the barn. She's showing him Feather Foot."

Maisy didn't answer.

"Callie's crazy about him," Julia said. "She knows he likes her. Then he gave her the puppy. That's all it took. An adult male who isn't trying to change her and likes her well enough to think about pleasing her. It's a rarity in her life."

"It's called a father," Maisy said.

"Yes, I know."

"You're going to tell him, aren't you?"

"I have absolutely no choice. Someone else will, or he'll figure it out."

"So that's your reasoning? You're going to tell him because you have to?"

"I'm going to tell him because he deserves to know. He's always deserved to, although when he was in prison, it seemed doubly cruel. Now it would be cruel not to. Those two belong together. They've already found each other without my help."

"Tonight?"

"No. I've got to tell Bard my decision first. I owe him that. It will change everything."

"And Callie?"

"I'll tell Callie when she's a little older. I don't want her to hear it from someone else."

"I'm so glad. Living a lie is the same thing as burning in hell."

"Maisy, you don't believe in hell."

''What would be the point? We make enough trouble for ourselves. The devil doesn't have to lift a finger.''

''You don't believe in the devil, either.''

''My point exactly.''

''What will Christian say?'' Julia stared in the direction of the barn. She could hear Callie's high-pitched laughter.

''What do you think?''

''He didn't just lose nine years of his own life. He lost all of Callie's, too. And he's going to blame me.''

Maisy put her hand on Julia's shoulder. ''Having children changes everything. It changes the way we look at life, the decisions we make, the choices we're presented with. We do things for our children we would never think of doing for any other reason.''

Julia covered her hand. ''It changed me. It will change him, too.''

''Here they come.''

Julia lowered her voice. ''How do they look together?''

Maisy's voice was sad. ''Like matching pieces of a puzzle.''

From the unpublished novel *Fox River*, by Maisy Fletcher

After Ian left I lay awake until dawn, planning how I would leave him. I was young, but not without common sense. I'd done nothing wrong, nothing I'd had the power to change, but Ian had beaten me anyway. All my struggles had been for nothing. I would never find a way to please him, not because I was foolish or inadequate, but simply because that task was impossible.

If he had hoped to convince me I was worthless, he hadn't yet accomplished it. He had made me doubt myself and feel responsible for everything that went wrong in our lives. But Ian had stepped over a line when he raised his hand to me. I knew what he had done was wrong, far worse than misguided, perhaps even evil. I knew men sometimes beat their wives. I had even been taught that sometimes a wife deserved it. But now that I had joined that hateful sisterhood, I realized that what I'd been taught was wrong.

No man should raise a hand to a woman. Not for any reason.

When my fear faded, fury replaced it. When fury faded, sadness seeped in. I thought sadly of the Ian

Sebastian I had first seen on a great black stallion, the Prince Charming who had scooped me from the ground and galloped away to his Virginia castle.

I rose at last, a plan half-formed in my mind. I would wait until Ian left Fox River, then I would go to Annie. I knew Ian would watch me carefully until he was convinced I meant to do as he'd ordered. By then Annie and Paul would be back from their wedding trip to Spain. I would stay with them until plans could be made to return to New York. My mother and brothers wouldn't want me at home, but I couldn't stay in Virginia, fearing I might find Ian around every corner. And if my family refused to take me in, then I would accompany Annie and Paul to Chicago and make a home for myself there.

I would miss Ian. This seemed strange to consider, but it was true. When he wasn't angry, he was a charming companion, a wonderful lover, an interesting conversationalist. I admired his devotion to Fox River, to the hunt, to Virginia. I would always mourn the death of our mutual dreams.

But I would not allow myself to be beaten again.

I arose with that thought, determined to avoid Ian without arousing his suspicions. I was stiff and my body throbbed, more from my tumble into the bushes than from Ian's fists. But when I straightened, pain sucked at my abdomen, a long, terrible spasm that left me gasping. I fell back to the bed and bent over double, resting my head against my knees.

For a moment I was terrified. What internal organs had been damaged when Crossfire threw me? The pain threatened to cut me in half. Even the pain I experienced during my monthly flow was nothing like it.

Although recently there had been no flow and no pain to which I could compare this.

Slowly I lifted myself into a sitting position again, staring at the door that separated my bedroom from Ian's. I had been so busy that I had paid little attention to my body's cycles. When I had thought about it, I had assumed that unaccustomed exercise had delayed my flow.

Until that moment I hadn't considered I might be with child.

I moaned a little, and rocked back and forth at the thought of what might be happening. I might well be losing a child I hadn't even known I carried, losing it because the child's father had caused my horse to throw me. Perhaps even because the child's father had beaten me afterward.

As terrible as it was, I could still see the irony. From the beginning Ian had claimed he wanted a son. Now, because of his own actions, his son might never be born.

I waited for another pain to strike, but after a few minutes, when nothing happened, I got to my feet once more and started toward the door. I had to relieve myself and check for bleeding. I almost reached it before another pain impaled me. I gasped again, surprised anew by the intensity. I crossed my arms over my belly, in some inborn and futile attempt to protect the child who might be growing inside me. And I moaned when the pain and dizziness continued.

I don't know if my moaning awoke Ian, or if he had lain awake that night, too, swamped with guilt over what he had done or, worse, angry that he hadn't thrown another punch. The door opened, and he strode in. I reacted by straightening, despite pain, and holding out my hands to ward him off.

He looked as if *I* had struck *him*.

"Louisa..." His face was contorted. "Are you ill?"

"No. Go away. Please..."

"You are. Something's wrong. What is it?"

His voice was so gentle that, for a moment, I couldn't understand what he'd said. I was tricked by the voice, beguiled by what looked like guilt in his eyes. "I woke up..." I gasped again as another wave of pain threaded through my body.

"Where does it hurt?"

I touched my belly.

Before I could speak he scooped me up and carried me back to bed. "Don't get up again. You must lie still."

"I don't know... It might be—"

"Are you going to have a child?"

"I hadn't thought so. Not until this. But I might..."

He seemed to take stock of the situation. "I'm going to phone Dr. Carnes. He'll come immediately."

Unexpected venom rose inside me. "What will you tell him when he sees my face?"

He laid me carefully in place and dropped down beside me. "Can you forgive me for that?"

I saw something in his eyes I had never expected. Tears. For a moment I couldn't speak. He did, instead.

"I don't know what came over me yesterday," he said in a choked voice. "The devil possessed me. I tried to get you to hold up, and when you didn't—"

"Couldn't!" I looked away.

"When you couldn't, I thought you were deliberately trying to show me I'd been wrong about Crossfire all along and you had been right. I wasn't thinking straight, Louisa. I admit it. Then, afterward, when I was the butt of jokes about you and your unsuitable horse, something rose up inside me. It was like the devil was urging me on."

Perhaps if I hadn't looked at him just at the moment I would have been safe. I wouldn't have felt pity for him, or a rush of some sweeter emotion. But I did turn, and I did look at him, and I saw tears on his cheeks.

"Oh God, I love you," he said haltingly. "I married you because I do, Louisa. If you can just forgive me this one terrible lapse. If you can just..."

His hand settled over mine. All I had to do was turn my hand palm up and let him take it.

And I did, for I had never really been loved before. Not this way, not so terribly, so wrenchingly loved. To be loved this way, by this man, was worth whatever I had already suffered.

And I would suffer no more. I was sure of it. Most probably I was carrying Ian's child, and if I didn't lose it now, then soon we would be a family. I would give Ian something he had desired, and that would surely make all the difference.

"Tell me you forgive me," he murmured.

I reached up and wiped the tears from his cheeks. And I told Ian Sebastian what he wanted to hear.

I did not spend the next months improving my riding skills, as the furious Ian had demanded. I spent them in bed, feet propped high and Fox River life revolving around my every whim. I was indeed to have a child, and even Ian's prize broodmares received less attention than I did.

I was convinced the child I carried was a girl. I hadn't yet shared that belief with Ian, who always talked as if it were a boy. I dreaded an argument about something neither of us could influence. He had been so kind and considerate since Thanksgiving night that, could I have chosen, I would have chosen a boy, simply from gratitude. But secretly—and since I had no control over the outcome—I yearned for a daughter.

When two months had passed without further cramping, Dr. Carnes declared me fit to rise from my bed. By then the child was visible to anyone who cared to investigate. My walk was less spritely, my clothes were chosen for what they hid instead of what they revealed, I bobbed my hair so something about me would be simple and streamlined. We entertained again, and if my unfortunate behavior at the Thanksgiving hunt had humiliated Ian, my pregnancy soothed the gossips. Every man in the club knew how impossible it was to reason with a woman in my condition.

We gave Annie and Paul a small dinner party before they left for Chicago, and six weeks later followed it with another for the Joneses. I was saddened by their departures, but encouraged by Ian's attentiveness. Perhaps I wouldn't need a local refuge. And when my new offspring was old enough to travel, we could visit Annie.

I was well into the pregnancy before Ian took me to task for knitting a yellow sweater for our baby-to-be. It was late in the evening, well before my usual bedtime, and until that moment we'd sat companionably, enjoying the fragrance of honeysuckle from an open window.

"Louisa, you do know that no son of mine will wear such a frivolous garment?"

His voice was light and teasing, and my instincts, dulled by months of coddling, weren't aroused. "Perhaps I'd better knit something in Fox River Hunt colors? Dark green and the scarlet of his father's coat?"

"Better than yellow."

"You know, the baby could be a girl. And if she has my coloring, she'll look pretty in this."

He was silent, and I drifted back to my own thoughts until he spoke again.

"It had better not be a girl, Louisa."

I looked up. "You're not serious?"

"I told you, I want a son."

"Of course you do," I soothed. "But this won't be your only chance to get one, you know."

"I have no interest in a daughter. Perhaps later, when I have enough sons to content me."

"Darling, what we've made, we've made together. And I promise if it is a girl, we'll make her a rider and someone you can be proud of." If I heard myself giving away my daughter's dreams, it was the last thing I worried about.

"A daughter is never cause for pride. Women, in general, are silly creatures. My own mother was the silliest of them all."

I was torn between wanting a new glimpse into his past and feeling outraged for my own sex. "You've never said much about your parents, Ian. What were they like?"

"My father was a man who knew how to get everything he wanted. He built Fox River Farm into what it is today, turned it around by the sweat of his brow and an unconquerable will."

"And your mother?"

"Weak. If she'd found herself standing on a track with a train bearing down, she wouldn't have had the strength or sense to step off."

"I see you weren't close."

"I had my father. He was enough."

"Not all women are silly. If we raise our daughter to be brave and intelligent—"

He scoffed. "No more of this talk. You'll have a boy. I'm convinced."

I was unhappy enough to excuse myself a few minutes later, claiming I was particularly tired that night. In bed, however, I couldn't sleep. Ian's picture of his family both intrigued and upset me. His disdain for his mother seemed almost to border on bitterness. And what of his father? The man with the unconquerable will? Had he conquered his son's will, too?

I began to be afraid for my child, girl or boy.

A month before the baby was to make its arrival I was in the kitchen with Lettie, requesting a cool supper for a particularly hot evening. I asked for cold chicken and green salad, but my real reason for being there was to question her.

"Lettie, can you tell me anything about Mr. Ian's parents? I know so little."

Despite two large windows that were shaded by oaks and a small fan revolving on its axis, the kitchen was almost beyond tolerance. I fanned her to encourage storytelling.

"Miss Claudia, she was a good woman, but a little thing, too little to stand up to Mr. Andrew. He was a big man, bigger than Mr. Ian, and when he shouted?" She shook her head and grimaced. "That's a sound I don't want to hear again."

"She was afraid of him?"

"We was all afraid of him, you want the truth. Me, I'd have gone somewheres else, if I hadn't been raised here. But this is my home, and he didn't yell at me, anyways. He knew I'd be gone if he did."

"But you were still afraid of him?"

"A man like that? Takes one little thing and he could snap you like a twig in those big old hands. Stayed out of his way. And I danced a little the day he passed."

I lowered my voice. "Was he cruel to Ian?"

"Only takes a time or two and you learn, if you're allowed. He beat the boy, but not nearly as much as he beat Miss Claudia. There wasn't nothing she could learn that could stop him."

The room was sweltering, but I went suddenly cold. "He beat her?"

Lettie looked up. There was understanding in her eyes. "My man hit me once and I sent him down the road."

"Seth?"

"No, I took up with Seth afterwards. He don't hit women."

"Claudia... Mrs. Sebastian died before her husband?"

"She did. You ask me, she didn't have no reason for living."

I tried to imagine my husband as a small boy, locked into this terrible family drama. What had he learned? Worse, what couldn't he forget?

"You want that chicken whole or chopped up in little pieces?" Lettie asked.

I don't know what I answered. I had lost all appetite.

By that evening, I began to have intermittent pains in my back and distended belly. Ian, convinced the baby's arrival was imminent, phoned for the doctor and sent me to bed.

The baby didn't arrive for two more days, two sultry, indescribably miserable days when labor would stop for hours, then begin again with new and fiercer intensity. Ian and Dr. Carnes consulted in hushed voices. Dr. Carnes called for a nurse, and a soft-spoken woman in white arrived to keep watch and make me as comfortable as possible.

I was sure I was dying; then I was sure I needed to. The warm maternal feelings that had grown during the pregnancy fled with each expanded pain. The heat was unrelenting, the humidity as thick as honey. When I could sleep I dreamed I was a prisoner in hell and the devil was riding astride on my belly.

Ian stayed near. He bathed my face with cool water and promised it would all be over soon.

On the third morning, just as the doctor was telling Ian he would need to intervene, the pains began again in earnest. An hour later our daughter was born.

Ian wasn't in the room, of course. The doctor and his nurse delivered her as I clenched my teeth and bore down with what little strength I had left. The child, a tiny baby girl, made her way into the world, and I attempted to bleed to death in greeting.

I remember little about the next day. I was told only Dr. Carnes's skill had kept me alive. Later I was shown my daughter, a red-faced, wailing child with tufts of dark hair and a rash.

Even later, I was told to cherish that pathetic, wrinkled scrap of humanity, that complications from the birth would make it difficult, if not impossible, to carry a child full term again.

I cried for hours, then dried my tears. I had wanted a daughter, and I had one. Deep inside I had worried about the logic of having more children, and now I had nothing to worry about. I had gone through hell to have this child, and I would never have to reexperience it.

Another day passed before I saw Ian. I didn't ask how he had taken the news of a daughter, or how he had reacted as I hovered near death. I particularly didn't ask how he had responded when he learned that his wife, the only broodmare in his human stable, would probably never breed again.

I was holding our baby when Ian came at last to see me. I had been bathed, my hair tied back with a blue ribbon. The baby herself showed signs that, eventually, she might be presentable.

I looked up without a word and waited for Ian to say something. The nurse was in the room, and the doctor was still in the hallway. I was grateful for their presence.

"You're feeling better?" Ian asked politely.

I nodded. The nurse came and lifted our daughter from my arms and took her to Ian. I wanted to rise from the pillows and snatch her back, but I waited, hardly daring to breathe.

Ian didn't take the baby, but he looked down on her obligingly. "She's not much to look at, is she?"

"Not yet," the nurse said. "They seldom are. But she has a lovely mother and a handsome father. She'll be a pretty baby soon."

"Perhaps you could leave me alone with my wife for a few moments?"

"Just don't stay too long. Mrs. Sebastian needs her rest."

He smiled coldly, and the nurse, taking the hint, ducked out of the room, carrying our child.

"Have you thought of a name?" Ian said.

It was the last thing I'd expected to hear from him. I had been waiting for accusations. I had not been an obedient wife.

"I like Alice," I said. "Or perhaps Ann, for Annie? I don't want to saddle her with Annabelle, and Annie wouldn't want me to."

He seemed to have lost interest in the question already. "Do what you like."

"Perhaps Alice Ann?"

"Choose well, since it seems this will be your one and only chance."

My eyes filled with tears. "Doctors have been wrong, Ian."

"I suppose we'll see."

"I know you wanted a son."

He waved away my words. "It's customary at times like this to give a piece of jewelry." He reached inside his jacket pocket and presented me with a narrow box.

Bemused, I opened it and drew a sharp breath. "Ian..." Staring up at me was a string of perfect pearls.

"They belonged to my mother. I thought you should have them to pass down to...Alice." He said the name as if it was distasteful.

I lifted the pearls and thought of the woman who had first worn them, the woman who had not been able to please her husband.

"Did your father give them to her?" I looked up, still dangling the pearls in front of me.

"They were a wedding gift from her parents, I think."

I don't know what I would have done if the pearls had been a gift from Ian's father. But these had been a gift on Claudia Sebastian's wedding day, perhaps the last happy day of her life, although this wasn't something I would ever know. They were a symbol of hope, hope that had been thwarted for Claudia and perhaps even for me.

But not for little Alice.

"They are lovely, and I thank you." I tried to smile. "It does make me wonder what I might have gotten if I had managed to produce a boy."

"My undying gratitude."

"Worth more than any necklace, darling."

He gave me the same cold smile he had given the nurse, then turned and left the room. I didn't see him again until my convalescence ended.

25

Just after dawn the next morning Christian stood at the fence in informal hunting clothes as Samantha exercised a new filly. The filly was a roan, pretty as a picture and fast as a gazelle. Someone without an ounce of poetry in his soul had named her Mack's Girl Cousin.

Samantha pulled up at last, the filly sleek with sweat. Another of Peter's trainers was using the track, as well, and after they'd cooled down, Samantha walked the filly back to the gate to get out of his way. Christian followed.

"Looking good."

"Peter has hopes for this one."

"The two of you belong together. A matched pair, with that red hair."

"If Peter decides to make a chaser out of her, I might see what I can do about riding her myself. I'm too heavy to be anything but a jump jockey."

"You could stop eating again."

"Could but won't. I like feeling human."

"Tiffany's back in school today?"

"Uh-huh. I drop her off at a neighbor's in the mornings, and she takes the bus from her house." She dismounted as he held Mack's head, then took the reins and started walking back toward the stable, where she would unsaddle Mack and rub her down. "Bet you didn't get up this early to talk about Tiffany."

"I wanted to catch you before I head off. I figured I could

take a minute, maybe even two, to tell you what I discovered yesterday.''

''It must be important.''

''I'm not going to beat around the bush, Samantha.''

''You can call me Sam. I'd like it.''

''Sam. I spoke to Caroline Watson yesterday, along with some others on your list. Caroline was the most interesting.'' He hesitated. ''You aren't going to like this.''

''Thanks for the warning, but if it's about Joachim, nothing will surprise me.''

''She claims Joachim sold drugs to Fidelity.''

Samantha's jaw hardened.

''Did you know?''

''About the time I got pregnant, I figured something wasn't adding up. Joachim didn't seem upset when I told him I was going to have a baby, even though my work dwindled the moment I started to gain weight. But there always seemed to be money enough to meet the bills, which was odd. Joachim had extravagant tastes, and polo rarely makes a man rich.''

''And you suspected drugs?''

''I suspected he had a rich girlfriend, but I was young, pregnant. I was depressed the marriage was such a bummer.'' She shrugged. ''I guess I didn't want to know what was going on.''

''Do you believe it now?''

''Let's just say it's a nasty surprise. But I guess it's possible.''

''Okay.'' He believed her.

Samantha stopped just outside the entrance. ''I do know this. Joachim wouldn't have murdered anybody. He was definitely a 'make love not war' kind of guy. No temper, no grudges. That's probably why he wasn't the best polo player on the circuit. He just didn't have the killer instinct.''

''Okay, I'm reaching here, but what about this? What if Fidelity got fed up with him. Maybe she threatened to turn him in for pushing drugs—''

''Then she'd have to admit she'd bought drugs from him.''

''If he had to, was Joachim capable of hiring somebody else to kill her?''

''Karl Zandoff?'' She thought for a long moment. Finally she wrinkled her nose. "I don't know. It seems impossible. But I didn't know about the drugs, either. If that's true, then there must have been a lot I didn't know."

"Okay. Next question. When he died, did he leave anything behind? Letters, papers, bank statements? Anything that might give us more information?"

"That's the only easy question you've asked. I have his entire apartment boxed and piled in a storage locker. He didn't have any family in the States except Tiffany. When he died, the authorities asked me to be responsible for his stuff. I sold all the furniture. Leather sofas, chrome coffee tables. Nothing with any sentimental value. Then I had professionals pack and store everything else. I figured one day I'd go through it, keep the stuff Tiffany might want and get rid of the rest. But I haven't gotten around to it. I guess I don't really want to face Joachim again."

"Yesterday you said you wanted to spend an evening together…"

"Oh, terrific. You and me under the bright lights at Acme Storage."

"These days, that's my kind of date."

Julia liked Yvonne and trusted her implicitly. As her sessions progressed, she'd become more comfortable with the questions Yvonne asked and more secure about probing her own memory for answers.

This morning when Yvonne asked again about hypnosis, she tentatively agreed. "I'm sorry I overreacted before. I seem to be pretty good at that these days."

"Sounds like you've been thinking."

"I guess if I really want to see again, I have to do whatever it takes."

"That's a good step, although we'll have to work on your enthusiasm."

Julia's smile was strained. "Just promise you won't make me flap my arms and crow like a rooster."

"We're going to start slowly. You'll be completely aware of everything around you. The moment you feel uncomfortable with something I've asked, you'll come right out of it."

"I can do that?"

"I'll make sure you can. Today we're going to remember a good day."

At Yvonne's instruction, Julia made herself comfortable in the soft armchair, settling back and resting her head. She closed her eyes, and for the next fifteen minutes she went through a series of relaxation exercises, tensing and relaxing different parts of her body until she felt absolutely limp. So far it had been surprisingly easy and nonthreatening, and Yvonne's soft voice was like a river flowing through her.

"I'm going to count," Yvonne told her. "And as I do, I'd like you to pretend you're at the top of a grand staircase. It's not high enough to be frightening, just a perfect sweep down to a cozy sitting room where you can see comfortable chairs and a fire blazing in the fireplace. You want to get there and snuggle in front of the fire because your favorite television show is about to come on. It's the story of your life. But you're in no hurry, because the show will only start when you're comfortable and relaxed in front of the television."

Julia could visualize the scene, adding details until it seemed as comforting as home.

"Are you ready to start down?" Yvonne asked.

"Yes."

"Take the first step and pause. Breathe deeply as you go. You're in no hurry. The fire will burn all night, the television isn't on yet. The air is warm, and you're dressed in your most comfortable clothes. You feel like you're light as a feather and floating. And as you take another deep breath, you take another step."

Julia lost awareness of time. She felt herself relaxing more deeply with every step. By the time she was sitting in front of the fire, she felt as if she were wrapped in a security blanket.

"There's a remote control just beside your right hand, Julia. When you're ready, you're going to pick it up and turn on the television. You'll keep the remote on your lap with your hand on it as you watch the story of your life. When you get tired or don't want to watch anymore, you'll simply push the off button and the show will end. You'll sit quietly for a moment, then you'll open your eyes and you'll be back in this room. And you'll remember everything you saw and did.''

''All right.'' Julia was so relaxed it seemed odd to speak, but her voice sounded normal.

''As you watch the show, please tell me what you see. Since I can't watch, I'll have to depend on you. There are many channels on this television set and many shows. The one you'll tune into now is a happy day from your past, a day when everything seemed right and you felt like you had the entire world at your fingertips.''

''That long ago, huh?''

''As long ago as you'd like. When you're ready, go ahead and turn on the television.''

Julia knew she wasn't in the sitting room in front of a fire, but the room seemed real. She could feel the heat from the fireplace, and the television seemed real, as well. In a moment she reached for the remote and slipped it into her lap. Then she pressed the power button and watched her past unfold.

''You know, Julia. You and Christian really can be prigs sometimes. It's a joint. You won't go insane if you smoke it. No one's going to spring out of the bushes and arrest you. Right, Robby?''

Tonight Robby was dressed as if he'd just stepped off the tennis court. His white shirt and shorts set off his tan and dark hair to perfection. The four friends were lying on a hillside above Ashbourne.

''No one's ever arrested me for anything,'' Robby said.

''Somebody ought to arrest you for speeding so you'd take it easier on the roads,'' Julia lectured. She waved away the joint. She knew she was overly cautious about life in general, but avoiding drugs simply made sense to her. She had never indulged.

Christian, who didn't even drink, waved it away, as well, and Robby passed the joint to Fidelity, who drew the smoke deep into her lungs before she passed it back to him.

''What on earth do you two do for fun?'' she asked, after she exhaled. ''Oh, I know. Don't bother to tell us unless you're going to share all the juicy details.''

Christian laughed. ''Is anything sacred to you, Fidelity?''

"Sacred? Like in church?"

They bantered, and Julia's mind drifted lazily. It was a warm summer afternoon, heading toward evening. In a month they would all drift away to school again, Fidelity to Swarthmore, Robby to Yale, Julia to William and Mary, and Christian back to night classes at nearby George Mason, unless a last-minute scholarship came through. The four friends had gone swimming, then decided to sun themselves looking over the fields of Ashbourne. Except for the joint, which still made Julia uncomfortable, the day had been nearly perfect.

Robby tossed the spent joint into the lush grass and lay back on the blanket. They were like the spokes of a wheel, feet pointing to the four directions. Somewhere above them bees buzzed and crows cawed in chorus. A light wind drifted overhead, erasing the hard work of the sun.

"This is sacred," Robby said.

Julia was surprised. Robby was not one to talk about his feelings. His mental powers were awesome, but if he experienced the world on other levels, he rarely discussed it.

"Why, Robby, how sweet," Fidelity said. "You like being with us? I would never have known it."

"You have to spell things out for Fidelity," Christian told Robby. "She doesn't have a subtle bone in her body."

"Good old Fidelity," Fidelity agreed. "What you see is what you get."

"Julia now, Julia has hidden depths," Robby said. "She's more like me."

"And what are you like?" Fidelity said. "What *is* the key to Robby Claymore?"

"The key?" Robby was silent a moment. "I just want what everybody wants, I guess."

"And what's that?"

"My own place in the sun."

"You've got that right now." Fidelity gestured toward the sky. "It's right there above you." She squinted. "Well, maybe not above you anymore. Going down fast... But still there."

"What do you want, Fidelity?" Christian asked.

"Everything. As fast as possible."

"What's your hurry?"

"Oh, I don't know. It's a big old gorgeous world, and I want a big old gorgeous chunk of it. Is that what you meant, Robby?"

"Nobody wants as much as you do," Robby said. "Your appetites are terrifying."

"And just how would you know about my appetites?" Fidelity propped herself up on one elbow. She plucked a long blade of rye grass and tickled him under the nose.

Robby brushed it away. "I have eyes and ears."

"What about *your* appetites?" Fidelity said.

"What exactly would you like to know?" Robby grimaced.

Julia giggled. Fidelity was seldom out of flirtation mode, and for once it was fun to see Robby playing along with her. The teasing went with the day. Lazy and sensuous, the kind of teasing only good friends indulged in.

Christian stretched his arms to the sky. "I want more days like this one. I don't ever want to shut myself in a laboratory or an office. I want to be outside, under the world's bluest sky—"

"Sweltering in the Virginia heat," Robby said.

"Sweltering in the Virginia heat," Christian agreed. "Riding some of the prettiest horses God ever made. Making a life for myself and Julia—"

"Hey," she protested, "don't I get to help make a life, too?"

"Making a life for myself and Julia, with her as my full-fledged partner in all decisions," Christian amended.

Everybody laughed.

"And I want to stay here in Ridge's Race," Julia said. "I want us to have a home of our own—"

"Won't Ashbourne do?" Fidelity drawled. "Little old Ashbourne's not good enough for you?"

"A home," Julia went on, as if Fidelity hadn't interrupted, "children, horses, and both of you as close to us as you are now."

"Back to you, Robby," Fidelity said. "You've got to do better than a place in the sun."

"I want to feel like I belong."

Julia was surprised. She didn't know what to say.

Fidelity, of course, had no such problem. "Belong?" Fidelity tickled his nose with the grass again. "How could you belong any more than you already do? You're Mr. Claymore Park, son. You're Mr. Ridge's Race. There's not a girl in this town who wouldn't pull down her pretty little ruffled panties for you if you just asked. You're gorgeous, smart enough to converse intelligently with Einstein—"

"Who is quite dead," Julia pointed out.

"Heck, Robby's smart enough to figure out how to bring him back," Fidelity said. "And under that aloof exterior beats a passionate heart, right?"

Robby grabbed her hand, removed the blade of rye grass and tossed it. "Is everything funny to you?"

"You're not funny. I think you're the absolute best."

Unaccountably, Julia felt tears sting her eyes. Fidelity could be selfish and vain, but she loved Robby, just the way she loved Julia and Christian. Fidelity might hold out her arms to the world, demanding everything in it, but at the same time she was ready to smother it with genuine, exuberant affection.

"Well, that means something, I guess," Robby said at last.

"We all think you're the best," Julia said. "You belong with us. You always will. That's never going to change, Robby. I just know we'll always be together."

Acme Storage was an impeccably kept facility. Still, Samantha's locker smelled musty, as if whatever was left of Joachim's life was rotting inside boxes and crates. The light was too bright and seemed to bounce off the glistening strapping tape. The temperature was cold enough to make Christian glad he'd brought his heavy jacket.

"Are you sure you want to do this?" Samantha said. "It's not going to be a simple task."

"The boxes seem pretty well marked. We can forget the ones that say glassware and books."

Christian looked around. There was a lot to sort through, but the packing company had done an excellent job of listing contents on the boxes. He began to move things around, piling the most likely boxes at one end of the locker. "What do you think? Shall we start with these?"

"I think we should pile them in my truck and take them back to my house. We can sort at our leisure. I have a nice Bordeaux Peter gave me after one of my colts finished first at the Foxfield Spring Race Meet."

It was an extra step, but it made good sense. He realized they would tire of the cold and the smell very quickly. "Let's get going."

An hour later the boxes were in Samantha's tiny living room, the baby-sitter had been escorted home, and a sleepy Tiffany—dark-haired like her father, but freckled and extroverted like her mother—had been tucked back into bed.

"Do we have a system?" Samantha asked, reaching for the first box. They were sitting shoulder to shoulder.

"You open and look through each one. If there's something you don't want me to see, that's fine. Otherwise I'll browse. If there's nothing interesting I'll set it aside—"

"And I'll repack it," Samantha said. "That sounds like a system. Where does the wine come in?"

"After we've done some work. As a reward."

She muttered a protest, but she left and returned with a knife, scissors and a roll of packing tape. "You have to take all the boxes back and pile them in the locker. Promise?"

"You won't have to do another thing. And I really do appreciate this."

They started to work. Samantha's house was warm and softly lit, and it smelled like peach potpourri. He had been surprised at how fiercely feminine it was. Pastel walls, floral slipcovers, lace curtains at the window. He supposed this was the flip side of the woman who worked so hard in the Claymore Park stables. He found it enticing. She was enticing.

Professional packers did not sort. They went through rooms putting items carefully into boxes, then taping them shut. Samantha laughed at the contents of the fifth box. "Here's the wastebasket, trash intact."

"Not kitchen garbage, I hope."

"No, his office. Nothing here worth sorting through."

"I'd better have a look just the same."

He did, and she was right. "Joachim Hernandez, fan of Moon Pies and connoisseur of Post-it notes."

"He used them for everything. I'd find them all over our apartment. 'Call John. Wash car. Fold laundry.'"

"He helped with the laundry?"

"No, those notes were for me."

They hit pay dirt on box number ten. "Bingo. Bank statements," Samantha said. "Now I can find out if he was making enough to stay current on his child support."

"Didn't he?"

"Joachim was master of the grand gesture. We wouldn't see him for months, then, just as I was ready to go to court, he'd drop around with a check and plans to spend the next two weeks with Tiffany."

"I hope there was insurance."

"A little. That's how I bought this house. I wanted Tiffany to have a place she could really call home."

"It's cute. I like it."

"I'm ready for that wine, how about you?" Samantha went off to open the bottle as Christian began to sort the bank statements by date. Joachim hadn't been organized; he had been a pack rat. The statements went back three years from his death, which suited Christian perfectly.

He had piles in place by the time Samantha returned with wine and a platter of cheese and crackers. She set the tray on a wicker coffee table and sat cross-legged on the floor beside him, leaning against the sofa with her knee brushing his. "What shall I do?"

"I'm going to start with the oldest statements. Maybe you should start with the most recent?"

"What are we looking for?"

Christian didn't know. Unusual deposits or withdrawals, perhaps. He really didn't think luck would strike and he would find a check made out to one Karl Zandoff, but he supposed stranger things had happened. He told her to look for patterns or deviations from patterns, and they went to work.

Half a glass of wine later, he looked up. "Did Joachim have a regular job, Sam? Or I should say, was he paid regularly by a sponsor?"

"Do you know how polo players are paid?"

"It's not my game."

"In a nutshell, it's a rich man's game, and rich amateurs pay professionals a lot of money to play on their teams. When Joachim was at his best, he could make as much as ten or twenty thousand during a tournament. The best players made more."

Christian whistled softly.

"But Joachim also had extravagant expenses. Six ponies, all the expense of keeping and transporting them. Professional fees. And, of course, the costs of schmoozing with the idle rich."

Christian knew "pony" was the traditional term but not accurate. Players used Thoroughbreds, and he knew the cost of their upkeep. He could see why Samantha had worked so hard.

"From what you've said, it's unlikely Joachim would have made a regular paycheck."

"A regular paycheck would have been a blessing."

"There's a deposit twice a month, every month, of six hundred dollars."

"Let me see."

Christian handed her the statement. "It's been on the last three statements."

"It's an automatic deposit." She looked puzzled. "It's not a fortune, but it's regular. Odd."

"Check and see if it's on the later ones, too."

They sorted through the records. In the end, the automatic deposits were the most interesting figures they found. They had started in the winter before Fidelity's death and continued for a year. Then they had concluded.

"How do we find out who made the deposits?" Samantha said.

"You could contact the bank, but they'll probably refuse to tell you. Your name wasn't on the account."

"I knew better than to merge my earnings with his."

"None of the checks look particularly interesting?" Christian said.

"No, they're all pretty straightforward."

"Maybe we'll find credit card statements." Christian reached for the next box.

Halfway through his second glass of wine, he did. He'd gone

to prison before developing a taste for wine or social drinking of any kind. Now the pleasures of a good Bordeaux sang in his veins. The beautiful woman at his elbow was a bonus. "Credit card statements. Years worth. Did he ever throw anything away?"

"He was phobic about getting rid of things. When we divorced, he insisted on taking all the canned goods, sort of a hedge against starvation, I think."

"I'll keep opening boxes. You let me know if you want me to go through some of those with you," Samantha said.

Christian found nothing of interest as he paged through statements. After ten or so pages, his eyes began to blur and words stopped making sense.

"I have to take a break."

"Eye strain?"

He closed his eyes and let the wine do its work. "Brain strain."

"It's a lot to go through."

"Reading's never easy for me," he admitted.

"You graduated from college in prison, didn't you?"

"Unless I'm really tired I read well enough now to do anything. But I am dyslexic."

"You see words backward?"

"No, my problem was poor word recognition skills. Most people see a word and automatically recognize it after a few times. Some of us have to sound out the same word over and over again until it finally computes, and in the meantime the meaning gets lost. With Robby Claymore's help I got better as I got older, until I was reading at grade level by the time I got to high school. But when I'm tired, even familiar words look new."

"You know, Callie has the same problem. Bright as the dickens, but reading is agonizing. She and Julia go over lists of words every night."

That surprised him, although learning disabilities were far more common than people assumed. He supposed it was just as well Callie was Julia's daughter. At least she'd known a little about dyslexia before finding out her daughter had it.

He remembered something Callie had told him when he'd

stopped by to see her. "She said her grandmother bought her a picture book to help her train Clover. I thought it was just because she's only seven."

"Eight." Samantha's attention was diverted. She flipped open the last box. "Pay dirt."

"What?"

"Appointment books." She dug through. "The year Fidelity was murdered." She held up a slim leather volume. "Pre-Palm Pilot. Joachim kept notes about everything."

She handed over the book, but he shook his head. "Read it to me, will you? Start a couple of months before Fidelity died and see what you find."

She settled beside him, turning the lamp so it shone directly on the appointment book. "March?"

"Start there. We can page back if we need to."

"Polo game. Drinks with friends. Meeting with M.I."

"Any idea who that is?"

"They met at a bar in...Leesburg." She held the book up to the light. "A ways to go for a drink, and the wrong direction for the polo crowd."

"*I.* Not that common an initial. Iverson? Irving?"

"Ice? Ink? Let's see if it shows up again." She read through a couple of days where Joachim had done nothing more important than take a horse to the vet and play practice matches.

"Here's something in the margin." Samantha turned the book and squinted. "No luck on sale. Report to M.I." She lowered the book to her lap. "Sale of what? Drugs? A horse? That's another way polo players make their living. They raise and train ponies for amateurs."

"M.I. Initials of a stable? Middleburg..." Christian shrugged.

"I doubt it. If he was meeting someone in a bar, he'd have their name down, not where they worked." She continued reading, paging through until she came to another similar notation. "Tried sale again. F. threat."

"F? For Fidelity?" Christian sat straighter. "Try the back of the book. Most appointment books have blank pages at the end. See what he wrote."

Samantha kept her finger in the margin and paged forward to

the end. "Birthdays. He got mine right, the loser, but never remembered to get me a present on time."

She turned the page. "Here's a list of phone numbers." She was silent a moment. "Fidelity's," she confirmed.

"Anyone with the initials M.I.?"

"Miles Inchman."

"Someone's mother had a sense of humor."

"I guess she thought if he was stuck with Inchman, she could balance it with Miles."

"I suppose it's too much to hope there's a number for Karl Zandoff?"

"Nothing."

They went back to the appointment pages. There were appointments with Inchman scattered through the months.

She paged through. "Here's something. Oh, Christian, listen to this note in the margin. 'F. says she'll turn me in. Ha. Ha. M.I. will laugh.'"

"I have a friend in the sheriff's office. I'm going to call and see if he knows anything about a Miles Inchman." Christian started to look for the telephone, but Samantha pulled him back down.

"Look, do it tomorrow, okay? I'm wiped. This is just a start. You can show him the appointment book. But you know this is a long shot, don't you? Fidelity, Joachim, Karl Zandoff? You might connect two, but all three? You're looking for a needle in a haystack."

Christian rested his head against the sofa. "I guess I ought to get out of here and let you get some sleep."

"Stay a while and unwind. We haven't finished the bottle."

Samantha was still sitting beside him. Her fine-boned face was close to his; her lush mouth was only inches away. She leaned forward and kissed him, and his hand crept to the back of her head to keep her there.

When they finally parted, his breath was coming in uneven spurts. "It's been a while since you've done that, hasn't it?" Samantha said.

"I've lost the technique."

"Not on your life."

He pulled her close for another kiss, and this time she came with it, her breasts soft against his chest, her hip nestled against his. In prison he had tried hard not to fantasize incessantly about women. He had known thinking of them, dreaming of their soft, supple bodies, would make his hellish life impossible to endure. Now he felt as if a banked flame had reignited inside him. The touch of Samantha's hands, the soft give of her lips, the restless movements of her tongue, were enough to drive him crazy.

She pulled away at last, just far enough to gaze into his eyes. "Just tell me one thing, Christian. Are you still in love with Julia Warwick? Because if you are, this isn't a good idea."

"I wasn't gone more than a month before she married someone else."

"You were in for life. You didn't expect her to wait, did you?"

"I didn't expect her to marry someone else immediately."

"Well, she did have Callie to think about."

The moment had passed. Desire was disappearing as fast as it had appeared, but his brain was still clouded with it. "Callie?"

She stared at him, then her eyes widened, as if she'd just realized something. "You know, it *is* getting late, and I sense some ambivalence here."

He grasped her arm. "You said Callie was eight a while ago, and I didn't even think about what you were saying. When was her birthday?"

She shook her head. "Not a conversation for us to have, Christian."

"We are having it."

"There's nothing I can tell you. She's not my daughter."

And then he knew, of course. Would have known sooner if he hadn't been so immersed in readjusting to life on the outside.

Would have known sooner if Julia hadn't hidden her secret from him, right from the beginning. If she hadn't deceived him into believing Callie belonged to another man.

He closed his eyes. "How can one man be so stupid?"

"Christian, I never, never meant to bring this up. Whatever secrets Julia had were hers to keep. I don't know any more than you do."

He opened his eyes. "But you've suspected. For how long, damn it?"

"After I met you and heard your story, it seemed so obvious. She looks like you. I thought that's why you were spending time with Callie, why you'd given her the puppy. I'm so sorry." Samantha looked as if she wanted to cry.

"She's blond, and both Julia and Bard have dark hair. We have the same learning disability." He was shaking his head, and he didn't try to comfort Samantha. "And she's already eight. I thought Callie was seven. Maisy told me about her in a letter. She must have waited months after Callie's birth to mention it. I didn't connect the dates. I never even considered she might be mine."

"Maybe she isn't. Maybe—"

He waved her into silence. "I think I'd better go."

She rested her fingertips on his arm. "It would be very easy right now to do something you'll regret."

"I'll tell you what I regret. I regret losing my daughter's childhood."

"Julia must have done what she thought was best, Chris. Maybe it wasn't, but hindsight's always twenty-twenty, isn't it?"

He got to his feet. "I'll come back for the boxes, if that's all right."

She joined him. "Go easy. Listen to me. Go easy. Think before you go and see Julia."

But Christian had already lost more time than any man could afford. He had no intention of losing even one more night.

26

Tonight Julia had begged off when Maisy offered to read to her. She'd thought she needed a break. Louisa's life was beginning to obsess her. Every night she was torn between asking her mother to stop reading and asking her to read faster. Louisa was like far too many women who had given their hearts to the wrong men.

Now she wished she had agreed to listen. She wasn't going to sleep anyway. The house was quiet, and everyone else was in bed. She gave up and found slippers and a bathrobe to make her way down the hall.

There were no advantages to losing her sight. Now one faint silver lining presented itself. She didn't have to turn on the lights and risk waking anyone. She felt for a glass and filled it with water from the tap; then she made her way to the front porch swing.

The night air was cool, but her chenille robe was heavy. From the woods she heard the whirring and chirping of insects and the sound of a lone night bird. She was closer to nature here than at Millcreek Farm, which was manicured and landscaped and where no woods of any consequence remained. She liked having the woods so close, although as a child there had been patches of forest at Ashbourne that frightened her.

The woods were deepest well behind the house, where Jeb Stuart Creek poured over stones as large as the ones the house had been built from. She had forbidden Callie to play there, and even when Julia learned to ride as a teenager, she always discouraged Christian from taking that route when they brought Claymore Park horses to ride at Ashbourne.

Even now, when she was feeling particularly worried she dreamed that those same woods were closing in around her, that the sun could no longer filter through treetops, and that vines twisted around her ankles and the hoofs of an unseen horse.

She shivered and decided to go back inside. She had started to her feet when she heard a vehicle coming down the driveway. She fell back into the swing and listened. At first she thought it might be Bard's BMW. Although she'd left a message that she wanted to talk to him, he had ignored her. She planned to warn him that she was going to tell Christian the truth about Callie, but so far he hadn't given her the opportunity.

The sound grew louder, and she realized it couldn't be Bard. The BMW had a hum as mellow as an after-hours jazz quartet. This sounded more like Maisy's new pickup, but louder, as if the driver was taking the gravel driveway too fast. She tried to decide what to do. Teenagers sometimes drove the county roads, drag racing where the roads widened. But Ashbourne was so far off the beaten path it rarely happened here.

She listened, and the truck slowed in front of the house; then the engine died and a door slammed. She had just decided to go inside and call for Jake when she heard Christian's voice.

"It's me."

She sank back to the swing. "You frightened me."

His voice grew louder, and she knew he was moving toward her. "What are you doing out here?"

"Trying to convince myself to fall asleep. What are you doing here?" Her heart was pounding faster, and not from residual fear.

"Well, I've been asking myself the same thing. All the way over. I've been asking myself why you would tell me the truth tonight when you didn't tell me almost nine years ago."

She sat very still, but the swing continued to move. She knew better than to play dumb. She couldn't buy time. No one should ever cheat this man of another second.

"We have to go somewhere else." She got to her feet. "Everyone's asleep inside, and I don't want to wake them."

He kept his voice low. "My daughter among them?"

Her stomach knotted. "Callie's been asleep since nine."

"Then we'll drive somewhere. Come on."

"I'm in my bathrobe."

"I don't give a damn."

"Christian, I can't see to get down to your truck."

He was silent. At this moment she doubted he wanted to touch her, and if she fell headfirst down the steps, he probably wouldn't care. Finally, though, she felt his hand on her arm. "I'll help you."

She knew she had to go with him, but it was the last thing she wanted to do. "Just don't pull me. It sets me off balance."

"Come on."

She shook off his hand and stretched out her own to find his arm. She followed his lead, feeling her way down the steps and out the stone path to the driveway. He led her around to the passenger side of the pickup and opened the door. She put one foot on the running board and felt for the floor with her other. In a moment she was seated, and the door slammed behind her.

"Where are we going?" she asked when he got in and started the engine.

"Somewhere we can talk in normal voices."

"Where you can shout at me?"

He was silent.

They drove for a while. She had no idea where they might be going, but she wasn't afraid for her safety. She was desperate to explain, although she knew there were no explanations good enough. She had kept one man from a daughter he would have loved, even behind prison bars, and asked another man who couldn't love Callie to be her father.

Christian applied the brakes, and she heard gravel spinning under the pickup wheels. Then the truck rolled to a halt, and he turned off the engine.

"Where are we?"

"Down the road from the swimming hole."

"An odd choice, don't you think?"

"Why, because we used to park here and make love? That's

what it was, wasn't it, Julia? Or is that another secret you've kept all these years?''

"I was going to tell you, Christian. I've just been trying to reach Bard first to warn him."

"Warn him that Callie's real father was finally going to know the truth?"

"Yes."

He exhaled, as if he had been holding that particular breath for an hour. "So..."

"I was afraid at first after you came back. I didn't know what to think or do. I'd been through so many changes. I'd lost my sight, left my husband. I didn't know what you would think, or what it might do to Callie or my marriage."

"We can't have something as insignificant as the truth upset your marriage, can we?"

"That's not fair. I'm just trying to explain there were more people involved in this than it seems on the surface."

His voice was heavy with sarcasm. "Let's see. Me. My daughter."

"Christian, *I'm* involved, whether you want to acknowledge it or not, and so is Bard. His name is on Callie's birth certificate. He married me to give her that name."

"So that no one would know a convicted murderer had fathered her?''

"Do you think that would have been easy for a little girl to explain?"

"Here's something you could have taught her. 'My father was put in jail, but he's innocent. My mother says someday everyone will know the truth.'''

Julia began to weep. "After my day in court you hated me. I tried to tell you I was pregnant. Your lawyer said you didn't want to speak to me. I sent you a letter begging you to call me collect. Peter brought it back unopened."

He was silent.

"I didn't know what to do. You were in prison for life."

"So you turned to Bard Warwick."

"He supported me during the trial. He kept showing up when I needed someone the most. He made sure I ate and got out of bed and did the things I needed to. And he listened. To everything I said. The way you always had.''

''I was a little busy fighting for my freedom to listen to you, Julia.''

''After you were convicted, I realized I was carrying your baby. I must have gotten pregnant the last time we were together.''

''The night before they put you on the stand.''

She pushed on. ''Bard and my parents were the only ones who knew about the baby. Maisy wanted me to have it and raise it at Ashbourne.''

''You could have had an abortion. Better than having a murderer's child, wasn't it?''

''Do you think I would have killed your baby? She was all I had left. Don't you understand? She was everything to me, just the way you had been.''

She heard the sound of a window being rolled down. It was the only sound for at least a minute. Then he spoke. ''So you decided that since I meant everything to you, you would hide my child's existence from me.''

''I decided that if you knew you had a daughter you couldn't see or hold it might well drive you over the edge.''

''So you did this for *me?*''

She heard the sarcasm. ''I thought I did it for everybody. Bard wanted to marry me, and he said he could be a good father to the baby. I needed someone to tell me which foot to put in front of the other, and God knows, that's his forte. You needed some measure of peace. Our baby needed a life without prejudice. So I married him.''

''It seemed the thing to do, huh?''

''I was twenty years old.''

''Well, you're twenty-nine now.''

''I was going to tell you. I told you, I was waiting until I could tell Bard my decision.''

''You owed him that, but you didn't owe me the truth? Not anywhere along the way?''

''I owed you the truth all along.'' She began to weep again.

"Yeah, you did." He started the engine and pulled back on to the road.

"What are you going to do now?"

"What do you mean?"

"We have to talk about Callie and what this will mean to her."

"I don't know what I'm going to do."

"You can't tell her, Christian. Not now. Do you know how confusing it would be? She's going to feel like she's at fault somehow. Her relationship with Bard isn't the best."

"I guess he's not all that fond of raising another man's child after all."

It was too close to home to deny.

"He'd better not lay a finger on her," Christian said.

"It's not like that. He's just not a man who likes children."

"So you'd like me to stay quiet so they can work out their relationship? Then what? When she's older I slip in the back door and mention how much I wish I could have been her daddy?"

He was driving too fast. She could tell by the sound of gravel flying against the windshield, but she didn't ask him to slow down. He did, finally, on his own. He pulled to a stop.

"I'm going to tell Callie the truth when I think she's old enough to understand how this happened," Julia said. "She's already crazy about you. Once she's over the shock, she'll want to be your daughter."

"And in the meantime? Your husband's going to let me spend time with her? He's going to welcome me into the family fold?"

"I'll make sure you have time with her. We'll find a way."

"Right..."

She found his arm with her fingertips. "We'll find a way to make this right. *I* didn't keep you from raising your daughter. The Commonwealth of Virginia did that. But I can make sure you have all the time you need with her now. And I will. I promise."

"Just tell me one thing. How could you claim to love me, then do this?"

She heard the agony in his voice. She began to weep softly, remembering the perfect day under the Ashbourne sun that she had relived in Yvonne's office. "I loved you so much I've had to find myself again, one piece at a time, and it's taken years."

"Somebody asked me tonight if I still loved you."

She wiped her eyes on the sleeve of her bathrobe. "You'd better take me home. Or maybe you have. Have you?"

"Do you want to know what I said?"

"Was it before or after you realized Callie was your daughter?"

He didn't answer. He asked another question. "When did you stop loving me?"

"Never."

He said nothing. Then he opened his door and closed it again, quietly enough that she knew they must be back at the house. He came around and opened hers, then she felt his hand on her arm. "Be careful," he said gruffly. "I'll help you down."

"I'll do it." She set a foot on the running board, then reached for the ground with her other. It was farther away than she'd estimated, and she pitched forward. He caught her, wrapping his arms around her to steady her.

"Christian..."

His mouth came down on hers with such a fierce hunger that for a moment she was frightened. Then fear fled and exultation filled her. Even if she hadn't let herself think of this moment, she had dreamed of it. She fitted against him as if their bodies had never been parted. She couldn't see him, hadn't seen him for nearly nine years, but now she realized how little that mattered.

She opened herself to him as she never had to Bard, because Bard had never wanted this much of her. She whimpered and pressed herself tighter against Christian. Her lips parted as his did, and she felt the smooth thrust of his tongue.

He parted her robe, and it tangled at her feet. Her breasts were bare under her nightgown, and he cupped one, his palm rough and searching. Desire was a liquid force, and she pressed her hips against his, searching, too, and finding the tangible evidence of his arousal.

He pushed her away and held her there with his hands on her shoulders.

"What in the hell are we doing?" he said.

She could feel the night air closing in around her. She didn't know where they were. She had visions of the forest she'd thought about earlier, where Jeb Stuart Creek flowed over boulders and the canopy of trees blocked all light. She could almost feel the vines pulling at her, twining around her feet until she was imprisoned forever. She was disoriented, frightened, yearning for something she'd only had a taste of.

A taste that might have to last forever.

"Go inside, Julia. I'll help you to the steps."

"I..."

"Don't say anything. There's nothing you can say. Just go inside."

She took the robe he shoved at her and let him help her to the steps. Everything felt unfamiliar, as if she had ended up in a new universe. She was home, yet she wasn't. When he dropped his hand, she reached for it and caught it. She held it against a cheek still damp with tears until he pulled away.

"Tell your husband I intend to get to know my daughter," Christian said. "I don't care what else you tell him."

She stood on the porch and listened as he drove away.

27

Christian didn't sleep. By the time dawn rolled around he knew trying any longer was futile. Since he and Peter were scheduled to have breakfast with an old woman who was having her annual reservations about letting the Mosby Hunt use her land, he only had a brief window of opportunity to call Pinky. He wanted to tell him what he had discovered about Joachim Hernandez. When he had finished with that, he would manufacture a thousand new jobs for himself so he didn't have to think about Julia and Callie.

He showered and had a cup of coffee before he dialed Pinky's number. A sleepy Pinky answered the phone, but once he realized who was on the other end, his voice warmed. "How you doing, Chris?"

They chatted for a moment; then Christian launched into his reason for calling. First he told him about his abortive meeting with Davey Myers. Then he told Pinky about Joachim Hernandez and his connection to Fidelity. Finally he explained about Joachim's appointment book, the deposits to his bank account and the notations about Miles Inchman.

There was a long silence on the other end. Christian wished he could see Pinky's face. Then he heard a humorless laugh.

"Well, there's not much I can say about Inchman," Pinky said. "Except that you're barking up the wrong tree there."

"Why? Can you tell me that much?"

"Listen, we'll have coffee. Ten-thirty? By then maybe I'll have more to say." They made arrangements to meet at the same fast-food restaurant and hung up.

Christian got through the next two hours on stamina and forced patience. He and Peter made the required visit to Sally Foxhall, a woman of eighty-nine who thoroughly enjoyed their attention. But by the time he and Peter had convinced her to keep her land open, he felt as if he was ready to fly apart.

"You seem edgy," Peter said on the way back to Claymore Park. "Anything wrong?"

Christian wondered if Peter knew that Callie was his daughter. "It's not easy coming back to a life you left so completely," he said. "I'm trying to untangle a million threads."

"At least your job is a sure thing, and pretty soon you'll be so busy you won't have time to worry about much of anything."

Christian wondered if Peter really thought coming back could be that easy. He switched the topic to the opening hunt, scheduled in four days. Until they arrived back at Claymore Park they chatted about strategy, about where they would cast the hounds and which horses they would ride. Christian would hunt the hounds, but Peter would be right beside him if he needed help.

Peter headed back to the house, and Christian had started down to the kennels when Rosalita called to him. "You have a visitor."

For a moment he wondered if Julia had come to finish last night's conversation. Then he saw the familiar figure of a woman.

"Pastor..."

The Reverend Bertha Petersen opened her arms for a hug, and he scooped her into his own.

He stepped back. "What are you doing here? How did you find me?"

"The warden told me."

"He probably hopes you can talk me into turning myself in."

"Warden Sampsen knows you're innocent. He hated to lose you, that's all. He was afraid the program would fall apart."

"Did it?"

"Javier's running it and doing a fine job."

He was glad to hear it.

"I'm going to Ludwell now," she continued, "but I thought

I'd swing by on my way from the airport and see how you're doing."

Christian was touched. "I'm coping."

"Not as easily as you'd like."

Christian ran his hand through his hair and tried to smile. "You can tell?"

"It's never easy, but it must be even harder when so much of your life was stolen unfairly."

"How many other men and women are sitting behind bars when they don't belong there?"

"I don't know. Seems to me you could think about that a little and see what you could do about it."

He hadn't expected that. "Like what?"

"We have laws that need changing. And men and women who need help once they get out. Who's in a better position to know what's fair and what's not?"

His first inclination was to laugh this off. He didn't need to take on anyone else's problems. But who better?

"Tell me about yourself," she said, changing the subject.

"I wouldn't know where to start."

"You don't sound happy."

He wasn't, and suddenly he wanted to tell her why.

"I'm listening," she said, as if she'd heard his thoughts. "Just me, and maybe the man upstairs."

"If there's a man upstairs, he has his hands over his ears."

"God has better things to do than run every little moment of our lives. But things do happen, and people learn from them, whether that was the point or not. Through it all, you've never been alone."

"Then why do I feel like I'm the last person in the world?"

"No evangelism today," she promised. "Suppose you just tell me what's going on?"

They walked to the fishpond, and Bertha seated herself on a stone bench. Christian told her everything, about Julia, about his search for more information about Fidelity's murder, and, at last, about Callie. He could hear his own voice, but it sounded unfamiliar. He sounded like a man who wanted something, a man like any other. And when he'd finished, he was frightened.

"You can't understand why she did it, can you?" Bertha said. "You can't understand how a twenty-year-old woman, whose entire life had been turned upside down, made a decision that hurt you?"

He didn't want to answer.

"You do understand," she said, looking closely at him. "You just don't want to. You're afraid if you let Julia back into your heart, even that little bit, you'll be lost."

Then he told her the rest, the part he hadn't been able to tell Julia or anyone else. "I still love her."

"I know."

Now he had said everything, but he didn't feel cleansed.

"Christian, I won't advise you to break up this woman's marriage. Is that what you want me to say?"

"I know you can't."

"I will advise you to forgive her. Until you do, the past and the present will be struggling and tugging at each other forever. You have to clear the decks for a fresh start, whatever that means. She's the mother of your child."

She got slowly to her feet and held out her hand. "You can't remember this, because it's been so long. But sometimes life is sweet and easy. It's a gift when it happens, one you'll receive again someday. In the meantime, you've been given something to look forward to. You have a daughter, and soon enough she'll know she has a new father. You'll watch her grow and know you've done something wonderful. Julia gave you that much, didn't she? It would have been so easy to have stopped that little life before it began. But she chose a harder path, and even if you don't like the fork she took, I suspect she did her best."

He wanted to remain angry. Anger was safer and surer, a terrain and territory he understood. But anger was melting away, no matter how hard he tried to hold on to it. Because at its center was a child, his child, whom Julia had protected in the only way she knew how.

Callie. His daughter.

"I'm glad I came," Bertha said. "I felt the strongest need to see you again."

"I'm glad you came, too," he said, taking her hand. "Come again."

"Maybe you'll come to me next time. I'm going to keep my ear to the ground, Christian. There are things you can do to make this world a better place, and I'm going to find them for you."

"You do that, Pastor. Then we'll talk."

Pinky was waiting when Christian got to the restaurant. He held up a plastic foam cup for Christian, and Christian joined him. His stomach did a slow turn at the entwined smells of grease and steaming coffee. He was reminded of Ludwell.

"Black, right?" Pinky said.

"Thanks."

"I only have a few minutes." Pinky poured a pack of sugar into his own cup, then followed with two more. "Here's what I can tell you, but it didn't come from me, understand?"

"Perfectly."

Pinky lowered his voice. "Miles Inchman works undercover for the sheriff's department. Vice, mostly drugs. And he pays informers."

Christian looked up. "Joachim?"

Pinky confirmed with a nod. "Worked for Inchman for a year or so."

"Then he wasn't selling drugs to supplement his income from polo."

"No, he was responsible for a couple of major busts." Pinky stirred his coffee. "Fidelity Sutherland was on his hit list, but somewhere along the way she got smart and stopped using altogether. Went clean as a fresh-picked goose, according to what I hear. Was clean for months before she died."

Christian was happy to let this theory go. He was glad his old friend had come to her senses, and he thought Samantha would be glad to know Joachim wasn't as blackhearted as she'd feared.

"What if somebody was afraid Fidelity was going to turn him in?" Christian said. "What if she knew too much and someone decided to be sure she stayed quiet?"

"Joachim was in a good position to know. There was no indication anyone had been worried about her. She was small potatoes. Didn't know anything important and not worth a hit.''

"Sounds like that's a dead end, then." He grimaced at his own pun.

"You know how much chance you have of finding out something about the Sutherland girl's death that we don't already know?" Pinky said.

"I'd be happy if I just found out something you *did* know. Everything you know, in fact."

"Very little, you want the truth. The department never picked up the ball on this one, Chris. It's that simple. You were there holding the knife that killed her, and even though you told them you'd just picked it up off the ground, you couldn't produce your own. What more did they need to find out?"

"Who really did it, for openers."

"Except for the drug angle, the investigation was as basic as they come. I've just about memorized that damn file by now, so I know. They talked to friends and family and got statements and alibis for all of them. She didn't seem to have any enemies, no stalkers, no professional intrigues. And now nobody cares even that much about conducting another investigation. Nobody's going to come after you again, and all your so-called leads are probably going to turn out like this one. That's the main reason I came. To tell you that you don't have to keep up with this. You aren't going to find anything, and you don't need to. You're a free man."

Christian took a sip of his coffee. "What if Fidelity stumbled on something she wasn't supposed to know? Not drugs, but something?"

Pinky rolled his eyes. "You're playing the long shots."

"What would people around Ridge's Race kill for, Pinky?"

"Just about anything, like people everywhere."

"I'm thinking about land. You've seen the signs at this end of the county. Growth is the dirtiest word in the dictionary."

"I don't know what you mean."

"Davey Myers told me that about the time Fidelity was killed, he was supposed to build a development close to South Land, but the land didn't pan out."

"You're reaching, you know that."

Christian knew Pinky was right. He didn't have the tools nor the knowledge to conduct an investigation. He only had motivation, and it was eating him alive. "Zandoff claims he worked construction. Construction was supposed to go up near South Land. Then Fidelity was murdered by Zandoff. It's like a puzzle with all the right pieces, but I don't know how to put it together."

"Even if you do, the picture might be blank."

"I guess that's a chance I'll have to take."

"And you want me to see if I can find out something?"

"Just see if anyone remembers anything about developers in the area. Any tensions over property."

"Then you'll call it quits?"

Christian didn't know. "You're a good friend."

"Chris, this is the coldest trail south of Santa's Workshop. You know, you got to let go of the past."

The advice sounded like Bertha's. "I'll think about what you've said."

"You do that." Pinky toasted Christian with his cup.

By some standards Mosby Hunt was a small club, but it had a sterling reputation. Some of the best equestrians in local history had hunted with Mosby, as well as some of the wealthiest men and women in Virginia. Still, times had changed, and to survive, the club had changed with them. Formal social events were held at local country clubs or estates large enough for full-scale entertaining. More often socializing was informal. Tailgate parties and bottles passed after a hunt's conclusion. Summer picnics and trail rides. Evening bonfires at the season's conclusion, where the best chases were recounted and entered into myth.

This year, as the board scheduled fixtures—or locations where each hunt of the year would take place—they'd voted to have the opening breakfast at Claymore Park. Tents like earthbound cumulus clouds would dot the hillside where the hunter's pace had been run, and caterers with tureens of peanut soup and silver platters of Virginia country ham would feed the multitudes. Peter had supervised every detail.

The success of the opening meet itself was even more important. When Christian returned from seeing Pinky, Peter was waiting for him.

"You don't need to tell me this is overkill, but I'm going to ride the land we'll be hunting. Check the jumps one last time and see if there are any trouble spots we haven't planned for."

Christian was sure Peter knew every inch of the area the way a man knows a cherished lover's body, but Peter was the successful man he was because he never left anything to chance. "Want some company?"

"I was hoping you'd volunteer."

He caught Night Ranger and saddled him, then joined Peter in the stableyard. Peter Claymore, on a rangy bay named Jack's Knife, was the quintessential horseman, straight yet relaxed in the saddle, his clothes casual but elegant, his tack glowing from hours of saddle soap, Neatsfoot oil and plain old elbow grease. He took exquisite care of his mounts and his own equipment. He never left important details to another living soul.

They rode in silence to the area where the opening breakfast would be held. Then they turned south from that point, passing beside newly plowed cornfields to follow a wooded trail that opened into a meadow replete with chicory and Queen Anne's lace. They had purposely diverged from the course for the hunter's pace. Having just ridden that way, the club expected and deserved a new venue. In the weeks to come they would hunt all over their territory.

"Once you finally taught Robby to enjoy riding, we often came this way," Peter said. "Just the two of us."

Christian doubted that "often" was accurate. Robby and his father had coexisted, but never with real warmth. He wondered if Peter had learned to accept his son's death by deceiving himself about Robby's life.

"I always thought Robby would succeed me as Master of Foxhounds," Peter said. "It was the one thing I really wanted. My father was master, you know."

Christian supposed he had known, although he hadn't thought about it in years. "And after him Julia's father."

"Harry Ashbourne took over when my father died unexpectedly. And what a master Harry was. I wasn't living at Claymore

Park then, but I would come home to hunt as often as I could. And as good as my father was, Harry was that much better. He would take a jump and not a hair on his head would move. But he could be ruthless, too. He was a tyrant, our Harry. He could rant and rave, but he was always right, and we were better for it. An emotional man encased in steel.''

Christian wondered how much of her father Julia had inherited. ''In those days Maisy rode with Mosby Hunt, didn't she?''

Peter smiled. ''She was an unlikely choice for Harry. Small-boned and delicate—''

''Maisy?''

''Oh, yes. She gained all that weight in later years. She was a lovely girl. More than a few young men wished they'd seen her first, I'll tell you.''

Christian had to smile at that. So Maisy had been the belle of her day. He was glad to hear it. ''Why was she an unlikely choice?''

''Well, Harry was older. A stern man, in his own way. A hawk. And Maisy was a butterfly. But for all their differences, they were perfectly matched. He adored her, although her riding skills exasperated him. She was a good rider by most people's standards, but, of course, Harry's standards were that much higher. I remember the way he used to watch her when she wasn't looking at him. There was such pride, such devotion, in his eyes. He clearly would have given his life for her.''

Christian liked the idea of Maisy having a great love. Her marriage to Jake was solid and warm, but he was glad that early, in the bloom of youth, she had been swept off her feet.

''It was the saddest day in the history of Mosby Hunt when Harry was found dead in the woods,'' Peter said.

A lot of years had passed since Christian had heard that story. He tried to remember. ''He was riding alone?''

''Yes, and when he didn't come home, his stablemen went out looking for him. His horse didn't come home, either, but they found him, a big gray like Night Ranger, with his reins tangled in a thicket. He was wild with distress. It took three men to free and settle him. They knew then that something had happened to Harry. It took hours to track him down, even when they put the foxhounds to it. That's not what they're bred for, but one of the dogs finally did find him in the woods by the creek. He was lying on the other side of a particularly vicious jump on Ashbourne property, a jump most of us never tried when we hunted that way. But Harry always took it and always as if he were floating on air. His neck was broken. He must have died instantly.''

"That must be why Maisy closed Ashbourne."

"Understandable, but not a suitable memorial to her husband."

They rode for a while in silence along the remnants of an old logging road and beside a creek that fed into Jeb Stuart farther up the line. Peter got down to check a coop—a jump that really resembled a chicken coop—to be certain it didn't need repairs. Christian didn't know what Peter was thinking about as he examined the sturdy boards, but Christian was thinking of another ride with Peter.

"There's a den not far from here," Peter said when he got back into the saddle. "That's one of the reasons I want to cast down by the creek at the opening meet. Would you like to see it? You should know where it is."

"Do you have time? Didn't you say you were going out this afternoon?"

"I have to ride back. But you go ahead." Peter gave him directions. "I saw three cubs in the spring, but I never saw them again. I don't know if they just didn't make it or if they were moved to another location."

"I'll see if I can spot the den."

Peter lifted his cap in salute, then started back toward Claymore Park. Christian turned and followed Peter's directions, riding for another fifteen minutes beyond the coop.

He halted at the edge of the woods and dismounted, tying Ranger to finish the trip on foot.

At first he didn't see anything out of the ordinary. The terrain was wooded and gently rolling, and he followed a path through brush and alongside the creek for a quarter of a mile until he reached a stand of luminous birch trees that Peter had told him to watch for. He scanned the immediate distance. Just as he was about to push forward again, movement fifteen feet to his right caught his eye.

A young gray fox—a teenager in fox years—was shifting sleepily on a flat rock bathed in sunshine, its sleek coat glistening. Christian drew a silent breath, but it was enough to alert the animal. It rose to all fours and stretched out its lithe body. Then it looked directly at him. Christian stood perfectly still. The fox waited; he waited. At last the fox turned and disappeared into the forest.

The last time he had seen a fox at such close quarters had been on the morning of Fidelity's death. He and Peter had taken a ride together that day, too. And on the way they had come upon a younger fox than this one. At the time he hadn't thought much about it. He'd expected small miracles in his life. He hadn't known then that his trip with Peter that day would be his last ride as a free man for many years to come.

"I'll have to remember this place," Peter had said that day, as the young fox turned and scurried behind rocks. "Looks to me like a family's living here somewhere."

Christian and Peter had set out early for South Land, where Fidelity's father had a mare he wanted to sell. Christian had been asked along for company and advice. He had taken the mare out for a ride while Frank and Peter discussed a price, then started back with Peter after the closing of the deal.

"They're beautiful animals," Christian said, hardly thinking about his own words. He was looking forward to a date with Julia that night. He had a million things to think about, but somehow Julia Ashbourne was always at the top of his list.

"Speaking of beautiful animals, did you know Miss Sutherland was out riding with my son this morning? On Firefall? Frank mentioned it. He was surprised you'd allowed it."

"Firefall?"

Peter gave a dry laugh. "I see you didn't know."

Firefall was Christian's newest project, a fiendish chestnut who had vast potential as a chaser and none at all as a pleasure mount. "Fidelity knows she's not supposed to ride him. She's seen me training him. She knows he's green as grass."

"Apparently that's what appealed to her. And apparently my son didn't know any better."

"I'll be sure to talk to her. Today." Christian wasn't surprised Fidelity had conned Robby into letting her ride the big hunter, but he was steaming silently. She'd risked both her own safety and Firefall's, as well. If something had happened to Firefall, all his months of work with the hunter would have been for nothing. And if something had happened to Fidelity...

They were almost back to Claymore Park when Peter asked a troubling question. "Christian, did you ask Fidelity to have her father talk to me?"

Now Christian was completely in the dark. "About what?"

"Frank tells me you've been accepted to the University of Michigan for your final two years."

In the spring Christian had begun to grow weary of working full-time and attending night classes, so he had applied to several universities. He had a 4.0 average and glowing recommendations from all his professors. One of them had highly recommended Michigan.

"It's just one place I've been accepted," he said. "I'm really hoping to go to the University of Virginia. I applied too late for scholarships, so now it's just a question whether anyone who got one gives it up to go somewhere else."

"Frank suggested that I write the Dean of Admissions at Michigan and give you a recommendation for complete financial aid. I'm an alum, you know."

Christian did know, but he had purposely never brought up his future. He was determined to make it through college without anyone's help. He had repeatedly turned down Peter's offers of financial assistance, and even a recommendation had seemed like interference.

"I know my dad was a troubled man," Christian said. "But one thing he taught me was to make it on my own. He never asked anyone for help, and neither will I."

"If Gabe had asked for help, he might be alive today."

Christian was surprised. It wasn't like Peter to be so direct or personal.

"I'm going to write the dean," Peter said. "Unless you tell me not to."

Christian didn't know what to say. Through the years Peter

had been good to him. He had allowed Christian to stay on at Claymore Park, and even though Christian had worked in the stable when he wasn't in school, he knew he could never make up his debt. He had been treated almost like family, and he didn't want to offend Peter now.

"I like a man with pride," Peter said, when Christian still hadn't answered. "There's too little of it around these days. Pride and honor are worth dying for. A man's good name is all he really has."

"Sir, I appreciate the offer more than I can say, but I guess I'm worried that with your help I might just get that money. Then I'd have to take it."

Peter chuckled. "It's Julia Ashbourne, isn't it?"

Christian could feel his cheeks turning red. "Yes, sir." And now that he thought about it, it surprised him Fidelity would try to ensure his admission to a distant university. If he ended up in Michigan, he would see little of Julia except for summers.

"I won't write the dean, then. It sounds like Miss Sutherland's been misled."

"Misled?"

"Well, Frank conveyed to me that you and Miss Ashbourne were ready for a bit of a vacation from each other."

Now Christian truly was mystified. "No, sir, we aren't."

"I have connections at UVA, you know."

Christian was tempted, but in the end, he shook his head. "Thank you, but it will mean more to me if I get a scholarship on my own."

"Everything comes too easily to most young people around here. No one can say that about you. I'm proud of you, Christian."

"Thank you, sir."

They had ridden the rest of the way back to Claymore Park in silence, and Christian had spent those minutes wondering what Fidelity had hoped to accomplish with her interference. He'd been angry to discover she'd taken Firefall without his permission. Now he was growing angrier.

He mulled over her interference for the rest of the day. Once he had taken care of the horses he still had chores to do in town, but afterward, he decided to swing by South Land and find out what was going on. Fidelity was up to something. And Fidelity, when she was up to something, was as unpredictable and dangerous as the horse she'd ridden without his permission.

He had been young and impatient. He had been anxious to see her and find out exactly what she was doing, so he could put a stop to it.

He hadn't known, of course, what he would find instead.

28

Midway through the afternoon, Julia sat in sunshine on the front porch, a ball of clay in her hands. Callie and Tiffany were playing with Clover in the yard, and between the children's delighted squeals and the puppy's vocal serenades, Ashbourne rang with music.

The screen door banged, and Maisy spoke from that direction. "They are having fun, aren't they?"

"That puppy was the best present anyone's ever given Callie."

"May I join you?"

"Of course." Julia could tell by the creaking of chains that Maisy had lowered herself to the porch swing. Julia had told Maisy early that morning about Christian's discovery. Maisy had been relieved and uncharacteristically tactful about asking for details. Julia was glad, because last night's scene did not bear repeating.

"What are you working on?"

"I don't know."

"A bust of someone?"

Julia smoothed the clay into a ball. No matter what she did, it seemed to form itself into a man's head and face, at least in her mind. "I'm just keeping my hands busy."

"How did your session go this morning?"

Karen had taken Julia to Warrenton for another go-round with Yvonne. Julia had let herself be hypnotized again, with the same results. She had been remarkably relaxed, and memories had flowed.

"We talked about Fidelity and the way I felt when I found out she'd been murdered."

"I'm sorry. That doesn't sound easy."

Julia slapped the clay from side to side. "Do you know that Fidelity and I quarreled the night before she died?"

"Did you ever tell me?"

"It took hypnosis to make me remember."

"Do you remember what you quarreled about?"

Julia began to mold the clay. "Christian and Robby."

"That's not uncommon, is it? Young women arguing about young men."

"She thought I was stupid to tie myself down. I should be playing the field, the way she was. She told me Bard was interested, and she thought I ought to go out with him and see what happened. She just couldn't understand that it was different for me, that I'd found the man I wanted."

"Was it a serious argument?"

"Serious just wasn't in her makeup."

"Why were you quarreling about Robby?"

"Fidelity thought Robby needed more confidence."

"That was certainly true. For a boy as smart as that one, he was remarkably inept around people."

"Robby was so involved in his thoughts that when he came out of them once in a while, he'd missed a lot and didn't know how to pick up the pieces."

"A good analysis. But what was wrong with Fidelity building his confidence?"

"She was flirting with him. Nothing big time, but she said she thought if she made a fuss over him, he'd feel better about himself. Fidelity had no reservations about her own powers."

"You can't see me, but I'm shaking my head."

Julia realized she was molding a man's face again. She had pinched out a nose, smoothed spaces for eyes. She rolled the clay in her hands and dropped it on the table beside her. "We all knew Robby was trying to find his place in the sun. Fidelity believed in simple solutions, that's all."

"That girl needed a job."

"She was after Christian, too, nagging him about going to a better college."

"And that's what you quarreled about?"

"She was like that all summer, making waves whenever she could to liven things up. I just got sick of it and told her to leave us alone."

"So that was your last conversation."

"She laughed it off. But I was angry when I left that day, and I told her so. I left in a huff. I wish I hadn't. That's not the way I want to remember our friendship."

"How many times did you quarrel with old Fiddle-Dee-Dee?"

"Not often. Who could stay mad at her?"

"And what kind of impression did your anger make that day?"

"Not a bit."

"So you don't really think she lost sleep on the last night of her life over this?"

Julia felt her throat closing. "Maisy, why don't we ever have a chance to tell the people we love goodbye?"

"We do, sometimes."

"I never have."

Despite a sleepless night, Christian threw himself into physical exercise for the rest of the afternoon. He washed horses and walked miles with the hounds. By evening he should have been exhausted, but he wasn't.

After an early dinner of Rosalita's fiery tacos and the prospect of another long night, he knew what he had to do.

He had a daughter, and he needed to see her. Not to tell her who he was. Not to begin the long process of turning himself into a real father. Just to see her and know, for the first time, that she belonged to him.

The puppy was his excuse. Amazingly enough, like all dogs, it seemed Clover was good for something after all. He decided he would stop by for just a few minutes to see how the puppy was getting on.

He called ahead to avoid trouble and got Maisy on the line.

She assured him that they were all there and would be glad to see him.

He started to hang up, but decided to add something while it was still only the two of them.

"I understand why you didn't tell me about Callie," he said gruffly.

"I'm glad."

"I'll be there in a little while."

He showered and shaved as if he was going on a date. But this date was with a little girl. He wondered if he would know what to say to her tonight. He changed into clean clothes and new hiking boots. Then he set out for Ashbourne.

Callie was outside with Clover when he drove up. He parked a distance from the house and got out, but he didn't walk up the driveway. He watched her throwing sticks for the puppy, who gaped as they sailed overhead. Obviously Clover thought Callie was providing some canine version of fireworks, because the puppy didn't move so much as her tail.

The sun was on its way down, and Callie was dressed accordingly. Blue jeans, blue sweater with a bright yellow jacket over it, sneakers with soles that lit up like fireflies every time she moved. She caught sight of him and came running, sneakers twinkling.

"Hey, Christian!"

He caught her just before she plowed into him. He didn't want to let her go. He thought he could hold her for the rest of his life, just this way.

But he did let her go, and she jumped back, laughing. "Did you see that? Clover watches the sticks. Next time, she'll catch 'em!"

"Think so?"

"I know it. Did you come to see me?"

"Sure did."

"Cool! Come on!" Callie dashed back to the puppy and Christian followed. "Wanna see what else she can do?"

"I can't wait."

"Watch this!" Callie got right in front of Clover and stared into her eyes. "Sit, Clover."

The puppy wagged her tail but stayed on all fours.

"Sit, Clover," Callie repeated.

Christian was about to warn her this particular command might take some time when the puppy dropped to the ground.

"Wow!" He really was impressed. He wondered what the child could do with a smart dog.

"You just have to get her attention," Callie said. "I don't like to pay attention in school, so I know how it is."

Christian squatted down to pet Clover. "I had trouble learning to read, so I didn't pay attention in school, either."

"Really? Me, too."

"You want to hear some good news?"

"What?"

"I did learn. Now I like to read."

Callie was definitely interested. "What? What do you read?"

"Books about dogs, for one thing. All kinds of books about dogs. And horses. Newspapers. Magazines. Novels. I like mysteries, because that's solving a puzzle."

"Reading is like solving a puzzle for me."

Again he was impressed with her intelligence, but this time pride followed closely. She was his daughter, and bright as polished brass. "It *can* be. But once you've solved it, it's worth it."

"I'm good at math. I can add anything in my head."

"I'll just bet you can."

"And I can draw. Like Mommy." She lowered her voice. "Before, when she wasn't blind."

"I remember how well she drew. She drew pictures of me a long time ago."

"You were friends."

"Yes, we were."

"Are you friends now?"

That was harder to answer. "A lot of sad things happened, Callie."

"Like Fidelity dying."

"Yes. That was very sad."

"Very sad," a voice said behind him.

Christian got to his feet and saw that Julia had joined them. He had been so fascinated by his daughter that he hadn't heard her footsteps. "Julia," he said in greeting, following it with a nod she couldn't see.

"Christian." Her arms were crossed over a fuzzy purple jacket. Her hair was pulled back in a braid exposing the same horse head earrings he had noticed at the hunter's pace. She carried a gnarled branch she probably used like a cane in the yard, to test her path.

"I guess I'd better be going," he said, looking down at Callie. "I just popped by to see if you and Clover were still doing all right."

"Christian." Julia stretched out her hand and found his arm after a moment of trial and error. "I want us to do something together. The three of us."

His heart was beating faster. He saw Callie's expectant expression and knew she was hoping to drag the evening out a little.

"What's that?" he said.

"I want to take flowers to Fidelity's grave."

Callie looked interested. He was surprised. "Now?"

"You missed the funeral."

At the time he had been in jail. Two months had passed after his arrest before Peter pulled enough strings to get him out on bail. But even if he had been free, he would have been the last person anyone wanted to see at the service.

Julia seemed to understand. "You never got to say goodbye. In a way, neither did I. I'd like us to do this together. Callie can bring Clover. It's a beautiful place. There's lots of room for them to run. Has the sun set yet?"

"Nearly."

"Then we ought to hurry. Will you do it?"

He couldn't say no. He decided not to lie to himself. He couldn't say no to Julia. "You have flowers?"

"Maisy's cutting some. Chrysanthemums, asters, whatever she can find. Of course Fidelity would prefer orchids, but this will have to do for tonight."

"Callie, you'd like to come?" he said.

"Me and Clover."

"Clover, of course. Maybe she'll find a fox."

"Really?"

"No," he said with a smile.

She grinned back at him, and he saw that one of her bottom teeth was missing. It nearly broke his heart.

Maisy came out with the flowers and offered the keys to the new red pickup. They piled in, dog and child in the middle, pressed against him, Julia on the passenger's side. The truck started with a lion's robust purr.

Christian knew where the Ridge's Race cemetery was, but Julia instructed him to turn in at South Land instead. "They buried her in the family graveyard," she said. "No one told you, I guess."

"They didn't ask me to do a eulogy, either."

"It was the hottest day of the summer. Tears dried on people's cheeks. Some girls from Foxcroft sang 'Amazing Grace.' A friend from Swarthmore played the flute. The priest refused to make sense of it. He said there was no sense to it. It was the kindest thing he could have said."

Christian was glad he had been in jail.

"Mommy, do you believe in ghosts?" Callie said.

"No, why?"

"Fidelity might be a ghost. She might be waiting there to scare us."

"Fidelity is an angel," Christian said, before he thought about his words.

"An angel?"

Julia laughed a little. "Fidelity would be the first to disagree."

"She was our friend," Christian said, "and now she's Callie's guardian angel."

"I have a guardian angel?" Callie sounded thrilled.

"I don't see why not," Christian said. "Fidelity is your middle name, right?"

"Uh-huh."

"Then she has a special interest in you."

"I have my own guardian angel," Callie told Clover. She looked up and aimed her next remark at her mother. "Christian says I'll learn to read like he did."

He hadn't said that exactly, but he didn't disagree.

"Christian can read anything," Julia said.

"Maybe Fidelity will help me."

It was a new take on guardian angels, but Christian figured the idea wouldn't hurt. He slowed as they approached the entrance to South Land. He told Julia where they were as he turned.

"The graveyard is off to the left, up a steep hill," Julia said. "The road runs between two weeping willows."

"Appropriate."

"You follow it to the top, and the plot's beside a creek."

He watched for the willows, then made the appropriate turn, slowing to a crawl as they wound their way uphill until he saw a white picket fence surrounding an area that bloomed with simple stone markers. He parked and turned off the engine.

"We're here."

"The sky is a big giant rainbow," Callie said.

"Sunset," Christian told Julia. "A really spectacular one tonight."

Julia rolled down her window. "It's so quiet out here. We should have buried her under the dance floor at a nightclub."

"An exclusive nightclub," he said.

"You can't bury people in a nightclub," Callie told them. The puppy was wiggling, and Christian knew Clover had had too much of a good thing. He opened his door and reached for her. Callie scooted under the steering wheel and took off with the puppy as he went around to open the other door for Julia.

She was clutching the flowers as if they might ward off everything from evil spirits to Martians. He rested his hand on her forearm. "If you take my hand, we might avoid what happened last night."

She looked up at him as if she could see every passing expression on his face. "I'm so sorry about last night. About everything, Christian."

"Why did you want to come here with me? With Callie, too?"

"We're going to be sharing her. It's important that she thinks we get along, that she doesn't worry about keeping things secret from either of us."

"Sharing her?" He gave a humorless laugh. "Bard Warwick is going to share?"

"Right now we're talking about you and me, and I want Callie to see us acting like grown-ups. This way, when we're ready to tell her the truth, she'll accept it.''

''What made you think of this place?''

She bit her bottom lip, white teeth sinking into soft tissue he had probably bruised last night. He couldn't seem to look away or think of anything else.

''I'm seeing a therapist,'' she said at last. ''Maybe you think that's silly? Or overdue?''

''A good idea, under the circumstances,'' he said gruffly.

''I...well, she's hypnotizing me....''

''Mommy?''

Christian turned to see Callie swinging from the lowest branch of an old maple tree at the cemetery's edge.

''What's she doing?'' Julia said.

''Hanging from a tree, trying to get her toe up so she can sit on the branch.''

''Should I be worried?''

''Not unless you're raising a little debutante.''

''No chance of that.'' She cupped her hands to yell. ''Just be careful....'' She lowered them. ''You'll tell me if she falls?''

''I'll pick her up. You were telling me about hypnosis?''

''It sounds like so much mumbo jumbo, doesn't it?''

''Not if it helps.'' He realized they were having a conversation like old friends. No matter how hard he tried not to, he just slid back into past habits.

''I don't know if it will. I think I'm supposed to remember things I've buried.''

''Things that keep you from seeing?''

''Maybe. But today I thought about the last conversation I had with Fidelity. We fought over you—''

''Me?''

''And Robby, too. Fidelity wanted me to play the field, to date other guys.''

''I know.''

''You do?''

''That was one of the reasons I was angry at her the day she died. One of the things I went to South Land to confront her about.''

"You never told me."

"It didn't seem important, not with Fidelity dead. And explaining anything from jail was impossible. By the time I got out on bail, I was more worried about whether I was going to prison. Or worse."

"You told the police you were angry because you discovered she had been to Claymore Park that morning and persuaded Robby to let her ride a hunter you were training, a horse you had told her nobody else was supposed to ride."

"Firefall. A big chestnut brute. Yeah, I was angry about that, too."

"I never understood why she did it."

"Sometimes if she got up early enough she'd come over for a morning ride, a change of pace from South Land's horses and trails. Sometimes we'd do the same thing and go over there. That morning she and Robby went out, and she probably told him I'd given her permission to ride Firefall. She was just looking for excitement, and Robby didn't know any better. I was upset when I found out, and I got angrier as the day went on. Late in the day, when I finally got a break, I went to confront her...."

"Christian, you said Fidelity wanted me to date other guys? How did you know?"

He told her about his conversation with Peter on the morning of Fidelity's death. He debated whether or not to tell her what had come next, but in the end, he decided to tell her all of it. There had been too many secrets. "I saw Bard in town that afternoon, when I was making a run to pick up some tack we'd ordered."

"Bard?"

Christian remembered the afternoon as if it had happened yesterday—he'd had years to go over each moment in detail. He had driven into town in one of Claymore Park's oldest pickups, a veteran that was usually relegated to the hayfields. He'd been hot and dusty, and the ride without shock absorbers or air-conditioning hadn't helped his temper. There had been one parking spot in front of the saddlery. As he'd turned into it, a sleek silver Jag had beaten him to the punch.

He had parked behind it, blocking the Jag's exit, and stepped down from the pickup.

Now, ironically, he realized how symbolic that moment had been.

"You might say we started off on the wrong foot," Christian told Julia.

"What happened?"

They'd had words. Bard had seen nothing wrong with taking the space, even though Christian had gotten there first. And when Christian refused to move the pickup until his errand was done, Bard threatened to go inside and call the police.

"We argued about a parking space," Christian said, keeping it simple. "And before we were done, he managed to tell me that he had his eye on you, and that Fidelity had told him you were ripe to play the field."

"I didn't know this conversation ever happened."

"Just out of curiosity, were you ready to play the field?"

"You were the only man I wanted. Why was Fidelity stirring up trouble?"

A question had been asked and answered, and he believed her. Now he thought about *her* question. His probing into Fidelity's life had paid off, after all.

He leaned against Maisy's pickup, watching Callie climb higher. "I know why she was stirring up trouble, but it's not pretty. Do you want the truth?"

"Please."

In as few words as possible he told her about Fidelity's involvement with drugs. "She pulled back while she still could, but that meant staying away from everybody and every place she'd gone before for excitement. She lived in two worlds, Julia. The one she inhabited with you, me and Robby, and a more dangerous world."

"How do you know this?"

"I've been doing some checking since I got out. I'm afraid I know this part for a fact."

"And you're saying that she was stirring up trouble...?"

"Because she was bored and probably a little angry about what her life had come down to. She was restless because she was fighting a craving that scared her. She had the good sense to back off before her life got out of control, but it gave her a lot of time and a certain kind of energy to mess around with the only people she could still afford to be close to.''

Julia was silent, digesting his theory. When she spoke, she sounded as if she wanted to cry. ''She was unhappy, so she wanted to make us unhappy?''

''I think she just thought she knew what was best for every-body, and she didn't have anything better to do. Maybe on some level she was jealous of what you and I had together, but if so, I can't believe it was a conscious thing. I don't think she wanted to hurt us. I just think she wanted control over something in her life.''

''Why didn't she tell me what she was going through? She never let on.''

''Fidelity had no weaknesses, remember? That's what happens when you raise a kid to think she's perfect. How can she ever admit she's not? To anyone?''

''I miss her so much.'' Julia's tears glistened in the fading light of day. ''I would have been there for her.''

''Well, I wasn't there at the end, when she really needed me. After I had my little encounter with Bard, I did my errand, then I left the saddlery hell-bent for leather and headed straight to South Land.''

''And that's when you ran into me?''

Julia had been on her way into town to get groceries for Maisy, and she'd waved him down. He'd been preoccupied and curt, and when she'd asked why, he only told her he had a score to settle with Fidelity. The words had come back to haunt him when she took the witness stand.

''That's when I ran into you,'' he acknowledged.

''And you refused to tell me what was wrong.''

''I didn't want to involve you.''

''Ironic, isn't it?''

His throat felt tight. ''If I'd only made it to South Land even twenty minutes before I did...''

Julia found his hand. ''Let's put her to rest, Christian. Both of us. We're not at fault for what happened. A crazy man killed her and left you to pay the price. We were her best friends, and we still love her. Maybe she is an angel. Who knows? Maybe she's still trying to meddle and bring all this to a better conclusion.''

"If Fidelity had any say in things, I wouldn't have gone to prison, and you wouldn't have married Bard and raised my daughter as his.''

"Maybe she just got her wings.''

"We used to watch *It's a Wonderful Life* every Christmas at Ludwell. There wasn't a man who believed the world would have been a worse place if he hadn't lived in it.''

She started to pull her hand away, but he gripped it and held tight. "I'm sorry.''

"For what?''

He was silent.

"Will you come with me to say goodbye?'' she asked.

"Yeah, I'll come.'' He tucked her hand under his arm and led her slowly to the little cemetery. Callie swung down from the tree and joined them. Clover tumbled through the long grass, every blade a challenge.

"Callie, will you put the flowers on Fidelity's grave?'' Julia said. "Christian will show you which one is hers.''

They walked down one row and up another. He found the plot at the end. It was lovingly tended. Someone had planted a bright red rose, and despite the onset of autumn, it still had one bloom sending sweet perfume into the air. "We're there,'' he said tersely.

"Fidelity,'' Julia said, "we still miss you. We wish you were standing right here in the flesh, but wherever you are, I hope you're at peace.''

"These flowers are for you,'' Callie said. She leaned over and carefully laid the bouquet at the base of a simple marble head-stone bearing Fidelity's name and the words: Beloved Daughter.

"And if you want to be my guardian angel,'' Callie added, "I'd be proud to have you.''

Christian knew it was his turn. He felt foolish, yet he also felt Fidelity's presence. She had been in his thoughts so strongly that he almost felt he'd conjured her.

"I'm sorry I couldn't save you," he said. "But I'm glad I knew you, and you were my friend."

A breeze rustled the bush, and Callie took Christian's hand. "She's not sad," Callie said. "Look, the rose is dancing. She's making it dance. Don't you be sad, okay?"

They stood together, watching Fidelity's rose waltz in the dying light.

29

This time Pinky's call woke Christian before dawn. At the first ring Christian felt for the telephone, knocking it off the nightstand. The guest wing at Claymore Park had a private line, and he had no doubt the call was for him.

"Chris? Got *you* up this time. Good going."

"What's happening?" Christian sat up, pushing his hair off his forehead. Pinky had obviously set his alarm to make this call, probably to pay Christian back.

"I wanted to catch you before you went out to the stables."

"Uh-huh." Christian forced his eyes open.

"I found out something you might like to know."

"I'm waiting."

Pinky laughed. "I got an old buddy of mine drunk last night. He used to work for Davey Myers. Went to work for him back in the days when Myers used to be somebody."

"And...?"

"You'd be surprised how easy it is for a cop to get somebody drunk. They figure, they're with you, nobody's going to do anything funny. You know?"

Christian yawned. "I'm sure I would if I were awake."

Pinky took pity on him. "Here's the thing. He remembered that deal Myers was talking about, the one up near South Land."

Christian was suddenly more than halfway toward consciousness. "What did he remember?"

"That's the thing. He said a lot of people would have been

pissed as hell if it had worked out, that a lot of rich folks would have woke up one morning to find bulldozers practically in their backyard and houses multiplying like horny little bunnies. He kept saying there'd be bunnies, not foxes there anymore. I guess that was the bourbon talking.''

Christian whistled, and, encouraged, Pinky went on. "He didn't want to say any more than that. I got the feeling maybe he'd been paid off to keep quiet. Half a bottle of Wild Turkey and he still didn't loosen up much more. He said he had things he had to think about, and maybe he didn't remember anything after all. That was the best I got.''

"Who's the guy?''

"An old hunting buddy of mine. Name of Lester Morgan. From down near Warrenton. He lives up here now, though. Works for Virginia Vistas.''

Christian was fully awake now. Virginia Vistas was the development firm where Bard Warwick was legal counsel.

"How long has he had that job, do you know?''

"Oh, a good long time. I remember when he moved up here. I helped him look for a place to live. Now he's got a wife and a house, but back then—''

"Do you remember exactly when that might have been?''

Pinky was silent. Christian could almost hear him counting backward. "Just about the time they sent you to jail," Pinky said at last. "Give or take a year. Is that close enough for you?''

It was close enough. "What does he do for Virginia Vistas?''

"Inspects properties. Hires contractors and oversees the work when it needs to be done. Truth be told, I was surprised he got the job. He's good with his hands, but not so good with his head.''

"Would he talk to me?''

"No. You'll have to go about it some other way.''

"Maybe I'd better look into what Virginia Vistas was doing back then.''

"You do that. And good luck. 'Cause it sounds like that's what you'll need from this point onward. I can't think of another thing I can do to help.''

Christian thanked Pinky and hung up.

* * *

Julia had worked out a routine that gave her a sense of security. Although she still needed help for errands and paperwork, she was growing more and more self-sufficient. In fact, Karen had been offered a job in a surgeon's office and planned to leave at the month's end.

This morning, though, Julia was glad to have Karen's assistance. Maisy was helping at the gallery, and Julia had an appointment in Leesburg with an internist who had examined her during her hospitalization at Gandy Willson. It was a routine visit to find out the results of lab work he had run. She almost canceled, but at the last minute she decided to go. Her own doctor was usually so overbooked that making an appointment to go over another doctor's tests could take months.

They went in Karen's car and chatted like old friends as they took the back way into town. Julia knew all about Karen's life now, and had told her a fair portion of her own.

"You know," Julia said as they stopped at one of the few lights between Ashbourne and the doctor's office, "you've made me realize how few women friends I really have."

"I have?"

"I...well, I guess I just haven't wanted another close friend."

"You had your husband, didn't you?"

"No." Julia was finally coming to terms with the fact that her marriage to Bard had seemed so acceptable because she had known they would *not* be friends. She hadn't been ready for another relationship where she would have to share her heart. And she was afraid Bard would *never* be ready for one.

Karen stepped on the accelerator. "Well, I married Brandon's father because everybody else was getting married, and I figured the time had come. Poor Walter was the first guy who asked once my time clock started ticking."

"And I married because I was pregnant with another man's child."

"Aren't you glad you had her, though? I don't know what I would do without Brandon. He's worth what I had to put up with from Walter."

Julia knew from prior conversations that during their marriage Karen's husband had collected lovers the way some men collect sports memorabilia. "I don't know what I would do without Callie. Just imagine what would have happened if I hadn't had her. I never got pregnant again. I might never have had the chance to raise a child."

"I don't know. There are lots of new treatments out there."

"I hear the nurse inside you talking," Julia said. "But I'm not even sure what the problem is. My periods are erratic, which is the most likely cause. Bard never wanted to bother with a real fertility workup. I don't think he likes children enough to try that hard."

"That seems funny to me."

"Why?"

"Well, you told me once that you thought he couldn't learn to love Callie because she wasn't his."

"That's part of it."

"Seems like he would have moved heaven and earth to have his own child, then."

"Maybe he would have if I'd wanted his child." Julia realized she'd never formed those words before. "I don't think I really wanted his baby, Karen. That's why I never pushed."

"And it's too late now?"

It was too late for a number of things that had to do with Bard. But that was a thought she wasn't ready to speak out loud.

They arrived early at the doctor's office, and Karen helped Julia into the waiting room. Julia had accustomed herself to not fully knowing what was going on around her, and even though Karen filled in some of the picture by describing the room, she was comfortable with what she couldn't see.

When it was her turn to talk to the doctor, Karen helped her inside and offered to wait. The nurse appeared and asked Julia to change into a gown.

"I'm just here to get the results of some tests," Julia explained. "Do I really need to do that?"

"The doctor wants to do a quick pelvic, Mrs. Warwick. Will that be a problem?"

Curiosity piqued, Julia said no. Karen helped her into the gown, then left to give Julia and the doctor privacy.

She was sitting on the examination table when the door opened and a voice boomed a hearty hello. Except for the obnoxious Dr. Jeffers, all the doctors who had examined Julia since her accident had run together in her mind. Neurologists, opthamologists, retinal specialists. Dr. Forrester, the chipper internist, seemed like a total stranger. She answered his queries about her health, the weather and whether she'd had any encouragement about her eyesight.

"You know, I saw your husband last year," he told her. "I just realized the connection. His doctor was out of town. Mr. Warwick is quite a powerhouse."

"I thought this would simply be a routine visit," she said, once she had the chance to initiate a sentence herself. "Is an exam really necessary?"

"I hope you'll bear with me. But I'm a little perplexed about something, and I thought I'd just do a follow-up exam before we talk."

"Mind telling me what?"

"I don't mind at all. But I'd be happier to talk after I've checked again. Not trying to be secretive, just thorough. I can tell you it's not anything to worry about, though."

She shrugged. "Fine. I'm not going anywhere dressed like this."

He seemed to think that was funny. She had to smile. Her own internist was humorless and aloof, and Julia had always intended to find another. Maybe she had.

He went out in the hall to call his nurse, and Julia lay back on the table.

Maisy had been heartened by what had seemed like a gradual return of Julia's appetite. Tonight, though, Julia barely tasted a supper of fresh greens and corn bread.

"Not hungry?" Maisy asked, as Julia carefully scraped plates into a compost pail for Jake to take out to the garden.

Julia took her time answering. "I guess I can't think and eat at the same time."

"You've seemed preoccupied."

"I still have a lot I need to sort through."

No one knew that better than Maisy, and no one knew better when Julia was keeping secrets. She went back to washing dishes.

"I've been thinking about your book," Julia said.

"Have you?"

"What made you decide to write this particular story?"

"Every author has to start somewhere."

"When I stand at my easel, I don't simply pick up a paintbrush and starting dabbing on paint at random."

"Never?"

"You're saying that's what you did? You sat down at the typewriter—"

"Computer. Little old modern Maisy."

"You sat down and started to type and the words came from nowhere?"

"No, they don't come from nowhere. Relationships fascinate me. They always have. And, like anyone my age, I've witnessed dozens of marriages, maybe hundreds, up close."

"Ian is a terrible man."

"If you see him that way, then I haven't done my job."

"Surely you aren't saying he has any redeeming features? It's possible to be too liberal."

"Blasphemy."

"I'm serious."

"Okay, picture this. A truck drives through an open field. The field is muddy, and the truck sinks a little. The next truck slips easily into the ruts the first one made and follows in its path without incident. Three or four do the same. Then the next truck comes along. All's going well, but suddenly the driver realizes he wants to make a turn. He tries, but he's so deep into the ruts he can only go in that direction. No matter how hard he tries."

"I believe the expression 'stuck in a rut' would be a quicker way to say the same thing."

Maisy smiled a little. "Unless you picture it, you can't see how impossible it is to change. How hopeless."

"Are you saying Ian Sebastian couldn't change his behavior? You're actually condoning the way he treats Louisa?"

"I'm just saying life is difficult, and answers are never easy."

"Bard would be surprised to hear that."

"You've insisted from the beginning that Ian is based on Bard."

"There are many different ways a man can raise his hand to a woman."

Maisy watched her daughter. Julia's chin was set, the way it had often been as a child. To others she had seemed an overly sensitive, malleable girl, but Maisy had seen firsthand what her daughter was made of.

"Stories, like paintings, have a way of taking on a different cast, depending on who hears them," Maisy said.

"Or who tells them."

Maisy acknowledged that with a nod Julia couldn't see.

"Does Ian change after he has a child?" Julia said. "Is that why you're defending him?"

"It's a while before bedtime, and I'm not defending him. You don't want me to give away the story, do you?"

"Why don't you read to me out on the porch tonight after we finish the dishes? Unless you have something else you have to do?"

"I don't."

"With Callie at Tiffany's, the evening's going to seem too long, anyway."

"I can read to you."

Julia faced her mother, almost as if she could see her. "When I paint, I always have a clear idea what I want to show."

"Some of us just fumble along, sweetheart. No matter how hard we try, no matter how much we need to say."

From the unpublished novel *Fox River*, by Maisy Fletcher

In moments of blinding rage Ian continued to strike me, and I continued to find ways to take what he had done and make it my fault. Forced to choose between an uncertain future and a husband who claimed to love me, a husband who later promised not to hit me again, I took what I thought was the easier path.

Although Ian still lashed out at me, he ignored our Alice for the first years of her life. I was secretly pleased, since I found her so utterly perfect myself. I doted on the tiniest things about her, the shape of her fingernails, the soft dark curls that covered her head, the eyes that were the green of my own. She was six weeks old when she first smiled up at me, and I was glad Ian wasn't there to share it. She was my child. He had abandoned her at birth. Had he lived in ancient Rome, he would have left her to the wolves.

As she grew, I was the one who witnessed her first faltering steps. I was the one who taught her to count, and the names of all the flowers in our gardens. Alice was my joy, the purpose of my existence, and the reason why my marriage to Ian Sebastian wasn't a complete failure.

Then, after time went by and Ian was sure at last that I would never give him a son, his attitude toward Alice began to change.

Until that time he had only noticed his daughter in passing. When I returned from taking her to visit my mother who was sick and growing sicker, Ian hardly seemed to have noticed Alice had been gone. She called him Daddy in her childish voice, and he dutifully showed her off to guests as a proud father was supposed to. But I had been certain if I stood Alice in a row with other little girls of her age and coloring, her father would not have been able to pick her out. Now, suddenly, he noticed everything.

"She's a timid child," he said one night after supper, when Alice was playing with three new puppy hounds Ian had brought up to the house.

I watched our daughter trying to evade puppy teeth. "Well, they do nip, and she's not even three. She'll be used to them soon enough."

"I can't imagine you were that shy."

"Every child is different. There's no comparing."

The next evening the scene was repeated. "Alice," he commanded. "Stop whining. Push them away if you don't want them biting you."

Alice's eyes grew huge. Until that moment Ian had hardly spoken to her. "Dey hurt!"

"Push them away!"

She tried, but her hands were small, and she was still frightened of their teeth. Ian got up and went to her. "I told you to push them away." He shoved the puppies back. What had been a game with Alice was something else with Ian, and the hounds understood. One went belly-up, the other two slunk away.

"You must always be brave," he said sternly. "Animals know when you aren't, Alice, and they will take advantage. You must always be strong and brave."

She looked up at him with her heartbreaking eyes

spilling over with tears. He shook his head and walked away.

I realized then how easy Alice's early years had been. Ian's detachment had caused no problems, but now this sudden attachment might. She hadn't pleased him at this first test of courage. And there would be other tests that she would fail. She wasn't a weak child, but she was a sensitive one. Colors were brighter; noises were louder; tastes were so strong she preferred only the blandest foods. She was acutely aware of the moods of those around her, and they affected her own. I expected her to be a poet or a musician, but never the brash, courageous athlete that Ian certainly wanted.

I saw trouble ahead.

The trouble began in earnest when Ian decided it was time for Alice to learn to ride. Alice was fascinated by horses. It would have been difficult to survive at Fox River if she hadn't been. But horses, large, lightning-quick creatures that they were, frightened her. She respected their hoofs and lithe long legs, and although she liked watching them from a distance, she understood that distance was best.

The week before our daughter's third birthday, Ian returned from a trip to a local auction with a tiny pinto pony. "Come see what I've bought Alice," he told me that evening. I followed him down to the stables and exclaimed over his choice.

"But don't be hurt, darling, if she isn't excited at first," I warned. "As small as that pony is, it will still seem huge to her."

"You coddle her too much. Someday this farm will belong to her, and she'll need to know everything about horses and riding to make a go of it."

I marveled that he had moved this far in his thinking, but I worried all the same. Our daughter was not the tomboy he hoped for.

On the day of Alice's birthday, neighbors arrived to celebrate. The Carroltons, a family with two young boys, were leasing Sweetwater in hopes that the Joneses would sell to them eventually. Ian admired Bob Carrolton, who had hunted extensively in England, and Etta Carrolton was a fine horsewoman herself. Alice was dumfounded that the boys, Dick and Gil, five and six respectively, could make so much noise, but she liked to watch them from the protection of my lap.

Lettie served ham with a variety of salads, then a huge coconut cake to celebrate Alice's birthday. The evening had cooled by the time Ian led Alice's pony to her for inspection. Wide-eyed and cautious, she allowed her father to lead her to the pony's head to pat his nose. Then, the moment Ian let go of her hand, she threw herself at me.

The boys thought this was hilarious. They were already vying to ride, although by their standards, Alice's pony was much too tame.

"You may have a turn, but Alice first," Ian said. He lifted Alice from my lap and seated her on the pony's bare back. The pony wore a simple halter, but since it was well-behaved, it needed nothing else. With Alice clinging to the scrap of mane within her reach, Ian led the pony around the yard.

I was thrilled that Alice did so well. I had expected tears if Ian tried to put her on the pony's back, but Alice stared straight ahead, not moving so much as a muscle in protest. After several turns around the yard, Ian lifted her off. Only then did I realize just how frightened she had been. When Ian deposited her in my lap, she was trembling so hard I couldn't hold her still. She put her arms around my neck and wept. Most telling, her skirt was damp.

Ian was disgusted. I could see it in his expression, although he politely supervised rides for the two little boys. But when the party had ended and the Carroltons had gone home for the night, he exploded.

"It's your fault," he told me. "You want her to cling to you."

"I don't," I insisted. "She's just three, Ian. She'll love the pony when she gets used to him. She's a real little soldier. She rode him even though she was scared. She'll be fine if you just give her a chance."

"You coddle her! I won't have it. You're useless to me, and now you've turned my only child into a scared little mouse."

I half expected him to grab Alice for another riding lesson that night, but he strode into the house, and in a few minutes our groom came to take the pony away. I put our daughter to bed by myself, just as I always did, but she had little to say and nothing about the pony. I told her that her daddy had bought the pony just for her, and that soon she would learn to ride him like a big girl.

She turned her face away and popped her thumb in her mouth.

Ian was waiting for me in my room. My heart sped when I saw his face. He was still angry, and I knew all too well what that might mean. But this time he didn't strike me.

"Alice spends too much time with you," he said. "Beginning tomorrow, I'll spend part of each morning with her, teaching her to ride. You don't seem pleased with the prospect," Ian said when I didn't answer.

I knew better than to provoke him. So far he hadn't taken his fists to me, but I recognized his struggle. "I was just thinking how much a girl needs her father," I said truthfully. "Alice needs to spend more time with you."

"I won't have you interfere with anything I do."

"She's your daughter. I know you'll take good care of her. Just…please remember the things that happen to her now can mark her for life."

He looked disgusted, as if that notion was old-fashioned instead of the latest thinking. "I'll come for her after breakfast. See that she's ready." He left the room without a word, and I knew, from experience, that he wouldn't be back. Tonight I was unworthy of his attentions.

The next morning I tried to prepare Alice for her first riding lesson.

"Your father's going to take you to visit your new pony."

She looked apprehensive. "Mommy's coming, too?"

"Not this time, sweet pea. Daddy wants Alice all to himself."

She didn't look happy at that. I continued. "Daddy found the pony just for you, and he wants you to learn to ride him. You'll be safe. Daddy will take care of you."

"Don't like ponies." She stuck out her lip.

I knew I had to be firm. "You will learn to like ponies, and you will learn to like this one. Daddy wants you to, and you must listen to Daddy."

Whatever she heard in my voice convinced her. Her eyes got bigger, but she didn't argue.

She was ready when Ian came for her. He never smiled at Alice, tickled her under her chin, swung her around and around, demonstrations of affection I remembered from my own stern father. Ian rarely looked at her and more rarely spoke to her. But this time he examined her closely, as if he wanted to be sure every part was present.

"Alice, we're going riding. Did your mother tell you?"

"She said I mus' learn to like it."

He looked at me, and I shrugged. "I said exactly that, Ian."

"There's not a child alive who doesn't like ponies."

I was afraid there might be one. "I told her she would be safe and you would take good care of her."

"That sounds like a warning to me."

I was too frightened for my child to be frightened of him at that moment. "Please be gentle with her," I said softly. "We females respond best when we're handled with care."

He lifted Alice in his arms and carried her out of the

house. If I could have snatched her back and run away with her, I would have.

They came back together about an hour later. "Today we just had a look," Ian said grudgingly. "She fed him a carrot, and I taught her what a saddle is."

"I petted the horsey's nose," Alice told me solemnly.

"And did he pet yours, sweet pea?"

She didn't giggle, a sure sign that the hour had taken its toll. She ran off to her room, but Ian stopped me from going after her.

"She's afraid of everything. Of me, of the pony, of the shadows in the stable!"

"This is all very new to her. But I'm sure you made headway."

"She had better shape up quickly." He stomped off, and my stomach knotted.

The next day's lesson must have gone much the same. I followed her once Ian had gone back to the stable to see what I could learn.

"Did you ride your pony today, sweet pea?"

"S'name's Patches."

"Is it? Did you name him?"

"He has patches."

"He certainly does. Big patches." She was sitting cross-legged on her bed, and I joined her. "Did Daddy give you a ride around the yard?"

She didn't answer.

"Alice?"

"Don' like Patches."

My heart sank. "Alice, Patches is really a nice pony. Will you try to like him, for my sake? He's not going to hurt you. And once you learn to ride him, you and I can go for wonderful long rides all over Fox River Farm."

She looked up at me with the same stubborn expression I had too often witnessed on my husband's face. "Don' like him."

"You must learn." I left her to think that over.

By week's end it was clear Ian had no patience left.

When he came to give Alice her lesson, he told me he had saddled the pony and Alice would ride that day, whether she wanted to or not.

"Ian, this will go better if you just wait until she's older."

"Alice is a very bright child, Louisa. She's just being stubborn."

I was desperate. "What are you going to do to her? Hit her the way you hit me when I don't do what you want? She's a little girl. You could hurt her badly."

His eyes narrowed. "Go upstairs and get her, or I'll drag her downstairs."

I didn't know what to do. If I refused, he would make good on his threat. If I continued to argue, he might become so infuriated he really would harm her. In the end, I went for Alice. On the way downstairs I told her she must do whatever Daddy said today, but I knew this day wasn't going to end happily for any of us.

"I'd like to come and watch, if I might," I said, as Ian took Alice's tiny hand.

"Not today."

"But I could cheer her on."

"Louisa, go up to your room and remain there until we return."

"A prisoner in my own house?"

"I won't have you interfering. Go upstairs."

Alice was looking at us with widening eyes. I knew if we continued to argue, she would be even more frightened. "All right," I said as cheerfully as I could. "You two have fun, please. Alice, be a good girl and do whatever Daddy says."

I started upstairs, but the moment the door closed behind them I stationed myself in the parlor, which had the best view of the stableyard. Ian kept opera glasses. I tried to remember where he stored them, but panic clouded my mind. Finally I found them in a walnut secretary. At the window I held them to my eyes and adjusted the lenses for clarity.

Alice leaped out at me. She was walking beside her father, reluctantly holding back the way a prisoner must on his way to the hangman's noose. Ian was saying something to her and shaking a finger. My heart sank.

I tried to think what I could do. Ian was so easily provoked that if I tried to interfere again, he might do something terrible to our child. There was no one close by who might interfere for me, certainly none of our staff, who depended on him for their daily bread. The neighbors wouldn't involve themselves in a domestic argument, and besides, the men might well agree with Ian. I was alone and unable to defend my daughter.

Patches was saddled and waiting outside the stable. Ian appeared to have said everything he planned to, because the moment they arrived, he lifted Alice off the ground and dropped her on the tiny sidesaddle he'd bought for the pony. She proceeded to launch herself into his arms before he could retreat. I could see her face clearly, and she was sobbing.

I put a fist to my mouth to stifle a cry. The glasses wavered. When I put them back to my eyes, I saw Alice in the saddle once more. Again she tried to remove herself, but this time Ian held her in place. I saw his mouth moving and could well imagine what he was saying. She shrank back, but the moment he stepped away, she tried to dismount again.

Ian turned and shouted something, probably to one of the stableboys. He held Alice in place as she squirmed to get down, but to my relief, he didn't hit her. Minutes seemed to pass as he held her there. Then the boy arrived carrying something under his arm. He passed it to Ian. As I watched in horror, Ian took what looked like leather cord and began to bind his daughter to the saddle while she pitched and fought him, sobbing all the while.

I felt physically ill. My stomach heaved, and I swallowed bile. Ian stepped away, and although Alice struggled, she could not remove herself from the pony's back. Then, as I watched, he began to lead her around the yard. And when he had finished, and as she continued to scream, he tied Patches to a tree and left my terrified daughter to battle her fears alone.

30

During the weeks of her blindness, Julia had waited for people to come to her. When she awoke this morning, she knew that this, too, had to change. She was blind. Although the doctors were convinced she would see again, she had no reason to believe them. Each tiny revelation had given her hope she was finding her way toward the light. But this morning, when she opened her eyes and the world was as dark as the end of time, she realized she couldn't put her life on hold. She had used the fact that she couldn't see as an excuse not to act.

There was no relevant connection.

She showered and dressed before anyone else arose. By the time Jake had gotten up to make coffee, she was ready to go.

"You're up early," he said. "And you look like you're going somewhere."

"I'm going to Millcreek."

"You need a ride." It wasn't a question.

"Do you mind?"

"Shall I bring my coffee and paper?"

"I'd be grateful if you'd stay while I talk to Bard."

He must have heard how much she hated to ask, because his tone was thoughtful. "You know, Julia, nobody minds helping you. Least of all your mother and me. I used to wish you needed me more. I like feeling needed."

"I'm glad you'll be there with me. There's no one I could want more."

"Let me put the coffee in a travel cup and we'll go. Would you like some first?"

"No, I'll do this without, thanks."

The ride was short and silent. Julia expected to find Bard home, but she knew she was taking a chance. She hadn't wanted to announce her visit. For once Bard could be the one caught off guard.

At Millcreek, Jake helped her to the door and she used her key. From inside she heard Bard's voice coming from the direction of the dining room and Mrs. Taylor's deferential tones. He breakfasted early, and at the end of his meal he usually gave Mrs. Taylor a list of things to do that day. Julia had rarely eaten with him, hoping, she realized now, to escape a similar fate.

She wondered if, like the fictitious Louisa Sebastian, she had accommodated herself to Bard's whims to keep peace. Louisa from fear, Julia from guilt and gratitude.

"If you'll get me to the door of the dining room, I can do the rest," she told Jake in a soft voice.

"I'll be out on the porch waiting for you. Will Mrs. Taylor help you to the door?"

He had assumed, quite logically, that Bard wouldn't be in the mood. "I'm sure she will. Or I'll find my way. I can visualize the layout of this room."

"I'll be waiting. Take all the time you need."

She let him lead her through the room, memorizing the steps and turns as he did. When he stopped, she dropped his arm.

"Hello, Bard."

Bard was obviously surprised. "Julia?"

She heard Jake's footsteps departing, then the sound of the front door.

"Was that Jake?" Bard sounded closer now. He was coming to greet her.

"He brought me over. He's going to wait outside."

"Why? Have him come in. I'll get Mrs. Taylor to make him breakfast. He can join us."

"I don't think so. This isn't a social call."

His tone dropped several degrees. "No?"

"I'm sorry, did you think I'd come back?"

"So? And now you're here to deliver the bad news?"

"I'm here to ask a question."

"You've heard of the telephone, I'll bet."

He resorted to sarcasm to get control of a conversation. She knew that, but she didn't retreat. "I prefer standing in front of you, even though I can't see you."

"I guess I don't have to offer you breakfast, then."

"Let's cut to the chase. Why have you lied all these years about the reason we didn't have a child together?"

She could almost hear him picking through possible answers, but the one he chose caught her off guard. "I'm glad you know. Does that surprise you?"

"Surprise, yes. Do I believe you?" She didn't answer her own question.

"Let's go in the living room and discuss this."

She didn't move. "Why didn't you tell me you'd had a vasectomy?"

"I know you're angry. I don't blame you. I—"

"I want an explanation. Not an interpretation of my feelings. Just give me the facts."

He didn't speak for a moment. She waited, refusing to break the silence as she had so often during their marriage.

When he spoke, his voice was an echo of its robust self. "When Callie was two, I realized I didn't want any more children. I was losing sleep over it, worrying every time we had sex, even though we were using birth control, so I decided to do something about it."

"Just like that? Without discussion?"

"There wasn't any room for discussion. At the time there was nothing you could have said to change my mind. I didn't like being a father. I didn't like the mess, the noise, the time. I sure didn't want to double all that with another baby, even if the next one was mine. So I had the procedure when I was out of town. I was going to tell you."

"Well, that was considerate. Did you just forget to mention it?"

"I regretted it later. I was too impulsive. You should have had some say. I know that now."

She didn't trust herself to respond.

"How did you figure this out?" he asked.

She kept her voice level. "The internist I saw at Gandy Willson was concerned about my irregular periods and wondered why I wasn't on the pill. I told him there'd been no reason for birth control. *I* meant because we'd hoped to have a baby, but *he* thought I meant your vasectomy. His name is Forrester. Does that ring a bell? He saw you last year for a urinary infection, when your own doctor was out of town. He remembered the vasectomy because you were convinced it was the cause of the infection and you wouldn't listen to reason."

Bard's tone changed. "As bad as this sounds, I did feel justified."

"I'd like to know why."

"I knew you were in love with another man. The chances you'd want my baby were slim to none. If you ever *really* did, I figured I could try to have it reversed."

"And if that didn't work? You'd have a test and claim the mumps or something else had left you sterile?"

"It was stupid. I admit it, but maybe I got tired of being the man you married to give your daughter a last name. Maybe I didn't see any reason to tell you the truth. You didn't want my baby anyway."

"If you'd told me you didn't want another child, maybe it wouldn't have mattered. But you kept the vasectomy a secret because you wanted me to think it was my problem."

"I made a mistake."

"That's your idea of an apology?"

"Don't be so self-righteous! I married you, didn't I? I've never liked kids, but I took responsibility for somebody else's little bastard so we could have a life together."

The words seemed to have power well beyond syllables and enunciation. One moment there had been a marriage, of sorts. The next it was over.

"I didn't mean that," he said immediately.

The words could not be called back.

He touched her arm, trying to make amends. "I married you because you were the wife I wanted, Julia."

"I have suspected for more years than I can say—" she cleared her throat and took a deep breath "—that a large part of my attraction for you was Ashbourne. When Maisy died and it became mine, it would have been yours, as well. But I never realized how easy my pregnancy made everything for you."

"I imagine it looks that way, but—"

"I had the property, the name, the background. I was acceptable in every way, and I needed you. Except for somebody else's little bastard, it was a perfect situation, wasn't it?"

"I married you because I wanted you to be my wife."

"You married me because you're a coldhearted son of a bitch who saw an opportunity and grabbed it! You were every bit as emotional about me as you are about a prime property that comes your way. A piece of land like Ashbourne, for instance. And you've been even less emotional about Callie."

She turned to go, but he put a hand on her shoulder. "We fit in every way. And we were good together, the way I knew we'd be. Maybe we didn't love each other at first, but I do love you now. I'll do whatever it takes to get through this. I'll see your therapist with you, if that's what you want. I'll spend more time with Callie. If you'll just move back and let me take care of you, we can work this out. But we'll never work it out with you living at Ashbourne. You've got to come home if we're going to make a go of this."

"Why?"

"Why?" He sounded perplexed.

"Why do I have to come home?"

"So we'll have more time—"

"So you can control me," she corrected him. "So I won't be influenced against you, right? So I won't be tempted to do things you don't approve of."

"I don't know what you're talking about."

"I think you do. I made one terrible mistake in the past weeks, Bard. I didn't tell Christian that Callie is his daughter. Well, he found out anyway. And coming back to Millcreek isn't going to turn back the hands of time. Nothing is the way it was. To be honest, I'm not even sure I *know* how it was. But I do know this. You say you love me, but even if it's true, love's nothing compared to making the past come right. You're not ready to commit yourself to that, and I don't think you ever will be.''

"You're saying this is final? You'd give up nine years of marriage because of one lie?''

"Our whole marriage has been a lie.''

"How convenient, Julia. You needed a husband to give your baby a name. I played the part. Now you don't need a husband anymore, because the baby's real father is back on the scene. Enter Christian Carver. Exit Lombard Warwick.''

She searched her heart and knew she was telling the truth when she said, "Christian could go back to prison this morning and my decision wouldn't be any different. Our marriage was over before it started. It just took nine years and the loss of my eyesight for me to see that clearly.''

Maisy knew about Julia's trip to Millcreek that morning, but neither she nor Jake knew any details. She had watched Julia all day, pale and strained but otherwise herself. Now Callie was in bed and Julia was sitting on the porch, despite evening temperatures that had dropped into the low fifties.

"You're going to freeze," Maisy said, coming out with a granny square afghan from her needlework phase. She saw that Clover had chewed a hole in one block and thought it was probably an improvement. "I don't suppose I can get you to come inside?''

"You're sweet, but I'm okay. Fall's really here, isn't it? Are the leaves falling?''

"Faster than I'd like. Jake's building a fire in the fireplace. If you'd like to hear another chapter, we could sit in there when you're ready.''

"I'm looking forward to the next chapter.''

"Are you?''

"I want to see if Louisa has what it takes to leave Ian.''

"I won't give it away.''

"It's one thing, isn't it, when a man mistreats a woman? Another entirely when he mistreats a child.''

''Women and children have been possessions for too many centuries. Attitudes change slowly.''

''Have they changed in your lifetime?''

Maisy joined her on the swing. ''Not fast enough.''

From the unpublished novel *Fox River*, by Maisy Fletcher

"Mister Ian wasn't even as old as Alice when his own daddy tried to teach him to ride." Lettie was setting the table for supper, and although I hadn't said anything as I arranged roses with trembling hands, Lettie knew what was upsetting me.

"It was a sad day for all of us when he learned," I said bitterly. Alice was asleep upstairs, and we were expecting guests. I knew I would spend a good part of the evening soothing her nightmares. Ian had left our daughter tied to the saddle for nearly an hour, and by the time he returned her to me, she had been incoherent. I had spent the day rocking and calming her. She'd fallen asleep at last from sheer exhaustion.

"His daddy taught him the way Mr. Ian's teaching Alice."

I didn't really care if Ian had learned his unforgivable behavior at his father's knee or if he had learned it from a heavenly visitation. He had harmed a sensitive child who wouldn't easily recover. Perhaps he had been the same sort of child himself, but I didn't want my Alice to become anything like Ian, the adult.

"It won't pay you none to try to change him," Lettie said. "That's all I'm saying. Some things run deep."

"I can't exactly send Mr. Ian down the road the way you sent your first husband, can I?"

"I'm just the cook."

I closed my eyes. "I'm sorry, Lettie. You're more than the cook. You're a friend, and I appreciate it."

I thought she was finished giving advice, but I was wrong. "Sometimes, you can't send them away, you go away yourself."

I lowered my voice, although Ian was still outside, and told her the decision I'd reached. "I'm going home to my mother. She's growing sicker. I'm taking Alice. Tomorrow, before Mr. Ian comes to get her for another riding lesson."

"You want Seth to take you to the train station?"

I had planned to walk to Sweetwater and throw myself on the mercy of Etta Carrolton, but Seth's assistance would make the escape much easier. "I don't want to get him in trouble."

"Then don't tell him why you're going. I won't tell him, neither. He won't know Mr. Ian don't approve."

I squeezed her hand. I had an ally, the very eyes and ears who had watched Ian develop into the man he was.

I was as charming as I could manage that evening so that Ian wouldn't suspect anything. I avoided him, something he surely expected under the circumstances, but I was a good hostess and the dinner party went well. Alice slept through it and only awoke as I was going to bed myself. I went to her and soothed her back to sleep. When I reached my room, Ian was waiting for me.

He was pacing and didn't stop when I entered. "You may think what I did was harsh, but it was the only way to break the cycle. She won't be nearly so afraid tomorrow."

I knew that if I acquiesced, his suspicions would be aroused. "Is that right? And if she is?"

"Then, by God, I'll do the same thing all over again until she isn't. And you won't stop me."

"Oh, you've made that abundantly clear. Nobody tells the great Ian Sebastian what to do, particularly no one weaker. We're at your mercy. Just the way you want us."

"There's no need for hysterics. There's not a scratch or a bruise on that child."

"There are bruises on her heart."

"My father was a hard man, and I survived. No, I thrived!"

"You have bruises on your heart, as well. And they keep you from feeling the things a father needs to feel for his child."

He moved as if to strike me, but I stood without flinching. I knew if he did, I would have proof when I returned to New York that my husband was a brutal man and my daughter and I were in danger.

Perhaps the day had taken an emotional toll on him, as well. Perhaps he had some unidentified guilt about what he had done. Instead of striking me, he stomped past and slammed the door.

There had been laughter in our marriage, tender kisses and beautiful gifts. This was the man who had given me pleasure in bed and a daughter I adored. Suddenly none of that mattered. I hoped this was the very last time I would ever see Ian Sebastian.

The next morning Alice and I arose to threatening skies, and I packed a few things for each of us. Then I explained what we were doing. "You and I are going away," I told her. "Far away from Fox River Farm."

Her green eyes widened. "And Patches?"

"Especially Patches."

She showed the first enthusiasm I'd seen in twenty-four hours.

"We're going to see your grandmother, and you can

play with your new cousin Joseph." My brother George had just welcomed his first son into the world, and I knew she would enjoy him.

"Will Daddy find us?"

I knew better than to turn a child against her father, but my own outrage was too great. "Daddy can't come to New York."

She seemed satisfied at that.

I knew Ian had an appointment in town, and he left without saying goodbye. I watched him disappear over the hill on Equator despite the oncoming storm. Then I told Lettie we were ready. In minutes we were in the Packard, with Seth at the wheel, heading for the train station. The thunderstorm broke when we were halfway there, as if to end my life in Virginia with one terrible flourish.

The trip to New York was long and arduous, but as each new mile separated me from Ian, my aching heart began to ease. Whatever happened next, I was free of Ian's abuse and, more importantly, so was Alice. We might be poor. We might never find a place in New York society. But we would be safe, and by leaving Ian I was teaching Alice the most valuable lesson she could learn. Her life was hers, not the property of a man. She had the power to make something of it, if only she dared.

I had telegraphed ahead to George to let him know when we would arrive and why. He was waiting for me at the station, dressed in solemn black. I took one look at him and knew my mother had passed away.

I handed Alice to him for an uncle's hug. "Mama's gone?"

"Last night about ten. I'd hoped she could wait for you."

"Was it peaceful?"

"She seemed glad to go."

"Did you tell her why I was coming?"

"No."

I was relieved. Mama had died without knowing about my disgrace.

"There's more," George said heavily.

We were standing on the platform. I knew that George, even as practical a man as he was, would not have kept me there unless he had good reason.

Instinctively I reached for Alice and clutched her to my breast.

"Ian has been in an accident," he said.

I waited, lips clamped, for the weight of the world to fall on me or lift forever.

"Apparently, after you left, he came back to the house for something he'd forgotten. He discovered you were on your way to the train station, and he tried to head you off by riding through the woods. His horse threw him. When the horse came back to the stable without Ian, his men went in search. They found him unconscious."

"And now?"

"He was still unconscious, Louisa, when last I spoke to the doctor."

This was incomprehensible. Ian was the finest horseman in Virginia, and Equator, older now and steadier, was not a horse that spooked easily. Ian must have been riding like a madman to catch up to us. He must have thrown all caution to the proverbial wind.

My duty was clear, and I didn't question it. "I just need to know," I said. "If I had stayed, George, would you have given me a home?"

"You're a married woman. Go back to Virginia and try again."

"And if I try and he continues to beat me? Continues to abuse your niece?"

"Then try harder."

"Will you really be able to turn us away, if it comes to that?"

"I hope never to find out."

So did I. I hoped that when I returned to Fox River Farm, Ian Sebastian would be dead or changed forever.

I did not bargain for what sort of changes there would be.

31

Christian wasn't cut out to be a detective. An entire afternoon at the courthouse had gotten him nowhere. He hadn't found any relevant reports, permits sought, documents relating to a land deal in the general area of South Land. He had discovered new restrictions on land use that made subdivisions next to impossible now. The county was fighting growth tooth and nail, and right now the county was ahead.

He made an early night of it and rose at dawn to work in the kennel, then exercise Night Ranger and walk a select group of hounds to ready them for tomorrow's opening hunt. Peter and the kennel staff would walk the rest of tomorrow's pack later in the morning. With his mind on other things, he was almost at South Land when he realized where he had been headed.

With no wish to revisit the site of Fidelity's murder, he turned away and headed up a hill, cutting across the border of South Land and skirting Ashbourne, since he doubted Maisy would welcome the hounds on her property. He'd come this way with Peter when they had breakfasted with Sally Foxhall. At eighty-nine, Sally was still spry, with a crystal-clear memory of her past, if not of present day. She had lived alone until recently, but now her granddaughter had joined her, a woman in her thirties who loved the country.

Sally had said that Lucy, the granddaughter, would inherit Foxhall when she died. Lucy was intrigued by foxhunting, and Peter had been thrilled when she showed an interest in riding with the

Mosby Hunt. If she did, the club could probably count on Fox-hall's sprawling acres for many years to come.

At the top of the hillside, Christian reined in Night Ranger and stared into the distance. Foxhall was a good twenty minutes by this route, but only a short distance as the crow flies. He hadn't paid much attention the morning of their visit, but something Sally had said nagged at him now. She'd been extolling her granddaughter's virtues. Apparently, compared to the rest of Sally's family, Lucy was a saint.

"Lucy here came through for me," she said. "She's the only one who cares."

At the time Christian had assumed Sally meant that Lucy was the only relative who'd been willing to uproot her life to care for the old woman. Now he wondered if she had been referring to Lucy's love of Foxhall, instead.

Sally had been transparently pleased to have visitors. He suspected she would be even more pleased to have an impromptu visitor today.

"Bunnies instead of foxes," he said, patting Ranger's neck. "Or instead of Foxhall, huh, boy?"

In the third year of his sentence, Christian had shared a cell with a confidence man who'd swindled senior citizens with the enthusiasm a politician or circus performer has for his job. He had shared his secrets with Christian until Christian had threatened to tie the man's tongue into knots.

But Christian had learned one thing. Always pretend to know what you don't.

He reached the offices of Virginia Vistas just before closing. He knew Bard Warwick was there, because he spotted his BMW in the parking lot. For old times' sake Christian parked his pickup against the back fender of the Beemer.

The office itself was overdecorated, a la English country house, but he recognized one painting, a particularly fine landscape, as one of Julia's. Her style had ripened and grown more sophisticated, but she hadn't lost her preoccupation with horses and hunting. Her talent was immense, but her scope was larger. She painted the perfection of nature, the joys of camaraderie, and values like honor and respect, which had fallen into disuse. She did not paint foxes and hounds, she painted hope and expectation and man's quest for the elusive.

When the receptionist asked for his name, he told her that Bard was an old friend and he wanted to surprise him. She pointed out Bard's office and turned her back.

Bard was on the telephone and didn't notice when he entered. Christian closed the door and waited until the call was over. He watched the surprise on Bard's face when he spun in his desk chair, ready to reprimand whomever had interrupted him.

"We're going to have a conversation," Christian said.

"How'd you get in here?" Bard's gaze flicked toward the door.

"I knew the password."

"I'm about to have it changed." Bard lifted the receiver.

"Go ahead. I'll be more than happy to share what I have to say with an audience. We'll start with Callie and work down from there."

Bard put the receiver back in place. "Who do you think you are?"

"I'm the man whose daughter you stole."

"I married your daughter's mother. Hardly the same thing."

Christian noticed Bard didn't seem surprised that he knew. "You claimed her as yours. Your name's on her birth certificate."

"Julia had a little something to do with that."

"I've already spoken to Julia."

"Is that all you've done?"

"What are you asking?"

"Julia moves out of the house. You get out of prison. I can put two and two together."

"Not very well. Whatever's between the two of you is between *you*. Leave me out of it."

"I'll bet she ran right straight into your arms yesterday after she decided she was leaving me."

Christian didn't betray surprise. Julia had left Bard. If he stopped to think about it, he wouldn't be able to think about anything else. "You seem to be putting in a full day's work."

"You can count on a good business deal. You can't count on a woman. Remember that, if she does the same thing to you."

Christian crossed the room and sprawled on the edge of Bard's desk like an old friend. He hooked one boot over the crosspiece under Bard's chair and folded his arms. "You've counted on a lot of business deals in your time, haven't you?"

"Get out of my office, Carver."

"For instance, there was that deal you tried to negotiate with Sally Foxhall. Remember her? She's almost ten years older than she was when you lavished all that attention on her. She still speaks highly of you, even though she can't figure out why you don't come around to visit, the way you did after her heart attack."

Bard was as good as Christian about keeping his feelings hidden. "I know Sally Foxhall. I grew up here, remember? She was old when I was born, and a little dotty even then."

"When did you get the idea she should sell her land to you? When she thought she was at death's door?"

"To my knowledge Sally hasn't sold Foxhall to anybody. Have I missed something?"

"Not a thing. You're good, as a matter of fact. If you'd pulled off that deal, I'll bet you'd be a rich man." He paused. "But then, you're already a rich man, aren't you?"

"I told you once, get out of my office."

"When I do, I'm going straight to the sheriff."

"With what?"

"Well, I'll start by telling them that on the morning Fidelity was killed, you were at Foxhall sweet-talking Sally. She had just about decided to let you handle the sale of her land. She'd lost hope she'd be able to keep up with it. None of her heirs wanted it—until Lucy came along. Of course, you would have bought the land yourself without putting it on the block, but your name wouldn't have appeared on any documents. I'm guessing a consortium of one kind or another would have been named. And nobody could have traced the impending development to you."

"You're guessing."

"I'll let you in on a little secret. Here's what it took me the longest time to figure out. I couldn't understand why you'd tolerate a housing development in Millcreek's backyard. But you wouldn't have, would you? You knew that was never going to be an issue, because as soon as the word of a development got out, you knew the Sutherlands and Peter Claymore and everyone else in earshot would band together to buy the land back at ten or twenty times what you'd paid Sally for it. Maybe you'd have thrown in something on the deal yourself, just to deflect suspicion. In the end, there would have been no development and lots of profit for your consortium of one.''

"You have a rich fantasy life.''

"Or Sally does. She told me how much she liked and trusted you and knew you'd do right by Foxhall. Too bad her health improved and she decided to stay on. You were set to make millions, weren't you?''

"You couldn't prove any of this in a thousand years.''

"I don't know. Sally's in surprisingly good health still, and she loves to talk.''

"If I wanted to buy Foxhall, it was just to add to my personal holdings. Better one of us than one of them, I always say. And you can never prove otherwise. Nobody would believe a thing Davey Myers said.''

"There's always a paper trail.'' Christian smiled thinly. "I've been out of jail for a matter of weeks and look what I've discovered.''

Bard leaned back in his chair. "I'll take my chances.''

"Is that so? With the sheriff, too?''

"Nothing I did was illegal.''

"Sally Foxhall is just so happy to talk about the things she remembers. She remembers Fidelity, you know. But who could forget her? I never have.''

"Are you leaving yet?''

"Fidelity came to see you at Foxhall that morning. Sally remembers that, too. With stunning clarity.'' He was guessing at the date. He didn't add that Sally had forgotten a few things, too. The fact that Fidelity was dead, for instance.

Surprisingly, Bard didn't try to deny it. "I did see Fidelity that morning. No revelation there. She came to find me.''

"And she was upset, according to Sally. Very upset, but who

wouldn't be? She'd figured out what you were up to. She was busy snooping and meddling that summer. She had time on her hands, and she was nobody's fool.''

"Even if Fidelity had known I wanted Foxhall, she wouldn't have raised an eyebrow. Like I said, better me than some outsider. She knew I wouldn't let developers in. We were cut from the same cloth.''

"Not by a long shot.''

"No? You might have been raised here, but you're nothing but the son of a drunk.''

"Oh, I don't know. I was good enough to stand at stud for you, Bard. That must say something about my bloodlines.''

A flash of anger brightened Bard's expression. "And I was too good for your leftovers, but I took them anyway.''

Christian grabbed Bard's shirt and pulled him forward. Bard was a big man, but he seemed to know better than to resist. "You didn't want to get your own hands dirty, so you hired Karl Zandoff to kill Fidelity because she had learned what you were doing. You probably met him through Davey Myers.''

"Never did.''

Christian tightened his grip. "Fidelity planned to warn your neighbors, and that's what you were fighting about at Sally's that morning. So you decided to have her killed. I'm going to prove you conspired with Zandoff, and I'm going to make sure they send you straight to my cell at Ludwell.''

Bard didn't move. He didn't even try to push Christian away. "You'll never find any link to Zandoff because there isn't one. He didn't kill her.'' He smiled a little. "But I know who did.''

Christian knew when a man was bluffing. It was another thing he'd learned in prison. And he knew when a man was telling the truth.

He released Bard's shirt and leaned back, but he didn't relax his guard. "Sally says the two of you stood in the road that day, arms waving like windmills. Then Fidelity drove off, and not long afterward you followed her.''

"She wasn't upset with *me*. She was angry at someone else. The person who killed her, as a matter of fact.''

"Who?''

"Do you think I just figured it out?"

Christian didn't blink, and he didn't move anything except his foot. With one flick of his boot he sent Bard's chair lurching across the room.

Bard got to his feet. "I've known from the beginning who killed Fidelity, and it wasn't Karl Zandoff. You never figured it out because you're every bit as blind as my wife."

Christian knew he didn't have a chance of making Bard name the murderer. Whatever this man knew would die with him unless Christian figured it out on his own. "Then you knew I didn't kill Fidelity, but you let me go to prison. You must have wanted Julia awfully badly."

"Julia was a pretty prize. Almost as good as snagging Foxhall. I contented myself with one instead of the other."

Bard was taunting him, hoping Christian would try to beat the truth out of him. The sheriff would be called for certain then. Christian would go back to jail.

He practiced the last and most important skill he had learned at Ludwell. He got to his feet.

And he walked away.

Julia missed riding. She missed the smell and feel of horses, the creak of saddle leather, the brief moments of flight when she soared over a jump. She and Callie had managed several more rides when Ramon wasn't busy, but before the accident, horses, like painting, had been a daily part of Julia's life.

To compensate, she visited Sandman, now comfortably ensconced in Jake's barn. He was gentle enough that she'd finally taken to slipping inside the stall to groom him. If she kept one hand on Sandman's side, she always knew where he was. She was becoming so confident at judging spaces that she never felt crowded or threatened.

Tonight, after she tucked Callie in, she went outside to the barn by herself, making her way with the walking stick in front of her. The gravel crunched under her feet, warning her when she strayed from the path. She didn't take a direct line to the barn, but she got close to the door without incident and felt her way inside. She slipped into boots she kept by the door, fed

Feather Foot a sugar cube, then made her way to Sandman. Something brushed against her leg, and she started. A cat yowled, and she realized she'd stepped on a paw or a tail.

"Sorry," she murmured, sure whichever cat had blocked her path was long gone.

She liked the sounds of a barn at night. The insect nocturne just beyond the walls, the stirring of large, sleepy equine bodies, the crunch of straw under her feet. There was no music playing here, no one to worry that she was bored.

No one to hear her tears falling.

She wasn't sure why she was crying. Because her marriage had ended. Because her sight had not returned. Because once she'd had dreams of a life filled with love and the deep satisfaction that comes from sharing the smallest things.

She found Sandman's stall and slipped inside. He was lethargic, sleeping perhaps, and he didn't seem to mind when she stroked his muzzle. She wasn't sure how long she stood there sobbing before she heard a voice.

"Julia?"

She wasn't sure where the voice came from, or even, for a moment, whose it was. Then she realized Christian was somewhere in the barn. The lights were probably off, and she suspected he couldn't see her.

"I'm here with Sandman." She cleared her throat. "What are you doing here?"

He was closer when he spoke again. "I don't know."

"Well, who would know better than you?"

"You're crying."

"No, I'm not." She wiped her cheeks with her fingertips, until she found a tissue in her pocket.

"You always did that. We'd go to a sad movie, and you'd refuse to admit you were crying. Then you'd wipe your cheeks with this look on your face that said you were surprised to find it was raining."

"You haven't forgotten a lot, have you?"

"I had a lot of time to remember."

That made her want to cry even more.

"Can I come in?" he said.

"I don't know. Is there room for all of us?"

"As stalls go, it's the Hilton." He joined her. She could feel him beside her. Their coats touched, but they didn't.

"Nice enough horse," he said.

"He's gentle. A good horse for a blind woman."

"You've been riding? Besides that one day, I mean?"

"The day you met your daughter for the first time?" She cleared her throat again. "Uh-huh. When I have help."

"You probably turned into quite a rider over the years."

"You should know. You made it happen."

"*You* made it happen. I just stood by and gave a few pointers."

"You practically had to hold me on the horse, Christian."

"You were a natural."

"Natural coward. But maybe I knew something back then. I wouldn't be blind if I hadn't learned to ride, would I?"

"Even so, you still miss it. I know how it feels. I'd wake up at Ludwell sometimes—" He didn't go on.

"Please, tell me."

She felt him shrug. "I would dream I was riding again. I'd wake up and find out I wasn't."

He didn't have to tell her how that felt. Her voice was soft. "After you went away, I dreamed we were making love. I always woke up."

He sounded as if he'd turned away. "When you were awake, did you ever think about me?"

"I was married to somebody else. When the sun was out, I was loyal to him. Funny how we can split ourselves up. I worked so hard to forget you, but at night you were right there again. And when I woke up after dreaming about you, I didn't feel disloyal to Bard, because the darkness belonged to you. I'd wonder how you were, or if you still thought of me with anything except anger. I'd remember...the good times."

"You've left him. He told me."

She was surprised, but she didn't want to know how that had come about. "I should have left him years ago, or tried harder to make our marriage count for something. But I just drifted along. I thought staying married was better for Callie, but it wasn't. She's a little girl, but she already feels responsible for the problems she senses.''

She faced him, reaching out to find him and be sure. Beside her, Sandman shifted his weight. ''Christian, I didn't leave Bard because you're out of prison. I don't want you to think I did. I left him because it was past time to go, and I've finally found the courage.''

''Why are you telling me?''

''Because I don't want you to think I'm flinging open a door and trying to drag you through it. I don't want you to feel responsible for the breakup of my marriage.''

''Let me take you for a ride. On Night Ranger.''

''What?''

''On Night Ranger. I rode over here. He'll carry us both. He has before.''

She was confused and only too aware he had sideswiped what she tried to tell him. ''Now?''

''Right this minute. You want to ride. I have the horse for it.''

''Did you hear what I'm saying?''

''I got the gist, Julia. Do you want to ride or not?''

She was hurt, then she was angry. ''No, I don't. This is what you did to me before. You shut yourself off. You thought I'd betrayed you on the witness stand, and you went off to prison without letting me explain. You left me with a hole in my life as big as the one they threw you in!''

''And now you have another.''

''I'm not asking you to fill it!''

''No, you're just telling me that leaving Bard has nothing to do with me. I guess you think I might feel guilty, and you sure don't want that to happen. Well, here's the truth, since you seem to need it all spelled out. I don't care why you left the bastard. I don't care if you had a vision, or your doctor convinced you he was hazardous to your health, or you simply wised up and realized he's the worst kind of bad news.''

She was stunned into silence, but only for a moment. ''Then why are you here? If you don't care about me, why did you want me to ride with you?''

''I'm not a saint, damn it. Don't you get it? I'm telling you

I'm not one bit noble. I can't make myself care *why* you left him. I just care that you *did*."

She felt as if she were floating, as if the weight of nine years had begun to lift. She reached out to touch his cheek. He took her hand and guided it there, holding it in place.

"We're a long way from talking about anything except the past and present," she said as she let her fingertips glide slowly up to his cheekbone.

"Agreed."

"But right now, in the immediate future I see a man and a woman and a horse. Do you?"

"The woman behind the man, her arms around him?"

"There's nothing I'd like better."

"I'll warn you. I don't know where we're going."

She wondered if he was talking about the ride or their lives. "Will you tell Maisy we're riding?"

"I already did."

"Let's fly, Christian."

He took her hand, not lightly, but the way he once had when they'd been lovers. He steered her carefully from the barn, warning her when they changed direction or skirted obstacles. Outside, he boosted her to Night Ranger's back; then, with one athletic heave, he settled himself in the saddle in front of her.

The saddle wasn't really large enough for two, but that didn't matter. She could feel Night Ranger moving restlessly beneath her and Christian's warm, strong body supporting her weight. His feet were in the stirrups, but hers dangled freely. She wrapped her arms around him and rested her cheek against his back.

He reached around and rested his palms along her thighs. "You weigh less than a hummingbird."

"Night Ranger probably doesn't think so."

"He's happy to have you here."

She leaned more fully against him. "Is he?"

"Yeah." Christian straightened and gathered the reins in his hands, nudging the horse forward. The horse began to rock beneath her as he started through the stableyard. Outside, in open pasture, he picked up speed.

The night was cold, but she was not. She was floating, with

the crisp Virginia air sweeping over her and the man she had always loved close against her. If she could have held time in her hand, stopped it at that exact moment so that nothing would ever change, she would have.

As Night Ranger stretched his long legs and began to canter, she thought that she and Christian were reliving their dreams, only this time together.

Christian was riding, and she was making love to him.

Maisy was waiting up when Julia got home.

"Your cheeks are as red as apples," Maisy said.

"I'm not surprised." Julia still felt as if she were flying. She and Christian had not exchanged another word until he helped her off Night Ranger and walked her to the door, but her body was singing and her heart was full.

"Come sit by the fire and warm up. I'll come down later and make sure it's banked for the night."

"Read to me, Maisy."

"Now?"

"Uh-huh. I'm not going to sleep anytime soon."

"You know, the story can wait. It's not going anywhere."

"I want to hear the rest of it."

"It's not all written."

"Read me what you have, then."

Maisy hesitated. Julia cocked her head. "You're reluctant. I'm sorry, are you too tired?"

"No, I'll get the next part."

"I want to find out what happens to Louisa."

"She's gone back to Ian, you know."

Julia realized the time had come to tell Maisy what she'd done. "*I'm* not going back to Bard. I told him yesterday morning."

"I suspected."

"No, you hoped."

"Julia, I hope for your happiness. I don't pretend to know exactly how you'll find it."

"I'm learning to hold on to the moment. That seems to be the only thing we can really count on."

"You're wrong there. We can change our future. Not everything, but maybe more than you've realized."

"I hope Louisa changes hers."

Maisy took Julia's hand and squeezed it. "That's the good thing about stories. We can make them turn out any way we want."

From the unpublished novel *Fox River,*
by Maisy Fletcher

Ian lay as if dead for five days after we returned. On the sixth he opened his eyes and stared at the same nurse who had helped attend Alice's delivery. "What in deuces...are you doing here?"

She backed away and let me take her place. I leaned over the bed. "You've been in an accident. We weren't certain you'd wake up."

He licked his lips as I told the nurse to pour a fresh glass of water. He stared up at me, trying to put the puzzle of his life back together. Dr. Carnes had warned me that with a serious head injury of this type, his memory might be spotty, perhaps nonexistent at first.

I fed Ian water by the teaspoon until the whole glass was gone. He closed his eyes and fell asleep.

After that he woke on and off for two days, confused each time, but docile enough. On the third day he struggled to sit up, and we helped him until he was propped against a nest of pillows. I brought him Lettie's cold tomato soup, which he devoured, then a bowl of rice pudding. He finished that, too.

"There was a storm," he said at last.

I supposed it was good his memory was returning,

although there were certain things I hoped he would never remember. "You were out riding. We think a tree fell and spooked Equator." I plunged on, as if my next sentences meant nothing. "Alice and I were on our way back to New York. Mama took a turn for the worse, and we were trying to get to her in time to say goodbye."

He frowned. "Your mother?"

"Yes. She died. George says it was peaceful."

"How long?"

"Nearly ten days since the storm."

"Equator?"

"He's fine."

"I didn't know...any horse could throw...me." He tried to smile, and for just a moment I saw a glimpse of the man I'd married. "Did I break...anything?"

"Your collarbone. Possibly your ankle. Definitely a wrist. You're wearing two splints and a sling, in case you haven't noticed. Mostly, though, that hard head of yours took a beating. Things may not make sense for a while. You may have trouble remembering. But don't worry. Dr. Carnes says eventually most things will come back to you. You just have to be patient."

He frowned at that, as if one thing that he did remember was his own impatience. "Alice..."

"She's fine. I can bring her to see you later, if you'd like."

"Is there...a pony?"

My breath caught. "There is. Patches. He's over at Sweetwater, so the Carrolton boys can ride him. He needs exercise."

"Alice...doesn't mind?"

"No. She's willing to share."

He took that at face value and closed his eyes. I wondered how long before he remembered everything and brought Patches back to Fox River.

Ian grew stronger gradually. A week after he regained full consciousness he was able to make his way to the stable under his own power. He made arrangements to have Equator sold at auction the following Friday.

My own fate hung in the balance those first months. Ian's recovery was so paramount, I couldn't begin to visualize my future. Although he was often irritable, he was too weak to hit me and too weary to renew Alice's riding lessons. He refused to talk about his injuries, retreating at times, as if he was still in pain. Patches stayed at Sweetwater, and Ian seemed to forget the pony's existence. He came to my room regularly and slept in my bed most nights. He helped in the kennel and the stable. The enforced truce was tentative, but welcome.

One day, while I was visiting Sweetwater, now officially the property of the Carrolton family, I mentioned Alice's fear of horses to Etta. Etta was a large woman, blunt and no-nonsense, but a wonderful mother. I enjoyed her company, although I knew that in any dispute she and Bob would take Ian's side. Good relations with neighbors are the only insurance country people can count on.

"I've had luck teaching children to ride," Etta said. "Dick was frightened himself. It nearly drove poor Bob to distraction. But now I can't keep him out of the saddle. Sometimes I wish I hadn't succeeded so admirably."

"Etta, could you teach Alice not to be afraid?" This was a solution that hadn't occurred to me. If Alice got over her fear before Ian attempted to teach her again, then perhaps we might avoid disaster. "I know it's a lot to ask...."

"Ian doesn't want to? When he's well, I mean?"

I hesitated, then told her the truth. I knew she wouldn't be able to help me in a crisis, but I wanted someone to know what my marriage was like. If the worst ever happened and Ian killed me in a fit of rage, I wanted someone to suspect what he'd done, if only to tell the authorities and perhaps save Alice.

"Lou-i-sa..." She shook her head.

"You can't tell anyone else. If he discovered I'd discussed this with you, I don't know what he'd do."

"Of course I'll teach Alice. It will be my pleasure." Clearly she wanted to do what little she could.

Etta's strength as a teacher was infinite patience. A week passed before Alice would go to the Sweetwater stables willingly. Two passed before she agreed to sit in a saddle again. But Etta saw each small change as a triumph. I was confident now that my daughter could avoid her father's wrath.

As soon as he was able to ride again, Ian insisted on resuming his duties as Master of Foxhounds. To celebrate, we had the board of governors to Fox River Farm for a Sunday picnic on the lawn. I was worried because he wasn't yet himself. There were gaps in his memory, and he tired quickly. Whenever he was under even moderate strain, I noticed he reacted by stiffening and staring with a fixed gaze into the distance. At those times he was impossible to converse with, and afterward his temper always flared.

I did everything I could to make life easier so Ian would stay calm. I wondered if throughout history women had bargained for their safety this way with the men who were supposed to love and care for them.

The day of the picnic Ian seemed like the man he had been. He was energetic and attentive, the consummate host. We sat at long tables under Fox River's ancient oaks. Lettie had corralled a daughter to help her serve, and Seth doled out corn liquor from a neighbor's still. So far the party was a success.

"Ian, we've been worried about you," one of the wives told him. "It's so good to see you up and about again. Now I'm completely certain you'll be ready for the season."

"And who will you ride at the opening hunt now that Equator's been sold?" her husband asked. "Will you take Crossfire from the little lady?"

Although the more mature Crossfire and I had come to terms several years before, my horse seemed like a reasonable solution for Ian. He was a big, showy animal, and Ian would look well on him, while still being subdued enough to control until Ian recovered entirely. But Ian grimaced at that possibility. "Crossfire? No chance of that. I have my eye on Bill Jackson's gray."

"Shadow Dancer?" Another of the governors looked shocked. "He's only half-broken, isn't he? And with those bloodlines, he'll be hell on the hoof." He looked around the table. "Excuse me, ladies."

"What's this about a new horse?" I asked.

"Barring complications, he'll be mine by the end of next week. We need a new stallion, and Shadow Dancer is the best horse to stand at Fox River."

I knew better than to question his good sense. I only hoped that when it came time to ride to hounds, Ian would have a change of heart.

After the others were gone, Ian told me he intended to trade Patches to Bill Jackson as part of the deal. Bill had a small son, and the pony was just right for him. I thanked him, but his next words worried me.

"He wasn't right for Alice. I can see that now. We'll wait a bit and buy another pony when she's ready to ride, something she can keep longer."

"She may not be ready for quite some time," I warned. The secret riding lessons were going well, but I was afraid the moment Ian began to put pressure on Alice again, her fear would return.

He stared at me—*through* me, in fact—as if suddenly he was grappling with an invisible enemy. His body went rigid, and sweat beaded his forehead.

"Ian, sit down." I tugged at him, and with relief, I realized I could lead him to a chair. I fanned him once he was sitting. He was still staring sightlessly, but as a minute passed, he seemed to focus. Finally he looked up.

"Ian, are you all right?"

He made a sudden swipe in my direction, as if I had enraged him. He missed me, but only because I'd been on my guard. I stepped just out of his range. "Please calm down. You're not feeling well. You—"

"Don't tell me how I feel!" Unexpectedly, he lunged forward, grabbing me by the shoulders and shaking me until I cried out. Then he shoved me hard.

As I stumbled backward, he fell into the chair and put his head in his hands. I remained silent—and distant—watching him.

"This has happened before," he admitted at last. "Did you know?"

He was speaking as if he hadn't just shaken the life out of me. I tried to breathe, but the words took moments to form. "I've been worried. But Dr. Carnes doesn't seem to think—"

"What does he know!" The volume of his own voice seemed to cause him pain. He winced.

"He's a doctor."

"He's a medicine show quack."

"He said head injuries can be touchy, and sometimes it takes a long time to recover completely."

"Yes, and does he know I have headaches so crushing they suck the life out of me? That when they begin, everything goes black? When I'm riding—"

"Ian, this happens on horseback?"

"I told you it's happened before!"

"But how can you continue to ride? How can you control a difficult horse like Shadow Dancer if you're in this kind of pain? You have to tell the doctor."

"You won't tell anyone, do you hear me? Not Dr. Carnes, certainly none of the governors. They'll say I'm unfit, and I'll be removed as master. You've never understood. For you, the hunt is simply something to occupy the time. For me, it's everything."

His voice was shrill, and he was trembling. Ian healthy was enough of a threat. But this man, under the force of pain he couldn't discipline, was terrifying. What little self-control he'd practiced before the injury might well disappear forever.

Despite that, I still tried to help. "Why don't you just rest a while? It's cool here on the terrace. I'll bring you something to drink, and when you're feeling like yourself—"

"This is myself! For God's sake, can't you understand? I'm this man with demons in his skull. If Dr. Carnes knew how bad it was, he would lock me away."

"Of course he wouldn't."

He straightened. His eyes narrowed. "And you would stop him? You want me locked away. You're my worst enemy."

I'd had enough. "I won't be shaken again or beaten because you can't control yourself. If this keeps up and you don't get help, I'll leave you."

He laughed humorlessly. "Just where would you go?"

"Someplace you'll never find me."

"I have you watched, Louisa. Don't you think I know you were leaving me the day of my accident?"

I wondered where I might find sanctuary. My mother was gone. My brother believed I should work out my problems in Virginia. And Annie, after a difficult pregnancy, had given birth to a healthy baby girl, Virginia Louisa, but her own health remained in jeopardy. I couldn't burden my dearest friend or her parents with my troubles when they had so many of their own. I had no one to turn to for help.

Now it seemed Ian was having me watched. I wondered which servants had this onerous duty. If running away had been a difficult feat, now it would be nearly impossible. And if I tried and wasn't successful, Ian might kill me in retaliation.

"These headaches will pass," he said. "I'll make sure of it. Then you and I will settle our little problems, once and for all."

"I'm going upstairs," I said. "Seth will check on you in a little while." I left as quickly as I could. I knew if I stayed and his strength returned, I might not be allowed to.

32

Christian was awakened by the telephone again, this time just minutes before his alarm was to go off. He considered ripping the damn thing out of the wall.

"Hi," Julia said on the other end.

He changed his mind about the telephone. He sat up straight, combing his hair off his forehead with his fingers, and wondered if there was anything sexier than waking up to Julia's soft voice. "Is anything wrong?"

"Nothing. I know I took a chance calling this early, but I was pretty sure you'd be getting ready for the opening meet. I just wanted to wish you luck. I'd give anything to be there watching you hunt the hounds."

He settled back against the headboard, cradling the receiver against his ear like a beloved object. "I have a lot to learn. Peter will probably do most of the work."

"Robby always said Peter was happiest when he was in charge."

"That was part of the reason Robby and Peter never got along."

Julia was silent a moment. "That's odd. You know, that was one of the last things Robby said to me, and I haven't thought about it for years. I told you I didn't see much of him. He turned me down every time I tried to get together. He wouldn't even come to Callie's christening. But I ran into him in town just a week or maybe two before he died, and when I told him how much I missed him, he said something about the way Peter had taken over his life."

"Well, you said Robby was depressed. If I know Peter, he was just trying to snap him out of it."

"You're probably right, but that day Robby seemed almost philosophical."

"What do you mean?"

"Well, he told me he'd finally become the perfect son." She paused. "I'm trying to think how he put the next part. It didn't make sense, so it stuck with me. Something about how he'd only done two things in his life completely on his own, but that had given Peter enough to keep himself busy for the rest of his days."

It didn't make sense to Christian, either. "Did he explain?"

"No. It was such an odd thing to say, I asked him what he meant. But instead of answering, he asked if I still missed you and Fidelity. And when I said I did, he said maybe it wasn't such a bad thing that Fidelity had died when she did."

"I hope he explained."

"He said Fidelity had died at the height of her powers."

Christian tried to put the pieces of the conversation together.

Julia continued. "I don't know. It's the kind of thing people say to rationalize the death of someone they care about, isn't it? She was spending a lot of time with him that summer, remember? In fact, I thought the flirting had gotten a little extreme, and I told her to ease up. When he lost both of you at the same time, I think he came unhinged a little. I've thought for a long time..."

"What?"

"That maybe his death wasn't an accident."

"Suicide?"

"Maybe. But if Robby was that disturbed, surely Peter knew and was getting him help."

"Sometimes all of us are blind when it comes to the people we love most." He heard his own words and realized where he'd heard some that were remarkably similar. From Bard Warwick.

I've known from the beginning who killed Fidelity, and it wasn't Karl Zandoff. You never figured it out because you're every bit as blind as my wife.

His hand tightened on the receiver as he realized exactly what Bard had meant.

Julia's voice grew even softer. "I'm afraid that sounds like something my therapist might say."

Christian's mind was going in a million directions. "I'm sorry. Not the best expression to use, under the circumstances."

"The right one. You'll be careful today? Bard's going to be at his worst."

"Maybe not."

"What do you mean?"

"Maybe he's not quite the bastard I thought he was."

"Christian?"

He was treading water, not sure which shore to swim toward. "I'd better go. There's a lot to do before we head out."

"Just take care."

"I will."

"Last night was wonderful. Thank you for the ride."

He thought of all the changes in his life, the way the simplest things had been snatched from him and how little control he'd had. He thought of all the things he'd never said to those who weren't alive now to hear them.

"Julia?"

"Uh-huh?"

"I didn't just dream about riding. When I was in prison. I dreamed about you, too. Every night, until I was afraid to go to sleep. Every night for nine long years."

He hung up softly and sat staring at the wall, trying to put the pieces of his life together once again.

Then he made his final phone call to Pinky Stewart.

Julia made the coffee before anyone else got up. Callie and Tiffany were spending the day and evening with a schoolmate's family at their cabin in Shenandoah County, and Samantha was going to drop Tiffany off on her way to opening hunt. Jake would drive the girls to the cabin after breakfast.

It would be quiet without Callie's sunny chatter, but for once Julia was looking forward to the silence. She knew what a big day this was going to be for Christian. She doubted she would be able to concentrate on anything else.

"You're up early."

Julia turned at Maisy's words. "Well, so are you. This is historic."

"I couldn't sleep."

"Welcome to the club. I've made coffee. It should be ready in a few minutes."

"Anybody watching you wouldn't realize you were blind. You've mastered the place."

"Which means as long as I stay at Ashbourne twenty-four hours a day, I can function."

"You're frustrated."

"I'm becoming resigned. Have a seat and let me fix your breakfast."

"I love being waited on." A chair scraped.

Julia opened the cupboard and felt along the bottom shelf for bread. "Whole wheat or white?"

"How can you tell the difference?"

"The whole wheat comes with a twist tie. The white comes with a little…thingie. That little tab with the slot. You know."

"Thingie is as good a word as any. But I'll take whole wheat. No butter. I'm on a diet."

Maisy's diets were legendary. "What's it this time? High protein, low protein, no protein?"

"Just good sensible eating habits and a decision not to hide behind these extra pounds anymore."

Julia stopped fumbling with the tie. "Why, Maisy?"

"Do you remember when you stopped calling me Mommy?"

Julia didn't remember that she ever had. "No. Weren't you always Maisy?"

"Oh, no. You stopped when your father died. I was Maisy ever after."

"You never complained."

"There were many more things to think about."

Julia forced herself to work on opening the bread bag again. "I can imagine."

"Can you?"

Julia hesitated, then her hands were still again. "Yes," she said softly. "I'm afraid I'm beginning to."

Maisy was silent.

"Have you finished your novel, Maisy?"

"It's finished."

"I'd like to hear the rest."

"Yes, I know. I'm glad."

"Will you read to me when Jake takes the girls to the mountains?"

"I will."

Julia faced her mother, the toast forgotten. "Has Jake read your book?"

"Jake only knows I've written it. He's a patient man, your stepfather. He's waited a long time for me to finally come into my own."

From the unpublished novel *Fox River*, by Maisy Fletcher

Several weeks after the picnic, I took the shortest route to Sweetwater, where Alice was having a riding lesson. A groom rode with me, as one always seemed to now. I knew better than to resist his company. The grooms were under orders, and Ian would hear if I made a fuss. I was just grateful my husband hadn't inquired as to why our daughter was spending so much time with the Carroltons. I hadn't enlightened him. The less said about Alice, the better.

When I arrived, Etta beckoned me to the riding ring. "We have a surprise for you, Alice and I."

I looked around for my daughter and saw her emerging from the stable into the ring, emerging on the back of Dick's Shetland pony.

My Alice, riding at last.

I felt tears in my eyes. Despite everything, Alice had conquered her fear. I clapped softly. "Etta, you've made a miracle."

"No, she's a tough little thing under those pretty curls. When she decided she was ready, she just did it. She's more her father's child than he knows."

Or ever *would* know, I thought. Because Ian would

never see Alice for what she really was. She was, after all and before anything else, female.

"How can I thank you?" I asked.

"By taking good care of her." Etta turned to look at me. "By keeping her safe. If there's ever a doubt, send her here. We'll teach her how to find the way."

I waited to show Ian Alice's accomplishment until she was more secure in the saddle. She was comfortable enough on Dick's Cricket, but still refused even to be led on a larger horse or ride in front of me on Crossfire. Etta said that small children were often afraid of falling, a sensible fear, since for them the back of a horse was as high as a hayloft. That would change with time.

Time was always the healer.

At last, on a night when Ian seemed at his most mellow, we visited Sweetwater and Alice rode for her father.

Etta, whose enthusiasm for my husband had cooled perceptibly, stood with us as Alice and the pony walked around the ring. She turned to Ian. "As Aesop said, slow and steady wins the race."

"It's nice to see she's not sniveling." Ian watched Alice with a practiced eye. "I suppose we'll have to buy her another pony now."

Etta glanced at me. "Why not borrow Cricket until you find something that suits her better? We have no use for her. Then you can take your time, Ian."

I knew what Etta was thinking. Cricket would be an appropriate mount for some time to come.

He shrugged. "That's kind of you."

I thanked Etta for everything. On the way home, Ian told Alice he was proud of her. It was the only time she ever heard those words.

In another month the hunting season was upon us, and with it Ian's decision about which horse to ride at the opening hunt. He had purchased Shadow Dancer to stand at Fox River Farm, but before the splendid gray would attract the best mares, he needed to be seen in action by local horsemen. Bloodlines weren't enough. Performance was the key.

Even had Ian been at the peak of health, training Shadow Dancer would have been a challenge. But with Ian's health impaired, Shadow Dancer, with his lethal hoofs, his unnatural strength, his powerful will, was a potential calamity.

Despite this, Ian rode brilliantly in the opening hunt, impressing the field with Shadow Dancer's extraordinary ability to sail over obstacles. We had one of the finest chases ever, ending when the fox considerately went to ground in time for a breakfast prepared and served by Lettie and her daughters. I had arranged the flowers ahead of time. They were scarlet roses and sprays of greenery, and the tables were clad in white linen with forest-green borders. Even Ian could find no fault.

By that evening, though, Ian was exhausted. He remained so for the rest of the week, and by the end, judging from his demeanor and temper, he was suffering several headaches a day. On the third hunt of the season he suffered one in the field. We had crossed from Sweetwater to Fox River Farm, and we were waiting for our huntsman's signal. The field behind us was chatting amiably when I saw him stiffen as if he'd been hit. Ian was lucky the headache hadn't come on during a run. With my heart pounding, I dismounted and went to his side.

"Darling," I insisted loudly enough for several of the field to hear, "I'm afraid Crossfire's picked up a stone. Will you come and see?"

He managed to dismount. We stood together, Ian leaning against the skittish Shadow Dancer while I held the horse's head, until Ian was able to move again. Then, as I led Shadow Dancer, he followed me to Crossfire and pretended for long moments to examine the nonexistent stone.

"I've imagined it, haven't I?" I shook my head. "I'm sorry."

"Did you need an excuse...to stretch your legs, Louisa?"

He helped me mount. I could feel his arms tremble. I wondered if he would be able to mount Shadow Dancer and lead the chase when it began again. He did both, but the run was lackluster and his leadership confusing.

Ian was not at his best, and I knew the others sensed it as well.

The worst part of the day came at a particularly difficult jump not far from our house, one I had never taken, not even with Crossfire. Ian easily could have altered the jump, since it sat on our property, but it was the biggest and most discussed challenge of every season. The best riders insisted we keep it exactly the way it was, since it was something of a coming-of-age ritual to clear it.

A horse had to soar over a split-rail fence of four chestnut logs directly on to the slippery bank of Fox River, which sloped away sharply on the other side of the jump. Footing was precarious, and the jump was extraordinarily high. Balks were common, and even when a horse cleared the jump, riders often didn't. There had been injuries and one near-death at the site.

Luckily, only a handful of riders felt equipped to try. The rest of us picked our way through the surrounding woods, taking a lesser jump over a modestly trickling branch of Fox River. Even Ian, the stern taskmaster, had never insisted I attempt it, although he always took it with ease.

I believed he would be cautious today, taking the safer jump while joking of the sacrifices he made for the field. But Ian's crusade to pretend all was well continued. He headed straight for the jump while my heart lodged in my throat. Shadow Dancer was in his element. The jump was no more trouble for him than brushing flies with his tail. He sailed over the jump perfectly, but my exhausted, suffering husband looked like the rankest amateur, bouncing in the saddle and toppling backward as Shadow Dancer launched himself forward. Had the great horse not possessed so much heart, Ian's poor horsemanship would have caused a grave accident.

I was not the only one who saw.

He slept most of the next day, but when he arose for supper, he denied anything was wrong. When I fussed over him, he became furious, and had Lettie and Seth not been in the room, he would have slapped me.

My position was becoming more precarious. I understood, as I hadn't in the earliest years of our marriage, that Ian's emotional life was a series of contradictions. At all times he was a man at war with himself, the man who "should have been" locked in combat with the man his father had made of him. In my own pathetic way, I served as the referee. And, like anyone so close to the fight, I was always in danger.

But never so much as now.

As the season progressed, Ian suffered more headaches in the saddle. Like other men before him, he turned his resentment toward the one person who could least resist it.

Alice had continued riding Cricket, growing in confidence and courage. She hadn't, however, lost her fear of larger animals, including a pony, Duchess of York, that Ian found for her. I knew he planned to buy Duchess as a test. She was a pretty palomino, too large for Alice and too spirited. But as Ian had so often done with me, he was going to put his only child in a situation where she was destined to fail. If there was no target for the considerable anger he held inside himself, Ian created one.

So often in the past I had believed, foolishly, that I could prevent Ian's fury. I'd been sure I had the key, if only I could find it. Now, sadly, I knew that no key had ever existed. At best I could delay him, and once again that was what I tried to do.

We were in bed together, and Ian, who had found a quick release in our lovemaking, was nearly asleep. I rubbed his back like a loving wife, although my thoughts were of survival, not affection. "Ian, Etta knows of a suitable pony for Alice. I think we should go look at him before we decide on anything."

I could feel his muscles knotting under my fingertips. "I found a suitable pony for Alice. What does Etta Carrolton know that I don't?"

"Of course she doesn't know half what you know, darling. But this pony only just went up for sale. He's much showier than old Cricket. She had only the highest praise for him. In fact, she was considering him for Dick."

"Then let Dick have him."

The pony was too small for Dick, which made him perfect for Alice. I just didn't want to tell the story quite that way, since it would doom the outcome. "The Carroltons have a full stable. They had to decline. That's when she thought of us."

Ian rolled to his back and sat up. "What are you trying to do?"

"I'm trying to tell you about another pony Alice might like better than Duchess." I realized I'd chosen my words poorly, but it was too late to call them back.

"Is that so? Etta knows our daughter better than her father does?"

"That's not what I said."

"It's damned close."

"I was just presenting another option. I thought you'd be pleased I've become so interested in horse trading."

"Duchess comes first thing in the morning. Alice rides her tomorrow, whether she wants to or not."

I envisioned another terrible scene like the one that had sent me fleeing to New York. As Alice grew, how many of those would I witness? How many times would I fear for my daughter's health, or even her life?

My horror must have shown in my face. "Don't look at me like that!" Ian said. "Frances, goddamn her, used to look at me the same way."

"Frances and I have more in common than I ever imagined!"

"What does that mean?"

"Frances left you because you beat her, didn't she? Just like you beat me? Did you beat her when she was pregnant? Is that why your son died?"

He stared at me, and his face turned a sickly white. "How...dare...you?"

He lifted his hand to strike me, but I didn't flinch. "I've *told* Etta about the beatings, Ian. I've told her that if I die, she's to go straight to the sheriff and have Alice removed from this house. For all I know she'll go to the sheriff if I show up at the next hunt bruised and battered. How long do you think you can keep this up without someone stepping in? For foxhunting's sake, if not for mine?"

"You are expendable!"

"I could go to the board, you know. I could tell them the truth!"

"I will not be challenged in my own home. The ice is thin, Louisa. Be careful where you step."

"You are heavier than I and far more likely to crash through it! And if you do, who will care enough to pull you out?"

He was silent. I wished I could read his mind, although I was certain I would hate what I found.

He surprised me by falling back to the bed. He stared at the ceiling. "Oh God, what have I become?"

I was stunned. He couldn't fake the agony in his voice. No one was that good an actor. I didn't know what to say. How could I answer? He had become a man like his father, dooming his marriages, destroying his wives, year by year, piece by piece. He had a monster living inside him.

He had a young boy living inside him, crying for his mother.

"I did hit Frances," he said. "But I didn't know she was pregnant. I swear I didn't. She hid the pregnancy from me. She was planning to go home to her mother, and she didn't want me to know. We fought one night, and she told me she was leaving. I shoved her, and she fell against the wardrobe and hit her head. I carried her to the bed and undressed her. That's when I discovered she was carrying my child. She'd had no problems until the fight. After that, everything went wrong. She was sure it would all come right if she could just get away from me. In the end she did, and both of them died."

I began to weep. He pulled me to his chest and stroked my hair. I don't believe he apologized again. What was there to say that hadn't already been said? He made no promises, told no lies. It was the finest, most honest moment of our marriage.

"I could have loved you," I said at last. "At the beginning I was so very, very close, Ian. A hairbreadth away."

"I do love you." His voice trembled. "But, of course, you can't believe it."

"No, I do. Things might have been easier between us if you hadn't. You might not have tried so hard to push me away."

"I fell in love with you that first day. Your hair straggling, your riding habit torn. I thought of you facing that bear and I said to myself, 'Perhaps she can face me, as well. Perhaps this is the woman who will set me free.'"

I wept harder, and at last, he wept, too. We fell asleep that way, holding each other with no illusions and no barriers.

When I awoke late the next morning, it was to a commotion in the stableyard. At the window, I saw Duchess being led into a ring and Ian giving instructions to a groom.

33

With Fish's help, Christian placed the hounds selected for the opening hunt into a run to be loaded into the hound truck. The distance to the meet was short, but Peter had decided to truck in the animals. As they entered the run, each hound was fitted with a tracking collar, and the number was recorded on a list of names that Fish would carry in the pickup. If Christian wasn't able to locate a hound, Fish could track it and hopefully pinpoint the animal's location.

Gorda fed and comforted those hounds remaining as Christian and Fish opened the door and waved the chosen ones into place. From inside the truck one hound—Chipper, Christian guessed from the timbre of his voice—loudly proclaimed his excitement.

The day was cold, exactly what Peter had hoped for. Clouds as gray as Williamsburg pewter hung low, and dawn worked under heavy mists to lighten the sky. Under his cape-shouldered oilskin Christian was warm enough, but Fish complained bitterly as they latched the door.

At the barn, Samantha had tacked up the horses and was probably loading them now. As superb a rider as she was, she had never hunted. Today she was coming along to see what the fuss was about. Peter hoped to make her a first-class whipper-in.

They completed preparations and started up the hill from the kennel. With a wave, Samantha pulled a custom gooseneck trailer into position behind the hound truck, and the little caravan drove to the starting point.

Christian arrived as the inevitable stragglers backed their horses down ramps and made frantic last-minute searches for gloves, stock pins and riding crops. Hunting with Mosby meant strict adherence to rules of dress and etiquette, but never more than at the opening meet. Everything white had been bleached to perfection. Everything metal had been polished until it glowed. Buttons on coats had been counted—three for subscribers, four for the master, five for hunt staff—and stocks pinned vertically for staff or horizontally for the field. A few scarlet weaselbellys and black cutaways worn with top hats were in evidence, some of which had been handed down through generations of Mosby hunters.

The riders who had earned it wore Mosby's royal-blue on their collars, but there were also guest riders from neighboring hunts, wearing their own colors. The field was larger today than it would be again for some time. Some were riders who were either out of practice, out of shape or simply beginners. More were first flight, and clearly Peter, as their leader, would have his hands full today. There were foot followers, too, dozens of them in country casual clothing. Christian wondered if the entire population of Ridge's Race had come for the event, but he knew at least one person was missing. Julia.

There was no time to dwell on that. The Sutherlands had made certain Christian would be welcomed as huntsman. He was greeted with deference, and when Samantha brought Night Ranger down the trailer ramp, the horse was admired for his gleaming silver coat and tightly braided mane and tail. Christian had debated the pros and cons of using Night Ranger, but in the end he hadn't been able to leave the horse behind on opening day. Christian knew the value of friendship.

"Looking good." Samantha examined the horse with a practiced eye before she handed over the reins.

She was looking good, too, in tan breeches and a black coat she had borrowed from a club member who would never be size three again. "Thanks for helping this morning," Christian told her.

"Something tells me it's the only thing I can do for you these days." She smiled to let him know she wasn't hurt. He was grateful.

Christian glimpsed Peter, who had ridden over on Jack's Knife. He was chatting on horseback with a group of directors, including Bard and Frank Sutherland. Peter touched his hat with his crop in salute, and Christian nodded before he turned away to unload the hound truck. He had glimpsed the stern set of Bard's jaw and remembered Julia's warning.

The hounds seemed to sense the importance of the moment and stayed on their best behavior as they exited. New hounds who were just being entered this season seemed to look to the experienced hounds for protocol, just as the new hunters looked to the older ones. There was a strict pecking order for both groups, and by now Christian was convinced Mosby's hounds were nearly as intelligent as its riders.

"Christian?"

He looked up to find Peter, still mounted on Jack's Knife, beside the truck. "Good morning, Master."

"I've asked Bard Warwick to take the hilltoppers."

Christian was glad. With luck he and Bard wouldn't have much to do with each other, since the hilltoppers rode at the rear. He suspected this had been Peter's point, since Bard was normally a whipper-in. "Thanks."

Peter named two men who would work as the whippers-in instead, both experienced and reliable. The men came over for instruction, then took their positions, flanking the pack to keep the hounds under reasonable control. Their function was to keep them together, off the roads and out of danger. Christian stayed at the front and waited for Peter's signal, then started toward the cornfield where they planned to assemble before casting the hounds. The procession was both gay and solemn, enthusiasm bubbling just below the elegant surface. Christian held up his hand when Peter motioned to him. "Hold," he instructed the hounds, and, like the well-trained animals they were, they did.

Peter waited until everyone had arrived and quieted. "Just a few words before we start," he said to the assembly. "We come together this season to participate in a sport that is older by far than this country. The first time a caveman gave chase to a fox who raided his pterodactyl coop, foxhunting was born.''

Laughter rippled through the riders, and Peter nodded. He was particularly handsome today in his scarlet swallowtail, the white vest he had inherited from his father and gleaming top hat. The formal garments, ludicrous on lesser men, suited him perfectly.

''Honor is a word we seldom hear today,'' he continued. ''I'm sad to say it's disappeared in the halls of Washington. Take a drive around the Beltway and you'll see for certain that it's disappeared among the drivers of Virginia and Maryland.''

He waited for the next wave of laughter to end. ''But honor hasn't disappeared among foxhunters. So let us behave as honorable men and women today. Let's watch out for each other and do the right thing in every instance.''

Christian watched Peter's expression and knew that Peter believed what he was saying. Peter's gaze fell on him. ''We have a new huntsman today, a young man who, from this day forward, deserves only the best this community can offer. Give him your allegiance, allow him mistakes, applaud his successes. I know beyond the shadow of a doubt that someday he will be the best huntsman Virginia has ever produced.''

He paused, then nodded at Christian. ''Huntsman.''

As tradition demanded, then, and only then, did Christian set his cap on his head, the ribbons trailing down his neck to signal his position on staff.

''Ready?'' Christian asked the hounds.

They came to attention, necks arched, heads held high, twenty couple of hounds as perfect as any in Virginia. Despite a mind filled with other things, Christian felt a stab of pride. He turned and started along the dirt road that ran beside the first cornfield. The hounds followed joyously.

They bypassed the cornfields, made their way through the shallow slice of woods replete with hickory, oak and black locust, and turned into the meadow where cows grazed on the western edge. A ridge ran along the northern boundary, and beyond and below it, the narrow creek that was a tributary of Jeb Stuart.

Although he'd thought of little except the morning's telephone calls, Christian had to concentrate now, unable to think of anything except the job ahead. He was responsible for the safety of his pack and the success of the hunt. He knew his hounds, but not well enough. His tasks were to keep track of them, to encourage them and to let them work using their individual strengths. The whippers-in spread out as they started through the meadow and up to the top of the ridge. Peter had decided to cast here, where thick brush had harbored many a fox and the narrow branches of the creek made for good jumping when the banks weren't muddy.

One of the whips trotted to the gate and dismounted to open it wide, making way for Christian. Christian moved the hounds ahead, not allowing them to stop or wander near the cattle. They were trained to ignore other prey. They did their job now, moving toward ''covert'' or the location where they would be cast.

Mosby's riders were well-trained, too. The first flight stayed well behind Peter, who kept them at a distance so the hounds could work. The hilltoppers stayed behind Bard, and the foot followers stayed well behind them. Most likely they would perch at the top of the hill and watch the fun from their vantage point.

Christian and the pack crested the ridge, then continued down toward the creek. The scrub brush ahead was dense, and he knew he had to be careful not to lose a hound, particularly one of the newly entered who might become confused or pursue its own line of investigation. The wind blew from the west, and with any luck a fox's scent would be drawn toward the hounds. The whippers-in spread out, giving the hounds room to work.

At the bottom and at the thicket's edge, Christian spoke to the hounds. ''Hello, friends, he's in there.'' He lifted the huntsman's horn, which had been used by generations of Mosby huntsman, and blew a few notes, motioning the hounds into the brush as he did.

He was relieved the notes came out true and clear. Mosby's former huntsman, Samuel Fincastle, had taught both Robby and Christian to blow the horn signals, and although Robby had lost interest, for Christian the training had paid off.

The hounds bounded into the brush, noses fixed to the ground. Not all of them were visible. Christian could dismount to cast them, but there was no need as yet. Most of them were visible, and a quick perusal told him that those who weren't were his most reliable. With little to be done about either, he waited for success or failure.

The field was quiet behind him. When moments had gone by, he called out encouragement. "Find him, my friends. He's in there, I know." Aware that the hounds were most comfortable knowing his location, he continued to spur them on with sporadic reassurance. "You'll find him, friends, just keep trying. Move along now, do your work."

Most of the hounds moved forward and closer to the creek. The others fanned out, as if they had planned this pleasing formation late at night in the kennel. But Christian had no reason to hope they were on a line. They were as silent as the field of riders, noses nearly buried in the earth, seeking anything to start the chase.

Then Darth, the hound that Robby had named, opened with a baritone aria. Christian hesitated, aware that the hair-trigger Darth couldn't always be trusted, but the hound was joined by a littermate, Daisy, who took up the song. For uninterrupted moments the two sang a spectacular duet. "Ho there, Darth," Christian called. "Go find him, go find him, go find him...."

The pack began to sing in chorus, and Christian, affected despite himself, raised the horn to his lips again and blew a series of quickly repeated notes. "Forward," he called as he lowered the horn. "Forward, friends. Let's find our fox."

"Holloa!"

Christian looked right and saw the whipper-in at the left flank pointing his hat and turning his horse in the direction of the creek. A fox had been flushed out of hiding and was making its way toward the water. Christian doubled the notes on his horn in the classic "Gone Away" and began to canter in the direction of the creek, the pack in full cry before him.

The hounds bounded through the shallow water, sending spray into the air like showers of diamonds. Night Ranger bunched his powerful body and cleared the creek without so much as a splash.

Christian could see the fox now. He was a big gray, far enough ahead of the pack to give good chase, but not so far that they were about to lose him. He streaked up a hill, brush waving in the wind, and the dogs, noses to the ground, followed behind, leaping over logs and boulders, then scrambling up the bank to make their way through a thicket of blackberry canes and brush.

The terrain was hillier here. The hounds dipped into a hollow lined on each edge with stands of tulip poplars as straight and tall as schooner masts. Some of the hounds gave tongue as they ran, crying their enthusiasm and certainty that they were on the right track. Others were silent until they caught the scent again, then rejoined the chorus.

Night Ranger was reveling in the run. They'd had some good chases during cubbing, but none as exciting as this. The horse stretched out his long body and ran as if he was on the last lap at the Middleburg Spring Races. Christian glanced behind him and saw Peter and a portion of the first flight just far enough behind to give the hounds working room. The rest of the field would straggle in. He was sure the creek had slowed some of them, the blackberry thicket even more. If the chase was strenuous and lengthy enough, some would drop out altogether or, worse, be left behind in the dust.

A stone fence, patiently constructed centuries before, appeared on the perimeter. Christian had lost sight of the fox, but his hounds hadn't lost the scent. They continued their steady pace toward the fence, scampering over it while Christian watched from the distance and counted tails. All the hounds were accounted for, thanks to the expertise of the whippers-in, who had urged some of the younger hounds along. When it was time to jump the fence, Night Ranger soared like a great gray bird.

The chase, a spectacular picture-perfect run, continued for more than thirty minutes, over grassland and dry creek beds, through thickets and a patch of sparse forest. Like most foxes, this one doubled back and looped in wily figure eights, confusing the pack, but only momentarily. Christian was so absorbed in keeping track of the hounds that it took him precious seconds to realize they had slowed at last. He pulled up just in time as the dawdlers stopped altogether, and he held up his hand so Peter would hold back the field.

The check gave everyone, horses, hounds and riders, a chance to catch their breath. The quick burst of scent followed by the fox sighting had been the ideal beginning to an opening meet.

Christian let the hounds range farther without accompanying them. He didn't want to chance crossing the line of scent, which would make it harder for the hounds to find it again. He would cast them again, if need be, but for now, he let them work.

He glanced behind him when he heard hoofs approaching and saw Peter closing in. Peter spoke in low tones, so as not to disturb the working hounds. "I've seen this happen in this place before. What do you think's going on?"

"I think our fox took a detour through that fallen log over there." Christian pointed with his whip. "Climbed up along what's left of that old stone fence and took a leap into the creek. What's your take on it?"

"Just about the same. He's a gray, so he climbs. Might even have walked along that low limb over there and not scampered over the wall at all."

"I doubt he's gone to ground." Christian, like a lot of fox-hunters, was convinced that foxes—American foxes, anyway—relished the chase and only went into a hole or den when they grew too bored or tired to continue. There were hundreds of such escapes in any territory, and the mere fact that there were chases at all seemed proof the fox enjoyed himself.

"You're doing a superb job, son."

Christian met Peter's gaze for a long moment. "Your son is dead, sir."

Peter looked surprised. "I'm sorry, Christian. I didn't realize calling you that disturbed you."

"There was a time when it felt like the greatest of honors. But this morning I realized that, with your help, your real son stole nearly nine years of my life."

Peter was silent. The two men sat, gazes locked, until a hound, Chipper this time, began to speak.

"He's found something," Peter said, turning his horse toward the field.

"I know how he feels."

"We'll talk later." Peter kicked Jack's Knife into a canter.

His mind straying in a million different directions, Christian moved in on the hounds, but not too close. Chipper, nose buried in fallen leaves, was dashing toward the creek. In a moment Lizzie joined him, aiming her musical support toward the sky, which was growing lighter as clouds dispersed. The conditions that had kept the fox's scent strong were changing, and the scent would rise and dissipate as the ground warmed.

The rest of the pack moved in to see if their pals knew what they were talking about. In moments they were in pursuit, splashing across this new and wider part of the creek bed with Christian and the whippers-in following.

Christian heard the pursuit behind him as he and Night Ranger took the creek in an extended jump. As he skirted the pack, he could see the first flight, Peter in the lead, crossing after him. Peter cleared easily, but one of the ladies didn't and lost her seat as her horse scrambled up the opposite bank. Unhurt, she picked herself up and darted quickly out of the way. Peter, who was closest, went after her horse, and Christian lost sight of them both as he stayed with the hounds, who were making their way over another stone wall into a pasture of black Angus cattle.

The cows fouled the scent, and the confused hounds grouped at the other side of the wall as if to say "What next, boss?"

Christian stayed behind the wall and remained quiet, circling Night Ranger so they would have an easy approach when they needed it. The pack split but stayed well away from the cattle. Some went east and some west, noses working as they tried to discover the familiar skunklike odor of fox. One graceful willow adorned the pasture, and the pack met again just beyond it, noses still to the ground.

Christian cleared the wall, and from the corner of his eye he saw the whippers-in taking it, to flank the pack from a distance. Cows lowed in protest but the bulls were in a separate pasture close to the house today, courtesy of the considerate farmer.

Even though they were gathered in a loose knot, the hounds were clearly still confused, casting here and there and coming up with nothing.

"Cheers to you, Charley," Christian muttered. Charley, the foxhunter's name for his quarry, hadn't grown large and sleek on good fortune. He was crafty and confident enough to fool one of the best foxhound packs in Virginia.

Christian rode closer, calling out to the hounds to reassure them. He could sense their frustration. He knew it well, the premonition that there was something more to be discovered, a trail to follow, a conclusion to be won. Like them, he resented anything that interfered.

Beyond the pasture was a deep stretch of forest, rising slowly up craggy Little Sergeant Hill. An old logging road gave laborious access, but few tried the road except on horseback. Christian had hoped to avoid this eventuality—the one negative about this particular fixture—but he'd prepared himself. Even the best riders could lose their way or their seat on Little Sergeant, and the best pack could split. The forest had never been clear-cut. Some trees were as old as Virginia, huge canopies still clinging to remnant leaves. Scrub had grown up around them, as well as sapling locusts and dogwoods. But Christian knew the fox was in there somewhere, laughing at his hounds.

One of the hounds knew it, too. Darth, who had already acquitted himself well that morning, opened his throat and sang like an angel. More noses to the ground, a crowd gathered, and the line was rediscovered. Off toward the forest they ran in full chorus. Christian blew the horn, then followed after them.

He and Night Ranger sailed over a coop placed along the pasture's edge for such a moment. He could hear hoofs thundering behind him, but he was too intent on not losing the hounds to spare a glance.

He started the climb. The hounds took the fastest path directly into the woods. He jumped a ditch and guided Ranger around a downed tree. The hounds were ahead of him, some straying to the right, as if they had lost the line, some moving with purpose through the undergrowth. Behind him, he heard the voices of riders making a steady climb. He imagined that by now they had lost the least valiant hilltoppers, who had gone back to enjoy the hunt breakfast. Some would wait at the pasture's edge in case the climb proved futile and the hounds were cast again on flatter land.

He sounded the horn and called to the pack, encouraging them. From the corner of one eye he saw Lizzie and her littermate,

Lego, cut off from the others, bouncing along at a fair clip. He debated whether to bring them back or let them investigate. The decision was moot when Lizzie gave tongue, joined immediately by Lego. They were on a fox, but which fox? The other hounds were preoccupied, even annoyed by Lizzie's racket. They were pursuing their own course, and before Christian could decide which group held the most promise, Lizzie and Lego streaked through the brush and headed up the hillside.

Only one of the whippers-in had joined him. The other was preoccupied with dawdlers. Christian saw the hounds fanning out and knew that if he didn't bring Lizzie and Lego back, hours might pass before he found them again. Their collars would be little help, since Fish was far away on the paved road well below them.

His decision was made when three more couple joined the littermates. He signaled to the whip, and took off after the errant hounds, calling them by name and cracking his whip in warning, but the hounds were on a line they refused to abandon. They were well-trained not to "riot," or track other game, but the littermates, at least, were young enough that their training might have been eclipsed by the excitement of the moment. They could be after deer, bobcat or, worst of all, bear. Coyote, invading this region like others throughout the country, was also a possibility.

The hounds, lower to the ground, could find their way through brush, over boulders and around fallen trees. Christian and Night Ranger were at a disadvantage. The big horse, at his best out in the open, had to pick his way slowly through the unkind terrain, and before long the hounds were out of sight.

Christian cursed softly and followed their voices. He called to them again and again, cracking the whip when he had the room, but they were in full-scale rebellion. Had he carried a gun, he would have fired it over his head, a signal hounds rarely disregarded. But he couldn't ride armed, as yet. Until he was out from under all suspicion and a permanent release from prison was official, he knew better than to be caught with a gun in his possession, not even a .22 filled with bird shot for emergencies.

Minutes passed, and he began to regret chasing the rebels. He should have waited for the other whipper-in and sent him. Once upon a time he had roamed every hill and hollow of this countryside, but he was at a disadvantage now. On his rides with Peter they had not come up this hill, hoping the hunt would proceed in a different direction. The territory was unfamiliar, the forest dense. He knew he wouldn't lose his way; he simply had to head down in order to find his way back to the logging road. But he wondered if he would find the hounds before whatever they were after did.

He reached a clearing, and just over the next ridge the hound symphony crescendoed. He spurred Night Ranger on, calling and cracking his whip as they charged through the open space, down into another hollow and up the side. At the top he peered down.

Peter, on Jack's Knife, waved him forward. Peter, who was holding a .38 pointed directly at Christian's chest.

34

Christian stood next to Night Ranger, loosely holding the horse's reins. On the ground at his feet the rebel hounds, exhausted from their long run and climb, lethargically sniffed for a new line.

"Bobcat," Peter explained. "Disappeared into that cave over there, just as I rode up. They're pretending they put him to ground, but none of them are stupid enough to go in after him. Still, I'm surprised at their lack of discipline." He sounded like the Peter Christian had always known. Nothing was different except for the gun that was still pointed at his chest.

Christian remained silent.

Peter studied him, then grimaced. "I told you to leave it alone, Christian. I told you not to stick your nose any deeper into this business than it was already. I got you off. That's all you needed to know."

"I needed to know the truth."

"What made you figure it out?"

"A lapse in loyalty."

Peter didn't seemed surprised. "All the pieces were there, weren't they? You just never let yourself put them together. You loved him too much."

"Not quite all the pieces. I didn't know Fidelity had been leading Robby on, not until Julia mentioned how close they were that summer. It never occurred to me that he'd have any reason to kill her."

"Not leading him on. If only it had been that. She was fucking him, pure and simple."

The word sounded incongruous on the tongue of a man dressed in formal hunting attire. It was a measure of Peter's complete disgust.

Christian theorized out loud. "I'm guessing she called it quits that last morning, when she and Robby went out riding together. Julia told her to stop flirting with him, and she must have taken it to heart. Telling him goodbye must not have gone well. Afterward she went to Bard Warwick for advice."

"He was a passionate man, my son. He loved deeply and forever. Robby thought she felt the same way about him. Foolish, foolish."

"So he killed her in a fit of rage."

"He didn't plan it. He went to plead with her, and she was getting ready for a date with somebody else, selecting jewelry from that collection of hers. He just...snapped. Afterward he grabbed the jewelry, to make it look like a robbery. He buried it on the way home."

"He used his own knife, didn't he? You gave him one that Christmas, too. I'm guessing he couldn't make himself pick it up again after he killed her. When he got back to Claymore Park, he found mine on a window ledge in the barn or in a stall."

"No, I found your knife and told him to say it was his. And that meant all the knives and the people who owned them were accounted for, except for the one you had your hands all over when they found you. They found prints other than yours on the blades, but Robby's prints weren't on file anywhere and he wasn't a suspect. Besides, that was easily explained by the prosecutor. You passed your knife around to anyone who wanted to use it. You always shared."

"Robby and I didn't share my time in prison."

"No. But Robby got the death sentence, didn't he? He drove his car into that tree on purpose. He left me a note before he took off that night. He couldn't stand what he'd done and the way you'd had to pay for it. He still loved you, you know. Right up until that last breath."

Anger burned in Christian's chest. "Why didn't he just come

forward and have me freed? Why not admit what he'd done if he felt guilty enough to kill himself?''

"I wouldn't let him. It's that simple. He was torn between his love for the two of us.''

"You couldn't stand the dishonor.''

"You know me well.''

"So you dishonored yourself.''

"It seemed a small enough lapse. I truly believed we would get you off and nobody would ever have to know what Robby had done. I hired the best attorney. There was so little evidence, not even a good motive, but in the end the fact that you were standing there with the murder weapon was damning.''

"You could have spoken up then.''

"I was sure we'd get you off on appeal.''

"How did Zandoff fit in?''

"How do you think?''

Christian remembered his conversation with Bard. "He had nothing to do with it.''

"When years passed, and it looked like you were going to serve your whole sentence, I knew I needed nothing less than a confession. So I worked through Zandoff's attorney. Who better to confess than a man about to die anyway? I told Zandoff what to say. In return, I promised to take care of his family after he was executed. He's an oddly sentimental man when it comes to his family. I knew no one would ever find a record of his having been in Virginia, but the chances they'd find records of him living anywhere for those months was almost nil. He was a drifter. I was certain I'd be safe.''

"It all fit so neatly together. I called my friend in the sheriff's department this morning. He told me you and Robby had airtight alibis. Each other.''

"Robby came to me right afterward. He was distraught. I told him to be a man, that we would fix this, too.''

Christian felt the hair on his arms prickle. "Too?''

Peter was silent.

Christian was feeling his way now. "The last time Julia spoke to Robby, he said that he had done *two* things in his life that would keep you busy for the rest of yours.''

"He resented me. I tried to make him strong. I wanted him to carry on our family's traditions."

"From my vantage point, I'd say you failed miserably."

"Pretty courageous for a man with a gun pointed at his chest."

"You've already done your worst. You took away everything I ever loved. You and Robby."

"I'm afraid he took more than you know."

Christian suddenly realized what else his boyhood friend had done. "My father?"

"Yes."

"Why?"

"Because Robby loved you. Gabe beat you, don't you remember? You told Robby and made him promise not to tell anyone else. You claimed Gabe was drunk and didn't know who he'd hit. But Robby couldn't stand the fact you'd been hurt. He hated Gabe for what he'd done."

"So he set a fire in the tack room after my father passed out the next night."

"I did everything I could to make it up to you. I treated you like a second son."

"God..."

"Robby was both passionate and impulsive. A cursed combination."

"He was sick. He was a time bomb. And you could have done something about it then. You could have gotten treatment for him. Instead, by not reporting him, you let him go on to murder again!"

Peter didn't defend himself. "We're Claymores. We've been here for centuries. In the end, after all the tragedy, defending our name was the only thing I had left."

"So what now? You've got a gun pointed at me. Are you going to finish what the exalted Claymore family started when Robby murdered my father? You'd better do it quickly, before somebody else finds this place and catches you in the act. Would you like me to kneel so you can say you shot me when you were trying to ward off the bobcat? You're good at covering tracks. What'll it be?"

"You've never had the pleasure of foxhunting in England,

have you? It's different there. They kill their foxes. They have too many. If they didn't hunt them, the farmers would trap or poison them, a worse death by far.''

Christian realized he didn't have much of a chance, but he was gambling that Peter wouldn't shoot him right there, not with Night Ranger behind him and the hounds at his feet. Peter loved his animals almost as much as he loved the Claymore name. And if Christian was forced to move, he had a fighting chance to lunge for the gun.

''Would you say so?'' Peter prompted him. ''People believe what they're told?''

''I certainly believed what you told me all these years.''

''In England they don't let the hounds tear a fox to bits,'' Peter continued. ''When a fox goes to ground, the staff digs him out and shoots him. One clean shot. Good sportsmen, the Brits. Then they give him to the hounds.''

''You're planning to dispense of me with one clean shot? Like a cornered fox?''

''Christian, you're a bright young man, but you've missed the point. This time you are the hunter and I am the prey.'' Peter stepped back, away from Jack's Knife and the hounds.

Christian realized what he was going to do. ''It doesn't have to be this way, Peter. Don't do this.''

Peter smiled sadly. ''Son, don't pick up the weapon this time. Show some sense.''

35

Julia was alone when she heard Bard's BMW pull into the drive. Maisy was out for the afternoon. Maisy's way, Julia supposed, of giving her the gift of silence.

She had hoped to hear from Christian about the opening hunt, but he hadn't called. She knew she would have been welcome at Claymore Park for the breakfast, but there had been too many reasons not to go, not the least of which was the man knocking at the door.

She got to her feet and found her way, opening it to face him.

"Hello, Bard."

"You knew it was me?"

"I know the sound of your car. Do you have anyone with you?"

"I'm alone. May I come in?"

She stood back and allowed him to enter.

"Maisy and Jake home?" He sounded as if he hoped they weren't.

"Maisy's gone shopping. Jake took Callie and Tiffany to Lilith's cabin in the mountains for the day." She made her way toward the living room, managing it with only one shoulder bump. He didn't try to help her, for which she was grateful. "I could get you tea, or something stronger, if you'd like. But you've probably just eaten."

"As a matter of fact, no, but I don't want anything."

"Oh? You didn't stay for the breakfast?" She felt for the big armchair in the corner and sat.

"There was no breakfast."

She knew she was frowning. "I'm sorry? Did I hear you right? Peter had caterers setting up tents and—"

"Julia, let me talk, okay?"

"What's going on, Bard?"

"I... This isn't easy. I'm sorry to be the one to tell you this—"

"Oh God." She envisioned Christian hurt. She brought her hands to her face, forcing herself to breathe. "What—"

"Peter's dead."

She was stunned—and fervently glad at the same time that it wasn't Christian.

"There was a chase up Little Sergeant Hill. The pack split. I was in charge of the hilltoppers, but they couldn't make it that far. Most of the first flight didn't even make it. The woods are thick, and it's as steep as a tree. We should have stayed away from the area entirely and gone after another fox. But that was Christian's call, wasn't it? A goddamned mistake."

"What happened?"

"The pack split, like I said. Christian took off after a couple of the younger hounds. I guess he can't be faulted for that. They were rioting, and he knew he had to bring them back. Unfortunately they were charging uphill, through some of the worst terrain. Peter rode after Christian."

Julia knew how unusual that was. The huntsman was in charge of his hounds and the master his riders. "What happened? Did he fall?"

"No, he took a bullet to the head."

She couldn't think of anything to say.

"A couple of riders went after the two of them when they didn't return. They heard the shot before they reached the clearing. Peter was on the ground, and Christian was standing over him." He paused. "The gun was in Peter's hand, Julia."

Her mind was scrambling wildly for an explanation. "Whose gun?"

"Peter's. Christian wasn't carrying one."

"How can this be?" She couldn't imagine the scene Bard had

described. Peter, dead, a gun in his hand. Christian standing over him, watching Peter's blood pool on the rocky ground.

Almost déjà vu.

"They've taken Christian to the sheriff's office," Bard said.

She got to her feet in a panic. "They've arrested him?"

"I wouldn't call it an arrest. They asked Christian to accompany them for questioning. Very politely, too, from what I was told. Christian called them on his radio. It took the deputies a long time to get up there. You can imagine it, can't you? They barely made it up the old logging road, then they had to walk the last five or six hundred yards. They led him away. Someone took his horse, a couple of us gathered the hounds. One deputy stayed behind."

"Peter was like a father to Christian. He couldn't have killed him."

"You don't have to tell me."

Julia lowered herself to her chair. "You don't think he killed Peter?"

"Me, of all people, huh? No, Peter killed himself. Peter was the reason Christian went to jail all those years ago. Robby killed Fidelity, and Peter covered it up at the same time he was trying to have Christian freed." He gave a harsh laugh. "Talk about leading a double life."

She felt physically ill, dizzy and nauseated, as if her body was trying to reject this latest tragedy. "How do you know this? Is that what Christian said?"

Bard didn't answer right away. When he did, there was an edge to his voice she had heard a thousand times before. "And if he'd said it, it would have been law, wouldn't it? He could say anything and you'd believe him."

"Yes, I would."

"But not me."

"You're right again."

She heard him get up and begin to pace, restless, as always, and anxious to get on to something else. "The morning of the day Fidelity died, she came to see me. She'd been having an affair with Robby—"

"Affair?"

"Yes, Julia, they'd been sleeping together all summer. And neither of them told you, did they?"

"I knew she was flirting. I..."

"She confided in me. She was short on friends she *could* tell, I guess."

And Bard had been safe to talk to. Not one of Fidelity's closest circle, who would criticize her behavior, not one of the drug crowd she was trying to avoid. Someone comfortably at the edge of her world, the way Bard had been when Julia herself needed him.

Her voice wasn't much louder than a whisper. "She was trying to build his confidence. That's what she told me when I cautioned her to leave him alone. I didn't think Robby would understand the way she was flirting with him. I didn't know how far it had gone."

"You were right. He didn't understand. All those years of watching Fidelity sleep around, and he still didn't get it. So when she called it quits, he fell apart."

"It's my fault. I asked her to leave him alone. I—"

"Robby Claymore had the self-control and emotional resources of a gnat. He loved her. She didn't love him. He killed her. Period."

Once upon a time she had been grateful to this man for telling her what to think. Now she felt another prick of gratitude. This time Bard's narrow view of the world was right. No one had been at fault except the tortured young man she had called her friend.

"This is such a mess," he said.

"You said Fidelity came to see you. What did she say?" She paused as the truth formed into something darker. "And why didn't you ever tell anyone?"

He sighed. Not the sigh of impatience she had so often heard, but something deeper and more revealing. "She said she broke up with Robby on their ride that morning and he acted like a wild man. She said he was so unreasonable, he frightened her. She rode her horse back to the stable right away and took off to find me."

"And what did you tell her?"

He cleared his throat. He wasn't a man who suffered the pangs of guilt often, but she heard guilt now. "I told her that any man she broke up with would act like a wild man. I flattered her into feeling better. And I told her he'd get over it."

"And how did you feel when you found out she was dead?"

"How do you think I felt?"

"Not bad enough to report the conversation. You kept silent, didn't you? You let Christian go to prison when you knew it was Robby who'd killed her."

"I didn't know. Not for sure. There was no proof he'd done it. Christian was on the scene. It was Christian's knife in Christian's hand."

"You knew who killed her!"

"I suspected, okay? But I didn't have one shred of evidence. Just a private conversation with Fidelity about a man with a childish crush on her. Robby had an alibi. Peter said they were together all afternoon. No one ever reported seeing Robby near South Land at the time she was killed. And he was Christian's best friend. I thought if Robby *had* killed her, he would come forward to save Christian from going to prison."

"I don't believe you."

"And how would it have looked if I tried to finger Robby and I turned out to be wrong? The Claymores are my neighbors. Peter was Master of Foxhounds. I would have been drummed out of local society as fast as you can say Mosby Hunt."

"You had a duty. Not to the club, but to decency. You kept silent because you wanted Christian in jail."

"I really don't know anymore. I didn't think it would go as far as it did. I thought if Robby killed her, the truth would come out. Meantime, I was making inroads with you. When Christian was convicted, I thought he'd get out on appeal...."

"And you kept silent!"

"Yes, damn it. I kept silent."

"I want a divorce, Bard."

"I had that part figured out."

"I want a quick one. Go somewhere and do it. Nevada. The Caribbean. Just make sure it's legal in Virginia."

"We have a lot to work out first. Property, for instance."

"Keep your damned property. I don't want a thing that has your name attached to it. You can make a cash settlement, if you want, so you won't look bad to all those people you have to impress, but I don't need your money, either. Just get me out of this marriage. Immediately."

"We have a child to consider."

"Do we? Since when has Callie's welfare mattered to you?"

"You're being unfair."

She tried to tamp down her fury, and managed to a little. "So what do you want? The occasional weekend so you'll look like a real father?"

"I'm not going to pretend I love Callie the way you do. But I'm the only father she's known. You can't believe it would be good to have me simply walk out of her life, can you?"

She closed her eyes. "Can you tell me the truth for once? Why do you care?"

"Because on paper she's my daughter, and right now she doesn't know any different. I haven't been a great father. I don't have it in me. But I'd miss her, and she'd miss me. That's the important part, isn't it? She wants to make me proud. Maybe I can find a way to let her know that she has. At least until she doesn't need me anymore."

She wanted to rage at him, and she wanted to cry. Everything he'd said was true.

"Can we work it out?" he asked.

"For Callie's sake." She hesitated. "And with Christian's permission."

"Christian..."

"The man your silence condemned to prison."

"I doubt it."

She knew Bard had taken as much responsibility as he was capable of. "There's one more thing you can do for me."

"If I can."

"I want you to take me to the sheriff's office. I'm going to tell them what you told me. I will not let Christian stay in jail for one more night."

"Save your breath. They aren't going to listen to you. Besides, it's obvious Peter's death was a suicide. Christian's not going to be charged—''

"Are you going to take me, or am I going to walk? Because I will, if I have to. I'll walk down that driveway and find my way to the main road, until somebody takes pity on me or runs me over.''

"I'll take you.''

"I'll get my coat.''

"Julia?''

"What?''

"I wish things had been different.''

She knew it was as close to an apology as he could come. "So do I. In a million different ways.''

"I did love you.''

"Bard, if that was love, I never want any part of it again. I hope you don't, either.''

Christian remembered the first time he had sat in this particular nine-by-twelve room at the sheriff's office. He had been shuddering violently, plagued by the vision of Fidelity's torn and bleeding body. He had wanted nothing more than to go back in time, to wake up again that morning and personally reshuffle the hand fate had dealt her. He had been too innocent, too convinced the world worked the way it was supposed to, to realize what danger he was in himself.

He realized it now.

The door opened, and the two deputies who had been questioning him arrived and pulled up chairs at the table again. They had come and gone, come and gone, for hours, and unfortunately today was Pinky's day off so there had been no respite. It was night by now, and he hadn't eaten anything except a vending machine candy bar since just after dawn. Someone from the club had left clothes for him, and he'd been allowed to change into jeans, a shirt and a sweater. He was grateful but not fooled. It was bad for Mosby's reputation to have their fully attired huntsman sitting in an interrogation room.

"I'm ready to sign a statement,'' Christian said. "I've told you what happened.''

"Your lawyer's on the way. We're under instructions not to question you or let you say another thing."

"Mel Powers?"

"He's the one you called, isn't he?"

No one had been at the office or Mel's home. He had left a message, but he hadn't expected to reach Mel before tomorrow. "How long is that going to take?"

"Shouldn't be too much longer."

"We could play cards."

The older of the two men spoke. The younger one had hardly said a word. "You're pretty damned calm."

"I'm pretty damned innocent."

"I thought Peter Claymore was your friend, Carver. You don't bleed a little when a friend shoots himself in front of you?"

Christian was bleeding. Through all his years in prison, Peter had been his one link to the world, the one person he had permitted into his life.

The one person he had trusted with it.

He gazed up at the two men, strangers, who wouldn't understand. Still, he tried. "Peter did what he had to do. He couldn't have gone on. He knew he wouldn't survive the exposure. Pride was everything to him. It was like air filling a balloon. When it was gone, there was nothing left."

"He was a pillar of the community."

"The mightiest pillars can be brought down."

There was a scuffling sound in the hallway, and Mel entered. "This place is a zoo. I thought they were going to check my teeth, spray me for ticks and fleas—" He headed straight for Christian. "Did you say anything?"

"A lot."

"You need a refresher course in Screw-You-101?"

"I didn't say anything to incriminate myself. Not nine years ago and not now. Circumstances did it for me."

"It's the principle of the thing." Mel turned to the older deputy. "I'd like to confer with my client," he said. "Alone?"

"Want some coffee? Another Twix?" the deputy asked Christian, rising slowly to his feet.

"No, thanks."

The two men exited.

"That's a good sign," Mel said. "That coffee-Twix thing. Or maybe they're just playing good cop for a while, hoping to trip you up. But it doesn't matter." He fell into the chair across the table from Christian. "You're safe, Chris. You don't have a thing to worry about this time. I've already spoken with the sheriff."

"And?"

"Suicide. No question."

"Yeah, I know. I got to watch." Christian closed his eyes, then opened them quickly, because the image was still there. He wouldn't rest easily again for a long time. "So I can go?"

"Not yet. They want your statement about the Sutherland girl's murder. They want it in writing. Are you willing?"

"Why? Does anything I say matter around here? Everybody who could have confessed to the murder or the cover-up is dead now. Maybe the sheriff could find some proof for Peter's story if he dug around, but he isn't going to bother."

"They don't have to do much in the way of digging." Mel folded his hands. "I have written corroboration. A letter from Peter, dated four years ago. And I have Robby Sutherland's suicide note. He confesses and asks for your forgiveness. I guess he was hoping his father would do the right thing and take the note to the sheriff."

Exhaustion washed over Christian in waves. He was almost too tired to put it together. "How did you get it?"

"Peter left an envelope in my care to be opened at his death. I didn't know what was in it until today. I thought maybe it was stock certificates signed over to you. Something like that. It was better, though. He told the whole story, Chris. Signed, sealed and delivered to my safekeeping. The son's suicide note finishes it with a bang. You'll want to read it."

Christian couldn't speak, and had he been able, he wouldn't have known what to say.

"There'll never be another question about who killed Fidelity Sutherland," Mel said. "Even your worst enemy is going to be sorry he doubted you."

"Then it's over."

"No question it's over." Mel hesitated. "There's a pretty

young woman out in the reception area who'll be glad to know it's over, too.''

"Julia?"

"Still as pretty as she was all those years ago. They've been trying to get her to go home for hours. The sheriff told me she threatened to call the newspaper and tell them he was trying to throw a blind woman out in the street.''

Christian shook his head. The faintest of smiles tugged at his lips; then he sobered. "I don't even know where to go tonight. I don't have a home anymore. I guess I never did.''

Mel reached across the table and put his hand on Christian's. "You've had one helluva day. I hesitate to tell you anything else and rock your boat even more. But here it is. I think you do have a home.''

Christian looked down at his hand, then up at Mel's face. The human contact felt strange.

"What?" he said. "What are you talking about?''

Mel withdrew his hand. "It's like this, Chris. I don't have Peter's will. His private attorney has that. But in the letter he left with me, he said he was leaving Claymore Park to you, and everything that goes with it. He asks you to consider it a token payment for nine years of your life.''

36

Julia heard a tangled chorus of voices coming down the hallway; then she heard Christian's, solo and strong. She got to her feet, but she was afraid to move, since she didn't know what was in front of her. She had been rooted to the chair for hours. She had used her cell phone to leave Maisy a message, but she hadn't told her mother where she was. Except for a few pointed exchanges with the sheriff, she hadn't spoken to anyone. Until Mel Powers arrived.

Mel had assured her that Christian would go free. But Peter had assured them both of the same thing for months before Christian was sent to prison. By now she was an emotional train wreck.

"Christian?" She waited, hoping he heard her.

At first there was no reply. Then she was swept into a familiar embrace. "Hey, Jules, have you been giving these folks a bad time?"

She held on to him as her heart beat faster at the old nickname. "Are you all right?"

"No. But I'm free. For good."

She thought he kissed her hair. Tears welled in her eyes. She held him tighter.

"Let's get out of here." This time she was sure he kissed her hair.

"I'll drive you wherever you want to go," Mel said.

Julia could feel Christian's hesitation. "Ashbourne?" she offered. "You know you'll be welcome."

"No. Drop us at Claymore Park, would you?" he asked Mel.

"You're sure?" Julia said. "You don't have to go back there tonight."

"I have to be sure Night Ranger and the hounds are okay." His arms tightened convulsively. "I guess Peter taught me well, huh?"

She swallowed tears. "I know what he did."

"Yeah, and in the end it killed him." Christian cupped her face and lifted it. "You can ease up a little now. I'm not going anywhere."

Reluctantly, she unwrapped her arms. "Who could blame you if you did?"

"I have a daughter in Ridge's Race."

She tried to smile, although her lips trembled. "Yes."

"You two wait out front," Mel said. "I'll pull my car out of the lot."

The sheriff spoke. "In your place I'd be bitter. None of us feels good knowing we put an innocent man in prison."

"It didn't feel so good to the innocent man, either," Christian said.

"'I'm sorry' is pretty inadequate. I wish things had been different."

"We agree on that."

"Let me know if I can help with anything in the coming weeks."

"Thanks." The word sounded as if Christian had chipped it from granite. He put his arm around Julia's waist and guided her toward the front door.

She found it easy enough to walk beside him, although clearly he was in a hurry to leave. He gave her room to move but expertly guided her through the darkness so she felt she was floating instead of slogging through mud. When the cold wind slammed against her, he pulled her closer to keep her warm. "When did you eat last?"

"Hours ago. I don't know what time it is."

"About eight. I'll get Mel to pick up something on the way back."

"He'll drop me off at Ashbourne if we ask. I can get something there."

"Don't go. I'll take you home."

"Christian... I don't want to get in your way. I just had to make sure you were all right. I just couldn't let them take you away again."

"Do you want to come with me?"

She recognized a turning point. They were beyond simple questions. "Yes."

"Then come back to Claymore Park."

She gripped his arm tighter in answer. The pressure of not knowing his fate changed subtly into something else, more pleasurable but just as uncertain.

Christian helped her into the front seat beside Mel and took the back seat for himself. They stopped once for take-out hamburgers and soft drinks, but the trip to Claymore Park was mostly silent. Even Mel, who would probably gab away his last breath, had little to say.

"You're sure this is what you want to do?" Mel turned into the long driveway leading back to the house and barns.

"I remember the first time I saw this place." Christian leaned forward, his breath warm and ticklish against Julia's neck. "I was ten. I took one look at it and knew it was so far beyond reach I didn't have a chance of living here."

"Maybe you'd be better off if you'd just kept going," Mel said.

Christian brushed his fingertips against Julia's shoulder. "Maybe. Maybe not."

"Well, it belongs to you now," Mel said.

"What?" Julia turned instinctively, as if she could still see Christian's face.

Christian sounded annoyed. "That would be good to keep to yourself until it gets out naturally, Mel."

"I'm sorry." Mel sounded genuinely contrite.

"What did he mean?" Julia said.

"It appears Peter left Claymore Park to me."

She let out a long breath. "Well, of course he did. Who better?"

"You think so? He said it was payment for nine years of my life."

"It was also quintessential Peter, wasn't it? Nobody else knows or understands everything he was trying to do here or has the emotional ties. Now the land will never give way to development, even if the law changes, and for years to come Claymore Park horses will win shows and races and the Mosby foxhounds will still have a home. You'll carry on his legacy."

"I'll be damned..." Mel turned a corner. "She's right, you know. Absolutely right. That crafty old bastard."

"I'll bet when the will's read," Julia said, "there'll be a condition that you can't change the name."

"I wouldn't change it anyway," Christian said.

"Why not?" Mel said. "The Claymores ran you into the ground."

"They died for it."

Mel gave a humorless laugh. "You're a better man than either of them." He slowed and asked where they wanted to get out. Christian directed him to the barn where Night Ranger was kept. The car came to a stop. "You're sure about this?" Mel said.

"We'll be fine. Thanks. For everything."

"Don't forget your hamburgers."

Julia heard the back door, then the passenger door opened, too. She unhooked her seat belt and swung her legs to the ground. "I... Thanks for taking care of Christian, Mel."

"I could have done a better job of it if somebody had told me the truth a long time ago."

She got out, and Christian closed the door behind her. They waited as Mel drove off. Only then did she notice how chilly it was. A frost-tinged wind blew through the windbreaker that had seemed appropriate that afternoon. Instinctively she curled her arms over her midriff. Winter was on the way.

"Let's get inside. You'll warm up." Christian took her arm.

She let him lead her through the door. Out of the wind the barn was snug. She smelled hay and manure and warm horseflesh. Somebody whinnied in greeting; there was a restless stamping of hoofs and the clanking of metal mesh gates. Somebody else snorted impatiently.

"Night Ranger," he said. "Waiting to be noticed."

"You knew he'd be fine."

"I know. But he's an old friend. He would never let me down. I have to return the favor."

"And next you'll go down to the kennel and check on the hounds."

"Not right away. Let me make sure he's really okay. Then we'll eat."

She used the closetlike bathroom while he checked on Night Ranger, washing up as best she could. She wondered how she looked and how different she seemed from the girl he had loved. How much had she changed since her sight had failed? Did she look older? Sadder? She brushed her hair, wishing she could take stock and gather courage. When she emerged, he was right there.

"Night Ranger okay?" she asked, as if she wasn't a seething tangle of nerves.

"I closed the wooden gate to his stall. To keep him warm. Old bones."

"Not so old. He'll be around a long time."

"Peter gave him to me." He paused. "I guess that's a moot point, huh? If Mel's right, every one of these horses is mine now.... I can't begin to think what that means."

"Nobody better." She stood waiting. She had no real sense of where they were, but she wasn't afraid. Christian would make sure she was all right. The loss of her sight had taught her valuable lessons about taking care of herself, but it had also taught her to trust the people she loved.

"This is the only building that still has an open hayloft."

"Does it?"

"The others are walled in, with chutes into the stalls. Very efficient. We're in the Mosby barn, mostly hunt staff horses and tack. It's so small Peter never got around to remodeling. Too many other fish to fry, I guess."

She knew what he was suggesting. "We'd be warmer up in the hay."

"You'll have to climb. I'll be right behind you. Can you do it?"

"Just tell me how many steps."

"Let me get blankets."

He stayed one rung below her, his body a barrier if she needed one. She climbed fearlessly.

"You're almost at the top. Next step, just lean forward and reach out with your right hand. Then feel your way. I'll be right here."

She managed to get from the ladder to the loft on her knees, wiggling aside so Christian could join her.

"Don't try to stand straight," he warned. "The ceiling's peaked, but you could knock your head on a rafter."

"How far do I have to move?"

"Not very. Take my hand and lean over."

They stopped what seemed like a few yards away. He dropped her hand. "Let me make a little nest here for you."

She could hear the rustling of hay as he spread the blankets. "It's warmer up here. Is it as cozy as it seems?"

"Yeah." He reached for her hand. "Come on down and see."

She lowered herself to soft, fresh-smelling wool. The hay was fragrant and, if not soft, at least supple.

"We came up here once before. Remem—" She clamped her lips shut.

His voice was heavy. "I remember. You, me and Robby."

"We were going to play some trick or other on Fidelity. Swoop down on her or yell or make silly noises." She refused to cry, although the urge was there.

"Are we going to reach a point when the good memories don't hurt anymore?"

"Probably not."

"What have we got left, then?"

She reached for him, bringing him to rest against her, although he was half again her weight. "All the days and years ahead. We both have Callie. And you have this place. I know it'll be tough for a while, but you were meant to live here. And you'll have the support of most people in Ridge's Race. They're a little full of themselves sometimes, but they're fair."

He twisted, and suddenly her face was in his hands. "What else do I have? Be honest. I can't take another drop of dishonesty. My cup runneth over."

"You have *me*. If that's what you want."

"So many years went by. How can you know?"

"Because I never stopped loving you."

He kissed her then and she circled his neck with her arms. It was a surprisingly gentle kiss, as if he was afraid of anything more. She felt as if she was falling back in time to lazy summer days when the hardest decision they'd made was whether to go out for pizza or scavenge for leftovers in Maisy's kitchen. He tasted the same; his lips were as warm and as firm. Hers gave with the same sweet fire.

She fell back against the hay, taking him with her. He covered her, angling to one side so his weight didn't smother her.

Desire rose inside her, but it hadn't had far to go. Now she knew she had wanted this since the moment she'd heard his voice in Maisy's garden. She had wanted him since the last time they had made love.

"Jules..." He traced one eyebrow with a fingertip.

She shuddered. "Can you see me?"

"Not very well."

"That's better than I can see you. You don't know how much I've missed that, how much I want to open my eyes and see your face."

"I'm the same old me, just older."

She stretched out her hands again and found his shoulders. She let her fingertips drift to his collarbone, into the open neck of his shirt, up his throat where his pulse was pounding like hoofbeats on racing turf, and finally to his face.

She cradled his face in her hands as he had cradled hers. She could feel her own hands trembling. Her entire body seemed to resonate to an inaudible vibration. "I've wanted to do this since the first moment I heard your voice again." She cleared her throat. The tears were still lingering there. "It's as close to seeing as I get these days."

He didn't speak. She felt the tension in his jaw, the strain of a man holding himself back. She let her trembling fingers drift slowly. He hadn't shaved since early that morning. His cheeks were rough and firmer than she remembered, as if the malleable flesh had toughened into the final portrait of the man. She found an indentation that hadn't been there before, a scar about an inch long along the ridge of one cheekbone.

"What happened?" she asked.

"I got in the way of somebody's fork in the commissary."

"I'm sorry."

"Don't be. It taught me to duck."

"That's a skill you've needed, isn't it?"

The skin under his eyes was softer, folding slightly but only just. She had always thought he would be equally handsome as an old man because he had strong bones and character written over them. He had aged, just as she had, but his face still felt timeless.

"Is your hair as light as it was?"

"I don't know."

"Did it turn brown?"

"I guess I don't stand at the mirror and evaluate."

"No, you wouldn't." She moved her fingers higher, tracing the broad sweep of his forehead. His hair brushed the backs of her fingers. He had always worn the top just long enough that he could plow it back when he was anxious. She wondered if he even realized he did it.

At last, with a sigh, she cupped her hands behind his head. "Just the way I pictured you. Except for the scar."

"You're finished?"

"Yes."

"You know me again?"

"I've known you forever."

"Do you know how badly I want you?"

"As badly as I want you."

"Protection was the last thing on my mind this morning when I set off for the hunt."

She pulled him closer. "I'm on the pill. We're safe until we don't want to be anymore."

"Jules..."

"Have I told you how good I've become at doing things by the sheer feel?"

"It's a good thing you didn't. You were driving me crazy as it was."

"I'm going to take off your sweater. Hold up your arms. Admire my prowess." She slipped her hands under the hem and, with one deft twist, pulled it over his head. She could feel the firm muscles of his chest under thin cotton. She tugged the shirt from his jeans and slid her hands under it. The hayloft was cool, but Christian's skin was not. She could feel his muscles bunch and his nipples tighten. He groaned.

She rolled to her side, and he went with her until he was on his back and she was lying half on top of him. "Next the shirt. I'm particularly good with buttonholes."

"Not good or fast enough."

"No? Are we in a hurry?"

"Some things never change."

She smiled. "Like your impatience?"

"Like your ability to make me come apart at the seams."

"Right now it's your shirt that's going to come apart. Only a shirt."

"You'll be lucky if that's all."

She finished the last button. "I think we're both going to be lucky."

As she spread her hands against his chest, he pulled her down and kissed her hard. Then he held her away. "I love you."

"Oh..." Tears filled her eyes. "I am so grateful...after everything, that you do. That you still can."

This time there was no way to tell who initiated the kiss. It was anything but subdued or gentle. Julia might have trained herself to accomplish things by feel, but Christian's instincts compensated for any skill he lacked.

"I want to let you play," he said, the words harsh and pulled from somewhere deeper than his throat. "I want to take it slow. But I need you now."

"Now is wonderful." She stripped off her windbreaker and tossed it over her head.

They fought the rest of their clothing as if each piece was a sworn enemy. His shirt, her turtleneck, the lacy scrap of bra that kept her breasts from sinking against his chest. Jeans and boots took longer, but nothing was too difficult. Not now, when so many years had kept them apart and they had found their way back together at last.

She had never forgotten how right it felt to have his skin hot against hers, his weight pressing against her, her body sleek and sinuous over his. His lips slid over hers, again and again, teasing and probing until she captured them and opened for him, tongue thrusting against tongue. Under him again, her hips rose to meet his, but he turned to his side, pulling her with him.

His tone was harsh with self-denial. "I want this to last forever, but I don't want it to last another minute."

"You don't have to take your time. We'll have time from now on. We'll have all we need." She trapped him against her with one leg, sliding it over his hip until he was as close as he could be without entering her. He was hot and hard against her and about to explode. It was a mark of enormous self-restraint that he had lasted this long. She reached down and took him inside her.

He groaned and turned her to her back. And he lasted just long enough to return the pleasure she so obviously gave him.

Wrapped in extra blankets, they ate cold hamburgers. Christian thought he'd never tasted anything so fine. As they'd made love, he'd been haunted by the fear that Julia was taking pity on him, offering her body as solace, perhaps. Now, looking at the same triumphant smile Eve had aimed at Adam, he knew it hadn't been pity nor comfort nor even something she'd indulged in for old times' sake.

The mother of his child loved him.

"I'm moving back to Ashbourne for good," she said, licking her fingers in lieu of a napkin. "We'll be neighbors again. Will you sneak over and see me like you used to?"

"I might not even sneak. I might just ride over in broad daylight."

"I'll be that infamous divorcée and Bard will be the wronged husband. Can you afford the scandal?"

"Scandal is my middle name."

"Then I'll be perfect for you."

Christian knew they would take things slowly. They hadn't

talked about it yet, but he knew how important it was to get things right this time. They had Callie to think about. He could content himself looking forward to a future that seemed, now, almost certain. But right now he had to be honest.

"Bard led me to Robby. He told me I was as blind in my way as you were in yours. He meant for me to figure it out." He told her the gist of the conversation with Bard and the way Bard's words had finally opened his eyes.

"It's nice to know he was capable of that much honesty, but it doesn't change a thing," she said.

"I'll resign as huntsman," Christian said. "I won't have time for it anymore."

"I'm sorry I never got to see you hunt the hounds." Her smile faltered. "But I guess I'm not sorry I wasn't there today when you did."

"I'm glad you weren't."

"Everything has changed so fast. Some of it wonderful." She held out her hand, and he took it. "Some of it so terrible. Will you really be able to live here?"

"I have an idea for the future. Do you want to hear it?"

"You know it."

"When I was at Ludwell I saw what a difference Pets and Prisoners made for the men who were picked to work in the program. Reverend Petersen always tries to find them jobs when they get out, but it's not easy getting employers to take ex-cons. I'm going to see about starting an extension program here. Something simple, at first. Just a place for parolees to come when they're released, the good guys, the ones with potential." He thought about Javier and Timbo. With the right kind of help, both men had a shot at changing their lives.

"And what would you do for them?"

"They'd have a job and a place to stay, some training to help them move ahead. But down the road a little, maybe we could phase in the next part of the Pets and Prisoners agenda. As prisoners, we never got to see the guide dogs go on to their new homes or help train the new owners. Maybe we could do that here."

"This is ambitious. And you just thought of it?"

"No, I've thought about it ever since Bertha came to visit. I was trying to think of a way to broach it with Peter. Now I don't have to."

"You know it's going to be controversial in town, don't you?" He grinned. "Yeah."

She smiled, too. "I love it."

"We have ex-cons working in the horse world. With this setup, we'll just know who they are for a change."

"Don't let Maisy get wind of it. She'll move the program to Ashbourne and take it over. She'll bake the guys cookies, counsel their wives about birth control and make sure all their children's immunizations are up-to-date."

"She's hired."

"You know, that's not such a bad idea."

He filed that away for another time. "You have hay in your hair."

"That's the disadvantage of being blind. I can't respond in kind." She sobered. "Christian, there's no guarantee my sight will ever return. You know that, don't you? You'd better take that into consideration when you..."

"When I what?"

"When you sneak around with me."

"I'll take you any way I can get you, Jules."

The Eve smile reappeared. Her blanket slipped from one shoulder. She lifted a brow. "Is that a promise, or are you just taunting me?"

"I keep my promises."

"Do you remember promising me a little while ago that we could play a little, when the time was right?"

"Yeah."

"Maybe we really can learn to play again. Maybe we can learn to be young again. Starting now."

He tossed his hamburger wrapper into the hay. And he made sure he kept his word.

Christian kissed Julia good-night in front of a silent house. The front light was on, but there were no sounds from inside the cottage. On the porch she listened to Night Ranger's hoofbeats die away before she went inside.

"I was hoping that was you."

Julia closed the front door quietly before she faced her mother. She'd been certain Maisy would wait up for her. "Please don't be mad I didn't call again."

"I know what happened. I've had half a dozen messages from Mosby members. And Bard called to tell me you were at the sheriff's office. Christian?"

"He's free, and he's going to be fine. How much do you know?"

"More than I can absorb. I can't believe Robby killed Fidelity. It's going to take some time to get used to all of it."

"I bet you didn't hear that Peter left Claymore Park to Christian."

Maisy didn't speak. Julia knew she was in shock.

"Did Callie get home all right?" Julia said.

"About an hour ago. She was exhausted."

"Maisy, may we stay here a little longer, Callie and I? At least until we find a place of our own. I've told Bard to get a divorce. He'll be efficient and quick."

"This is your home. Ashbourne belongs to you."

"I thought I could count on the future, but I know better now."

"When you and Christian are ready, you'll find your happy ending. I believe it deep in my heart. I'm a romantic. I guess I never stopped believing."

"Do you really think so? I want to believe that more than anything. After all this...sadness."

"I believe it."

They stood facing each other. Julia stretched out her hand, and Maisy took it. "We've reached the end of your book, haven't we?"

Maisy didn't seem surprised at the change of subject; then she, of all people, realized that the subject had actually stayed very much the same. "There's only the final chapter."

"I'm ready to hear it."

"Are you? It's been one of the roughest days of your life, sweetheart. The ending will keep."

"I need you to finish it. Tonight. Please."

"We'll sit by the fire. Everyone else is asleep upstairs." Maisy put her arm around her daughter's shoulders. "Would you like to change into your nightgown while I make tea?"

Julia nodded. "I'm going to take a quick shower."

"I'll be waiting."

Julia found her mother's cheek and kissed it. "I think you've waited a long time already."

From the unpublished novel *Fox River,* by Maisy Fletcher

I begged Ian not to make Alice ride Duchess that day. She had taken one look at the pony and fled to her room. I had hoped our confessions of the past evening would mellow him. But, of course, they'd done the opposite. He was angry anew, angry that he had let down his guard, angry that I had witnessed the most vulnerable part of him.

As I pleaded with him to reconsider, he barely looked at me. "We will do this quickly," he said. "You will get her now, or I will. The sooner she sees there's nothing to fear, the better."

"Ian, please. Let her get used to Duchess slowly."

"I'll get her, then."

I didn't know where to turn. The stable staff had discreetly disappeared at the first hint of raised voices. Ian strode toward the house, and I ran after him and grabbed his sleeve.

"Ian, are you trying to make her hate you? Is that what you want? For both of us to hate you?"

He stopped, and his eyes were cold. "I am the man of this house, Louisa. I know what's best for Alice."

"You don't have to prove anything to her or me or

anyone else. She's just a little girl. She only wants to love you."

"I understand what you're trying to do to me."

"I don't know what you mean. I just want—"

He shook off my hand. "You want me to be less of a man. That's what all women want, isn't it? Well, you can't have your way. I'm in charge here. You'd better remember it from this moment forward. Because I won't... I won't..."

His eyes began to glaze over in a way that was growing familiar. I knew another headache—brought on by his anger—was beginning. I turned and ran toward the house, determined to get Alice and take her to Sweetwater until Ian was calmer. He would make her ride Duchess eventually, but perhaps I could delay until he had less to prove.

When we emerged, Ian was waiting for us, white and shaken but capable of movement and determined.

"I'll take our daughter."

"Please. Why don't you wait until you're feeling stronger? We'll go down to the stable and visit Duchess together. Maybe Alice can feed her an apple."

He held out his arms. I could hand over Alice as if I approved, or I could continue making a fuss and upset her further. He solved the problem by wrenching her from my arms.

"Go into the house. You'll make this more difficult."

"It doesn't have to be difficult at all. Please—"

He turned and started toward the ring where Duchess was saddled. Alice began to whimper, but he ignored her. He didn't speak to her or try to calm her in any way. When she began to struggle, he shook her hard. She cried out, and he shook her again.

"Stop it, Ian. You're going to hurt her!"

He stopped, but only to push me away. I fell to the ground, and by the time I'd picked myself up, he was inside the ring.

"Don't come inside," he warned. "I won't be responsible for what happens if you do."

I was as chilled by his tone as his words. I had done everything wrong, so far. If I hadn't intervened. If I hadn't argued.

If I hadn't married him.

Yet there he stood, our daughter in his arms. His only child. His legacy.

He lifted Alice to Duchess's back and settled her in the saddle. She was as pale as a summer cloud, and she was sobbing softly.

"Why are you crying?" he demanded. "Tell me why!"

"I fall... I fall..."

"So? What if you do? It won't kill you, Alice. Is that all that's worrying you?"

Her eyes were huge and terrified. "I...fall..." She held out her arms to him.

My heart nearly stopped as he lifted her from the saddle. But he didn't hold her close. He didn't comfort her. He didn't reassure her. He simply dropped her to the ground. She landed in a heap at his feet. "There, see? Falling is nothing. Falling won't hurt you."

She was sobbing in earnest now. She scooted away from him, but he picked her up, held her higher this time and dropped her to the ground once more.

"Ian, stop it! Stop it or I'll get the grooms to stop you."

He laughed. "What will you tell them? That you don't like the way I'm teaching my daughter to ride? I'm the best horseman in the county." He bent and scooped a screaming Alice from the ground, held her higher and this time threw her to the ground.

I started inside the ring, determined to stop him. The ground was soft from a light rainfall, but Alice was small and delicate. I knew she could be hurt. Worse, I knew that even if her body survived unscathed, she would never forget this terrible ordeal. I grabbed his arm when he lifted her again, but he struck me hard enough to send me flying. Then he set Alice on the pony, and before I could stop him, he knocked her off the saddle and to the ground once again.

I was screaming for help by that time, but no one came. I was a woman, after all, a notoriously hysterical creature.

"We'll leave you, Ian! Stop this, or we'll leave you."

"You can't and you won't. And if you manage it somehow, I'll find you and take Alice. I have the money and the power to do it, and don't forget it."

"You wouldn't!"

"If you don't get out of here," Ian warned me through gritted teeth, "I won't be responsible for what happens to her. Do you hear me?"

"Please... Please stop this!"

He hit me again as I tried to reach my daughter. Alice held out her arms to me, but there was nothing I could do. As I fought him, he lifted and threw her again. Farther and with more force. And finally I knew that if I didn't leave the ring, he would kill her.

He would kill his daughter to prove he was as much a man as his father had been.

I backed away, horrified.

"Better, Louisa," he said, scooping Alice from the ground. "But not good enough."

I ran to the gate and outside, closing it behind me.

"To the house, Louisa."

Behind me, I heard Alice's screams. I ran as fast as I could, praying my departure would stop the violence. By the time I reached the house the screams had stopped.

But not until he brought my sobbing, battered daughter inside at last, did I know for sure whether the screams had ended because Ian had stopped throwing her to the ground or because Alice was dead.

He insisted we go riding that afternoon, despite a cold, heavy wind from the north. Ian on Shadow

Dancer, I on Crossfire, Alice on Duchess. He assured me this was just the thing to put the unfortunate morning behind us and to show me how wrong I had been. Alice had not spoken since coming inside. When I told her we were going for a ride she simply stared at me. I knew there was no reasoning with Ian. If I resisted, we might well have another horrifying scene.

I spoke softly to my daughter as I dressed her for the ride. "We won't go far. And Duchess is a good pony, sweetheart. I'll be right beside you."

She looked up at me with an expression I had never seen on her face. Then she turned away from me. She would not be comforted.

She was surprisingly quiet when Ian lifted her to the pony's back.

"See?" He stood back and sent a smile that chilled me to the bone.

"You've only proved that you're bigger than she is and stronger. Nothing else."

"She'll do well to remember it."

"How could she not? You'll never let either of us forget it."

I was beyond caring if he hit me, but he just shrugged and helped me mount Crossfire; then he followed suit on Shadow Dancer.

Ian led the way, riding ahead at a gallop, then riding back or stopping to let us catch up with him when necessary. Because of the weather, we couldn't go far. We headed toward the river, to the area of our farm where we had hunted last. Although the wind howled, the ride was relatively easy, and I prayed it would be short.

Shadow Dancer hadn't been exercised that morning, and spirited was a tame word for his behavior. As we neared the river, Ian took several jumps, going back and forth across them to take the edge off his mount's considerable energy. The horse seemed frightened by the wind, his ears flat and his nostrils wide. Ian controlled him with some difficulty.

I concentrated on my beloved daughter, encouraging and helping her when I could. I knew from her expression that she had moved beyond fear to something worse. Annie had told me of coming across a rabbit in a trap as a child. I knew how it must have looked before Paul Symington set it free.

"We'll do these rides often," Ian said, coming back once again as we neared the river. "Our picture-perfect little family." Irony dripped from his words. "Alice, sit up straighter!"

She jerked upright, her eyes widening.

"Leave her alone." I rode closer, leaving Alice just behind me. "Haven't you done enough damage for one day? She's here. She's riding Duchess. What more do you want?"

"I want a son. But since I can't have one, I want a daughter who doesn't snivel or whine."

"She is already too good to be your daughter!"

Fury clouded his features. There are some words that penetrate straight to the marrow, that leave scars so deep they can never be ignored again.

I had found them.

Ian lifted his crop. I knew he meant to bring it down across my shoulders. But before he could, a groan was wrenched from his throat. His body locked into position, and he stared straight ahead.

Shadow Dancer, sensing the change in his rider, began to dance beneath him. The wind already had him on edge, and Ian's sudden loss of control spurred him on.

I was torn for a moment, watching him fight his bit; then I dismounted. Shadow Dancer edged away from me as I approached. I tried to soothe him, but he pranced nervously farther and farther from me until, at last, I lunged for his reins. The leather slid across my gloved palms, blistering them, but I held on.

Ian's crop fell to the ground, and the reins fell from his hands. He lifted his hands to his head, aware, in spite of his agony, of what was happening. Shadow Dancer backed away, half rearing as he did, and finally Ian, consciously or perhaps only instinctively, managed to grab for his mane.

I heard Alice cry out behind me. It was a sound I had heard too many times. The sound of my terrified daughter. But I couldn't take my eyes off Ian. I fought Shadow Dancer, who reared once more. As he came down, precariously close to my feet, I scooped Ian's crop from the ground.

I dropped the reins, and as my husband watched helplessly, I snapped the crop hard against Shadow Dancer's left flank. He took off through the woods in a panic, and as I stared at what I had done, Shadow Dancer sailed over the four-rail jump to the bank of Fox River. Ian landed in a crumpled heap at the edge of the bank as Shadow Dancer galloped away. From his position I like to think Ian died quickly, that his neck snapped and he never knew what had happened to him.

But I remember the expression on my husband's face when he realized what I was about to do. I wonder, sometimes, if I imagined the faintest flicker of relief in his eyes. The knowledge that the fight inside him had ended at last.

I'll never know. Like many women, I am not above seeing things that aren't there. Perhaps, from the beginning, I saw things in Ian Sebastian that never existed. But perhaps they did after all.

I put Alice in the saddle with me and led Duchess home through the woods. We traveled slowly, since I wasn't sure Ian was really dead. I knew that I would tell our staff he had decided to ride farther by himself and should be home by suppertime. I didn't want a search party looking for him until dark. I wanted to give my husband enough time to die.

Alice didn't speak for weeks, not at Ian's funeral, where he was praised by all who knew him. Not afterward, as I sold Duchess, then Ian's horses, one by one until none was left, not even Crossfire, who was a gift to Etta Carrolton.

When Alice began to speak again, it was never of her father. It was as if Ian had never existed for her. As for me, I removed as many signs of Ian Sebastian's existence as I could. I posted Fox River Farm and forbade anyone to hunt there again; then I took an extended trip to Chicago with Alice to see my dear Annie, who was recovering at last.

I didn't tell Annie what I had done, but I think she suspected. She asked me to stay on in Chicago, to abandon Fox River Farm to its ghosts and sorrows.

But, oddly, I could not.

There are autumn mornings now when I awaken early to the sound of foxhounds in the distance. As I stare at the ceiling I can almost feel the frost-tinged air, the exhilaration of the chase, the moments of flight on the back of a great white horse.

I can see the Master of the Hunt on a proud black stallion, waiting to scoop me into his arms and our fairytale life.

I rise, and I go into the next room to see if the hounds have awakened the master's daughter. She is always awake, sitting up in bed, waiting for me to soothe her.

I will be there for Alice as I could not be for her father.

Always.

37

Julia stared sightlessly at the flames. "My father was a large man." She cleared her throat, as if she were fighting tears. "I had forgotten, but now I remember how I felt when he carried me. His grip was firm, but I would look down at the ground, and it seemed a million miles away. If I cried, he held me higher. He hated for me to be afraid."

Maisy sat silently. She was trembling, and now that she had finished reading, her breath was coming in uneven spurts.

"He tried to teach me to ride," Julia said. "He threw me to the ground when I cried." She put her head in her hands.

Maisy gathered herself for what was to come. "How long have you known this was our story?"

"I don't know. Not at first. Gradually. There's been so much going on besides this. And I guess... I guess I didn't want to know."

"You stored it away deep inside you. You haven't wanted to remember."

"He was a bastard!"

"Your father could be a cruel man. He could also be funny and kind and charming. I was kept off balance."

"Why didn't you just tell me straight out? Why did you make the whole sordid drama into a novel? How much of what you've written is true and how much is fiction?"

"Too much is true. I loved a man. I married him. He had a

demon inside him that few people ever saw, but I saw it all too often. You don't need all the facts.''

"You weren't married at the beginning of the twentieth century, like Louisa. You weren't a stranger without friends. You were a modern woman from Baltimore. You could have gotten away."

"That's so easy to say now. But I wasn't that different from Louisa. I was alone. My parents died when I was a child. The aunt who raised me died just after my marriage. I was pathetically young and innocent, and I loved Harry past believing. By the time I realized what I'd done to myself, the trap was set.''

"You could have left him."

"I had no useful education, no financial resources, and little by little, step by step he convinced me and everyone who knew me that I was useless. Silly Maisy, foolish Maisy. It's a terrible thing, an unbelievable thing, but it happens more often than anyone realizes. It happened to me. I believed him when he said I would never make it on my own, Julia, and he made threats. He had a priceless gun collection. He would take out each gun and make me sit there while he cleaned and fondled it, aiming it at me and pretending to pull the trigger. Nowhere to run and nowhere to hide.''

"Why have you kept his memory sacred, then? Why tell me the truth about him this way? And now?''

"When you were growing up I couldn't see the point. Why tell you that your father had hurt you? You couldn't remember it. Why make you hate him? Then I began to block it out, too. I asked myself if it had really happened. Everyone knows how silly I am, how flighty. Maybe I had imagined the worst parts. Maybe there were other explanations. I couldn't bring myself to believe I had settled for nothing in my marriage except fear and self-loathing.''

"And now?''

"There have been too many lies and too many secrets. Look what they've done to you. I watched your marriage to Bard and realized that, in some ways, you had picked a man like your father. Sometimes we accept what's familiar, even if it's not good or safe. Bard tried to control you, not in the same ways, but with variations on the theme. I finally faced the fact that I had been part of a conspiracy, and I had allowed you to repeat the same patterns because you didn't know better.''

Maisy got up and went to sit beside her daughter. "I've wanted to tell you for years. I just didn't know how to do it."

"So you put it in a novel."

"Julia, Yvonne knows the truth. She told me to take this slowly. We agreed you should see the truth a little at a time."

"And the ending?"

Maisy wrung her hands, ineffectual hands covered with sparkling rings. Hands that had not, despite her best efforts, been able to shield her beloved daughter.

"It's true," she breathed. "I whipped Harry's horse across that final jump."

Julia shook her head. "I remember a scream."

"Only mine." Maisy stretched out her hand, withdrew it, stretched it out again, but she didn't touch Julia. "Your father died instantly, I think."

"And was he glad that the demons would be stilled at last? Or is that fiction, too?"

"I don't know. He was a tormented soul. I don't believe he wanted to be the man he was."

Julia reached out, and Maisy took her hand. "I don't expect forgiveness," Maisy said.

Julia clasped it hard. "Have you forgiven yourself?"

"It's taken most of my life."

"I was so afraid of horses, so afraid of learning to ride. And still, I loved them."

"You came by the love naturally. You came by the fear at your father's knee. You have Harry's good qualities and none of his bad. You overcame your fear with his tenacity. You wear it well."

Julia brought her mother's hand to her cheek. "I have to be alone now." She stood. She started across the room as Maisy watched; then she turned. "Maisy, does Jake know the truth?"

"No. I've never told anyone except Yvonne."

"Are you going to let him read your...novel?"

"I'm going to feed it to the flames."

"I think that's a good idea." Julia hesitated. "But you should write another." She hesitated again. "Are you going to tell Jake?"

"Yes. I'm going to tell him tonight. Jake's waited nearly as long as you have to hear the truth. I think he's run out of patience."

"You said you didn't expect me to forgive you."

"I don't."

"Is that my father's legacy, too?"

Maisy couldn't answer.

"You were always there for me, Maisy. Always. But until tonight I never realized how much."

Maisy watched her daughter find her way out of the room, Harry Ashbourne's only child. Maisy wanted to believe that the Harry she had fallen in love with, the man deep inside the raging beast, would be proud of the woman he had sired.

But she was proud enough for both of them.

Half an hour later she was still sitting in an armchair, watching flames die in the fireplace. Tomorrow she would clean out the ashes and sprinkle them in Jeb Stuart Creek. Fox River, Harry had nicknamed the creek, because of the multitude of dens near its banks.

"Fox River. The place where the hunt always begins..."

She began to cry.

"Maisy?"

She heard Jake before she saw him. She opened her eyes and saw he was kneeling beside her chair. "Maisy, are you all right?"

"I'm going to be. I'm really going to be."

He took her hand. "Come to bed."

"I have a story to tell you."

"Tonight?"

"Yes. Will you listen?"

He put his fingertips under her chin and lifted it. Jake had the kindest eyes. The first time she'd looked into them, she had thought that perhaps she had found a man who could love her at last.

Now his eyes were filled with concern. "I've just been waiting to listen. I can wait as long as it takes."

"You already have."

He got to his feet and held out his hand. She took it and held it against her cheek, the way Julia had held hers.

* * *

Sometime during a sleepless night the door to Julia's room opened and bare feet scurried across the floor.

"I can't sleep. Can I sleep with you?"

No request had ever been more welcome. Julia moved to the edge of the bed and opened her arms to her daughter. "Sure, sweetums. But what's wrong?"

"Maisy and Jake are talking."

"They are?"

"I hear whispers. It's weird."

"I guess it is." Julia pulled Callie against her and kissed her hair. She thought of Christian and cuddled her closer. "You had fun at the cabin?"

"Uh-huh," Callie said sleepily. "I love you, Mommy."

"I love you, too. Sleep tight."

Julia didn't know what time it was, and she didn't expect to fall asleep herself. She had cried away all her tears, but fragmented memories still paraded through her head. She no longer had the luxury of opening her eyes to ward off bad memories. Darkness was her companion, and with it now, the past.

The warmth of Callie's small body began to seep inside her. She thought of Maisy, who had risked so much, suffered so much. And Callie, whose challenges were still ahead. She thought of the father she'd known so briefly and the terrible impact he'd had on her life.

She had witnessed Harry Ashbourne's death, although she still couldn't remember anything except Maisy's scream. But "Alice" had been silenced for months, and Julia was afraid that that part, too, wasn't fiction.

As a child she had been mute, and now she was blind. She had a body that acted out the dramas locked inside her head, and still, despite all her flaws and turmoil, she was loved. By Jake. By Maisy. By Callie.

By Christian.

She slept at last, and in her dream she was in familiar woods far behind the stone cottage, riding unwillingly toward Jeb Stuart Creek. A giant on a horse in front of her turned and shouted something that made her cower in her saddle. Suddenly the giant sailed off the back of his horse and through the air, soaring with the wings of a great black vulture, until the sun was blocked by his immensity.

Then he was gone, and the world was a brighter place.

She woke with a start, frightened and breathing hard, until she heard Callie's soft breathing beside her. She was afraid it might still be night. She opened her eyes, as she did every morning, as if opening them might make a difference.

The room seemed unfamiliar. She stared, refusing at first to believe what she saw. *That* she saw.

Callie slept on beside her, beautiful Callie, with sunshine-colored hair, like her father's. Callie with rosy cheeks and dirt under her fingernails. Callie, her perfect little daughter.

She sat up and realized that light was streaming through a window. She heard birds singing and something else. The *clip-clop* of a horse's hoofs on the driveway.

She rose, such an easy task for the sighted, afraid she was still dreaming. Her gown was pale blue and tumbled to her feet. She'd thought it was yellow. The floor was heart of pine, the bed frame maple. She took a step, disoriented at first, but she didn't fall. She took another, clasping her hands to her cheeks.

She opened the window to a rush of cold air, but it couldn't wake her, because she *was* awake. She leaned out and closed her eyes, and the sunshine disappeared. Open again, the world was light, filled with blue sky and the last autumn leaves clinging to spidery branches waving in a morning breeze.

A man was on the road outside, a man on a huge gray horse. His hair shone in the sunshine. The face was older but every bit as dear as she remembered. His shirt was blue, his jeans faded.

She could never know the future, and the past was gone, but that moment, that priceless, perfect moment, was everything. He looked in her direction, head proud and high.

"Jules?"

"You look wonderful! I'm going to paint you just that way. Wait for me!"

She didn't linger to witness his surprise and joy as he realized she could see again. She simply ran through the house to meet him.

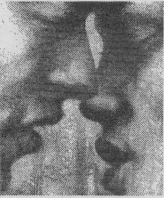

EMILIE
RICHARDS

66570	WHISKEY ISLAND	___ $6.50 U.S.	___ $7.99 CAN.
66492	BEAUTIFUL LIES	___ $5.99 U.S.	___ $6.99 CAN.
66273	RISING TIDES	___ $5.99 U.S.	___ $6.99 CAN.
66152	IRON LACE	___ $5.99 U.S.	___ $6.99 CAN.

(limited quantities available)

TOTAL AMOUNT $_____
POSTAGE & HANDLING $_____
($1.00 for one book; 50¢ for each additional)
APPLICABLE TAXES* $_____
<u>TOTAL PAYABLE</u> $_____
(check or money order—please do not send cash)

To order, complete this form and send it, along with a check or money order for the total above, payable to MIRA Books®, to: **In the U.S.:** 3010 Walden Avenue, P.O. Box 9077, Buffalo, NY 14269-9077; **In Canada:** P.O. Box 636, Fort Erie, Ontario, L2A 5X3.

Name:_____
Address:_____ City:_____
State/Prov.:_____ Zip/Postal Code:_____
Account Number (if applicable):_____
075 CSAS

*New York residents remit applicable sales taxes.
Canadian residents remit applicable GST and provincial taxes.

MIRA®